Kenny

The Making of a Serial Killer

- A Trilogy -

Patrick Laughy

__Dedication__

To the memory of Vancouver Police Service Dog, Duke III.

<u>Acknowledgement</u>

Without Suzy's help, this book would never have been written.

Thanks to Linette and Joe for their editing.

The characters and events in this book are fictitious. Any similarity to real persons, alive or dead, is coincidental and not intended by the author

- PREFACE -

This book is a work of fiction.

I write it from the perspective of a cop, because I was one and that has provided me with the experience and credibility to realistically describe both sides of the fictional accounts of the two main characters involved in this story.

This narrative is a description of the making of a serial killer, coupled with the background experience of the cop who eventually brings him to justice.

To help you set the stage for what is about to take place, I think it is only prudent for me to provide you with some basic facts before we begin our tale.

- What is a Serial Killer? -

What motivates him or her to kill again and again? What, if any, are the common denominators found among serial killers?

Serial killers are not the same as, and should not be confused with, people who commit mass murder, which is described as killing numerous people in a single incident. Nor is it the same as spree-killing, where murders are committed in two or more locations over a short timeframe.

Generally-speaking, a serial killer is a person who, suffering from abnormal psychological gratification, murders three or more people, committed as separate events usually, but not always, by a single offender acting alone.

These murders normally take place over a period of more than a month and include significant breaks or cooling off periods in between. The average age of a serial killer at the time of the first killing was just over twenty-seven years and they are typically white males.

Female serial killers are likely to kill husbands, relatives, or people in hospitals or nursing homes where they work. Their murders usually take place in one specific area. Poison is frequently used on the victims; money is often the motive. Male serial killers are more likely to kill strangers. They tend to be geographically mobile, are likely to torture or mutilate when killing, and report having a driving sexual motive. While the motivation for serial killing can include anger, thrill-seeking, financial gain, and attention seeking, psychological gratification is the usual object of the serial killer. Most serial killings involve sexual contact with the victim.

These murders will often be attempted or carried out in a similar fashion, and the victims frequently share something in common, such as age group, appearance, gender, type or race.

There are exceptions to these tendencies however. There have been examples of serial killers demonstrating extended bouts of sequential killings over periods of weeks or months, escalating, while having no apparent cooling off periods or a significant return to normalcy.

There are several oft found characteristics among serial killers. One of these is the exhibition of a degree of mental illness or psychopathy which can contribute to the killings - psychotic periods, during which the killer believes that he or she is another person, someone who is compelled by other entities, to commit murder.

Psychopathic behavior common to many serial killers can include predatory behavior, the need for control, impulsivity and the absence of feelings of guilt or remorse. It is important to keep in mind that psychopaths can seem normal and often are considered as quite charming.

Serial killers have often been abused by a family member, either emotionally or physically and frequently, sexually. They tend to be more likely to engage in fetishism, partialism or necrophilia and have a strong tendency to experience the object of their erotic interest as a physical representation of the symbolized body.

Many young serial killers display one or more of the following tendencies in their early years: a fascination with setting fires, involvement in sadistic activity with animals, and bed-wetting.

While children, and in early adolescence, they are frequently bullied or isolated socially. Some will become active in petty crimes and have trouble as young adults in seeking and keeping a job. A serial killer is no different from any other individual in seeking approval fromparents, sexual partners and their peers, as a child.

In early life, having a loving, supportive and nurturing family or lack thereof, is of utmost importance. Interaction with family plays an important role in a child's growth and development and is what they identify with on a regular basis. The quality of their attachments to parents and other members of the family is critical to the future way these individuals will interact with and value other members of society.

The need for approval influences children to attempt to develop social relationships with their family and peers. If they are rejected or neglected, they cannot achieve this end. This failure results in the lowering of their self-esteem and can lead to the creation of a fantasy world in which they are in control.

Early trauma, followed by contributing factors such as the use of pornography, alcohol or drugs, serves to fortify this situation. It is common for a serial killer to come from a family which has experienced divorce, separation, or the lack of one or both parents.

Additionally, many serial killers have experienced emotional neglect and some type of physical or sexual abuse. If a child receives no support from those around him or her, then he or she is unlikely to recover successfully from an earlier traumatic event.

Children who do not have the physical or mental strength to control the mistreatment they suffer often create a new reality to which they can escape. This new reality, one of pure fantasy, then becomes their method of total control and becomes part of their daily existence. From that point on, it is from within the confines of this fantasy world that their emotional development is guided and maintained.

In this sociopathic state, the child fails to develop the normal concepts of right and wrong and the ability to experience empathy towards others is arrested. Safely ensconced and self-centered he resides in his/her own little dream world, in which they can do no wrong. The pain of others is of no consequence. Only the needs of one person, that of the child, matters. It is a haven in which the child has complete control, leaving only an outer shell that walks through the real world, a world to which he or she has no desire to commit.

In every sense of the word, the child is then emotionally isolated within those safe fantasies.

A head injury or some form of brain pathology is often a predisposing factor in the development of a serial killer. This will often occur if the individual in question has responded in a negative way to the traumatization while in the formative years, experiencing low self-esteem and developing increasingly violent fantasies.

Traumatic experiences and feelings from the past can be dissociated from conscious feelings, and the adult offender often expands an altered state of consciousness by using facilitators, such as alcohol, pornography, or drugs.

Eventually he or she commits murder as a way of regaining control and in so doing feels reinforced on a short-term basis, before low self-esteem reasserts itself. Shortly thereafter, the divisions between fantasy and reality are lost and when that occurs, the fantasy existence can begin to morph, leading to a need to assert dominance and continue the act of serial killing.

Do not forget however, that, as adults they may well appear as normal, part of a regular family and gainfully employed.

There are several psychological phases in the development of serial killers.

The initial phase consists of a withdrawal from reality and a heightening of the senses. This phase may last anywhere from a few moments to several months and will likely begin as a prolonged fantasy. During this time, the killer may attempt to medicate himself with alcohol or drugs.

In the next phase, the killer begins to act, identifying and stalking his first victim. This is followed shortly thereafter by the killer working at gaining the confidence of a victim in preparation to trapping that target.

The next step is for the killer to render the victim helpless, therein allowing for a reversal of the roles in a ritual re-enactment of the disastrous experiences of the killer's childhood. Now, finally in complete control, the killer savors his retribution.

The high from this is short-lived. Dead, the victim no longer represents what the killer thought he or she represented. Conversely, the horrific memories of the individual or individuals who previously tortured the serial killer in the past, remain.

For the most part serial killers fall into two main categories - organized or disorganized.

Organized serial killers usually have social and interpersonal skills that allow them to develop both personal and romantic relationships. They have friends and lovers and often a spouse and children and tend to plan their crimes methodically. They often abduct their victims and then murder them in one place before disposing of the bodies elsewhere. They usually have a fair knowledge of forensics and tend to sustain a high degree of control over their crime scenes.

Organized serial killers believe that they are smarter than the authorities and will have no difficulty in getting away with their crimes.

To them the entire exercise becomes a game of cat and mouse, a game which they firmly imagine they can win. This type follows the media coverage of his or her acts, taking pride in their accomplishments.

Disorganized serial killers are normally far more impulsive. They often commit their murders with whatever weapon is at hand at the time and usually make no attempt to conceal the body. This type is likely to have a history of mental illness, be either under-employed or unemployed and very likely a loner, with very few, if any, real friends.

The motivation for their crimes can vary widely. An examination of some of these variations is worth consideration. For example, so called *'Visionary Serial Killers'* suffer from psychotic breaks with reality. During these breaks, they may believe they are another person or are compelled to kill by superior entities like the Devil, or God.

'Mission-oriented Serial Killers' are generally not psychotic. They justify their acts as necessary to rid society of certain types of individuals that they believe to be undesirable. They target specific groups, for example homosexuals or prostitutes.

The motive for *'Lust Serial Killers'* is primarily sexual in nature. The lust may be satisfied with either a living or dead victim, and fantasy plays a major part in their murders. The level of sexual gratification achieved will depend on the amount of torture and mutilation they perform on their targets. These serial killers have a psychological need to have absolute control. Usually their victims are strangers. They must dominate and be all powerful over their victims. The infliction of torture and ultimate death is required to satisfy their need. These killers generally use their bare hands or sharp instruments to do the job. They relish close contact with their victims and the time between killings often decreases while the required level of stimulation required to fulfil their need often increases with each kill.

The primary motive of a *'Thrill Killer'* is to induce pain or terror in their victims. They seek the rush provided by hunting and killing victims and murder only for the kill. Their attack is usually swift and has no sexual aspect. They can abstain from killing for long periods of time while tending to become more successful at killing over time.

Beginning in 1979, this novel is set in the west coast city of Vancouver, British Columbia, Canada.

It contains a factual depiction of one of the so-called prostitution *'Strolls'* located in Vancouver.

There are several of these strolls, enough to satisfy most of sexual appetites one finds in large cities. There is the *'high track'* stroll on Seymour Street. It is upscale and operated by pimps and organized crime, unlike the *'low track'* stroll on the Downtown East side where you will find women who will turn a trick for the price of their next fix.

For different appetites, there is the *'kiddie stroll'* located on Commercial Drive, which is stocked with runaway girls as young as twelve working the sex trade and *'boy's town'*, situated at the foot of Homer Street, which caters to men who are looking for sex with teenage males.

There are approximately two thousand prostitutes working the combined strolls of Vancouver.

Those involved in the sex trade are likely to be targeted by a serial killer for several reasons.

Firstly, they are usually individuals who come from the bottom end of our society. Often these people have been forced by poverty, sexual abuse, alienation at home, bullying at school, and drug addiction, into the dead-end life of the sex-trade worker.

Unlike regular members of our society, the disappearance of one of these individuals is not treated, by either society in general or police, as being that surprising. If one of them goes missing it seems to all concerned that this should be expected, that it is *'par-for-the-course'*. They are rarely in regular touch with either family or friends, anyone who would be alarmed should they go missing.

Therefore, when they do go missing, it doesn't ring the same alarm bells with law enforcement officials that it would if it happened to you.

After all, under those conditions, people move on; life is like that on the streets.

Serial killers pick up on stuff like that. I mean, if you are thinking of killing people, you can't find a safer hunting ground than that of the sex workers, from which to choose your victims.

In Canada, the Criminal Code was changed in 1986 to make it illegal to communicate in public for buying or selling sexual services. Hence the existence of the strolls. Now those interested in partaking no longer must search out a hooker; they just drive to a specific stroll location and help themselves to take-out.

Now, let's step back a little in time and armed with this basic understanding of the complexities of what makes a serial killer, and a clear concept of the stroll situation in Vancouver, we'll follow one of these monsters from birth to the point where he is fully involved in his grizzly crimes.

Concurrently, we'll experience the life of the cop who is destined to become the central figure in the effort to successfully bring the serial killer's crimes to an end.

Before we begin I will also warn you that the novel begins sedately enough, but as it progresses it is not a story for the faint of heart.

You are headed for an adventure into the dark side.

CHAPTER ONE

- September 1979 -

When he came into the world, Kenneth Jacob Simpson wasn't necessarily predestined to be a serial killer. However, over time, he was to morph into one of the worst in Canadian history.

He was born to Karen Anne and Phillip Richard Simpson on September the first of 1979.

He had a big sister named Leanne. She was two when they brought Kenneth home.

His parents were prosperous, and he found himself warmly welcomed into a nurturing and privileged existence. His mom and dad called him Kenny.

For the first few months, his sister called him *'Kemmy'*. As she got older, she learned how to say it right.

His grandpa on his mother's side of the family had passed away from a heart attack a year and a half before Kenny was born. That left him with two Grammas and one Grandpa. All three of them doted on both him and Leanne.

The grandparents all came from old money.

Kenny's dad was an engineer and he owned a company that did contract work, mostly for the government. They lived in West Vancouver, an upper-class suburb of Vancouver, in a large house on several acres situated high up on a mountain ridge overlooking the city.

They had a big in-ground swimming pool, cabanas, stables, a riding ring and a tennis court within the fenced confines of the well-landscaped property.

His mother didn't work but she spent a good deal of her time involved with various charities and society events, as well as regularly playing tennis and riding horses. He and Leanne had a nanny. The family also had a full-time combination cook and housekeeper who supervised an outside cleaning staff, gardeners and a pool boy, who each spent two days per week keeping the family estate in pristine condition.

By his first birthday, Kenny had a full head of blond hair, a round and endearing face accented with bright blue, inquiring eyes. Otherwise he was of average intellect and looks. Nothing about him stood out especially. He appeared to function and act just like any other little boy.

Despite being physically active enough, he tended to be a little overweight in those first few years.

Edith, his grandmother on his mother's side, lived alone in one of the gracious turn-of -the-century mansions nestled in the treed, prestigious neighbourhood of Shaughnessy in Vancouver. She had inherited it from her parents. It was a big rambling place that required staff to keep it up, but she could afford it. Her father had been in sugar and she still owned the controlling interest in the company her grandfather had formed in the late eighteen-hundreds.

Edith had been born into a privileged environment and raised to fulfill her station in life, with little consideration for her ever having to make her own way in the world. Naturally she had married well. Early in her marriage, she and her husband had purchased a villa in the south of France and Edith now spent six months of each year living there and, despite her age, still played her part in the higher level of society life, when very comfortably ensconced in either of her residences.

While she felt affection for, and enjoyed, the company of her grandchildren, she had grown up in an era where, for the most part, children were seen and not heard, cared for by staff and experienced in short visits and only when convenient.

Kenny's father's parents also had money, but it had not been solely inherited. What they had been left when their parents passed had certainly entitled them to be considered as well off. However, for the most part their wealth had come as a result of a good deal of hard work. As a team, the couple had created a timber and sawmill empire that had grown exponentially over the years. A few years before Kenny's birth they had received an offer they couldn't refuse, and they'd sold their holdings off to a larger firm.

Although they were getting on in age, and didn't need to work in view of the fact that they still held a large block of shares in the purchasing firm, they were not the retiring kind. Instead they'd gone on to create a small tree trimming business which currently provided enough income to let them live very comfortably, without the need to draw on any of their other investments.

Just after selling off their large company, they'd purchased forty acres of forested waterfront property on Indian Arm. The parcel of land was thickly covered by mature second-growth evergreens, here and there interspaced with the odd copse of deciduous trees. It was in the undeveloped eastern portion of the Vancouver suburb of North Vancouver.

At the time of purchase, the property had only been accessible by boat, but a couple of years later, in conjunction with ten other owners who lived or had property on that section of the waterfront, they'd anteed up the cash required to put through a gated, private road which connected them with the populated areas of North Vancouver to the west.

Once the road had been built, they'd cleared just enough land, up on the small bluff overlooking the ocean where killer whales often frolicked, and pleasure craft plied the open water, to build their dream home.

After the house was finished, his grandfather had built a chicken house and run so they would have fresh eggs and chickens to eat when the hens got too old to lay. He'd also constructed a fair-sized piggery to produce pork, both for their personal consumption and some commercial sales. Attached to the building where the pigs could get inside in inclement weather, was a workspace grandpa used when he butchered pigs, and a couple of big freezers to keep them in once they had been cut up and wrapped in brown paper.

That accomplished, he and grandma moved on to clearing an area at the inland border of the property, just off the private access road, creating a paved, chain-link-fence enclosure to house their new company's small fleet of trucks and chipping equipment. Once the yard and fence were in place grandpa built a small workshop with its own bathroom and a row of garages to house the trucks and chippers when they came in each night after work.

They had planned to leave the remainder of the land in a mostly natural state, but because they liked to keep physically active, they'd soon decided to take on the task of leveling the parcel of any grossly uneven land, while endeavouring to leave the remainder in its natural state. They also planned to do some future landscaping around the house, along the edges of the long driveway, as natural screening between the house and the pig and chicken pens.

Some idea of how to do this without the removal of any of the old growth trees, which neither wanted to take down, held them up for a short period of time, but in the end, they decided to accomplish this by filling in and levelling all the natural depressions on the property utilizing the product from their company's wood chipping machines. They figured they could accomplish that by slowly working their way through the standing timber wherever possible.

To simplify the work required, they'd purchased a small excavator for use on the property. Kenny's grandfather now used the compact machine each day to spread the loads carried in by the trucks from the cleanup of the company's various jobsites and hauled back each night by the employees to be dumped in the storage yard compound.

As he grew a little older, Kenny became very close to the pair and loved to spend time with them on the property.

He could help grandma feed both the chickens and the pigs when he and his sister visited and unlike Leanne, he watched when Gramps selected the older birds for the table, then got out the chopping block and the axe and cut their heads off.

The chickens were still alive for awhile after the axe had done its job, and they ran around like crazy, spraying blood everywhere. His sister found the whole process kind of gross and unsettling. She hid here eyes and cried the first time and after that she didn't take part. Kenny found it exciting to watch. When it was over, he would find himself eagerly anticipating the next time the culling process would take place.

Once he was finished with the chopping job, Grandpa would take the chicken heads and legs down to the pig pen and throw them over the fence. Kenny didn't think the animals would eat them, but Grandpa just laughed and told him that those pigs would eat anything.

He was right. The pigs gobbled them up.

On these visits, his grandfather would also let him help drive and work the trucks and the excavator.

They visited regularly, Grandpa and Grandma Simpson happily taking the young fellow and his sister in for weeks at a time, unlike Grandmother Edith, who only occasionally had him and his sister, accompanied by their mother, over for afternoon tea.

Grandma Simpson was his favorite grandparent. She was a practical, down to earth, no nonsense woman, but very caring and she adored him, lavishing him with love and steadfastly granting his every wish.

At this early point in his life, Kenny may have had some problems, but then what kid didn't?

He had been born into the good life and in those first few years, he certainly, gave no outward indication of becoming the monster he would eventually turn out to be.

At the time Kenny was born, Dave Richards was twenty-five years old.

He stood six-two, was strongly built, and weighed in at one hundred and ninety pounds. He had recently graduated from the Vancouver Police Department Academy and was currently undergoing practical training under the supervision of a senior constable.

Dave wasn't what most people would describe as handsome, but his chiselled features, thick brown hair and blue eyes, coupled with his physical bearing, often drew a second look. He was happily married to his wife Jennifer, who was a stay-at-home mom. They had two kids, a boy, Philip who was four, and a girl, Alicia who was two. They lived in a new three-bedroom bungalow in the Vancouver suburb of Richmond, which they shared with a cat named Murphy.

Prior to joining the police force, Dave had been a member of the Canadian armed forces working as a radioman. He'd spent four years on the east coast while serving in the Navy but had never gone to sea, instead being posted to the large naval radio station situated just outside of Halifax.

Looking for employment more rewarding, and a return to the west coast where he had been born and had family, and at the suggestion of an uncle who was a member of the Vancouver force, Dave had talked it over with Jenny and they had decided he should give the police force a try.

From the day Dave applied to join the force he'd loved every second of what that meant. He seemed to be a natural and looked forward to every day he went to work.

Everything wasn't coming up roses of course, but he was a realist and didn't expect that kind of perfection from life. Dave had always been able to roll with the punches. There were bound to be ups and downs and his new job would certainly not be everyone's cup of tea.

That said, all and all he found the job both challenging and rewarding. His first posting was to what was designated as District Two, one of the four police districts covering the City. This north-eastern section of Vancouver had long ago been coined the *'Downtown East Side'* and contained the skid road zone, most of the drug activity, and was rampant with run-down hotels, cheap flophouses and homeless - and of course the addicts, or, in police jargon, the *'hypes'*.

Eight marked police units served District Two. The eight cars were designated with call numbers seven to fourteen. This was without doubt the toughest part of town. All the cars in D2 were two-man units, except for car seven which was a small one-man wagon. The city's biggest wagon, a large and much employed two-man van, was also part of the district.

Dave was assigned to do his practical in car nine and his partner was a grizzled old veteran, by the name of Jack Edwards. Edwards was long divorced and had been passed over for promotion numerous times. He also had a serious drinking problem, which he managed to keep under control when on duty for the most part, with some exceptions.

Jack had long ago come to terms with the fact that he was going to stay a constable until he retired, and it could be argued that he was just *'putting in his time'*. Initially that's what Dave thought, but after they'd worked together for a few months, he changed his opinion about that.

It quickly became apparent to him that Jack lived for his job simply because he really had no other life. The realization was a little depressing and sad when it first sank in, but eventually Dave figured it was as good a reason as any and it drifted to the back of his mind.

Jack didn't look for trouble, but he didn't back away from it either. He was prepared for what was necessary, and was very streetwise and a pretty good role model for a new cop.

Dave had to laugh when he related to others what had happened the first time he and his partner had climbed into a black and white.

Jack had paused at the back of their assigned unit, a seventy-six Chevy that had seen better days, and dangled the car keys in front of him. He then spoke for the first time since their introduction in the squad room.

"I'll be doing the driving, son. You can sit in the front seat beside me for now, but if you even think about touching either the emergency switches or the radio mike, you'll find yourself riding in the back so fast it will make your head spin. We clear on that?"

Over time, it got better.

After a month of observing what went on inside the unit, Jack tossed him the keys one morning. Dave, who hadn't been expecting it, damn near dropped them. Jack managed a small grin.

"Don't do anything I wouldn't do kid. I'll be watching you. Oh, and what I said before about the emergency switches and the mike still goes, for now."

CHAPTER TWO

- December 1984 -

At the tender age of five, Kenny suffered what was unquestionably very serious trauma, both in a physical and psychological sense. He was involved in a serious road accident and, as a result, his life changed exponentially.

When they'd set out on that fateful day Kenny, as usual, had fought against wearing his lap belt. In the end, he had only agreed to wear it if it was fastened very loosely and not restricting him too much.

Looking back on it later, he would come to realize that demanding that slackness had probably saved his life. If the belt had been as firmly fitted as his mother had originally ordered, he would very likely have suffered the same fate as the rest of his family.

The details of the accident would repeatedly haunt him for the remainder of his life. He would suffer routinely from flashbacks of the entire incident, haunted by horrible, detailed and highly animated recollections, which varied little over time.

The initial screech, coupled with the smell of tortured, burning rubber as his father fought to control the careening car. The rending shriek of metal grinding against metal as the vehicle struck the guardrail. His loss of balance as the car tilted slightly as the wheels on the driver's side lifted clear of the pavement. The sensation of helplessness as it scraped along the length of the extended barrier.

The sounds, sights and smells of it once again overwhelming his senses. The inability of his young mind to take it all in. The whole thing becoming surreal. Time dragging and, from that point onward, everything happening in slow motion.

Recalling becoming physically sick as his stomach knotted up with fear.

His mother in the front beside his dad. Both she and his older sister, who was seated next to him in the back, were screaming. His father was frantically struggling with the steering wheel in an ineffectual attempt to bring the heavy vehicle back down onto all four wheels. One of the guardrail posts finally succumbing to the intense pressure and snapping under the strain, shearing off and rocketing through his sister's window. It struck her a glancing blow on the shoulder before narrowly missing his own head as it flew past him and hurtled out through his window.

That initial impact of the thick post had been enough to shove the car back onto its wheels and when the spinning rubber had grabbed at the road surface again Kenny had been thrown up and sideways, slipping out of his belt and to his horror, following the path the post had taken, out through the shattered side window.

Kenny had come down hard on the pavement and then rolled into a lifeless ball.

Even when Kenny reached adulthood he'd often relive every little detail of the accident. Mostly it was in nightmares, but sometimes the recall seemed to be triggered when he was fully awake, when he was under any kind of stress.

After the fact, he'd learned that at he time of the accident his head had taken a serious hit on his forehead, knocking him unconscious. As a result, he'd been left with no first-hand recollections of the large car nosing into the next post, nor that it had then lurched upward and gone ass-over-teakettle up and over the remainder of the barrier; before becoming fully airborne and silently arcing out into the yawning emptiness of the nearly two-mile plunge to the floor of the gorge below.

Kenny had awakened in the hospital three days later. When he did, he had no memory of anything after he'd hit his head on the road. He had no idea of what had taken place after he'd been thrown clear of the big car.

His Simpson grandparents had been at his bedside in the hospital when he'd finally opened his eyes. He noticed immediately that they had both been crying.

They didn't tell him anything about the accident that day and for some reason he wasn't inclined to ask about it.

It wasn't until they could take him home a few days later that they told him everything. By then he'd already begun to get flashbacks and already had a fair idea of the important parts. He no longer had a mom, dad, or a sister, and everything had changed for him.

His grandparents had taken him home from the hospital, to their large house on the water. He'd been there several times before and he had enjoyed each stay. It was very big and nice, but it wasn't all fancy and fussy the way his real home had been. There was no pool, but in the summertime, he could fish and swim in the ocean under the watchful eyes of his grandfather.

This was to be his house now too. Grandma had told him so when they'd come home from the hospital.

Shortly after they had entered the house, she and grandpa had sat him down on the long couch, in what grandpa called the parlour. That's when they'd told him about what had happened after he'd been knocked unconscious and told him that he would have a new life now and that he would be living with them.

When they'd got to the part about his family being dead, Kenny sensed from their hesitancy and expressions that they expected him to cry, but even when he tried very hard to make them come, the tears just wouldn't flow.

He was mildly disappointed at his inability to be reduced to tears, but for some strange reason it just wouldn't happen.

Maybe that would happen later, he couldn't remember how those things worked. Anyway, it didn't seem all that important and he soon pushed that concern to the back of his mind.

Over the next nine months Kenny settled into his new lifestyle. Initially he'd spent almost all his time with at least one, and often, both of his grandparents.

The nights were the worst. That's when the nightmares were most prevalent, especially in the first month or so. Several times a night he would wake up, screaming, soaked in sweat and unsure of his surroundings. They had given him the bedroom just down the hall from their own and whenever the horrific dreams woke him, one or the other would quickly enter his room to comfort him.

It was about this time that Kenny had begun to wet his bed regularly. That really embarrassed him but he couldn't seem to stop, no matter how hard he tried. It began to register on him that he seemed to have less and less control of his life each day.

His grandmother told him not to worry about it, that he would grow out of it, but to Kenny that didn't make a lot of sense. He hadn't wet his bed before the accident. Heck, he had stopped that a least a couple of years back. It didn't make any sense to him that he was doing it again now.

These things aside, Kenny's days were cool though.

Each morning when he got up, he would have a long bath and by the time he got back to his room to get dressed, Grandma would have changed the bed, fed their calico cat, Fluffy, and would already be clattering around in the kitchen getting breakfast together.

Once the three of them had finished the first meal of the day, he and grandpa would head out to do whatever chores needed doing, feed the chickens and pigs, stuff like that, and then hop into the little red Ford pickup and drive down the long driveway toward the main road, accompanied by the family dog, old Sam, who kept them company wherever they went.

Grandpa loved that old dog an awful lot.

When they got to the spot where the driveway met the main road, they'd swing into the yard where all the tree machinery stuff was kept overnight and then he and grandpa would park the Ford.

The last thing they did was to use a high-pressure hose to wash down the vehicles, giving special attention to the big shredding machines. Grandpa said they had to keep the blades in them clean or they wouldn't cut properly. Before doing that though, they'd go over to the big pile of woodchips the incoming trucks had dumped earlier and use the excavator to load the old, unlicensed, yard dump truck, and use it to haul the material that had been brought in the day before to even out low spots on the property and dump it.

Kenny loved that excavator. Grandpa would start it up as soon as they got to the yard. Grandpa had rigged up a small seat right beside his and Kenny would sit beside him as the big machine chugged into life. Once it had warmed up, they would begin the job of transferring the pile of shredded material into the battered old dump truck.

They'd gouge up big scoops of the material and dump them into that old truck and when it was full, they'd pile into that noisy old thing and roar off into the bush until they found a low spot grandpa figured needed filling to make the ground flat.

Sometimes it would take several truckloads to fill a hole and once all the material from the yard had been scooped up and dumped, they'd park that old dump and get back into the excavator and then crawl out through the bush to level all the newly deposited chips.

Kenny enjoyed every minute of the work and grandpa let him pitch in all the time, even so far as to allow him to sit in his lap sometimes, to help drive the old dump or work some of the controls for the excavator.

When he wasn't out working or playing with grandpa, Kenny liked to spend time on his own.

He'd overheard his grandparents talking about him a couple of times and Grandma was worried about him having no other kids to play with and spending too much time on his own in his bedroom.

Kenny didn't ever say so, but he wasn't much interested in playing with other kids.

Shortly after that though, grandpa bought him an Atari VCS, so he would have something to keep himself occupied with when he wanted to be alone.

Kenny really liked it, especially one game, the one called Battlezone, where he got to shoot other tanks and things with his tank. He liked being in control, even if it was only a game and he got very good at killing the other stuff.

It had started off alright, but '84 turned out to be very a bad year for Dave Richards.

During his tour with his training officer Jack, working the skids, Dave had learned a great deal about what a patrol cop was all about.

Car nine's patrol area centered on the dregs of the city. While consisting of only about ten square blocks, it encompassed by far much of the street level drug activity that took place in Vancouver. Bar brawls, public drunkenness, run down rooming houses and low-level prostitution was rampant. The majority of the city's sudden deaths, primarily overdoses by heroin addicts, took place there, as well as the regular occurrences of knifings and deaths resulting from fights about, and for, drugs.

It was a real eye opener for a middle-class guy like Dave, who had been raised in the suburbs in a comfortable bungalow nestled on a half acre with two nurturing parents, two cars in the garage and a big brother to guide him.

During the 15 months that he spent there, Dave learned a lot about life on the other side of the tracks. When he looked back on it, he couldn't think of a better hands-on introduction to police work.

For policing purposes, the city of Vancouver was divided into four districts. District 1 and 2 worked out of the main police building which was situated downtown on Main street. Districts 3 and 4 split the southern part of the city and worked out of a substation located in central south Vancouver.

Once he was elevated to the rank of fourth class constable, Dave transferred from car nine, which patrolled in District 2, to car one, which worked in District 1, in what was commonly referred to as Vancouver's *'west end'*. There he worked in a two-man patrol unit with another old timer, named Jim Bird.

The west end of Vancouver is full of high-rises and as far as crime went, far less dangerous than the skids. B&E's were the most common calls. Those and parking complaints. Lots of report writing. Not a great deal of action.

Unlike his first partner Jack, Jim had only a few months left to retirement and he was just putting in time. He would, quite successfully, avoid any radio call he could. He didn't have a drinking problem but, unfortunately, he suffered from narcolepsy.

He'd never bothered to advise Dave of this fact.

After the third time, the old bugger had fallen asleep behind the wheel while they were working night shift and Dave had been forced to take control and shove his foot on the brake to prevent them from piling into stationary objects, it had become readily apparent.

There was not a lot Jim was capable of, or was interested in, teaching Dave.

His short three-month stint in car one was the most boring in all of Dave's career.

Dave had given a lot of thought to his future during the time he rode around in car one. He'd decided that he wanted to give the Dog Squad a try. It was an elite squad, and probably one of the most physically demanding for a young constable.

Among several other prerequisites, the department required that all potential dog masters must have at least two years on the job and have been confirmed in the rank of constable first class to apply.

Dave went on to spent two years in the Dog Squad. Although he and his partner had been very successful at catching the bad guys during that time and the team could well have stayed longer in the squad if they had so desired, it was not recommended for anyone who was interested in future promotion to spend too much time in any one position. It was common knowledge that a couple of years in one spot was about the maximum anyone should spend if they wished to be considered for higher rank in the future.

When Dave left the Dog Squad, he was thirty-five years of age and a confirmed first-class constable with several commendations to his credit. He was ambitious and already had his eye on the next promotion, which would be that of the interchangeable ranks of Corporal and that of Detective.

His uncle, recently retired from the force, had advised him to apply for a patrol position in D3, the south-east sector of the city, to expand on his general patrol experience, and had indicated that he would put in a good word for Dave there if he wished.

Dave did that and was assigned to work car twenty-two, another two-man unit.

His new partner was a ten-year man by the name of Cliff Spencer. Spencer had spent five years in the district and was generally accepted within the department as be a rising star. It was a plum assignment and Dave soon settled in nicely with his easy going, but very motivated and career oriented, co-worker.

They worked the car together for just over two years and then, again at his uncle's suggestion, Dave applied for a spot on the Youth Squad which worked out of the same sub divisional offices as both D3 and D4. His transfer was accepted.

Two-man teams worked the youth detail and Dave was coupled with an ex-academy comrade, Ed Hamilton, who viewed the world very much as he did. They turned out to be a very balanced and effective team. Good cop (Dave), bad cop (Ed) personified.

A total of four teams worked the detail, and within a couple of months Dave and his partner were at the top of the heap as far as clearances were concerned. They began to specialize in B&E's and quickly became very good at soliciting confessions from the young perpetrators of these crimes, clearing up numerous individual reported crimes, which often went back over many years and numbered in the hundreds. The number of recovered items they could return to the victims was the envy of the squad and got the department a good deal of positive media coverage.

An enviable pile of commendations for the duo resulted, and after two years both Dave and Ed were promoted to the interchangeable Corporal/Detective rank.

Ed was assigned to the uniformed patrol as a Corporal, but Dave managed a transfer to the elite serious crimes section, which was tasked with all Robbery and Homicide investigations undertaken by the department. He got a new partner and was assigned to Robbery.

By 1984, career wise, Dave was flying high. Unfortunately, in his personal life, disaster was about to strike. In early December of that year, while they were doing some last-minute Christmas shopping,

Dave's wife Jenny and both his kids, riding in the family station wagon, were T-boned by a drunk driver. The idiot had been traveling well over the limit and had run a red light. He not only killed himself in the resulting crash but also took the lives of Dave's entire immediate family.

For David, the whole world shattered. The grief was completely overwhelming, leaving him appearing to others as little more than comatose.

Nothing was any longer important to him. He was devastated, so deeply immersed in grief that he saw little reason to live.

CHAPTER THREE

- September 1985 -

Kenny turned six the day he started school. For him, things seemed to go down hill from there.

He hadn't want to leave the safety of the house and property. He worried about meeting strange people.

He couldn't sleep the night before he started grade one. His stomach was churning and he couldn't eat any breakfast the next morning either.

Grandma had done her best to settle him down, telling him he would meet a bunch of kids and have a lot of fun, but Kenny didn't see it that way. He said very little, keeping to himself. It wasn't until Grandpa had loaded him, old Sam and his lunch into the little Ford pickup to head out, that he'd ventured to talk a little about it.

Kenny had asked the old man why he had to go and Grandpa had thought for a few seconds before answering him.

"Well, Kenny, school is the place where you learn new things and get to spend time and play with other kids like yourself. You're getting to be a big boy now and its time you expanded your horizons a little."

Kenny had frowned at that and Grandpa had smiled.

"Don't worry yourself too much, son. All kids feel pretty much the way you do on the first day of school. It's something new and a little scary before you get there, but it'll give you a chance to make some friends.

"Trust me, you'll have a lot of fun. When you look back on this day later, you'll wonder why you were so het up about it."

Kenny didn't reply, but he didn't think he was going to like it at all.

And he'd been right.

From that very first day he just didn't fit in somehow. He was chubby. He didn't feel comfortable being around a bunch of people and was very quiet. He'd kept pretty much to himself. After the few attempts he'd made to relate to some of the other kids, he had been cruelly rebuffed. No matter what Grandpa said, he just wasn't like the rest of them.

His teacher, Mrs. Palmer, was OK. She didn't hassle him or anything, but she was always trying to get him to take part in stuff and Kenny did not like to be singled out and made the centre of attention.

As time passed, he was often made the butt of jokes, teased and bullied by the others in his class. He stood out for several reasons, none of them positive in the eyes of his classmates. He didn't know how to deal with these affronts, never spoke up for himself or responded in kind. He just did his best to avoid setting himself up for a repeat.

Kenny didn't have a mom and dad like everyone else, just a grandpa and two grandmas. He was overweight and not well coordinated and hopeless at games and team sports. After those first dismal failures at trying during recess and lunch, he never again attempted to play with the other kids.

Instead he sat alone and well away from the remainder of them.

After a couple of months Mrs. Palmer sent a note home with him and after Gramma read it she and Grandpa seemed worried. That night when Kenny went to bed, he could hear them talking quietly for a long time, on the other side of the wall.

Something about social skills. He had no idea what that meant, but obviously they were worried about him.

The next day, when Grandpa came to pick him up from school, Sam was not in the truck but Grandma was. She got out and held the door open for him. Before he could say anything, she spoke.

"Hop in, Grandpa is going to take you for a burger."

Grandpa moved off as soon as the door closed and he had his seat belt fastened. They left her standing in the parking lot waving.

Kenny didn't have to inquire about what was going on. It was pretty evident that Grandma was going into the school to see Mrs. Palmer about him. Grandpa was putting a good face on it all, talking away cheerfully about their adventure out to McDonalds.

Grandpa didn't usually do a lot of talking, so Kenny picked up on the fact that the old man was uncomfortable with what was going on, but he knew better than to ask about it. That would just make matters worse.

So, he played along, saying he was looking forward to the burger.

That's all it took to take the pressure off. The strain in grandpa's shoulders eased and the old man grinned as he ruffled Kenny's hair with one hand.

Edith Simpson met with Mrs. Palmer in a small conference room just off the principal's office.

She liked the woman right from the start and after the initial awkwardness of it all, the two of them settled down with a cup of tea and got right into it.

Mrs. Palmer explained her concerns about Kenny's difficulty relating to the other children in the class, matter-of-factly telling it as she saw it and expressing her concern over the situation. Edith, having expected to hear pretty much what she was receiving from the teacher, appreciated the woman's sincere interest in Kenny's wellbeing.

After some discussion of the finer points of what had been happening in the class, plus Edith's frank input as to what the boy had experienced with the loss of his immediate family in the horrific accident, they both agreed that they should perhaps seek some professional help for Kenny.

Mrs. Palmer provided some names for Edith to consider for possible counselling and promised to keep an eye on things in the classroom in the meantime. The two of them agreed to keep in touch on a regular basis.

Two weeks later Kenny had his first appointment with a psychologist. He and Grandma spent an hour with him and after, as a reward for the boy's co-operation, the three of them stopped off at McDonalds, which had by this time become Kenny's favorite place to eat.

For the first little while the appointments were weekly, as was the hamburger offer. After a month of sessions, the psychologist advised Grandma that monthly get-togethers would suffice from then on and that she would no longer need to sit in for the entire hour. Instead, she would only have a few minutes alone with the doctor at the end of Kenny's sessions.

It was after that next appointment, when granny left Kenny in the waiting room while she went in to see the doctor, that he'd given her the lowdown.

Kenny was having trouble dealing with the trauma of the accident, coupled with the loss of his parents and his happy environment. He had lost most of his self-confidence and was beginning to isolate himself from the outside world. He felt that he no longer had any real control of his life.

This situation could well lead to serious consequences during adolescence and adulthood; however, as he was still young, it was hopefully not irreversible.

The grandparents were doing everything right and with continuing therapy and the maintenance of a stable home life, Kenny's prognosis for a long-term recovery was good.

After the accident, Dave went off work on compassionate leave for nearly two months. During that time, he sold off the house because he could not stand to enter it and moved in with his parents.

Loaded up on valium, he'd managed to attend the funeral held for Jenny and the kids, but when it was over, he remembered very little about it.

For several weeks after that he really didn't give a damn about much of anything. Overwhelmed by the feeling of grief and loss, he simply bumbled around in a fog, lost a good deal of weight and refused to leave the protective cocoon of his parents' house.

The Police Department was good about it. Staff Relations told him to take as much time as he needed and not to worry about anything but getting back to normal, whatever the hell that was supposed to mean.

During the sixth week of leave, his old partner, Ed Hamilton began to drop in and after a few days, managed to get Dave out of the house and into a pub where they had some brews and the first real meal Dave had considered eating since the accident. They also played a few games of pool.

Ed kept the conversation on a general plane for the first half of the evening but slowly over the next hour or so began to mention things going on in the department. Promotions, firings, interesting cases etc. By the time they climbed into Ed's car to call it a night and head home, Dave had unconsciously begun to allow the shell he'd been living within to crack open slightly, just enough to begin to ask questions about other departmental goings on.

Ed was the type of guy who valued good friends and knew they were few and far between.

After he had dropped Dave off at his parents' and on his way home, encouraged by what had transpired during the evening, he began to formulate a long-term plan aimed at getting his pal Dave out of his slump and back to work.

Within the department it was common knowledge that once Ed had something in mind there was very little that could sway him off a determined course of action.

His nickname was *'Bulldog'*, and there was good reason for that.

CHAPTER FOUR

- October 1988 -

For Kenny, three years passed by reasonably uneventfully.

He and Grandma attended the monthly sessions with the psychologist religiously. He had managed to become less of a target in the schoolyard, had grown a few inches and lost some weight.

He still did not seek out or have any real friends, but he was no longer simply shunned out of hand by his classmates. He remained quiet, kept his thoughts to himself and still spent a lot of time at home playing games in his bedroom.

Both Grandma and Grandpa had worked at keeping him wrapped in love and attention, a little of his self-confidence had returned and the nightmares had lessened over time.

Unfortunately, any gains he had made during that period were about to be reversed with a vengeance.

In October of nineteen eighty-eight, a few days after Kenny's ninth birthday party, his grandfather, Gordon, passed away. The death, very traumatic for a boy of Kenny's tender years, was compounded by where and how suddenly it had occurred.

Gordon and the boy had been doing what they enjoyed best, spreading chips and cuttings with the excavator out in the bush. By this time Kenny had graduated to operating the machine while Grandpa sat to one side and supervised.

It was late in the day that Gordon suffered the massive heart attack. When the old man cried out, put his right hand over his heart and slumped against him, Kenny knew something was seriously wrong.

He managed to move the bulk of his grandfather off himself so that he could shut off the machine, but when he tried to help the old man it didn't take long for him to realize that there was nothing he could do.

He found himself immobile, staring down at the inert form for some time, studying it with growing interest.

The sight was somehow peaceful. The situation seemed to empower him. Out here suddenly alone, he felt in control of everything. He didn't want to leave Grandpa, but he knew he should go for help.

Light rain had been falling for a couple of hours and they were a long way from the house. Dusk was settling in.

Eventually Kenny climbed down out of the machine and called old Sam to his side. The two of them then headed back to the yard along the tracks made earlier by the heavy machine, piled into the little Ford pickup that Grandpa had recently allowed Kenny to drive, and meandered down the long driveway toward the house.

When the got there, Kenny shut the truck off, and leaving the door wide open for old Sam, went to find his grandmother.

After he'd told her what had happened, everything was kind of a blur to him.

Grandma had called for an ambulance and all three of them had got into the little truck and headed back to the road to wait for the ambulance so Kenny could lead them back to the machine.

When it arrived, the ambulance driver said they couldn't go out of the paved area of the yard with the ambulance because it would get stuck, so the two ambulance guys grabbed a bunch of stuff and the four of them hurried off into the bush with Sam on their heels.

Once the excavator came into view, Grandma made Kenny stay back, telling him that he would have to hold old Sam while the ambulance guys saw to Grandpa. He watched from a distance and when he saw Grandma raise her hand to her face and sink to her knees to the dirt, he knew that he wouldn't be seeing Grandpa again.

He dropped dejectedly down on a fallen log and threw his arms around Sam's neck.

He didn't cry, but he did do a lot of thinking, the reoccurring theme being, '*everyone who tells me they love me always dies.*'

Once the ambulance had gone, Kenny and his grandmother answered some questions for the policeman who had been at the storage lot waiting for them when they came out of the bush. The policeman wrote down the stuff in a notebook and then got back in his car and left. Then he, Grandma and old Sam drove slowly back to the house, Kenny behind the wheel and Grandma crunched down in the seat beside him, crying her eyes out.

When they got back inside Kenny allowed Grandma to hug him for a few minutes and then asked if he could go to his room for awhile. The old woman stepped back from him, did her best to stop her tears and then nodded. Gordon's passing had hit her very hard, but Kenny figured that she would probably come out of her funk eventually. She seemed like she had changed, to have lost much of her self-confidence.

He left her standing forlornly in the kitchen and made his way back to his room, closed his door and fired up the Atari VCS.

Several hours later he heard the doorbell and paused his game, then got up off his bed to walk over to his closed door to listen.

He heard his grandmother speaking to someone, he thought it was a lady, and a few seconds later there was a knock on his door and he heard his Grandma.

"Kenny would you like to come out? There is a social worker here, she's come to help us."

Kenny had no desire to meet some stranger but he knew a refusal would simply make matters worse. He let out a deep sigh and opened his door.

The lady stayed for over an hour and Kenny sat sullenly through the whole thing, answering a question if asked but volunteering nothing. The gist of the conversation between her and his grandmother was something she called 'bereavement counselling'.

Kenny closed his mind to most of the gibberish.

By the time the woman left he had a headache.

Grandma had stopped her crying by then and she was obviously concerned about him. She said she was going to make them dinner and he nodded and headed back to his room. She was moving around kind of zombie-like and seemed to have lost her zest for life, quite incapable of making any major decisions.

The next morning Kenny ignored his alarm clock when it went off to get him up for school. When his grandmother knocked and then opened his door a few minutes later, he told her that he was not feeling well and asked if he could stay home from school.

His grandmother appeared to be somewhat back to her normal self. She nodded her head and told him that he needn't go until he felt up to it.

Kenny managed to cocoon himself in his room, except for meals, over the next four days. After that Grandma told him that they both had to get their lives back on track. He would have to go back to school and they would be going to his regular session with the psychologist the next week.

The night out had brought about enough of a change in Dave to encourage Ed to push forward with his plan.

Ed took a week's leave and, with a little help from Dave's parents arrived with a truck full of camping gear and fishing equipment and all but kidnapped Dave.

As they pulled out of the driveway Ed grinned over at his astonished friend.

"Ever been ice fishing?"

Nine hours later they were well into northern British Columbia at a desolate lake that had taken more than a little *'four-by-fouring'* to reach. The tent was up and a hearty fire was flickering below a slung coffee pot.

Slowly, in increments over the next five days, Ed laid out his plan for Dave's future.

Everyone knows that time and time alone is the best healer, but Dave needed to help the grieving process to work its way though. He needed to get his mind on other things.

In the department, there was an opening for a cop of detective level to be paired up with a social worker in a new car that was going to be an experiment in dealing with a recent dramatic rise in domestic calls.

The department was looking for volunteers

Over the past couple of weeks Dave had repeatedly said that he didn't want to go back to what he had been doing.

He'd said that he needed to put the past behind him and take on new things. Well, he had to admit that this was something entirely new.

Dave's first response to the suggestion was,

"A social worker for a partner! You've got to be kidding man, a cop and a social worker, teamed up…no way."

At the time, Ed had left it at that, but over the following days he'd kept enthusiastically nibbling away at Dave's doubts.

"Look, No one has volunteered so far; they are working with a short time frame here."

"This new car is supposed to roll out in two weeks and the media have been all over the idea with positive response."

"It would be very embarrassing for the chief if it fell apart before it even got started. It never hurts to make the chief happy. They say he has a long memory. A move like this sure as hell can't but help your career man! You said you wanted something new and completely different. You've got to admit that it can't get much different than this."

"Besides it's only going to run for a six-month trial. That's all you have to commit to."

There was no one within a hundred miles of them and Ed, as planned, had the opportunity to bluntly use Dave as a captive audience.

The surroundings were magnificently pristine. The quiet and isolation was restful. The companionship was strong. The food was simple, but cooked over an open fire, delicious.

They even caught some fish!

It took almost the whole week, but by the time they had started the drive out, Ed had worn Dave down with his never-ending keenness about the whole idea.

Two weeks later Dave arrived at the chief's office to be briefed on the experimental unit and to meet his new partner. An official press conference was to be held later in the day.

Dave was a little anxious about the whole thing, but the idea behind the emergency response car had taken hold of him. He thought it had merit and it was certainly going to be completely different from everything else he done in the department before.

He was committed to the idea and becoming absorbed with it.

His grief had not disappeared, far from it, but he now had other things to think about as well. He had been a little surprised, but pleased, to find that he could, albeit briefly, push those feelings of loss to the back of his mind if required to respond to outside influences.

The meeting went well, as he'd figured it would.

There was one exception however. His new partner, the social worker provided by the provincial government ministry, which was co-sponsoring the experimental project, was not what he'd been picturing at all.

He had been excepting it to be a guy.

Instead it was a woman. She was introduced as to him as Linda Carnarvon, and she smiled broadly as she firmly shook his hand.

Linda was young, he guessed in her early twenties. She was also gorgeous.

Tall and slim, about five-ten. An athletic build, but very nicely rounded out in all the right places. Thick, shiny dark hair, worn long, to just past the shoulders. Big brown eyes that seemed to sparkle and miss nothing. A bright smile that you couldn't ignore.

During the next hour, he also found out she was very well educated, smart, confident, outgoing and in general terms, a pleasure to be around.

The next six months went very quickly for Dave and then, when the project came to an end, and he and Linda were quietly married in a civil ceremony, much to the surprise of everyone, including him and Linda.

CHAPTER FIVE

- July 1989 -

For nine months Kenny and Grandma had been living alone in the big house. During that time, Kenny, had slipped into the habit of calling her Granny instead of Grandma. Granny seemed more fitting somehow.

The psychologist told Granny that Kenny's progress had taken a backward step due to Gordon's death. Kenny was not responding well during their sessions. He tended to remain aloof and withdrawn, not only when in the session, but pretty well all the time.

At home Kenny, without Gordon around to get him out working on the property, seemed to be living in his bedroom. At school, he had become sullen and uncooperative.

Granny was at her wits end as to what to do to bring the boy out of his shell, to be more active. She was unsure of herself for the first time in her life and seemed to second guess every thought she had.

In July of eighty-nine she sat Kenny down one night and then read him a letter that had come from Gordon's younger brother, Bob, asking if he might come and visit them.

She seemed to think it was a good idea to let him come.

At first Kenny didn't say anything one way or the other, but in his own mind he didn't think it would be a good idea at all.

Granny then went on to explain to him that she had good reason to allow the visit. His other grandmother, Edith was trying to get custody of Kenny. And that would mean that she and Kenny might be separated. And he would have to go and live with her instead.

Kenny didn't completely understand it all, but apparently Edith had hired a lawyer and was going to go to court. Granny told him that his other Grandmother was saying that Kenny should stay with her instead because she had the staff to help look after him and Edith was on her own.

Granny figured that if Bob did visit them, then she would have a better chance of keeping Kenny with her. Besides that, Bob was an ex -priest who had had a breakdown and had been unable to continue in his field. Together she and Kenny could maybe help him get better and he could spend a lot of time with Kenny, which would be a good thing. She said it would be a positive to have a man around the house who Kenny could learn from.

Kenny didn't like the idea of someone new coming into his life. It seemed to him that everyone who had cared for him, his parents and his sister and Gordon, had all died and left him. He could see no advantage to having this Bob character visit. He certainly didn't give a damn about trying to help some stranger.

On the other hand, he did not want to be uprooted and forced to endure a new environment. He was reasonably comfortable with the way things were with Granny.

Granny obviously wanted him to agree with the idea though, and he figured he should probably do that, if he wanted things to stay the way they were.

So, he said that he thought it might be a good idea to let Bob at least come and visit. If he was anything like grandpa Gordon, it might be OK.

A week after they'd had that little talk, Granny got called to go to the school on the Wednesday. When she got there, she found Kenny waiting in the principal's office and was told that he had been stealing things from the other kids in the class and had been caught red-handed.

Kenny would neither admit nor deny the thefts, nor would he agree to return items that had gone missing but had not been recovered.

Instead, he refused to speak, sitting mute throughout the entire session.

As a result, he was suspended from school until he was prepared to admit to the thefts and had also returned any articles that were still in his possession.

As they drove home in the little red Ford pickup, Granny tried to start a conversation with Kenny but he simply sat silently in the passenger seat and stared out the window.

Two weeks later, when Bob arrived for his visit, Kenny was still suspended.

Bob, who look very much like his brother Gordon, presented agreeably. He was well-groomed and neatly dressed in a suit and tie, and sported highly polished oxfords. Granny was obviously impressed.

To Kenny, who over the past few years had spent a good deal of time assessing others, Bob did not seem to be a person who had suffered a breakdown. He appeared to be confident, caring and very much in control of himself. Initially growling at the intruder, Old Sam had uncharacteristically made it clear that he didn't like him from the get go and Kenny thought the dog probably had the right of it.

Bob had arrived with a single suitcase only, but Granny had later explained that away to Kenny, saying priests lived a very simple life.

It was apparent to Kenny that Granny was very taken with the man. He figured that was probably because he looked like Gordon and gave the appearance of an upright, caring and amiable individual.

Kenny wasn't so sure about that. Nobody was that good.

He fleetingly wondered what might be beneath that polished surface. That said, he knew he would need more than this brief initial meeting to come to any serious conclusion about the newcomer.

As was his way, Kenny kept his thoughts to himself.

Within a few days, Bob had fully ingratiated himself with Granny.

Comfortably ensconced in living quarters located in the secluded far wing of the rambling house, Kenny and Granny saw little of him in the evenings, but during the day, he seemed to have all but stepped directly into Gordon's shoes.

Kenny didn't particularly enjoy this interruption of his earlier environment. He kept his thoughts to himself and while outwardly pleasant enough to the man, he figured he was losing even more of his life as Bob worked slowly but surely toward gaining the old woman's complete confidence.

Bob seemed to be no end of help and advice, fixing little things that needed doing, helping here, there and everywhere.

Two weeks into the visit the advice was coming in a flow. Bob advised granny that Kenny didn't need to go back to school if he didn't want to. He and Granny could easily home-school him, whatever that entailed.

Granny readily agreed.

When he and Granny went to the next session with the psychologist, Bob drove them in the Ford and waited for them outside. At the end, when granny went in for her short talk with the psychologist, he told her that Kenny was no longer responding to the sessions and that he felt Kenny needed to begin seeing a psychiatrist.

On the way home, they went to McDonalds for a burger, Granny having told Bob that Gordon had always taken them there. While they ate, Granny told Bob what the psychologist had said. Bob nodded solemnly and then said that he had had some experience along that line and wasn't overly supportive of the idea.

Kind of talking over Kenny's head, Bob suggested that Kenny probably only needed to build a little self-confidence and just needed some firm male bonding.

He felt that between him and Granny they could provide all the help Kenny needed to bring him out of his shell.

Granny seemed a little unsure of that, but she put the suggestion to Kenny directly, asking him if he wanted to do as the psychologist had suggested and begin sessions with a psychiatrist or instead try having just the three of them work it all out.

Kenny had no wish at all to see any more shrinks. Not surprisingly, he voted for the second choice.

From that day forth, Kenny was home-schooled.

Bob had some definite ideas about how the three of them would work on helping Kenny.

Kenny, in his bedroom, overheard them talking one evening that week after dinner. Bob was speaking confidently and with authority; Granny was mostly listening.

"The boy needs to be a boy and learn what it means to be a man.

"You mother him too much. Not that I blame you mind; the kid has been through a lot. However, he's getting older and that should stop now. The boy is too soft.

"I've had a lot of experience working with troubled youth. He should spend more time with me.

We should move him out of his current bedroom and place him in the wing where I'm staying. That way he won't always be running to you when he has those nightmares of his. I can console him when he needs it.

"He needs some discipline and a male role model, a man to look up to and help harden him up a little.

"You can school him in the morning and then I'll take him out and spend time with him for the remainder of the day, just as Gordon did. He can show me how to work the machines and the male bonding that will naturally take place while we are working together will do him world of good."

With everything that had been going on over the past few months, Granny was grasping at straws.

She welcomed Bob's suggestions as if they were a gift from God.

Dave returned to Major Crime after completing his six months in the emergency response car experiment, which had gone extremely well for all concerned and was now a permanent fixture in the Patrol Division.

He had moved into Linda's west end apartment after they got married. It was small and they both wanted to purchase a house somewhere in the suburbs. They were actively checking the real-estate listings.

After a four-month stint in robbery, Dave, who had impressed the upper brass both while in the trial patrol unit and as a robbery investigator, had then been selected by the chief to move over to the elite homicide section, as a replacement for a retiring detective.

Homicide had only six detective teams, and each of them were very good at their jobs. Detectives didn't make the grade unless their early detective work in other areas had been outstanding. Clearance rates by way of convictions were high. Anyone who was lucky enough to be selected to one of the six positions, rarely left the post by choice. Once into the prime job, the majority lost any interest in promotion and tended to stay put and ride it out until they retired.

The most senior members of this elite squad had worked together as partners for most of their careers and were looked upon with a fair amount of awe by the other members of the force.

As chance would have it, Dave was paired with the most senior man on the squad. Although he only got to spend a short time with his new Homicide partner, who was near retiring at the time, during their time working together, Dave learned a lot and the two of them successfully cleared a couple of tough murders. Dave loved the work and was more than ready to accept a new partner and continue in Homicide, but the Chief had other plans for him.

Dave was a little uneasy when the call came in for him to head upstairs. He had no idea why he was being summoned to the top of the building. And he had a good case of butterflies when he left the elevator and entered the boss's secretary's office. Luckily, he wasn't given a lot of time to worry about why he was there, as on his arrival, he was whisked directly into the Chief's office where he found him and the two deputies huddled together around the circular boardroom table at the far end of the spacious room.

The three of them stopped talking as the secretary closed the door behind Dave, turned to look toward him and the Chief rose and then beckoned him over.

"Grab a seat. We have an offer for you to consider."

The gist of the conversation that followed was that Internal Affairs appeared to be having some difficulty in dealing with some serious complaints which had been going nowhere and, would Dave be willing to accept an assignment there?

Dave heard them and took a few seconds to consider his response. He didn't want to seem ungrateful, but Dave who was often honest to a fault, went with his gut feeling.

"I'm not sure I would be comfortable with that. Investigating other members of the department is not exactly what I pictured myself doing as a cop. I really like Homicide…"

The Operations Deputy replied, "Fair enough, but we'd like you to think about it. It takes a very special kind of man for a job like this. You seem to be pretty well qualified for it."

The Administration Deputy stepped in.

"It takes a guy who is not only well-liked by all ranks, but trusted as a fair player. No one wants to work Internal; that's probably why the unit is currently doing such a lousy job."

They were team playing him. The ball bounced back to the Operations Deputy.

"We've taken a hard look at your service record and we are all of the opinion that the other members of the department certainly think of you as both honest and fair, although we admit that in consideration of your relatively rapid rise through the ranks, there is bound to be some who feel a certain amount of jealousy and as a result may well be detractors. That said, we think you're smart enough to handle that type of problem, should it arise.

"And a successful stint in Internal would certainly look good to any promotional board you might find yourself facing later in your career."

The chief dropped the clincher.

"While on your assignment in the emergency response car, you clearly demonstrated an ability to ingratiate yourself and the department when dealing with both the media and the public. I think you would do very well acting as the spokesman for a revamped internal unit. It wouldn't be for more than a year or so, just long enough to get things reorganized in there. Of course, should you agree to take it on, it would mean a promotion to Sergeant, as we would want you in a supervisory and leadership position."

He paused for effect before continuing.

"Unless memory fails me that would make you the youngest man ever to reach the rank of Sergeant in this department.

When Dave didn't respond, he expanded.

"While very important to the Department, Internal is a small squad. You'd pretty well be able to call the shots and while there, you'd only have the Inspector to answer to..."

He chuckled before continuing.

"...and the three of us, of course.

CHAPTER SIX

- March 1990 -

The custody issue regarding Kenny reached the court in early December of 1989, a couple of weeks before Christmas.

Kenny had not been briefed on the situation in any great depth but he did know that a decision as to who he would be living with in the future would depend upon the outcome of that court appearance.

Bob had arranged for a lawyer to represent Granny, and Kenny knew that the lawyer felt they didn't have as good a case as his other Grandmother Edith did. This knowledge depressed Kenny.

While he was not particularly happy about the current situation with Granny Gertrude seeming under Bob's thumb, it was at least something he understood and could deal with.

The idea of being uprooted and going to live with Granny Edith had no appeal for him whatsoever.

As luck would have it, Bob had an idea of how Granny Gertrude's position could be improved.

It was simple really. He and Granny would marry and then, as a stable couple, they would be in a far better position to argue the provision of a better home life than their opposition, and thereby stand a much better chance of winning the custody battle for Kenny.

Granny's lawyer had agreed with that suggestion.

Later, the deed accomplished, Bob had officially become his new grandfather.

As predicted, he and Granny won the custody of Kenny.

Christmas was a big celebration for the three of them. Bob was very pleased with the way things had worked out and as a result Kenny found everything he'd asked for under the tree that year.

After New Years had passed, life settled down and returned to normal in the rambling house.

If not particularly a happy nor well-adjusted boy, Kenny was at least more or less at peace.

The winter weather meant that he and Bob could not do much outside and that left him free to retire to his room and his Atari. Bob had convinced Granny to give in to his pre-Christmas request for more adult-oriented games and several new ones had appeared under the tree as presents for him.

A couple of these new ones provided him with the opportunity to indulge in a good deal more violence and this made him feel far more in control when he played them, feeling a great deal of satisfaction and pleasure.

He was now able to battle with, maim, and destroy numerous characters who challenged him on the screen. Life was relatively acceptable to Kenny.

Then that all changed.

At first Kenny didn't really pick up on anything out of the norm.

He and Bob had headed out to do the chores together after a morning home-schooling session with Granny. Initially, things went well.

They had some chickens to cull and Bob took him down to the pen and told him what chickens to bring out while he got the block and the axe. Kenny was then informed that part of Bob's program about teaching him to be a man was to have Kenny do the head chopping from now on.

Previously, Kenny had been grossed out by the sight of 'chickens-with-their-heads-cut-off' frantically spraying blood around, but that was not the case on this occasion.

Instead, the idea held a great deal of appeal for Kenny. He found himself eagerly looking forward to watching the chickens running around after their heads had been removed. Additionally, he thought that the idea of doing the cutting himself might be very stimulating.

Bob even let him toss the chicken heads and legs into the pigs after they were through and he wholeheartedly enjoyed watching the wildly grunting animals fight over the bloody scraps.

Kenny was also subconsciously aware that Bob was enjoying the activities too, or at least, enjoying watching Kenny's reaction to it.

When they had finished with the animals, it was time to head out to the front of the property to the yard where the equipment was kept.

Bob let Kenny drive the little Ford and the old dump truck, then asked him if he would show him how the excavator worked.

Kenny showed him how to start it and work the controls but once into the operator's seat, Bob was unsure. He asked Kenny to sit in his lap and run thorough everything with him again.

Kenny was enjoying the feeling of kind of being the boss and he readily agreed.

He clambered up into the man's lap, then began to run through the whole procedure again.

The guy seemed unusually dense. Kind of like he was in a fog and his mind was on something else.

Bob was kind of hugging him like, holding him steady and jostling Kenny around playfully as he explained stuff again. Then a few minutes later he noticed that Bob's breathing had became laboured. A few seconds later, Bob grunted and let out a deep sigh.

Nothing was said but after Bob's breathing had returned to normal, he lifted Kenny up and moved him over to the small seat Gordon had made for him earlier.

He then began to work the machine and Kenny offered advice as they worked and thought no more about the somewhat strange behavior that had taken place while he was in Bob's lap.

That experience wasn't going to be a one-off though. The next day Bob had again asked Kenny to sit in his lap and go over the machine's controls. It was a repeat performance of the day before.

Two nights later Kenny had one of the reoccurring nightmares about the car crash and woke up chilled and in a sweat. His room was dark but as he tried to settle himself down he realized that the door was slightly ajar. After a few seconds, his eyes adjusted to the dimness and he became aware of the fact that someone was standing at the foot of his bed.

He let out a little cry of surprise and Bob spoke. His voice was soft and reassuring.

"Having one of those bad dreams of yours, hey son? You were moaning and I could hear you. Nothing to worry about now. I'm here. It will be all right."

Bob moved up to the side of the bed and sat down on the edge, then reached out and hugged him. The embrace was something that Kenny was used to when he woke up from a nightmare. Granny had done it many times. It was comforting to Kenny and he accepted it.

Bob cradled him and gently rubbed his back as he spoke.

"Nothing to worry about at all. I'll stay with you until you feel better."

Eventually Kenny went back to sleep.

When he woke in the morning he felt a little strange about what had happened. At breakfast Bob was telling Granny Gertrude how he had heard him having the nightmare and had come in to comfort him.

Granny seemed pleased.

Kenny figured all was well and dug into his food.

The next night Bob was back in Kenny's room. While Kenny slept, he gingerly pulled back the covers and stared at the ten-year-old for almost an hour while he leisurely masturbated.

Kenny never even knew he was there.

Two nights later Bob was back just before dawn. He had the covers pulled back and was very lightly fondling the boy. Kenny came half awake and then sleepily shifted his hips against the pressure on his privates.

Bob kept stroking as he smiled down at him.

"Nothing to worry about son…you got a woody is all…very normal for a young fellow like you. I can help you with that.

It will feel good and it will be our little secret, just between you and me.

It's guy stuff; we won't tell your grandmother.

She wouldn't understand.

"Just close your eyes and relax."

From that night onward, good old Bob regularly visited Kenny's room several times a week.

Kenny found these visits strange and a little uncomfortable but felt powerless to do anything about them.

Now that Kenny had been moved away from Granny, Bob also discovered that Kenny was regularly wetting his bed.

He got very angry and told Kenny that it was a slovenly, dirty habit and that he had to stop. Whenever Kenny wet from that point on, Bob would make him change his own bed, and wash the soiled linen. Bob would then make him pull down his pants and proceed to use his belt on him.

Bob was careful to only demand this punishment when Granny was occupied elsewhere, and he told the boy that if he ever complained to the old woman, he would receive a much more severe punishment for his dirty ways.

From then on, Kenny tried very hard not to wet the bed. He was afraid to go to sleep at night and fought to stay awake so he could go to the bathroom often. He began to suffer from insomnia, lost weight and soon had dark rings below his eyes due to lack of sleep.

As time went on, good old Bob showed Kenny lots of other things that two guys could enjoy together. Kenny was deeply confused about the whole thing. On one hand, he hated it and wanted it to stop, on the other it did feel good at the end.

It wasn't his decision to make of course. He felt powerless to do anything about it.

Dave had taken the position in Internal.

Sergeant Dave Richards and his wife were now the proud owners of a two-year-old three-bedroom bungalow located on a half acre lot in Richmond, a Vancouver bedroom community suburb.

After a couple of weeks, he'd proven to his satisfaction that his initial concerns about accepting the job could reasonably be handled with a little determination and an open mind.

The Inspector in charge of the unit had had a meeting with the Chief before Dave arrived and had obviously been ordered to give him a free hand. That went a long way toward making things easier than Dave had anticipated

It didn't take him long to decide that the squad was in a rut, without doubt.

It consisted of the Inspector, him, a receptionist and four detectives. He found out quickly that two of the detectives were near retirement and while they tended to appear very busy, they accomplished little, if anything. They resented finding themselves suddenly under the supervision of a new and very young Sergeant brimming with new ideas and making changes, but this close to retirement, they had no desire to rock the boat.

Dave decided to put them on notice, letting them know that he felt they were just going through the motions and that he would be expecting them to either pull up their socks and get involved in the task at hand, or he'd transfer them out. For the two of them, the current assignment was, or at least it had been, a cushy spot. A good place to idle away their last months. Neither of them wanted to be bounced.

Dave sat them down in his office together, and read them the riot act, then softened it with the comment that both had been damn good detectives earlier in their careers and that he was quite prepared to let them stay, but only if they shifted out of low gear and started to produce some results.

They heard him out, looked at each other briefly, smiled and acknowledged that they had been floating and both committed to adopting a new attitude.

Dave agreed to give them two weeks to demonstrate they were serious.

The other two detectives on the squad were younger, one in his late thirties and the second in his early fifties. He called them into his office separately, the oldest of the two first.

Dave had studied their personnel files carefully and he'd determined the shortcomings of each, well before sitting them down. The older one had come to Internal directly from Patrol, after his promotion to Detective. He had been a good street cop out on the road and was certainly seen as a fair guy by most of the force. Those two things had probably been the driving force behind his selection in the first place.

That said, it hadn't taken Dave long to figure out why he wasn't effective in his current assignment. The problem was that he was also very much one of the boys and had no desire to ever be thought of as anything but that, by his fellow cops. Subsequently he had a strong, predetermined bias against finding any cop at fault. It was clear to Dave that there was no way he should be working the Internal detail.

Dave went straight to the problem and told him his chances of promotion were going to be seriously affected by his stint in Internal if he remained, and he told him why. Dave didn't fault him for the fact. He simply advised him that Internal was not for everyone and it certainly wasn't a good spot for a man who didn't want to hurt his fellow officers' feelings. His transfer would take place immediately.

The youngest Detective was another matter.

After reviewing his file, Dave was a little nonplussed. Lots of commendations, ambitious, good street cop. He was recently new to the squad, having been here only three months. That could be part of the problem. More likely though, it was because the more senior guy he'd just transferred out had been his partner.

Dave figured that the older Detective had probably been holding the younger one back.

When he interviewed this detective, Dave didn't pull any punches. He told him how he saw it and said he wasn't happy with what appeared to have been going on and that it had to stop. He was prepared to give the younger detective a second chance with a new partner, but if things didn't radically improve he would transfer him out as well.

He advised him that considering your own without a hint of bias was not an easy task for any cop, but it was what it was. A bad cop was something no one needed, not the public and certainly not the Department. He made it clear that if the man wanted to stay in Internal, he was going to have to be prepared to see things in that light and honestly do the investigations he was handed.

If not, Dave didn't want him. The choice was his.

On the home front things, if a little hectic, were going well for Dave and Linda.

After doing the stint in the police unit with Dave, she'd decided it was time to work on her Master's degree in social work. That meant taking courses during the day at the University of British Columbia. To facilitate this, she'd requested and been granted permission to work steady night shifts, and had been transferred to the after-hours Emergency Services Ministry office, which handled juvenile placements and after-hours family counselling and services.

That also meant working a good number of weekends as well as in the evenings, as that was when the normal Ministry offices were closed.

Working in Internal, Dave was nine to five Monday to Friday.

Because of their conflicting schedules, they were often living like ships passing in the night. It wasn't easy for them, and after a few weeks of it, Linda had offered to drop her schooling for awhile if Dave wanted her to.

Dave knew Linda well enough to know that she didn't really want to stop her schooling and he told her that it wouldn't be forever and they could handle it.

Despite the shift conflicts, like most newly married couples, they managed to spend quality time together and, on any weekend, that Linda managed to get off, they rarely got out of bed except to attend to the necessities of eating and visiting the bathroom.

Having a social worker in the family was very good for Dave; it helped him work through the grieving process. Being able to love again was a bonus he hadn't even seen coming.

All in all, life was pretty good.

CHAPTER SEVEN

- September 1991 -

By his twelfth birthday Kenny was living a double life.

He'd accepted his lot in his day-to-day existence because he couldn't do anything to change it, but he blocked that part out whenever he could and instead, lived in a new and separate fantasy world, a world which allowed him to be in control where he called the shots.

He'd become a quiet, reserved and unhappy boy who had learned how to fade into the background when in the real world. He was Bob's pawn and complied with everything the man demanded of him. Now, when Bob came for him, he simply shut down mentally, blocking it all from his mind.

He'd also managed to expand this new commanding and forceful fictional existence, in which he could escape from the real world, a place where he was in command, where he could deliver pain, injury and death to all who challenged him.

For a couple of weeks now, he'd been considering broadening his fantasies even more.

Starting destructive fires was his first innovation.

Several suspicious blazes in the neighbourhood occurred. Kenny had been careful to cover his tracks on those. Days later he'd strangled and dismembered a neighbourhood cat using a butcher knife.

Each of these acts had brought him a wonderful sense of expanded power and control. He had spontaneously ejaculated, without manual manipulation, while observing the last two fires rage and during the mutilation of the cat.

In so doing, he had found a new way to be in full control of at least part of his real life and found it a very wonderful and empowering achievement indeed.

In general, his day to day real life had changed as well.

Bob seemed to have Granny in the palm of his hand and now it was he who was making all the important decisions about what went on in the house and with the business. He'd decided they should buy a computer for the business, and promptly went out that day and bought one, arriving back at the house with not only the new machine, but also a brand new pickup truck.

Obviously, the ex-priest had also found his way into the control of the family chequebook.

From that point on, the new truck was parked in the garage and the little old Ford was relegated to sitting out on the edge of the circular driveway.

Bob had also begun to drink heavily and was quite often drunk by evening.

Granny was now spending a lot of her time in bed, feeling poorly, and any free time she had, she spent in the kitchen. Except for a little cooking, she had little enthusiasm for much of anything.

The old woman did worry about the boy, however, and took responsibility for his home schooling as Bob had directed. However, when she was with what was now a barely responsive Kenny, she found herself incapable of seriously relating to him, seemingly lost in a sort of dream world and just going though the motions.

Old Sam had begun to spend most of his time following Kenny around in the house and liked to sleep in Kenny's room at night. By this point Kenny considered the dog his only real companion.

But that was about to change as well.

Bob eventually took note of the time the two now spent together and began to complain that the animal was not well, had begun to stink and should be put out of its misery. A few days later he took the boy and dog out to the front of the property and told Kenny to shoot him with Gordon's old twenty-two and then made him use the excavator to bury the corpse.

For a split-second Kenny, who was familiar with, and had used, the gun on several occasions under Gordon's supervision, thought about turning the weapon on Bob and shooting him instead.

But Kenny wasn't stupid. He knew he wouldn't get away with shooting the man, so he did as he was asked. Did it without giving the act too much thought.

He had no real qualms about the execution and found watching the dog die and handling the dead but warm corpse strangely stimulating.

It gave him an erection.

The incident wasn't unsettling to him, and it only served to further confirm to Kenny that anything that warmed to him was destined to die. He thought nothing more of it, but from that day forward Kenny sank even deeper into his fantasy world and rarely left his room.

A week later Bob began chastising the boy for spending all his free time brooding in his bedroom playing stupid games and avoiding chores. He then decided that Kenny, since he already knew how to operate the dump truck and excavator, should now take over sole responsibility for continuing the process of leveling the property.

In front of Granny, he told the boy it would do him good to get outside and get a little exercise and fresh air for a change.

Granny didn't object; she hadn't even responded to the comment. At first Kenny, had wanted to rebel against the suggestion, but he quickly realized that it would allow him to get out from under from Bob's thumb, for at least part of each day.

The next morning, after he'd take his lessons with granny, Kenny got together some rain gear and hurried out to the little Ford, and then headed to the yard.

The rest of that day went well for him. He liked working on his own and while he was out in the bush, no one could intrude upon his fantasy world. That first day, he'd kept at it until the sky had begun to darken with impending dusk and he was forced to accept the fact that he would soon have to return to the house and face the night ahead.

This knowledge compelled him to reluctantly release his fantasy world and face the inevitable.

He briefly considered just getting back into little Ford and running away, but lacked the self-confidence to do it. Angry and frustrated by the unfairness of it all, he reluctantly drove the excavator back to the yard and dejectedly headed for the house.

When he arrived, Bob was sitting on the porch waiting for him. For a few seconds Kenny just sat in the cab staring at the man through the wipers as they slowly brushed back and forth across the windshield and then, accepting the preordained, he sighed deeply, shut the Ford down and got out.

Bob stood up unsteadily and started right in. His words were slurred and he was obviously half drunk.

"What the hell have you been playing at boy? Where in Christ's name have you been? You've missed your dinner. Well, now you can bloody well go without.

"Don't just stand there gaping like an idiot, get into the house. I have half a mind to take a belt to you. We'll deal with that later tonight."

The Richards family had grown by one, a calico kitten, who they had named Murphy.

Linda was getting to the end her studies on her Master's degree and Dave had Internal ticking over like a fine watch.

In the first six months of his posting to the new job, one of the older Detectives had come up to speed and the other, who had chosen not to change his ways, had been amicably transferred to stolen autos, where he could ride out the rest of his career in happy oblivion.

Dave had personally selected the man's replacement and for the past year, that new member of the team seemed to be doing very well.

All four of his men where showing signs of a committed effort and, as spokesmen for the squad, Dave had managed to keep a good balance with both the media and the public. The Chief and his two deputies were happy, and whenever he needed it he was receiving immediate support from them for any innovation he wanted to introduce.

The Chief had originally said he would be able to leave after a year, but it had taken a little longer for Dave to makes the changes he wanted, and to assure himself that these had done the job required, so he'd requested to stay with it until that had been achieved.

When he felt he had met that goal, he was asked where he wanted to go next and he'd chosen to go back to Major Crime. There was a currently an opening for a Sergeant in Homicide and he got it.

He'd no more than settled into his new office when he got called back upstairs for another meeting with the big three.

The Chief advised him that they were considering sending someone from Homicide down to the FBI academy at Quantico to take a course on Profiling and Serial Killer investigations and asked was he interested?

He was.

Three weeks later he was on the course.

The knowledge he gleaned over the term of the course completely absorbed and fascinated him.

He learned that the object of profiling criminals was to detect and classify the major personality and behavioral characteristics of an individual based upon analysis of the crime or crimes the person had committed.

This involved several steps.

The first of which was referred to as *'assimilation'*, during which all information available about the crime scene, victim, and witnesses, was carefully examined. This included victim profiles, police reports, crime scene evidence and photos, witness statements and autopsy reports.

The next phase was coined 'classification' and concerned integration of all the information collected into a framework which would allow the classification of the perpetrator as being either 'organized' or disorganized'.

In the case of serial killers, once the killer had been classified, an attempt needed to be made to reconstruct the 'behavioral sequence' of the crime. This required a reconstruction of the perpetrator's 'modus operandi'. During this process, the profiler had to look for the offender's *'signature'*, the thing that the perpetrator does to satisfy his or her psychological needs while committing the crime.

After further study of the 'MO', the offender's signature, and an evaluation of any presence of staging of the crime, the profiler then generates the profile. This document would contain detailed information regarding the offender's demographic and family characteristics, any military background, education, and personality characteristics. It would also suggest to the investigator an appropriate interview/interrogation technique, to be used after making the arrest.

To profile serial killers, it is first necessary to link crimes to a type of common offender. To accomplish this, the type of offender could be determined based on types of action committed at the crime scene. It is of prime importance that this classification be reliable and be verifiable through means of observation or experiment to assign an offender to one group.

This classification also needs to meet with the assumptions of a typology. It needs to be made according to specific types, occur together frequently, and be distinct from the characteristics specific to any another type.

The course wound up with a breakdown of how a successful serial killer investigation should be conducted, starting from the top.

Other than the assignment of knowledgeable and experienced homicide investigators to lead positions in the team, leadership must play a virtually non-existent role in the actual investigation. Its primary task is to establish and reaffirm the primary goal of catching the killer and provide support for the investigators.

The organization of the structure or task force of an investigation, is key to its success. Serial killers often commit their crimes in more than one law enforcement jurisdiction. Therefore, ensuring information sharing between other agencies and jurisdictions is paramount as is the collecting of all related information into a single location where it can be organized and easily accessed by other jurisdictions who are working toward the goal of arresting an offender.

Prior to being formed the need for it should be identified as either long term, or short term.

Short term needs, like the canvassing of a neighborhood or road blocks should only be called in on a short-term basis. When the task force's framework is expanded to include a new resource on a long-term basis, it should become permanent and not removed.

The decision of whether resources are needed short or long term must be made personally by the lead investigator.

If the investigation runs longer than eighteen months, there is a risk of burnout for individual investigators. While it is inadvisable to add and subtract staff from a task force under most conditions, leadership must remain vigilant to ensure that individual burnout in a member is not allowed to occur.

Inter-departmental and inter-agency communication, is paramount. Fluid communication within the confines of the task force is a no-brainer but it is also important to keep uniformed street patrol cops up to date and in the loop. This can be accomplished by having one or more of the task force team responsible for providing periodic summary briefings to patrol officers and field supervisors. Providing up to date briefings and information to officers on the street almost inevitably improves the chances or picking up solid leads in the case.

Another important activity in this type of investigation is the management of all the information that flows in to the task force from outside. The investigation of a serial killer generates a staggering amount of data. All of it should be reviewed and analyzed. Therefore, a standardized method of documenting and distributing information must be established up front and investigators must be allowed time to complete reports at the end of each shift, after investigating leads.

CHAPTER EIGHT

- December 1991 -

Overall, conditions had improved a little for Kenny.

He enjoyed getting out of the house and away from Bob during the day by spreading the chips and shredded material out in the bush. It allowed him to spend the entire time locked into his fantasy world.

Bob's drinking had increased. Not only was he normally drunk by late afternoon, he had taken to heading out to the pub for his dinner and often didn't return to the house until the early hours of the morning. Often, when he got back he was so drunk that he passed up the bath he normally took before he retired and instead, reeking of booze, passed out on his bed fully clothed.

Kenny did not miss his nocturnal visitor on these occasions and it made for a definite improvement when it came to the amount of abuse and beatings he had to endure, the situations that he had learned to block from his mind.

Those visits had become almost nightly, but now were usually only two or three times a week.

Granny seemed to be a little happier as well now that Bob was away for a good part of the time. She and Kenny sporadically had a chance to regain just a little of what had been their existence before the ex-priest had come into their lives.

It wasn't a big change of course. By now, Granny had been browbeaten into the ground by the miserable bastard and what remained of her was only a shell of her original self. But at least it was a small improvement.

On the other hand, by this point Kenny was spending most of his days deeply embedded inside his fantasy world. He was also spending a lot of that time trying to figure out some way to accomplish the commission of those delicious activities without the cops ever finding out that he'd done it.

December of ninety-one was the first Christmas that Kenny never received any gifts. The celebration was ignored completely; they didn't even have a tree.

It occurred to Kenny then that there really wasn't much reason for him to remain in the house and he figured that at twelve years old, he might just be old enough to make it on his own. He told himself that if things didn't begin to improve in the next few months, he might run away and take his chances out on his own. What the hell, cutting out had to be a better deal than the status quo.

Accomplishing that would take some careful planning and preparation on his part to pull off, and it would take time.

He would need a bunch of money. Enough to hold him over until he found some way to make some cash on his own. He would also have to figure out where to go, someplace where Bob couldn't find him, because he knew only too well that the twisted, drunken bastard would come looking for him.

When he was out in the bush working, he kept an eye out for anything he could find and began to set snares for rabbits and other small animals he could catch.

The first thing he now did each morning when he arrived, was to check the snares. If he had been lucky enough to catch something overnight, he'd enthusiastically kill it very slowly, savour watching it die, and then happily dissect it with his sharp penknife, before disposing of it.

Those days were the best days for him.

Four months had passed since Kenny's last kill and mutilation. He was beginning to feel an overpowering compulsion to do it again.

Granny was now spending most of her days in bed. She'd been recently diagnosed by her doctor with something called 'multiple myeloma' and seemed to be in a very bad way. She'd gone for several treatments and Kenny had overheard something about a remission, which was apparently likely to be temporary at best.

Kenny wasn't much bothered by that. It meant that he no longer had to do the homeschooling thing and he sure as hell didn't miss that. Bob didn't seem to give a damn about his not taking his lessons and that was just fine with Kenny.

Kenny was curious about a couple of things though. He'd never given any consideration to the fact that Granny might die. But, it seemed to him that that was likely now. If she did die, he'd be left on his own with Bob and that was a very chilling thought. Kenny decided that he needed to find out more about this *'multiple myeloma'* stuff, but he wasn't sure how to do that.

He sure as hell wasn't going to ask Bob, and Granny was being medicated and was kind of unresponsive these days, so he couldn't very well ask her.

Eventually he decided that he might try and see if he could look it up on the computer that Bob had bought for the business.

Bob used the machine almost daily, but only in the mornings, and then only after his hangover from the night before had begun to wear off. Kenny had no idea of how the thing worked, but he soon figured a way around that obstacle.

The computer was set up in a small alcove next to the kitchen, on a desk that overlooked the expanse of water beyond and below the house.

For over a week Kenny passed up working in the bush for as long as he could. Instead he would get things done as quickly as he could and then drive back down the driveway toward the house for about a half mile and then park the little Ford and make his way on foot back to the house.

He'd then enter quietly and wait until Bob sat down to use the computer. Then, ensconced safely in the recesses of the darkened room directly across the hall from the small office, he used binoculars to watch what the bastard was doing at the keyboard.

It took him while, but eventually he found an angle where he could see both the keyboard and the screen.

He concentrated on the start up procedure first and picked that up quickly. Early on, the stuff on the screen didn't interest him much, business stuff he figured. But on the second day of his spying Bob eventually shifted from doing the business stuff and the content showing up on the screen changed.

Kenny couldn't believe his eyes. Thanks to Bobs nocturnal visit to his bedroom, the content of the pictures that were scrolling across the screen was not particularly shocking to Kenny, but the fact that that kind of thing could be available on the machine certainly was.

After a week of watching the goings on in the small office, Kenny waited until Bob had gone out for his usual pub visit late one afternoon and then he went into the office and sat down at the computer. As usual, Bob had left the thing on and all he had to do was press the space bar to bring the screen to life.

Kenny learned all about Multiple Myeloma, although it had taken him a fair amount of time to figure out how to spell it right. From what he read, it was obvious that Granny was not likely to be around for much longer. She was going to die soon.

A scary thought…just him and Bob in the house.

This changed things for sure. Bob was going to have to die before Granny did.

Kenny managed to find the place were Bob was getting the kiddie porn he liked to watch, and he spent an hour having a look at what was available.

It was very appealing to him and he masturbated a couple of times before he'd finished watching.

That night in bed Kenny concentrated on what he had now coined as 'the Bob problem'.

Later in that week Bob had inadvertently left the machine open on a sadomasochistic kiddie gay porn site. Kenny found this new theme extremely stimulating. He'd masturbated repeatedly, until he could no longer do it.

Then he noticed the favorites list at the top of the screen and began to explore. Before long he was into sites that covered the same kind of material but also depicted dominance and even snuff portrayals.

He found these wildly stimulating and started adding them to his own private fantasy world, fleshing it out with glee.

He'd struck a gold mine, and things were looking up in his little private world. By comparison, video games were bland now. Kenny decided that he was going to be spending a lot of time sitting in front of the computer in the future.

Gone was any thought of taking off and trying to make it on his own.

The computer was in the house and he wasn't leaving it for anything.

There were a least a few reasons for him to stay now, but the computer was the most important one for him.

Bob was the one who was going to leave, and that needed to happen very soon.

He set up a new schedule for himself.

He started to spend his days out in the bush, avoiding Bob, and doing whatever happened to be in the snares, then as soon as he heard Bob drive out on his pub date Kenny would close everything down and go back to the house, quietly go inside and close the office door behind him, before he fired up the computer.

Eyes glued to the screen, he would masturbate repeatedly, for as long as he could keep it up. He found this new activity so enjoyable, that he sometimes even forgot to break for dinner.

Things were going so well for Dave and Linda, they decided to take ten days off over Christmas, for a much-needed break. Linda, determined to get them some quality one-on-one time together, booked them an all-inclusive Hawaiian five-star hotel for the trip.

A less than enthusiastic Murphy, who had by this point settled in nicely and had been nicknamed *'His Majesty'* and pretty much ruled the roost, found himself having to indoctrinate Dave's parents in the proper procedures required for his care, for the entire ten-day stretch.

Leaving from Vancouver International during a light snow storm and landing on the big island of Hawaii to experience waves of heat radiating up off the runway and humidity you could taste, boded well for the trip, and it only got better after that.

It was the first trip to Hawaii for both. The duo spent every second of the trip together. They had no itinerary and took each day as it came, doing everything that appealed. They did a lot of the usual tourist stuff, a luau, peering into volcanoes, scuba diving and snorkeling, visiting the Mauna Kea Summit, visiting a tropical botanical garden, hiking, a boat tour, museums, even a helicopter tour.

The rest of their time was spent within the confines of the hotel itself, mostly tanning, swimming, reading and sampling what the five restaurants had on offer.

They didn't get a great deal of sleep, but then they were in love, and didn't really seem to be suffering from the loss.

CHAPTER NINE

- April 1992 -

The dilemma of how to get rid of Bob was solved for Kenny mid-month.

By then, Kenny never went to sleep at night before he heard the garage door opening for Bob's truck, and the usual stumbling and bumbling along the hallway that followed his entry as he drunkenly made his way down the hall and into his own room.

Kenny would lie breathlessly listening for signs of whether Bob would take a bath in preparation for a visit to Kenny's room, or flop onto the bed fully clothed in a semi-comatose state. If it was the latter, Kenny could relax in the blissful knowledge that he wasn't going to be targeted that night. If not, he would begin the process of leaving the real world and closing his mind against what was to come.

On this night, Kenny heard the garage door go up as expected, but then nothing but silence.

Kenny waited for a good half hour for the bastard to come into the house, but he didn't.

Finally, he got out of bed, slipped into his jeans, grabbed the flashlight off his bedside table and quietly made his way though the house to the door that led out into the attached garage.

The small overhead light that automatically came on to illuminate the room for a short while when the door went up, had gone off. The big overhead door had settled back down and was closed.

The garage was in complete darkness.

As Kenny's eyes adjusted to the images in the dark interior he eventually made out the pickup sitting in the center of the garage. Intrigued, he slowly made his way over to the driver's door of the vehicle and looked inside. It took a second before he could make out the outline of a figure slumped down across the seat.

Bob was flopped over onto his right side and appeared to have passed out.

Kenny hesitatingly eased the driver's door open. The interior dome light came on, leaving Kenny shitting bricks, but Bob didn't so much as blink.

Kenny froze for a few seconds, convinced that the bastard would wake up. But he didn't.

He was obviously completely pissed. He was snoring loudly, out of it.

Kenny shifted his gaze to glance over at the gas gauge. It registered three- quarters full.

Kenny smiled and his stiff shoulders visibly relaxed.

What the hell, it's worth a try. He had nothing to lose and everything to gain.

He checked to confirm the truck was in park, then reached gingerly into the cab, grasped the ignition key, and holding his breath, turned it to the start position.

When the truck rumbled to life, the loud sound of the engine engaging echoed within the confined space and scared the living-bejesus out of Kenny.

It seemed loud enough to wake the dead, but even that wasn't enough to wake Bob. He didn't so much as move a muscle.

Kenny's smile broadened considerably as he carefully lowered the driver's window, using his knuckle on the button, and oh so gently, pushed the door of the truck closed.

The small garage wouldn't take long to fill up with the V8's idling exhaust.

Kenny turned, walked back to the door leading to the house, and opened it.

Standing in the doorway, silhouetted by the soft glow of a nightlight further down the hallway behind him, he gave the truck one more glance and couldn't hold back a soft chuckle.

Happy, he stepped backward into the hall with a satisfying sense of a job well done, then gently pulled the door closed behind him.

His first real kill!

Kenny whistled softly as he headed back to his room, all the while nurturing a picture of the idling truck in his mind.

Sweet dreams you twisted son of a bitch. God, I'm going to sleep well tonight!

And he did - for the first time he could ever remember.

Kenny didn't get out of bed until nine thirty the next morning.

Bob usually took Granny something to eat in in the mornings, so Kenny figured she'd be wondering where he was.

After he'd showered and made himself some breakfast, he made her a cup of tea, then went in to see her. She was sitting up in bed. After he'd given her the tea, he told her that Bob wasn't around. Granny hadn't taken her morning medicine yet, and she was still with it enough to carry on a reasonable conversation.

She seemed surprised and he told her he was going to go and see if Bob's truck was in the garage, suggesting that perhaps he was outside doing something.

Kenny had very carefully planned exactly how he was going to handle the morning. So far, everything was going exactly as he'd figured it would.

He headed out to the garage and the second he opened the door the smell of carbon monoxide hit him. The truck was still running. The truck was still running, Christ, he hadn't expected that.

Kenny reached around and hit the switch to open the overhead door, then closed the entry door and went back down the hall and then out onto the porch to cross over toward the garage.

He stood a few feet back from the open door, waiting for the noxious gas to clear enough for him to be able to breath safely, and then went inside.

He didn't touch anything, just peered in through the open window. He spent a good five minutes relishing the sight inside, then turned and walked back to Granny's room to give her the news.

Granny made the call and Kenny went back outside to wait for the emergency people. He knew he shouldn't, but he risked going back inside for another look at his handiwork several times anyway.

What a glorious sight!

Then they arrived.

A cop car and an ambulance.

A lot of good that ambulance was going to be.

Kenny put on his best sad face and sat down on the porch steps where he could watch and enjoy all the proceedings. He was disappointed when they brought Bob out on the stretcher and put him in the back of the ambulance. They'd put him in a plastic bag. Kenny would have liked to have had one final look at him.

The cop, an older guy, asked him a few questions, the answers to which he'd rehearsed carefully the night before, and when he'd finished he was certain that he'd done a good job.

'Yes, Bob went to the pub most nights and got home late. He and Granny went to bed as usual, and when Bob wasn't around in the morning, Granny had asked him to check to see if the truck was in the garage. He had, then he told Granny what he'd found and she had phoned for help.'

Things proceeded smoothly after that. Surprisingly, Granny rallied quite a bit. She seemed almost as relieved by Bob's death as Kenny was.

She was still weak and sickly, but she managed to get herself dressed and relatively mobile quickly.

Kenny stayed in the background while the old woman worked the phone.

Two hours later a permanent live-in nurse and a housekeeper had arrived to look after his and Granny's needs. She'd also arranged for him to have private tutoring five days a week.

An hour after that a representative of the law firm Granny used was sitting down with the two of them.

Kenny didn't say anything during the discussions that took place, but he listened to what was going on.

It was during that conversation between Granny and the lawyer that Kenny found out that Bob had managed to wrangle himself into the old woman's will and would have been the one who looked after Kenny and held the purse strings if she'd died before him.

Kenny was very pleased that he'd acted when he did.

The very thought of having to kowtow to that dirty old son-of-a-bitch until he was old enough to be on his own, was chilling.

From Kenny's perspective, except for the tutor, which he figured he could live with, things were looking up.

Linda finished her Master's and had been promoted to a supervisory position. That accomplished, she'd then requested and been assigned to work the day shift, securing a permanent Monday to Friday spot, at Covenant House in Vancouver.

Covenant House, a provincial office situated in Vancouver that responded, on an ongoing basis to the needs of street kids, runaways and so-called *'elopees'* from the various juvenile detention centers was located on Granville street in the center of downtown.

Linda felt that the services provided by the office were fulfilling a need, and considered the posting to be both challenging and rewarding. She was also very much looking forward to finally having weekends off.

Dave had been reassigned to Major Crime shortly after he'd returned from the Quantico course. The Chief had then asked him to take on the task of creating procedural manuals, setting the departmental standard policy on both profilers and on future *'Serial Killer'* task force operations. He was to be under no specific time restraint as to how long it took to get the two manuals completed.

Dave undertook the challenge with enthusiasm.

He was given a small office space in Major Crime and was told he could set his own hours. He'd chosen to work days, Monday to Friday, with weekends off.

Murphy, who had taken to terrorizing the available female cats in the neighbourhood on every opportunity, experienced his first visit to the vet for a clip job and for several days after that he was quite grouchy.

That eventually passed and shortly thereafter, the three of them settled into a comfortable weekly routine.

The half-acre lot they'd purchased was a part of the development of what had originally been a large orchard. On their property, there were several fruit trees which ran in neat rows behind the house.

They redecorated the place and decided to put in a vegetable garden at the very back of their land. They were planning what they would plant for the approaching growing season.

By this point, they had also discovered that there were good neighbours living on each side of them.

To the west was a nice Danish couple, a little older than they, who had two boys. The wife was a stay at home mother and Linda had worked out a deal with her to do light housekeeping for her and Dave once a week.

On the east side were a couple who also had two kids, a girl and a boy.

Dave and Linda were at the point of considering having some kids of their own, but not just yet. They were still enjoying the newness of their relationship and now, with both having weekends off, not quite ready to commit to taking on that level of responsibility.

CHAPTER TEN

- September 1992 -

There had been a new addition to Kenny's household by the time his thirteenth birthday rolled around.

With Bob gone, Granny, who was apparently still in remission and relatively mobile for most of each day but couldn't overdo things, had decided she needed someone who knew the business to take over the responsibility for the day to day management of the family company.

She had chosen Walter, one of the young truck drivers, to fill this new position.

The guy was only in his mid-twenties but had apparently been with them since graduation from high school and he knew the business inside out. Additionally, according to Granny, he was apparently really into computers and capable of handling all the necessary accounts receivable, payables, and other bookkeeping that was required to do the job.

At the time, Granny had offered Walter the chance to be a live-in employee, and Walter, who had no family, had accepted.

Kenny had moved back into his old bedroom which was just down the hall in the same wing as Granny's bedroom. The nurse had a bedroom next to the old lady's, and the cook/housekeeper and Walter were now quartered in the distant wing.

Kenny, who'd not been around strangers a lot over the past few years, initially found this expanded household a little daunting and restrictive. He thought about the fact that he was eventually going to be old enough to leave the property and wanted to do so, to enable him to fulfill his fantasies. When that time came. he would have to be able to do this with confidence. To achieve that, he concluded that he needed to work on developing an ability to manipulate new people who came into his life in a manner that would be to his advantage. That meant he had to work at improving his image in the eyes of others. Resolved to work toward that end, he began to experiment on those currently living within the household, using them as guinea pigs.

As he had no real basic social skills at the start of this experiment to target and successfully manipulate others, he figured that the whole process would have to be a matter of trial and error.

To get an idea of what worked and what didn't, he decided to take on a single person for a trial run. He intended to concentrate his full focus on that individual over a week, trying out different approaches to see what if any worked at improving his relationship with them. He knew he would have to take great care in his varied approaches to this person and go slowly, evaluating their responses before trying something new. He would use all his senses to read and carefully weigh what reaction each of his actions or words had engendered.

He decided to begin his trials with Granny.

He began by adjusting his schedule to begin making regular visits to her room, starting with a couple a day and then working it up to six or seven a day by the end of the week. Each time he visited, he would find an opportunity to inquire as to how she was feeling and then would commiserate with her whenever she responded that she felt ill.

That seemed to work well and he moved on from there by beginning to share first some, and then all; of his meals with the old woman. Their relationship began to improve and to add icing to the cake, he also began to read to her every night before she went to sleep.

He was amazed to find that just doing these few things made a world of difference in how she was now relating to him.

That confirmed to Kenny that he was on the right track and could indeed learn how to put on a false front for others and present himself in a manner they found pleasing. This would, of course, lead to a much better chance for him to manipulate any relationship in a manner which garnered trust and would serve him admirably in the future.

With things now going very well with Granny, it was time to shift his attention to the others in the household.

He took on the nurse next.

To date the woman had appeared to Kenny as self-absorbed, stiff, and standoffish in her crisply starched uniform. She'd hardly spoken to him unless she'd had to. She kept to herself and made it quite clear to anyone inquiring that her sole concern was the care of the old woman. She had no time for other activities and that included what she termed as idle chit chat.

At first, Kenny didn't know how he could break through that stiff exterior, but he noticed that his increased attention toward Granny had not only improved that relationship, but it had also caused just the slightest melting of the nurse's up to now frigid persona.

Using that little chink in her armour Kenny soon picked up on the fact that the woman was starving for praise and recognition. He began to ask her questions about Granny's condition and often expressed to her his respect for her dedication to the old woman. When that went down well, he took it a step further, telling her that she was probably the most important person in the house and that he was so thankful that someone of her ability and sense of calling had the responsibility of looking after his grandmother.

The change in the woman was almost instantaneous and it astonished Kenny. He excitedly milked it for all it was worth, and within a few weeks she had begun to warm a little and open up, beginning to treat him as a confidant regarding Granny's condition and starting to share with him her supposed expertise in maintaining the old woman's remission.

To Kenny, this concept was all important.

He knew full well that the longer Granny lasted the better it would be for him. Once she was gone, the freedom he was now finally enjoying would be restricted due to his age. For sure, he wanted her to last at least long enough that when she went he would be old enough to do his own thing, without further outside interference of any kind.

By the time he was ready to move on to the cook/housekeeper, Kenny was well on his way to perfecting his new assessment methods and using them to gain the good graces of others.

The housekeeper was a simple woman and in the end, all it took for Kenny to win her over was what appeared to be his supposedly sincere interest in her work and especially his complimenting of her cooking ability, something she was very proud of.

He soon had her eating out of his hand.

Kenny had saved the person he felt would probably be the most important of the householders he needed to have onside, if he was to be able to satisfy his future needs, till last.

He'd realized that he had to learn how to run the business if he intended to have the wherewithal to make it later his own. He knew that when Granny went he would be inheriting everything.

That was assuming, of course, that she lasted long enough for him to be legally old enough to assume control of the business, investments, and money without restriction. Therefore, a full understanding on his part of how to run the business would be paramount.

Walter would be the key to accomplishing that end.

It took a few days to figure out how to approach the guy. Kenny carefully studied him to isolate his strong and weak points before he began to work on him.

In the end, Kenny decided that what was most important to Walter now was his new position and that he would probably respond positively to an appreciation of his accomplishments when it came to his computer ability.

That decision made, he began to hang around the office during the day when Walter was sitting at the keyboard and solicitously ask the odd question about how to operate the computer. When that produced a positive response, he moved on to periodic enquires of how the business was run.

Walter was pleased to respond to Kenny's attention, happy to have the kid's companionship and to demonstrate his expertise with the computer. Soon the questions became more complicated and shortly thereafter Kenny began to help Walter with some of the business entries.

Within a month, Kenny was doing most the entries under Walter's mentoring.

With a better understanding of how computers worked, Kenny suggested that perhaps Walter should have a password to protect the system. He also asked if he could become a second user on the machine so he could use it for other stuff.

Walter thought the password was a good idea. He showed Kenny how to do it and then he set Kenny up as a second user and allowed Kenny to put in his own password, so that he could use the computer without somehow screwing up the business stuff.

Kenny was very pleased with this development. When he was alone, he could now look at what he wanted, with the knowledge that nobody else, including Walter, would be able to figure out what he'd been looking at.

Walter had various other responsibilities in the household. He picked up groceries, made bank deposits and did spot checks on the jobsites from time to time. When Kenny asked if he could tag along on these trips, providing of course his tutor had finished with him for the day, Walter cleared the idea with Granny. After that, the time the two spent together began to expand exponentially.

During the month of September, Kenny figured he had come a long way toward effectively manipulating everyone around him. From his perspective, it appeared that for them, he was turning into the golden child. And all it took from him was a little effort to provide each member of the household what they individually seemed to require emotionally.

For the most part, his daily routine was now his to control.

The maintenance of his new persona required a minimum of time. His evenings were his to do whatever he wanted.

There was plenty of time to make use of the computer after the work day had ended. He'd convinced Walter to have a new lock put on the office door as a security measure and only he and Walter now had keys. Once Walter, who had a regular girlfriend, had packed it in for the day, Kenny was free to indulge himself on the computer.

Earlier in the month, he'd also come across Bob's very substantial stash of booze in a cabinet in the garage and begun to partake of this bonanza when he was alone in his room or safely locked in the office.

Fortified with alcohol, he became lost in his fantasy world for hours each night. On these occasions, he would inevitably enjoy what was on offer on the *'net's'* darkest of sites; preferably snuff films.

It had taken three months for Dave to complete and edit the two manuals to his satisfaction. The Chief and his deputies had offered up a few minor changes to be made to the contents and inserting those additions and changes had taken another week to accomplish.

Twenty copies of each document were produced and then, based on the material, Dave was assigned to set up instructional courses for all the members of Major Crime. Each of the classes had to be small, as the workload of the section was heavy and only a small number of officers could be taken out of the normal workday routine at any given time.

When September rolled around Dave had finished with the courses and had been reassigned to duties as a supervisor in the homicide section of Major Crime.

His duties consisted primarily of assigning new cases to the various detective teams and keeping tabs on their individual progress. Most were straight forward, with an obvious perpetrator and sufficient evidence, often including a confession, to secure convictions.

When that was not the case, he would involve himself more, spending time regularly with the team assigned to those investigations.

The teams were, for the most part, well-seasoned and good at their jobs. He rarely found it necessary to advise them to try a new line of enquiry but acted primarily as a sounding board, providing specific direction only when he thought it was needed.

Dave found that he missed the street work a little but was buoyed by the fact that since his involvement with the section, clearances were up and the Chief had personally congratulated him on several occasions regarding specific cases he had actively helped put to bed.

Linda was garnering a great deal of satisfaction in fulfilling the duties of her new position.

She was really into kids. She was a realist however. She knew that the chances of saving very many of the sad cases that came to her attention were very slim. Kids that had lived through the deplorable early life experiences these ones had were usually far too damaged to hope for a chance at ever participating in a normal life.

While the failures saddened her, and she was never satisfied that enough was being done, she didn't beat herself up personally because of those realities.

Their relationship was such that both felt free to bring their work home with them and each encouraged the other to share and discuss their problem cases. With weekends and evenings off together now, they often spent a good deal of their free time advising each other in relation to difficult cases occurring at work.

Murphy had, by this point completely forgiven them for the vet visit and in his altered state, seemed happiest lazing around home, rather than venturing outside and taking his chances with the ladies. He had become a lump.

Over the past few weeks, Dave and Linda had been discussing introducing a more restrictive diet for him. Had Murphy been capable of understanding what they were talking about, he'd probably have offered some negative put down of the idea, but as he didn't, the cat found life was currently pretty good around the Richard's household.

CHAPTER ELEVEN

- September 1994 -

The newly created guise Kenny had formulated to hide his inability to feel empathy toward others in a normal fashion was working like a charm.

He was convinced that in the eyes of the other members of the household, he now appeared to be nothing more than a typical, well-adjusted and caring fifteen-year-old.

His daily regimen had changed considerably as part of this façade and the new routine had become second nature to him.

He shared all his meals with Granny each day.

Monday to Friday he took has classes until noon.   After lunch, he went directly to the office where he and Walter would make the required business entries. Walter let him do most of them now and rarely needed to correct anything or offer advice anymore.

Pretty well each weekday, Kenny would accompany Walter out to run whatever errands needed doing and to check on a jobsite or two.

During these site checks, Kenny would often watch the big commercial chippers chewing up the large tree branches being fed into them, while Walter was talking to the crew chief. He was amazed at how fast and efficient they were. Within seconds of being fed into the machines, the shredded remains of a thick branch would came blowing out of the exhaust hose in thousands of small chips and settle into the back of the attached truck.

Kenny being Kenny, it was not surprising that on these occasions it hadn't taken him long to slip into his fantasy world as he watched the machines work.

He was soon imagining what it would be like to feed a body into one of them.

He loved the roaring and rending sound of a chipper as it worked and imagined what those whirling blades would do to human flesh.

He reckoned that you'd have to cut the body up into several pieces first, but that wouldn't be a problem. After awhile he got a full-blown erection just thinking about what a segmented body would look like coming out the other end.

There would be nothing left but a bloody pulp, maybe a few bone chips and teeth.

It would be awesome to watch.

Later in the week, Kenny was with Walter on a site check - in response to the crew-chief complaining about a chipper that had broken down. To deal with the problem, he and Walter had picked up a backup chipper from the yard on the property and towed it out to the site.

They hauled it there behind the truck that Bob had bought himself earlier. The one in which the rotten bastard had eventually died.

Kenny had fond feelings about that truck. He loved riding in it.

After they had delivered the replacement machine, Walter hooked up the non-performing chipper and they then brought it back to the storage yard. He and Walter pressure-washed the old machine before seeing if they could figure out what was wrong with it.

In the end, Walter concluded that it was simply worn out, and needed to be replaced.

When they got up to the house he and Walter told Granny what had happened and she authorized the purchase of a new chipper. During the discussion between the three of them, Kenny suggested that the new one should be one that could handle larger capacity chunks of wood, as the old one had often taken too much time to shred the volume of material fed into it.

Walter had agreed with the boy and had then asked him if he wanted to come along when he went to select the new one. Kenny readily agreed to that idea. The two of them wandered into the office as they discussed it and once inside, Walter set Kenny to the task of surfing the web for prospective chipper dealers.

When he went to bed that night Kenny was pleased with himself. Life was getting better for him. His routine was set and working out well for him. He really did feel that he was at least beginning to pretty much run his own show.

These days, he and Walter would be back at the house from their running around by five and Kenny would then join the old lady for dinner. Once that ordeal was over with, weather permitting, he would head out to check his snares and work with the excavator for a few hours before coming back inside and reading to Granny before she went to sleep.

Then it was into the office for Kenny and an enjoyable session on the internet before he went to bed.

On the weekends Kenny would spend most of each day working outside and then, after reading to the old lady, he'd eagerly lock himself in the office for several hours of undisturbed pleasure at the keyboard. He was getting very accomplished with the computer and was amazed at what stuff he could find on it.

For his birthday that year, among other presents, he'd received an eight-week old German Shepherd puppy from Walter. Granny had given her support for the gift, believing that all boys should have a dog as a companion while they grew up. She thought it would be a good company for him when he was out in the bush and that caring for the animal would give him a new sense of responsibility.

When Kenny was out on the property he still set his snares, but the bunny population on the property was thinning out. It was beginning to be hit and miss for a catch. Besides, he was finding that these episodes had become a little old hat now, seeming to offer only short-term stimulation for him. The snuff films, which Kenny now watched obsessively, went a long way toward scratching the surface of the niggling new itch for heavier stuff he was feeling, but he knew that a need to experience some form of stronger stimulation was growing within him.

It had been a long time since he'd killed Bob. For him, doing Bob had been the highlight of his life. It had been extremely gratifying on so many levels. He still regularly masturbated to the image of that idling truck in the dark garage, but the reliving of the experience didn't get anywhere near to producing the level of high he'd garnered at the time of the original act.

What he really wanted was to repeat the awesome adrenaline-rush and subsequent sexual high that he'd experienced while killing that asshole, Bob.

Late in the month Dave found the time to begin to use his new profiling expertise.

Encouraged by those upstairs to begin experimenting with the process on some of the outstanding cases when he had any extra time, he began to work at applying the system to a few cases that seemed to be stonewalled for one reason or the other.

He was both surprised and pleased when he managed to achieve three promising outcomes, each pointing the way to an investigative lead, before the end of the month.

The first related to a series of robberies committed at jewelry stores.

In that case he could pinpoint a possible geographical area in relation to the robbery locations and the team working on the case used this information coupled with some other facts in the file, to set up surveillance at a likely target. That surveillance paid off and the three perpetrators were caught in the act within a week

The second involved a peeping-tom who was working a small area in south Vancouver. It was a small thing, but Dave found that the file held enough general information that it was worth a shot. After working on his profile over an afternoon he was able make some headway on a probable suspect. The team handling the case used this information to justify an interview and subsequently charged a sixteen-year-old who then copped to several offences shortly thereafter. Being a juvenile, the kid wouldn't do any time, but at least they had nailed him and given pause to anyone else considering wandering in the neighbourhood at night peering into windows. And the department wouldn't be getting the flood of calls that had been plaguing them over the past few months.

After these small successes, Dave created a profile for a rapist who was working in the west end of the city. Using the info his profile contained, the team of detectives assigned went back through the case files on it and found themselves newly interested in an earlier interview they'd conducted. It had been with a known convicted molester, who had been checked by a patrol unit in the general area of one of the rapes. Although they had 'liked him' for the crimes after that first interview, they had dismissed him as a suspect shortly thereafter because he had come up with a reasonably solid alibi for a couple of the earlier rapes.

Armed with Dave's info, they rechecked those two alibis in greater detail and found both had been provided by the same person, an old girlfriend. They paid her a visit and, under a little pressure, she buckled and admitted that at the time of the earlier rapes he hadn't in fact been with her as he'd claimed. He had told her he was being railroaded, hadn't done it, and asked her to do cover for him. She burst into tears and justified the whole scenario to them by telling them that she was living with the guy at the time and that he liked to get physical. She'd been too afraid of him to say no.

After leaving her apartment the team had gone to the suspect's place of employment, picked him up and hauled his ass back downtown for another interview.

Once there, they'd left the suspect alone to sweat for an hour in one of the small, overheated and windowless interview rooms. When they finally rejoined him, they casually dumped a thick file onto the table between them and the suspect, identified themselves, gave him the official warning and told him they were charging him with the rapes.

It took them a while to wear him down, but two hours later they came into Dave's office and presented him with a photocopy of a signed confession, covering the entire batch of rapes.

The charges of rape that resulted cleared up four old cases, and when word got back to the Chief, he was ecstatic and came downstairs to congratulate Dave personally.

During the visit, the Chief and David discussed the profiling process a little and then out of the blue, the Chief asked him what he could do to help him expand the process to more stalled cases.

He didn't respond for a second, then let out a deep breath and settled back into his chair before answering.

"Well, there is so much information to go through and then a study of that all has to be inter-related to produce results. It would be a definite help if we could manage to computerize the information we compile to produce a profile.

"I'm not all that conversant with computers, but I think if the significant information already gathered on any specific investigation could be entered by a clerk, after all the reports had been visually reviewed and culled by a detective, then the whole process could be handled much more quickly and effectively.

"The detective doing the initial assessment would need to be computer-friendly, and then he could teach me the fine points of how to use the results produced by to assist in building a profile."

The Chief thought for a moment and then shrugged.

"OK, you've accomplished quite a bit in a short time doing this profiling business. If you think using a computer to sort and store information will speed things up, I'll get one for you and send you a clerk with entry skills. In the meantime, you select someone of detective rank that you want to add to your unit and when you got that nailed down, I'll see to the necessary transfer."

The Provincial Ministry, where Linda worked, had been switching over a lot of their files and records over the past couple of years to a new computer system which, according to her, was streamlining a lot of their access to information and record keeping.

Unlike Dave, who only knew the basics, Linda was very comfortable sitting at a keyboard. She had been using them at work for some time, and it was she who had originally suggested the computerization of the investigative files.

When he got home that evening he told her what had transpired with the Chief and she congratulated him. They went out to dinner that night to celebrate.

CHAPTER TWELVE

- May 1995 -

Life for Kenny had not changed much over the past eight months. When around the others, his façade formed automatically now. It had become second nature to him. He no longer had to work at it.

As far as how each of his days were spent, little had changed. He still felt he had successfully managed to get a good hold on controlling most of his own life.

Kenny's puppy, who he had named *'Vicious',* because he was anything but, was now nine months old. For the first six months of its life, the dog the had spent most of its time with Walter during the day, while Kenny was in his classes, and out with them in the truck when they did their various errands.

Its nights were spent following Kenny around, and the dog slept in his room.

The dog idolized Walter, but didn't quite hold Kenny with the same level of reverence. That fact irritated Kenny to no end. Not because he particularly liked the dog, but because he figured the dog's strongest loyalty should be to him. It was his dog after all. Once again, he was being rejected.

Shortly after the dog's arrival, Kenny had asked to take him out with him when he went up to the yard in the evenings, but Walter had disagreed, saying the dog was too young to be out in the bush. It wasn't until April that Kenny could have the dog accompany him on his daily sojourns to the far end of the property.

Kenny had been toying with an idea of how to straighten the animal out, but that meant getting the dog outside alone and until April such an opportunity had not presented itself.

About a week into the month, he had been given permission to take the dog up to the yard and the bush with him. Kenny now had the opportunity to act out on one of the little fantasies he'd been formulating. The goal of which was, in addition to pure enjoyment, to teach it who was really in charge.

The afternoon after he gotten permission to take *'Vicious'* with him the two of them headed out. When they were deep into the bush using the excavator, Kenny called the dog to him, and led him off further into the bush. Then, using some of the fishing line he used to set up his snares, he tied the dog to a tree by one rear leg and left him.

The dog immediately tried to follow him but Kenny ignored the frantic barking and garnered a great deal of satisfaction when he was far enough away to be out of the dog's site line, and heard the animal begin to utter a plethora of pain-filled yelps.

Kenny began to whistle and calmly climbed back into the excavator to continued to work. He left the dog alone for almost an hour.

When he returned he found the dog laying exhausted, the tied leg extended, raw and bleeding where the fish line had cut into it as he'd struggled to be free.

Kenny was initially pleased with the results.

He stood watching the whimpering animal for a little while before he began to utter, what he thought the dog would consider to be soothing words, based on things he'd heard other members of the household use when comforting the animal, mimicking what he could remember of them, while he used wire cutters to free the injured leg.

Once freed, the dog was unable to use the leg, so Kenny picked him up and carried him back to the excavator, tossed him into the cab and leisurely made his way back to the yard.

By the time he'd arrived at the compound, he'd had time to think the whole thing through and had realized that, while the incident had certainly taught the dog who was boss, the sight of the injured leg was going to have to be explained away to those back at the house.

He loaded the dog into the little Ford pickup and sat for a few moments trying to figure out how he could rationalize the dog's injury in a manner that it would be acceptable to them as just a horrible accident.

Completely ignoring the dogs pitiful whining as he licked the injured leg, Kenny ran through some possibilities.

He could say that the dog was running around and got caught in one of his snares, but then he would have to explain why he had set snares in the first place. He wasn't about to do that.

He could say he had no idea of what had caused the wound. That the dog had wandered off and he'd had to look for him and when he found him the leg was injured.

He turned to look at the actual injury and figured, nope, that wouldn't fly.

In the end, he decided to tell them that the dog had been playing and had tangled himself somehow in some of the heavy brush. He had panicked and fought Kenny when he had gone to help him and, in so doing, damaged the leg.

He knew it was a little farfetched, but in the confusion of seeing the dog, he reckoned that they might not be thinking straight enough to question it.

When he got down to the house, he left the moaning dog in the truck and sat for a second preparing himself for how he should react when he went in. He reflected on how Granny had responded when Gordon died. He decided to mirror as much of her reaction as he could manage.

It went well. Everybody was so concerned and worried. They asked what had happened, of course, and, breathing heavily, he'd disjointedly given them his story.

They were so worried about the dog, Walter determined to get the dog to the vet as soon as possible, and the others tearing up and trying to soothe the dog, that they weren't even paying much attention to Kenny.

So far so good. It had occurred to Kenny, by this time, that the vet might not buy the story, once he examined the dog. He hadn't considered that angle before.

Walter was already carrying the dog to the other truck when Kenny asked, in his best pitiful voice, if he could come and hold the dog on the way to the animal hospital.

In the end, he was glad that he had decided to go with Walter and the dog.

While she was working on the dog, the vet, an older lady, asked how the injury had occurred. Kenny, standing in the background and doing his best to look devastated, stayed mute and let Walter speak.

Walter explained to her that the dog had got his leg caught in some heavy brush.

The vet paused in her work and turned to face him, a questioning expression on her face. Kenny bit his lip and held his breath. The vet said it looked to her like a wire of some kind had done the damage.

Kenny mumbled out a response. "

We have some old fences out there. They are all broken down barbed-wire."

It was bullshit of course, but it was the first thing that came to mind for him and he was desperate to bury the discussion quickly before it expanded. Walter wouldn't know one way or the other about any downed fences on the property. He'd never even been out in the bush at the back of the property.

Kenny didn't say a word. The questioning-look on the vet's face didn't exactly disappear, but she did turn her attention back to administering to the dog. As she cleaned the wound she spoke over her shoulder to them.

"I would have thought a smaller wire, but I suppose it could have been frayed barb. At any rate, you two might as well go back into the waiting room while I finish up here. You'll be able to take him home when I'm through. You will need to pick up a proper sized cone for the dog to wear to keep him from fussing with it until it has a chance to heal. Talk to the receptionist and she will fix you up. I will also be giving you a prescription to get filled, so you'll have to stop at a pharmacy and fill it within a day or two. Before you leave I'll give you enough medication to keep him going for a few days."

Kenny let out a sign of relief and, realizing that he'd been holding his breath while she spoke, gulped in some air. The Vet saw him do it and her features softened.

"Don't worry, son, there doesn't appear to be anything seriously damaged. Your dog will be running around again in a week or so."

It was a close call and Kenny remained mute on the way home. As he had anticipated, Walter just figured he was so quiet because he'd been really shaken up by the whole incident. Kenny was using the time to silently thank his lucky stars and give the whole screwed up scenario a lot of thought.

He had been stupid to do what he'd done without thinking it all out carefully. As result, he'd damn near been found out. He'd acted on impulse and that was damn stupid.

Before Walter left for the evening, Kenny overheard him ask Granny if she was aware of any old collapsed fences on the property. The old woman had thought for a moment and then said that she didn't think so. She then enquired of him as to why he had asked.

Walter had shrugged and told her that he was just curious.

Bloody amazing how gullible people were.

It had been a stupid thing to do but he seemed to have gotten away with it.

Kenny had learned a good lesson from it though. Acting on an impulse was not a mistake he would ever make again.

On May the sixth, Linda bought a computer for David on his birthday.

The past eight months had been busy for the two of them. Linda had been promoted again, this time to the position of Regional Manager for emergency services. It was a big jump in both salary and responsibility abut it also meant that she would have to return to working nightshifts and Monday to Friday.

Since Dave had been told that he could set his own hours in his new position, he was able to shift over to nights as well and, as luck would have it, the change in office hours surprisingly worked out very well for him.

The Chief had been very pleased with the results of the new unit to date.

Dave was now profiling about one-third of their serious cases and results were producing solid leads, which in turn meant more evidence and further lines of investigation.

This had occasioned the Chief to authorize an expansion of his manpower.

Dave now had three civilian entry clerks and an additional detective to help with the process of assessing files and culling the vital material available, prior to its entry into the new system. Dave asked for and was granted his request to have his old partner Ed Hamilton take up the position. Ed was both a computer nerd and a known entity and Dave was looking forward to working with him again.

With the odd exception, the remainder of Dave's staff remained on days, which allowed for witnesses to be interviewed more easily.

Dave, the new entry clerk and Ed, fresh out of the Drug Squad who was doing the file culling, worked nights.

Dave quickly found that he could work much more efficiently on all ongoing active files at night than he had been during the day, which seemed to be punctuated with constant interruptions.

The shift he'd chosen in the end allowed him to overlap the dayshift members of his team by one hour. This provided him with the opportunity to interact personally with all the working detective teams in Major Crime every morning at the start of their shifts, making it possible for him to point out to them any new line of investigation he'd picked up on while he'd been reviewing the files overnight.

His supervisory responsibilities were therein simplified, more immediate, and took up far less of his time.

The new computer system for the unit had been functioning well using the software that had come with it, but both Ed and Dave were finding themselves frustrated of late with some of the many program glitches. The system was also having difficulty handling the expanded volume demanded of it.

Linda had been spending a fair amount of time on the phone with him over the past few months helping him with some of those very glitches. Now, with a home computer for him, she could accomplish that more comfortably, with him sitting beside her in their off time and watching what she was doing.

Programming and software improvements to the system went much faster that way.

That aside, Dave was finding himself less and less enamoured about the capabilities of the basic software program they had been using.

Linda said he was probably right, that it had not been specifically designed to accomplish what he needed it to do. She suggested to him that she have a look at the setup and see if she could use her experience gleaned from having gone through similar problems at the Ministry. Then, perhaps, working together, they could design something better.

They were in the middle of that exercise now, and although far from confident that any such a thing was even possible, Dave was beginning to see some light at the end of the tunnel.

CHAPTER THIRTEEN

- September 1995 -

Having turned sixteen on the first of the month, Kenny had been eager to get his driver's licence and Walter had taken him in for it. Kenny had already been driving around the property for several years and he had been studying carefully for a couple of months to prepare himself to write the test. He sailed through it with flying colours.

And as luck would have it, Dave wasn't the only one who got their own personal computer for their birthday in '95. Based on Walter's recommendation, Granny got Kenny one too.

He was delighted.

From this point on he would not have to wait to spend time in the office after Walter had left for the day. Now he could nurse a drink while he accessed his stuff whenever he felt like it, night or day, and in the privacy of his own bedroom.

On the outside, he appeared to the others as a normal and well-adjusted teenage boy. Hormones were raging rampantly as part of a normal cycle of physical development, but to consider Kenny's reaction to these hormones in any sense as normal, would be to make a very big mistake.

There was nothing about Kenny's sexual urges that could be in any way construed to be within the norm.

By sixteen, Kenny had reached a full understanding of what, of all the sexual fantasies he could envision, provided him with the most satisfaction. His preferred a fantasy subject, the individual image of a sex partner that provided him with the ultimate stimulation, was that of a teenage boy, someone over whom he could demonstrate complete domination.

It was that combined representation he now envisioned whenever he fantasized about sex, which was much of any given day. A *'boy-next-door'* type. Handsome, with longish hair, a reasonably athletic build and surrounded by an aura of innocence. It didn't actually have to be real innocence of course, just the appearance of innocence was acceptable.

The itch to do someone again had not gone away - anything but. However, now having access to his own computer whenever he needed it was making it easier for him to hold it in check.

With a single exception, day-to-day life in the household was flowing smoothly. The only glitch was the fact that Granny was going downhill. Kenny had his doubts that the remission thing was going to last much longer.

If Granny kicked the bucket, it wasn't going to particularly bother him, but according to her will, which she had read to him, if she died before he reached twenty-five, he would again find himself under some adult's thumb until he reached that age.

He was actively taking two steps to prevent that.

Firstly, he had used his computer to look up multiple myeloma. He had read everything he could find about it on the net. Once he was confident that he had a good grasp of the subject he brought the topic up with Granny, one morning over breakfast, which she usually took in her bedroom.

Kenny waited until the nurse had left the room, leaving him and Granny alone.

At first the old woman was a little taken aback by the amount of effort he had put into his research. She said little, just nodded from time to time.

Kenny began to wonder how the whole thing was going down, but then he noted that her eyes were beginning to tear up. The stupid old woman was obviously filling with emotion, believing that he was seriously concerned about her health.

A sense of relief filled him.

He went on to explain to her that his research had indicated that there was a method of extending the life expectancy of people with the disease using stem cell therapy.

She responded by saying that her doctor had mentioned that but had also indicated that such treatment was only available for individuals under fifty years of age.

Kenny had known that response would be coming and he was prepared for it.

He told her that was indeed the case under the provincial medical plan but that he had considered it carefully and found out that there was another way to get that type of therapy. It was expensive of course, but if you had enough money, you could get it done at private clinics in the USA, regardless of age.

Granny's features softened and she smiled. She told him that she did have more than enough money to undertake such a process, but that would mean that she would have less to leave for him. Besides, at her age she didn't think it made a great deal of sense.

Kenny didn't push it this first time. He left it there and changed the subject. Of course, he had a definite goal to achieve with this approach. He needed her to last a few more years, and he was far from giving up on the idea.

At breakfast, a couple of days later he proffered his other idea. Didn't she think that having him unable to inherit from her until he was twenty-five was a little silly. Didn't she think that he would be able to handle it at nineteen, the Province's age of majority? Hadn't he already demonstrated that?

He now knew the business inside out. He was doing all the daily computer entries for Walter already and had been for some time. He'd been all over on different job sites and knew how the operation ran. Didn't she think he would be mature enough at nineteen to accept the responsibility?

Granny said she would think about it.

That had satisfied Kenny for the moment, but he fully intended to work at her until he succeeded in having the will adjusted to reflect this change.

For the next month, every couple of days he raised both issues with her. He didn't want to get her back up by harping on them, but he was determined to wear her down.

By the end of the month Granny had been down to the States to take her first stem cell treatment and a representative of the legal firm who looked after her needs had attended at the house.

Her will had been changed to specify that his inheritance would now take place on the Province's majority age of nineteen.

Now all Kenny had to do was to see to it that she lived until he turned nineteen.

After that he wouldn't have to give a damn about what happened to her. In fact, over the past few weeks, on more than one occasion, it had occurred to him that if and when that time arrived, he might just be prepared to personally assist her in making that final jump into the next world.

The new schedules adopted by Dave and Linda were working out well for them. They still had their weekends off and because of their past experiences of working various shifts, the change over from working days to nights was no big shock. If anything, both seemed happier on nights.

Murphy, on other hand, had initially found the switch in routine a little unsettling. However, after a couple of weeks the cat had adjusted to it.

Both Dave and Linda had supervisory responsibilities that occasionally dragged one or the other away on their off time, but each was used to dealing with that kind of thing and rarely found it a problem.

Linda was making good money now and her little old Dodge was beginning to show its age. She'd always wanted a red sports car, so the two of them had been shopping around for a replacement and had recently settled on a new '96, fire-engine-red, Audi Cabriolet.

Working the same shifts, they could go to and from work together. When the weather was good they took the Audi and when it wasn't, they used Dave's pickup. They only had a one-car garage and as Linda's Audi had dibs on that, the pickup had been relegated to the driveway.

Over the past four months, Dave and Linda had been working together steadily during their free time to create a software program that was specifically tailored to meet the needs of his unit. Dave laboured to determine the requirements he wanted the system to fulfill, and Linda used her programming experience to work toward producing an end-product that would accomplish the job.

The process was going well and by this point Dave was no longer a doubter. He really had little idea of what Linda was up to when she was tapping away at the keyboard, but he'd quickly realized that the idea of building effective software to assist in his profiling was now a genuine probability.

They worked well together and the project, which was in its final stages, seemed to be bringing them even closer together.

Everything was good on the domestic front.

Linda's new position carried a much higher level of responsibility than her last. Running the after-hours emergency services program meant that she was no longer solely supervising the needs of street kids, although that was a major part of it. She was now also overseeing the handling of all the after hours domestic violence and family problems as well.

She found the basic family stuff a bit frustrating, at least in the cases where just adults were involved, as it seemed that any intervention she had available rarely seemed to provide a lasting improvement. But most cases, included kids and kids were her thing, so she gave each case everything she had.

She and Dave often discussed each other's workload and when Dave heard about how desperate some of her so called *'client'* situations were, he would just shake his head in wonderment that she didn't simply burn out from the disappointment and hopelessness of it all.

When he'd expressed this opinion to her the first time, saying that it must be like banging your head repeatedly against a brick wall, she'd just laughed and told him that his was a strange comment, coming from a guy who spent most of his time trying to identify and convict the purveyors of serious crime.

Dave had smiled and agreed.

When they'd first become engaged, everyone who knew them had wondered just how well a marriage between a dedicated social worker and a cynical cop would work out, and to be honest, at the time, each of them had also had some concerns about the concept.

Interestingly, having to share their different experiences and perspectives on life was working out surprisingly well for both.

CHAPTER FOURTEEN

- September 1996 -

Over the past year, Kenny had been relatively satisfied to ride out the status quo. He had matured both mentally and physically. Realizing that he was now playing a waiting game until he reached nineteen, he had taken great pains to learn to control his growing inner urges to branch out and begin to sample some of his now well-developed fantasy scenarios for real.

Surprisingly, the twelve months had passed relatively rapidly and uneventfully for him. He had been careful to maintain the effective routines he'd set up in the household to ensure his ability to manipulate everyone.

That still gave him plenty of time in his bedroom, where he could enjoy a few drinks and surf his preferred sites. He could indulge more heavily in alcohol, because he was just going to go to bed later and would not be having to interact with anyone before he did so.

When he went out with Walter now for site checks and errands, he did the driving. He also went out on his own occasionally in the little red pickup, but only in the daytime, as Granny didn't want him driving at night yet.

The internet gave him a good deal of satisfaction and for now that, coupled with the intermittent success of the snares, was enough to keep his needs in check.

Well, with one minor exception.

When he and Walter had gone 'chipper' hunting, Kenny had been determined that they would get the biggest one they could find. As time went on, Walter had been a little surprised at how much resolve he had about it and had initially tried to get him to go for what was available at the dealership, but he was also impressed by Kenny's commitment to get the best.

In the end, they had agreed to do it Kenny's way.

Unfortunately, the model that Kenny wanted was not only extreamly expensive, but also had a huge capacity and was therefore not much in demand. It was not only unavailable at the dealership, but would have to be a purchased by way of a special order and that order would have to be sent to the head office of the manufacturer and from there to the factory, where the unit would be built from scratch.

The salesmen told them that the model Kenny had chosen was nicknamed the *'Behemoth'* and that it would take anywhere from six months to a year before it would be completed and shipped to the dealership for them to pick up.

Kenny didn't particularity like the idea of having to wait so long for the machine but that was balanced out by just how much he relished the sound of the chipper's nickname.

It had arrived four months ago. That led to his only possible misstep in judgement over the year - something which could have caused him to fail to keep everything sufficiently under control until he reached nineteen and his inheritance.

It was sort of a spontaneous thing.

Both Walter and Kenny were left speechless when they first saw the chipper. It was massive. At first sight, Walter had taken a deep breath, and then mumbled something about the fact that they were going to have to buy a bigger truck to pull the damn thing.

That proved to be an exaggeration of course, but at the time had certainly been within the realm of possibility.

Kenny was very excited as they towed the chipper back to the property. He kept turning in his seat to look behind at it and was grinning like an idiot.

Walter wasn't much better. Guys and their toys.

When they got it back to the yard, the two of then couldn't wait to test it out.

For a month or so, they had been piling up some deadfalls gathered from around the property and within minutes of getting the new machine into the yard they had it hooked up to one of the bigger trucks, one of the ones used for holding and transporting the chipped product, and were feeding a procession of large branches into the yawning opening that led to the whirling blades.

Walter was impressed by the amount the machine could handle in one feed. Kenny was exuberant beyond belief, not only for the capacity it could take, but by the real possibility that the *'Behemoth'* was probably quite capable of doing exactly what he had fantasized it doing.

He couldn't wait to find out, even if doing so might be somewhat risky.

When they were running low on stuff to feed in, Kenny asked Walter to take the small truck and go pick up some more material for the chipper so they could keep at it for a little longer.

Walter agreed, telling Kenny not to operate the machine until he got back. Kenny replied saying that he would only carefully feed what was left on the pile while Walter was gone.

Satisfied by that, Walter grinned and nodded. Kenny had been operating chippers since he was twelve and knew all about the rules for using them. Nevertheless, he reminded Kenny to be sure to let go as soon as the blades grabbed, because otherwise the chipper was powerful enough to pull him in with the branch.

That done, Walter hopped into the little red Ford and drove out of the yard to collect what he could find.

Kenny waited until the pickup had left the yard and then immediately walked over to the shed. He went behind it and quickly uncovered three rabbits that he'd hidden under a pile of leaves earlier in the week. At the time, he had not really admitted to himself why he had not mutilated and buried these animals, as he normally would have. It wasn't until now that he understood that he'd saved them for the specific purpose of conducting this experiment.

He hurried back to the chipper with them and quickly fed a large branch into the machine, then threw the three rabbit carcasses into the yawning hole on top of the tail end of the branch.

The machine didn't even hiccup when the rabbits hit the blades.

There was a wonderful red misting of the air coming out of the exhaust blower and into the trailer hooked up to the machine. That quickly disappeared and when he looked inside the trailer after feeding in a couple more branches, he couldn't even see any sign of bunny remains.

It was awesome.

Of course, the bunnies were small. He would have to try bigger bodies to see how it would handle them to be sure. But so far so good.

Oh, and then there was also the antifreeze thing too.

Early the next week, when he and Walter were in the yard, one of the drivers had been unloading containers and putting them into one of the garages. As he was moving the last one out of the pickup, it caught on something and tumbled out of the back of the truck. The plastic cap cracked and burst open, spilling some of its greenish contents onto the pavement.

Walter yelled at the guy and then, leaving Kenny behind, charged across to the man.

Although some distance away, Kenny overheard Walter telling the driver to be more careful and that antifreeze was poisonous to animals. That they liked the taste of it and if they drank it, it could kill them.

At the time, Kenny had filed that little tidbit of information away into the back of his mind. That night he got on his computer and did some checking. Sure enough, Walter was right.

There were lots of warnings about dogs loving the stuff and dying after they lapped it up.

Kenny was delighted.

The very thought of something the size of *'Vicious'* hitting the blades of the new chipper gave him an erection.

But he had already taken a big chance with the bunnies. That had been risky. He wasn't ready to blow his image with the householders at this crucial point in time. If anybody were to clue into something like that, his positive image would instantly shatter.

No, he had learned his lesson and he was not about to risk everything by acting on impulse again.

If he did decide to try such a chipper experiment, he would not act on impulse. He would plan it very carefully first.

Linda had installed the new profiling software into the computer system Dave's squad was using just over three months ago. It was pretty good, but his team was still experiencing some minor glitches that had shown up. With Linda's help, they had solved most of those problems by early September and by the end of the month it was running smoothly.

Once Dave's people got more comfortable using it, they began to apply it to a larger number of cases, almost fifty percent of the Major Crime investigations.

It was still too early to produce a statistical evaluation of how effective this tool was turning out to be when it came to the overall conviction rate, but several outstanding cases appeared to have produced some very positive results.

Predictably, these high-profile successes had produced a snowball effect in relation to how the other members of the department viewed the whole concept of profiling. When Dave had first come up with the idea, there had been many departmental naysayers, some of them that held relatively high rank, who had openly expressed the opinion that it was good street policing, not geek computer programmers, that caught crooks.

At the time, that faction had been in the majority, but by the end of September that was turning around.

As a result, the workload had increased yet again and the Chief had provided Dave with a second civilian entry clerk and an additional detective to expand his team.

Dave had personally interviewed and selected the young new detective.

He'd been looking for someone with a good street record, someone who also demonstrated a high level of computer proficiency, and who could hopefully and effectively deal with any little problems which showed in the software Linda had designed, and on an ongoing basis, upgrade segments to improve it.

His selection process had left him with a man who had turned out to be more than capable of dealing with any glitches, with a simple call to Linda, whenever they popped up.

Although the need for this kind of tweak was occurring rarely now, when it did, it was dealt with within minutes instead of holding up the entire process for days, as it had in the past.

Linda had turned thirty on July fourth and predictably, she was becoming concerned about her biological clock ticking away.

She and Dave had been discussing having children over the past few months and had recently decided that they should try to get pregnant.

CHAPTER FIFTEEN

- September 1997 -

Turning eighteen brought about several changes in Kenny's life.

Granny played a large part in these changes. She had been clearly going downhill again and he had begun to panic at the thought of her kicking the bucket before he made it to nineteen.

He decided he needed to persuade her to go through another stem cell treatment. He turned to the nurse for support to assist him in convincing the old lady to make another trip to the States.

Kenny figured that the nurse had it pretty good in her current position. She was very well paid and the job of looking after Granny wasn't all that taxing. That being the case, he reckoned it was in her own self-interest to support Kenny in his endeavour.

He'd managed to build up a pretty good relationship with the nurse over the past couple of years and he knew how to manipulate her. It only took him a couple of weeks to get her on board with the idea.

By the third week in the month, Granny was headed for the States. Kenny hoped to hell that he'd made the right decision and that the trip itself didn't kill her. All he needed was one more year out of her, then it wouldn't matter.

He was on pins and needles until she was back home.

Before the old lady left, impressed by his concern for her physical wellbeing, she'd informed Kenny that he would now be receiving a regular paycheque for his work with Walter and had also relented on her restriction regarding Kenny's not being allowed to leave the property at night.

Having some money of his own would be great and Kenny was very excited about the possibilities this would provide. Those two things would give him an opportunity to broaden his horizons.

He was too keyed up to take advantage of this newfound freedom while Granny was in the States. He did however spend some time surfing around on the net, looking for what he could find that would allow him to satisfy some of his growing sexual needs.

By the time the old lady had returned, looking a good deal better than she had when she left, thank God, he had already selected the place where he would make his first night trip. It was in Vancouver at a spot where teenaged boys apparently openly offered sex for money.

On the net, it was referred to as *'boy's town'*.

Kenny was very excited about the prospect of experiencing that, but he had been working on another idea for some time and after Granny had been back home for a week and things were mostly back to normal in the household, he decided that he was ready for the next chipper test.

Over the summer they had taken to leaving the dog out over night. For the past week, in the early evenings, Kenny had been taking *'Vicious'* with him up to the yard when he used the excavator to empty the work trucks and fill in depressions on the property.

In the last week of the month, Walter had instructed the drivers to check their trucks for antifreeze as the weather would soon turn colder.

The next day Kenny took the dog with him as usual and once they got up to the yard, Kenny let the him roam for a bit while he went into the garage where the antifreeze was stored and helped himself to a partial jug of the stuff.

He then carried the jug out to where the trucks were parked and set it down while he looked underneath the line of vehicles until he found what he was looking for.

Under the front of the third truck he spotted a few drops of green antifreeze on the ground where it had landed when the driver had filling the radiator. It was only a couple of drops but it was enough to fit into his plan.

He got the jug, opened it and then hunched down and reached under the truck and poured about half of the contents directly onto the spot where the drops were. Then he called the dog over to him and let nature take its course.

Just like the net had suggested, the stupid dog loved the stuff.

Kenny stood and watched to be sure the dog would keep lapping away and he did until it was all gone except a stain of green.

He then loaded the dog into the dump truck and began his usual work to dispose of the cuttings the trucks had brought in that day.

He kept an eye on the dog and after about an hour *'Vicious'* was beginning to react, wandering around like a drunk and drooling like crazy

Kenny had carefully memorized all the symptoms of an antifreeze poisoning and so far, everything was proving out. A couple of hours later, he finished up and found he had to lift the listless dog into the cab of the excavator for the trip back to the yard.

The dog had begun to vomit by the time he got there. Kenny left him in the cab lying in his own puke, while he pressure-washed the chippers, then he hauled the dog out and dumped him into the box of the little red Ford pickup.

As he was driving back down to the house he adjusted his rear-view mirror so he could keep an eye on the dog who was rolling around in the back and noticed that *'Vicious'* had begun to piss himself.

When he was about a hundred yards from the house he stopped the truck, and lifted the dog out of the box and carried him about twenty feet into the woods and then dropped him into the brambles below a large deciduous tree.

When he arrived back to the house for dinner he was whistling happily.

The next morning the housekeeper, who usually fed the dog in the morning, put his food out as usual. She wasn't particularly surprised to find that the dog was not at the door. Several times in the past, the dog had not shown up till later in the day.

Kenny was impatient, filled with eagerness to reach his final goal, but he forced himself to stick to his carefully worked out plan.

That evening, when he went out to get into the little pickup, he stood in the yard calling the dog loud enough to attract the attention of the housekeeper who came out onto the back porch. He crossed over to speak to her and asked if she had seen the dog. She glanced down at the food bowl and shook her head and told him she hadn't and that his food looked like it hadn't been touched.

Kenny reacted as he figured he should, frowning and slouching his shoulders and then went into the house with the housekeeper trailing along behind him and into the office were Walter was just finishing up for the day.

The three of them talked for a few minutes and then he and Walter went back out into the yard. Walter loudly called for the dog. When he got no response, he turned to Kenny and shook his head. Kenny looked as upset as he could fake it and let out a deep sigh. Walter rested a hand on his shoulder and suggested the two of them split up and look for the dog.

Kenny readily agreed and said he'd search the area around the house if Walter went up to the yard and had a look around there.

Walter took off in his truck and Kenny watched him disappear before he headed out into the bush. He found a nice quiet spot out behind the pig pen and settled down with his back to a tree.

About an hour later Kenny heard a horn honk and he roused himself, brushed the leaves off his butt, put on the sad face he'd ritually practiced in front of the bathroom mirror and headed back to the house.

He and Walter commiserated for a bit and then Walter told him not to be too worried, the dog would probably be back in the morning.

Kenny nodded and maintained the sad face until Walter's pickup was out of sight, then he headed into his room. Once inside he locked the door, dropped the façade and fixed himself a drink. He grinned as he sat down at his keyboard.

Experience had taught him that people who were really upset didn't have much of an appetite. He was hungry, but as part of his plan, he intended to beg off eating dinner. Earlier, he'd stashed a couple of sandwiches in his night table. They would do until the morning. Until then, as far as everyone else was concerned, he was moping because he couldn't find the dog. Before retiring, Kenny set his alarm so he could climb out of bed early enough to be sure to be up before anyone else was around.

When it went off, he dressed quickly and headed for the kitchen, where he wolfed down a large chunk of cheese and a glass of milk and then put on his sad face as he heard the housekeeper coming down the hall toward the kitchen. He solemnly passed on eating any breakfast.

Most of that day Kenny, depressed face fixed in place, shuffled along and was not very responsive as he and Walter did some more searching.

It was a big property and as Kenny had expected, they had no luck.

When they got back to the house, Kenny retreated to his room, although he did later allow himself to be coerced into coming out just long enough to eat a little dinner.

The next morning Walter was too busy to help him search and Kenny, carrying a couple of sandwiches the housekeeper had prepared without being asked, headed out on his own. He drove the little Ford pickup down the road to where he had left the dog and, after eating one of the sandwiches, he got out and walked into the bush.

The dog wasn't quite dead but when he kicked him with his foot, he didn't respond. Kenny lifted him and carried him back to the road and then dropped him into the truck's box.

He took time to leisurely eat the other sandwich and then, whistling softly to himself, he turned the truck around and headed back to the house.

Things went rapidly after he got there. In a matter of minutes, they were headed out the driveway.

The vet, a different one this time, said it was too late to do anything.

After speaking with a somber Kenny for a few moments, the vet told him and Walter that he couldn't be sure yet, but he thought it looked like antifreeze poisoning. He told them the dog was suffering and should be put down.

Walter was as mad as hell as they drove back to the property and he went directly into the yard and jumped out of the cab of the truck and stomped over to where the trucks were normally parked at night. It didn't take him long to find the large stain left where Kenny had dumped the antifreeze.

As Kenny had hoped, that really got him furious.

Kenny watched all this carefully from the cab of the truck, but stayed mute throughout, ensuring that the sad expression on his face was prominent.

When they arrived back at the house, Kenny told them that he wanted to bury the dog by himself and, taking note of his obvious distress, they acquiesced.

He then put on a good show for them. Gently wrapping the body in an old blanket before shifting it to the back of the little Ford pickup, and then he got in and drove slowly back down the driveway to the yard.

There he unloaded the dog and carried it around behind a shed and unceremoniously dumped it into the hollow where he had earlier stowed the dead bunnies. He stared at it for a few moments, then kicked some leaves over it.

After that he wandered around the yard to idle away a couple of hours, before he returned to the house.

When he got there Walter called him into the office and sat him down. Kenny, hoping he appeared suitably depressed, said little as Walter went on and on about death and how one needed to go through a period of mourning, but must get over that as soon as possible and get on with life.

At the end, Kenny quietly told him he would try.

That evening a more stable Kenny went into the office just as Walter was leaving and thanked him for the talk. He announced that starting now, he would do his best to get over the loss of *'Vicious'* and that he'd try to remember to stop moping. Maybe he would go for a long walk into the bush to think about things for a bit.

Walter was pleased with the turn of events and on his way out of the house, he told the housekeeper what had transpired between him and the boy. She'd nodded her head in understanding, saying that it was a good thing for the lad to keep himself busy now.

Kenny drove to the yard and promptly started up the *'Behemoth'*. He fed a few branches into it and then got the dog and tossed it in with the next batch.

What a power trip!

It worked awesome, not even a hiccup as the body went through!

That done, he happily carried out his usual routine for emptying the parked trucks.

Before he went back to the house, he did an extra careful job of power-washing out all the chippers, giving special attention to the new one.

When Dave had been assigned to his latest position by the Chief, the Inspector in charge of Major Crime, Jim Henderson, had been in the doubter's camp as far as far as the positive results of profiling went.

Thanks to the conclusive results now being produced by the new unit, that point of view appeared to have turned around several months ago.

Predictably, in the initial stages, and although it was under his direct command, Henderson had not paid a great deal of attention to the new unit. He was an old-timer, and he hadn't particularly welcomed the Chief's direct involvement from upstairs in setting up the profiling unit, which Henderson took as interference in his personal bailiwick.

He hadn't said as much publicly of course. He was only a couple of years away from retirement and he knew better than to openly buck the Chief. However, he was a tough old bird and once the new unit was in place, he'd made it quite clear to Dave, in a private one-on-one, that he wasn't going to hold his breath in anticipation of wondrous results from the new unit.

With Dave working nights of late, he and the Inspector very rarely crossed paths. That aside, there were small signs that Henderson had warmed up a bit to Dave, and had even begun giving him a receptive nod when they infrequently crossed paths, a definite improvement over the scowls Dave had previously become used to.

Additionally, Dave had heard through the grapevine that the Inspector had even begun to drop into the little office where his unit hung out during the day, occasionally sometimes spending up to a half hour chewing the fat with Dave's minions.

Recently Dave had been both surprised and a little unnerved when he'd arrived for work one night to find a note on his desk asking him to stick around after his shift ended the next morning and drop into the Inspector's office before he went home.

Dave had found it difficult to concentrate on his work that evening.

He kept drifting off, trying to figure out what he was in shit for. Henderson was not the type who delivered much positive news.

At the end of his shift he tided himself up a bit and downed a coffee, then he left his office and went down the hall to the Inspector's corner office.

Several unpleasant thoughts were raging a in his mind as he knocked at the door and a bellowed *'It's open'* sounded on the other side.

Dave had no more than got it open when that was followed by *'shut it behind you and grab a chair'*.

Henderson was hunched over reading. He didn't look up, but waved to the chairs on the far side of his desk.

Dave eased into one and sat quietly for a few moments, until the Inspector let out a sigh and leaned back as he deftly plucked the reading glasses off the tip of his nose and set them down on top of the pile of reports in front of him.

He looked at Dave briefly as if he was mentally shifting gears, and then he frowned.

"Where do you see yourself going in the department?"

Dave thought about that for a second, trying his best to figure out exactly where that remark might be heading. Before he could answer, Henderson frowned, waved his hand and shrugged.

"Loaded question I suppose. Don't answer it.

"I've been watching you lately and a thought occurred to me. You're doing a pretty good job with that new-fangled profiling thing."

Dave couldn't believe what he was hearing. Henderson was not the kind to toss those kinds of compliments around. His ears perked up for what was to come.

"You've got the Chief in your hip pocket, as I'm sure you are aware. Now, he's a relatively new chief, so having him on your side certainly isn't a bad thing for your prospects. Problem is, he's got a lot of new ideas about changing things and I was wondering just what ambitions you may have, when he decides to promote you again.

"Reason I asked you here is because I'm going to be putting in my papers in a couple of years and like I said, I've been watching you. The Chief spent most of his career in patrol. Very little detective experience. I can see him eventually moving you out of here and into patrol and frankly I think that would be a hell of a waste.

"That little squad of yours appears to be growing by leaps and bounds. Seems to me that if he does have a mind to promote you again soon, you might just want to try to finagle a Staff Sergeant spot here in Major crime. And, as I said, in a couple of years I'm out the door. If you are as ambitious as you appear to be, and if you happened to be a proven Staff Sergeant by the time that rolls around, well with all your experience in the squad - who knows…"

He paused for a couple of seconds trying to read Dave's reaction then continued.

"If that idea appeals to you, I could maybe put on a push for just such a slot within your unit, when it grows again.

"Anything I've said so far of interest to you?"

Yep…Dave was very interested.

Linda's doctor had confirmed her pregnancy in December of '96 and she had given birth to a healthy boy on June third of '97. They named him Shaun William. Both were delighted and within days, their set routine had been turned upside down, but in a good way.

After the birth, Linda had taken off a few months on maternity leave coupled with built up booked overtime hours. She'd also arranged to have her younger sister Cathy move in with them to help look after young Shaun, before she had to go back to work.

With the expanded household, they decided to do an addition onto the house, adding two new bedrooms and one and a half bathrooms. With all that was going on, their weekends were suddenly very busy.

Murphy's nose was out of joint. He wasn't particularly pleased with the upheaval bought about by these new additions to the family, however, he rolled with the punches and managed to adjust to the changes it caused.

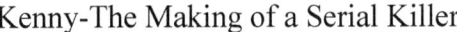

Book 2

CHAPTER SIXTEEN

- September 1998 -

Determined not to rock the boat until his nineteenth birthday, Kenny had been, rather reluctantly, relying on the internet to provide him with the stimulation he hungered for. But, as time passed, since then he was finding the 'net wasn't any longer quite enough to completely satisfy him.

For several weeks now, it had taken a good deal of personal resolve to repeatedly check his desires sufficiently to prevent a rising temptation to bring the fantasies to the reality of full fruition. The internal pressure to do so was definitely building, but so far, he had persevered in his decision to properly prepare before making that compelling move.

Kenny got several very nice surprises on, and shortly after his birthday in nineteen ninety-eight.

Having been told in March that she would likely not live to see the end of the year, the old lady had thankfully managed to hang in until the first of September, although she was now often drugged out, almost completely bedridden, and obviously on her last legs.

Kenny had been sticking to his now adopted routine of spending time with her over the past year. He had been pleased to find that the effort had apparently born fruit for him in a financial way when, in July, she'd surprised him with the announcement that he would now receive a fixed monthly salary from the business.

He was to get two grand a month.

Additionally, as a surprise birthday gift for Kenny, in the last week of August she had instructed Walter to take the old Ford pickup into the dealership and provided the cash for him to select a brand new full-sized pickup with all the bells and whistles. Walter had done this during his off time and arranged for delivery of the truck early on the first of September.

After Kenny had finished his breakfast with the old lady that day, she'd presented him with a little wrapped gift box. She'd wished him a Happy Birthday and told him to take it into the office to Walter before he opened it.

Walter was waiting for him with a big grin on his face and immediately ushered him outside onto the sun- drenched porch. The new, fire-engine-red truck, was parked in the driveway. Walter chin-gestured toward the gift-wrapped box and suggested Kenny open it up. Inside were two sets of Ford keys.

And there was more.

When he'd finished looking the truck over, Walter handed him an envelope.

Kenny looked at it, noted it was from a law firm and was addressed to him. He glanced up at Walter inquisitively.

"What's this?"

Walter's grin broadened.

"Open it up. It arrived last week. They phoned your grandmother a couple of weeks ago and said it would be coming. I think you'll be pleased."

Kenny sucked in a deep breath and then released it as he tore the envelope open and pulled out a single typewritten page. It was short and to the point.

On his nineteenth birthday, he was to receive a legacy that had been set up by his grandfather on his mother's side, before his death. Originally the legacy had been created on a shared basis with his sister, but since she had pre-deceased him, it was now to be his in its entirety. The amount of this legacy was not indicated; however, the letter described it as considerable.

It went on further to advise that a representative of the firm would be calling him with respect to setting up a meeting with Kenny at the house on that very afternoon.

Kenny was astonished.

He'd known from family gossip that the old fart had been loaded, but hadn't the slightest inkling that any of it had been put aside for him.

Suddenly Kenny's whole world had changed. His somewhat clouded future had begun to look very bright indeed.

The call from the lawyer's office came at just after ten and a meeting was arranged for two o'clock that afternoon.

After the call, Kenny's mind started racing. He was on pins and needles.

A new truck of his own. A regular amount of cash coming in every month. An undetermined inheritance from his grandfather. Granny was gonna kick the bucket any day now. No more worries. Very soon he would be able to do whatever the hell he wanted, and he had some very definite ideas of how that would go. Fantasies were going to be turned into reality for sure.

He couldn't wait to get started.

With Kenny hovering around him in the room, completely hyped and impatient for two o'clock to roll around, Walter found it impossible to get any work done in the office. After about twenty distracting minutes, he suggested to Kenny that the kid forget working for the day and instead take his new truck out for a little test run.

Kenny realized that he needed to do some serious thinking. Big changes were ahead for him. He needed to begin work on perfecting his plans as to exactly how to guarantee that he was properly prepared for the culmination of his fantasies.

He took up Walter's suggestion of a ride in the truck. It would give him something to do to fill in the time until the lawyer got to the house, as well as an opportunity to mentally isolate the steps he would have to take to be ready to safely turn those, by now well-developed, fantasies into reality.

His mind was more on anticipating the upcoming changes in his life, than on the truck as he drove.

The instant the old lady was gone he had to be ready to exercise the new possibilities now provided to him by his new-found situation. He would have to move very carefully when the time came to make that first big step.

He had managed to get away with murder once, but he fully intended to take that up far more than a notch, very soon. If he was to be ultimately successful in achieving his end goal, he was going to have to have a solid plan in place before he acted on his fantasies to ensure he avoided the attention of the police. He had no intention of being held accountable for his acts.

To accomplish that, it was imperative that he not act on impulse, not hurry these first few, very necessary steps toward the exciting result, no matter how fervent he was about finally being able to get started.

By the time he'd pulled back up at the house at one-thirty, he'd managed to settle himself down. He'd forced himself to rationalize his longing to get started instantly. He'd recognized and accepted the need to hold that craving in check until he was certain he was properly prepared.

He would not make the mistakes of other serial killers. He would be ready for any eventuality that might arise. Restraining the urge to get started was not going to be easy. He could almost taste the excitement of that first real kill, but he was determined to compartmentalize that excitement at the back of his mind, and take a sensible, balanced approach.

He would begin his quest very gradually.

That would mean testing uncharted waters sufficiently before taking each step. To ensure the complete achievement of his goals while not being caught by the police, it was imperative that his strategies were sufficiently perfected, before he made each step aimed at realizing his ambition.

The lawyer arrived a few minutes early for the scheduled appointment. He was an old guy, impeccably dressed and driving a new BMW. Once the introductions were completed, he and Kenny went into what granny had always referred to as the parlour. The housekeeper served them tea and once she had poured, she left the two of them alone in the room.

The lawyer set his briefcase on the table beside his chair and opened it up. He took out some papers and settled them on his lap.

Without further preamble, he asked Kenny if he wanted him to read the documents in their entirety or would a brief summery do. Kenny went with the second option.

In doing so, the lawyer didn't have a great deal to add to the gist of the letter Kenny had read earlier, but he did offer a few rather tantalizing specifics.

Kenny was to get four million dollars. There were some strings attached. Three million was to remain in trust until he was twenty-five years old. That amount was to be invested in trust under the auspices of the law firm, and held by them until he reached that age.

The remaining million would be his to use as he saw fit, albeit restricted to the withdrawal of amounts of less than ten thousand dollars, during any calendar month. This restriction would remain in place until his twenty-fifth birthday.

Before leaving, the crusty old bastard surprisingly presented Kenny with a chequebook on an account already made out in his name. The balance therein was listed as one million dollars. Kenny had never seen so many typed zeros in his life.

He was giddy with the prospect of what this would mean to him.

There was now very little left standing in the way of his being free to fully enjoy all the delights that an expanded world had on offer. That said, he cautioned himself to be disciplined and reasonably patient about making any major changes, at least until after the old lady was gone.

That wouldn't be easy, considering that he could envision a whole big world of pleasure out there, just waiting for him. However, he would be an idiot to upset the applecart at this point by alienating her somehow and having her change her will at the last minute, just because of some stupid thing he did.

No…it wouldn't be easy, but he would an idiot not to bide his time for a little longer yet.

Without doubt, this was his best birthday ever!

The renovations to the house had been completed. Cathy, rent free, was happily ensconced, at the far end of the enlarged structure, in her own, self-contained quarters.

Cut out of the same physical mold and a younger version of her sister to all intents and purposes, Cathy was twenty-four years' old. She was single and currently undergoing her medical internship at Vancouver General Hospital.

A very pretty woman, Cathy attracted males like flies to sugar and when she wasn't looking after Shaun or at work, she was rarely home. She was an outgoing and upbeat individual and almost compulsively clean and neat. Characteristics that made for very easy relationships with both Dave and Linda.

Shaun adored auntie Cathy and surprise of all surprises, she was a cat person. Even Murphy liked her.

On a regular basis and as necessary, Linda adjusted her work schedule to offset Cathy's, making sure that Dave, or one of them, was always home to look after Shaun. Both Dave and Linda were in positions that allowed them to vary their schedules if the need arose due to some sort of scheduling conflict, but in practice that necessity rarely arose.

With the new construction now out of the way, the recent weekend pace had slowed considerably for both Dave and Linda. Often, the two of them found themselves otherwise unencumbered and during their days off spent their time puttering around the house, enjoying time with their son.

All three of the adults enjoyed cooking and whoever happened to be home at the time, tended to prepare the meals for the entire household.

Most of the housekeeping seemed to fall to the two women; however, Dave balanced that responsibility by taking on the yard and any handyman jobs that came up.

Although Dave often quipped that he was now unfairly outnumbered by females, he did so in fun, regularly entreating his young son, in front of the two women, to hurry and grow up so he could have some much-needed vocal male support in the house.

A couple of months earlier, Dave had taken his Staff /Sergeant exam and interview. He'd passed with flying colours and was currently shortlisted for future promotion.

Inspector Henderson had been as good as his word. As part of his latest departmental budget for Major Crime, he had put in a request for a new position of that rank and it was currently under consideration by the powers that be.

With a view to using their expertise in profiling to assist the detectives assigned, Dave and his little crew continued to examine all current cases under investigation by Major Crime and were now routinely coming up with some excellent results.

In addition, over the past few months, chiefly based on some of the recently successful work done by some of the larger law enforcement agencies in the States, Dave had begun toying with the idea of setting up a separate section within his squad specifically assigned to reopen some of the department's still active, but cold and still outstanding murder and serious crime cases.

This idea of making a re-evaluation of the old cases, many of which had been collecting dust for decades, had also been recently prompted by David's interest in the growing media coverage of the recent successes in the introduction of DNA evidence into the Canadian courts. DNA was now being routinely used as a trusted method for positively identifying potential suspects.

That fact, coupled with the triumphs in court because of new evidence, which had been garnered using several other recent scientific advances relating to the analysis of old crime scene trace-evidence, now offered police forces a concrete opportunity to reassess old evidence. By applying these new scientific techniques to material that had been originally gathered at the time of the initial investigation, law enforcement could now often provide conclusive, court admissible, evidence which could then lead to the arrest and conviction of the perpetrator.

Dave figured his department was currently missing a bet in this area. That it should be availing itself of the opportunity to have a new set of eyes. Eyes cognisant of the recent scientific leaps achieved toward the analysis of trace evidence, take a second look at these cold cases.

Toward this end and in his own time on the weekends, he'd begun to review some of the successes being achieved by the other police forces throughout the world. The more he read, the more excited about the possibility of using this approach in his department he became.

He'd recently discussed the concept with Linda and she had been supportive of the idea.

Convinced it should be done, Dave kicked some ideas around in his mind for a couple of days before writing up a proposal for the creation of such a project and, with Henderson's blessing and endorsement, submitted it upstairs.

He did so, aware of the fact that any new investigative tool undertaken by the department was going to face an up-hill battle. New initiatives were routinely *catch-twenty-two* situations, in that they were rarely properly resourced until after they had proven themselves beyond question.

In the end, he decided not to ask for too much by way of manpower during the initially stages of the project. He reckoned a single team of experienced Major Crime detectives would be sufficient, at least to get the ball rolling.

Knowing that new hires would probably be kyboshed as too costly, he again recommended that these first staffing positions be filled by a couple of recently retired guys. Ideally, they would be retired Major Crime detectives that could be hired back, on a month-to-month contract.

Late in September he was given the go ahead to run a ninety-day trail of the project, at the end of which the department would evaluate the results and decide whether or not to continue with it.

Dave eagerly began interviewing recently retired Major Crime detectives to see if he could find a team capable of providing what he was looking for.

It only took him three days to come up with what he wanted. By the end of the month, after the concept had been given the green light, he had found two recently retired members who were eager to take part.

Dave then rearranged the furniture to make enough space in his allotted floorplan to cram in a couple of desks in the corner of what was already a crowded squad room. The two detectives arrived and on that first day, they promptly hauled up from the basement a couple dozen dust-covered boxes containing old cases and soon had their noses buried in stacks of time-worn reports.

At this stage, these cold cases were still very much on the back burner for the rest of his staff, but Dave, not surprisingly, saw this new task as a personal challenge. He encouraged his new cold-case specialist team to initially carefully cherry-pick from the cases, suggesting they look for ones that held sufficient crime scene evidence to make it likely that they would lead to successful DNA testing.

He continued to provide the new team as much of his own time as he could spare.

CHAPTER SEVENTEEN

- November 1998 -

The weather had turned dismal. Grey days, with a seemingly never-ending drizzle.

It was hard for Kenny to believe that it had only been two months since his birthday. Even though so much had changed in his life, to Kenny it seemed to be taking forever to have it all over and done with.

A terrific weight had been lifted off his shoulders when the doctors had determined that granny could no longer remain at home and would have to enter hospital. That had come about in late October.

It had only been a first step of course. She was still alive, but at least she would soon be out of the house and then he could at least begin to make some meaningful changes.

Kenny was confident about how he would handle this eventuality. While he'd hoped that she would just die at home and get it over with, he'd figured that it would probably not be that simple. He'd forced himself to be patient, continuing with the daily routine, spending time and meals with her right up until the decision to hospitalize had come.

Meanwhile he'd used his free time to do research on the computer.

He'd read everything he could find on serial killers. His main intent was to find out what mistakes they had made. How they had been caught. Kenny didn't intend to fall into that trap once he started his wonderful new life. He'd also learned everything he could about those who had never been caught.

His third research project over that period had revolved around the best way to initiate his scheme. Some stuff he'd already worked out – disposal of bodies for example. Few investigations ever got anywhere if no bodies were ever found. He was satisfied that he already had that aspect worked out.

Witnesses to the acts themselves. He was kicking that one around. It seemed to him that the best idea there was to ensure that there were no witnesses to the acts but him. However, it also seemed sensible for him to use a 'cut-out' in the initial procurement stages of selecting his victims. A single person who he could safely repeatedly use to seek out the right quarry and bring them to him. That way, he wouldn't need to have any direct preliminary tie to the victims. He was still working on that one.

But he had managed to pick out the actual source of prey. That was a no-brainer.

'Boystown', situated at the foot of Homer Street in Vancouver, which catered to men who were looking for sex with teenage males. This area would obviously provide him with plenty of delightful subjects, the clear majority of whom were apparently runaways, kids. Kids who would very likely to not be seriously missed once they suddenly disappeared from the face of the earth.

All the research had left him giddy with anticipation and now that the old lady was soon moving out of the house, he could begin to set things up in preparation for putting his plans to act out on his fantasy into action.

He was about to expand both his territory and his research.

Granny would be going into Vancouver General Hospital for assessment within the week, and he would dutifully visit her everyday. Visiting hours started at seven in the evening and Kenny was going to be there on the dot. After each visit, he was going to pop on down to the 'Boy's town' area and surreptitiously complete his research on how to safely go about selecting specific prey. He was very excited about the prospect of undertaking this portion of his preparatory work for victim selection.

He could hardly wait for the ambulance to transport granny so he could begin his provisions to rid himself of unwanted staff and have the house to himself.

When that day finally came, he rose early and had a hearty breakfast. On the porch, surrounded by Walter, the housekeeper, and the nurse, he did his best to play the part of a somber grandson as the old woman was loaded into the ambulance.

Once the ambulance headed down the driveway, he asked Walter to join him in the office.

There he advised him about the changes he was going to make.

He told Walter he was going to give him a raise and planned on building him an office and small house near the yard at the front of the property. Walter would then have the day-to-day responsibility for the running of the company. Kenny went on to explain that he wanted to keep his hand in a little and so he would continue to do the cleaning of the equipment and the spreading of the loads of chips that came in on the trucks each day, but he would leave most everything else to Walter.

Walter, who was currently engaged to be married, was excited at the suggestion and readily agreed to the idea. Kenny tasked him to immediately select an architect and contractor to begin work on the new buildings.

That out of the way, Kenny promptly terminated the employment of both the nurse and the housekeeper, giving them both excellent reference letters and generous severance packages.

Two days later the only sharing of the house Kenny faced was temporary, that of Walter from nine to five, Monday to Friday. Plans for the office and house complex had been selected and a contractor had been hired to begin work on the projects starting in two weeks.

The estimated time for completion of the construction was roughly six months.

Kenny wished it could be less, as he was eager to begin his program to reach his fantasy goal, but he counselled himself to be patient and make good use of the delay by way of continuing his research. Expanding that already done on the computer and taking some concrete steps toward physically studying the area from which he would be selecting his potential sexual playthings.

He had been sheltered from the real world for most of his life and it was time for him to spread his wings and educating himself on the street life of the big city.

He looked up maps and familiarized himself with the area where the teenage male stroll was centered and plotted out a route that would take him directly from the hospital to the area in question. He planned to make his first recon on the first night, after visiting Granny in the hospital.

Driving in the city was alien to him at the best of times and, typical of November, darkness fell early, and it was raining heavily.

Relying on his memory, he found it much more difficult than he had anticipated to follow the route that he had prepared for his first trip from North Vancouver to the hospital. He got lost several times, and had to pull over and park long enough to turn on the interior light in the pickup, find his current location on the map and refresh his bearings.

By the time he arrived and got parked in the massive, tiered garage adjoining the hospital, he was sweating profusely and so unnerved that he had to sit in the truck for almost half an hour, before he felt capable of making his way into the hospital itself.

He'd expected the building to be large but was astounded by its actual size. The hospital complex consisted of several buildings and it was huge! He wandered about for some time before managing to find an information desk where a chatty, half-witted, ancient crone with a name tag attached to her drooping bosom, identifying her as 'Mildred', finally understood what he needed to know and gave him directions to the correct building and ward.

It seemed to take him forever to make it to the correct building and once inside he immediately found himself lost in a sea of people. A seemingly endless maze of hallways, stairs, and elevators crammed full of bodies, all in a hurry and often impeding his comfort zone and the path ahead.

Kenny was not used to having to deal with large numbers of strangers. He found being jostled about among the throng very uncomfortable, uncomfortable to the extent that he was having some difficulty in breathing by the time he got to the right ward.

Once there, he had to pause for a few moments to compose himself enough to put on the proper face, displaying at least some semblance of sincerity and confidence before he was able to enter her private room.

The trip had taken him a good half-hour longer than he had anticipated.

Thankfully, Granny was heavily medicated, and although she did appear to recognize him when he came in, she kept drifting off and was unable to hold a train of thought long enough to carry on a conversation.

Despite that, Kenny stayed for the full half-hour remaining in the visiting hours, not to satisfy the old lady if she even noticed, but to give himself a chance to feel back to normal before leaving.

When the end of visiting hours was announced, he braced himself for the ordeal of running the gauntlet of humanity that would be required for him to make his way back to his truck and struggled his way through the jostling crowds and back to the parking garage.

It had been hell. He'd lost his way in the maze of buildings three times and had panicked on each occasion. In the end, he was forced to seek assistance each time.

Once safely ensconced inside the cab of the truck, he put his window down and lit a cigarette with shaking fingers. He immediately took several heavy drags.

He was worn out, stomach in a knot and sweating profusely.

The though of leaving and going into the center of the city to reconnoiter the 'boy's town' area rather than proceeding directly home, had completely lost its appeal. He decided he would leave that until tomorrow night when, based on what he'd had to endure on this first visit, he would be better prepared for the effort the whole thing would require from him.

He then checked the planned route for the return trip on his map, carefully, closed his window, and started up the truck.

It took a great deal of determination for him to force himself to maneuver back out onto the street and from there, into the darkness and pouring rain to begin the trip back home.

Over the past two months things on the home front had been going relatively smoothly for Dave.

Having Cathy around to help with keeping an eye on Shaun on the occasions when both he and Linda were working, was a godsend.

Of late, he was, however, a little concerned that his sister-in-law seemed to be burning the candle at both ends with the result being an obvious loss in weight and an inkling of burnout.

Cathy's workload was intense of course, but from Dave's perspective it wasn't her work schedule that seemed to be taking the toll, it was her excessive social activities. Those had recently been expanding. These days it seemed to Dave, that if she wasn't at work or caring for her nephew, she was out on the town partying.

Dave had never been particularly judgemental when it came to Cathy. After all she was young, single, very good looking and a definite extrovert. Live and let live was an idiom that had served Dave well for his entire life. That said, he did care for his sister-in-law and his concern for her wellbeing had reached the point where he figured he needed to talk to Linda about it to find out if she felt he had real cause to worry or was simply misreading the signs.

Linda had always been *'big-sister'* protective of Cathy.

With that fact in mind Dave knew he had to tread softly. He bided his time and broached the subject carefully one evening when Cathy was out as she, Dave and Shaun were sitting down to dinner.

"Cathy sure looks beat lately – is she eating properly? She seems to be losing weight and doesn't quite seem to be herself…"

He forked in a mouthful and let the question hang so Linda could have a chance to evaluate it before responding.

Linda, paused in cutting her meat and put down her knife and fork. She then let out a little sigh and frowned across the table at him.

Dave initially took the look on her face as one of displeasure, but when Linda's shoulders drooped, and she bowed her head, he realized that was not the case.

He kept his mouth shut and waited for her response.

"Yes...I've been worried about her for a few weeks now. Her workload at the hospital is heavy, but she's able to handle that with no problem. It's all the carousing and late nights that are wearing her out. There's more to it than that though. She seems somewhat driven to live her free hours to the full at a time when she should be more concerned with her education and workload...

Don't get me wrong, she's always been one to max out socially, but of late it seems that that aspect of her life appears to be more important to her that anything else."

Dave nodded.

"Well I'm glad its not just me who thinks so. What's it all about, has she found some special guy or something?"

Linda took a sip from her wine glass and shook her head.

"No, that was my first thought, but she says not. It's almost like she's seeing how many different guys she can party with. It seems to me its not about the relationships, its all about having as much fun a she can with as many men as she can."

Linda lifted her fork and pushed some food around on her plate and then sighed deeply again before continuing.

"However you look at it, its not healthy and she needs to take a good look at what she's doing to herself. If you've noticed the change too, I'd better have a talk with her. Leave it with me."

In mid November Henderson called Dave into his office and told him that the decision had been made regarding the new Staff/Sergeant position for Major Crime. It had been approved. He then told Dave that he had asked the Chief to fill the position by way of promoting Dave from within the squad.

Henderson hadn't yet received a confirmation of that possibility, but at the time, the Chief had informed him that there were several promotions being made before the end of the month to fill new vacancies, and that Dave would be making Staff/Sergeant when that came to pass.

When Dave left Henderson's office he was comfortably confident that he would be named as the new Staff/Sergeant for Major Crime and with that behind him, he began to think about who he would like to replace him in the position of Sergeant.

He had put so much of himself into the job and with the new cold case experiment almost two-thirds of the way through it's trial, he didn't want to see it fail.

By the time he got back to his own office he already had an idea of who he could rely on to fill the spot. Someone with the same energy he'd given it. Ed Hamilton, who he'd partnered with in the youth squad, and who had recently passed his Sergeant's exam and interview.

If promotions were coming shortly, it was likely that Ed would make the cut. Ed was a known entity for Dave. The two had always worked well together.

He figured if he approached Henderson to ask for Ed as his replacement (if and when he was successful at making the new Staff/Sergeant position), it was likely he would be able to get the Inspector's support.

The real question was, could he sell Ed on the idea of moving to Major Crime?

Ed was currently working in the drug squad and seemed to be happy there. Dave knew it was kind of early in the game, but he figured he'd sound out his old partner on the idea, sooner rather than later.

Dave gave Linda a call and discussed it with her. She suggested he invite Ed over for diner that night.

She pointed out that Ed was recently divorced, and Linda ventured to guess that he'd probably be up for a home cooked meal, which in turn would hopefully put him in a mellow frame of mind and more open to considering Dave's proposal.

Dave laughed and agreed that after a few drinks and a good meal, Ed would indeed probably find the idea more palatable.

As soon as he'd finished speaking with Linda, he called Ed to extend the invitation and as Linda had surmised, his old partner had welcomed, with open arms, the idea of a home-cooked meal.

CHAPTER EIGHTEEN

- December 1998 -

It had been snowing intermittently for days and there seemed to be a never-ending layer of slush covering the roads.

Despite the urgency he felt to get things rolling, try as he might for over a week Kenny had not been able to make that intended first recon trip down to *'Boystown'* after his visits to Granny.

It had taken him that long to become conditioned enough to feel reasonably self-assured about his ability to deal with all it would entail.

The traffic congestion and stormy weather, coupled with the idea of extending his time away from home by another half-hour to accommodate the additional side trip.

That after being subjected to the trauma of dealing with the suffocating mass of humanity afforded by attending the hospital itself.

He told himself that it was nothing to be overly concerned about. He had been insulated from this type of human congestion since birth and had accepted that a learning curve to deal with it now was only natural.

In early December, he finally felt ready, and after carefully studying his map, he left the hospital parking lot and made his way down to the foot of Homer street.

After circling the block twice, he found a parking spot on Hornby, hallway up from the intersection. With a sigh of accomplishment and relief, he shut the truck off and lit up a cigarette to quiet his nerves.

What the internet had told him was quickly confirmed.

Young men in small groups or on their own were irregularly spaced on the corners and along the street. There was no way to ignore the obvious, they were all provocatively dressed and clearly displaying their wares for the parade of slowly moving vehicles that, despite the mixed rain and snow, leisurely cruised by on the street.

Kenny let his eyes shift from individual to individual. He was ecstatic.

Just like the internet said, here they were, hot little numbers all. Most of them appeared to be in their early to mid-teens, with the odd older guy thrown in. Some unsavory lowlifes for sure, but that was OK.

There was very definitely a goodly amount of prime meat on show.

Just the sight of them gave him a throbbing hard-on.

It didn't take long for the side windows in the truck to fog up as he watched. He welcomed it as he felt safely concealed from view.

To keep the delectable smorgasbord of delicious boys being displayed, he simply had to turn on the wipers from time to time to clear the droplets and then wipe the inside of the windshield directly in front of him with his shirt-sleeve.

He felt like a kid in a candy shop.

He promptly unbuttoned his 501's, hauled it out, and began to masturbate leisurely.

He came quickly, but completely engrossed in the eye-candy before him, continued to stroke his still-swollen member with vigour.

He had no idea how long he had been happily enjoying himself, when his concentration was abruptly interrupted by a thud on the outside of his driver's window.

Incredulous, he quickly fumbled his stiff cock back into his pants as he twisted his head to see what had caused the sound. His startled gaze was met by the glare of a flashlight beam against the fogged glass.

He managed to get a couple of buttons done up before opening the window to find himself face-to-face with a uniformed cop who was standing in the open passenger doorway of a marked police car with its strobe lights flashing.

The cop spoke first.

"You can't park here buddy, you're in a loading zone."

Scared shitless, Kenny flushed and nodded.

"Sorry, I didn't know. I'll move."

Droplets of moisture were dripping from the brim of his hat as the cop glanced into the interior of the truck and moved the now very bright flashlight beam around the cab.

"Let's see your drivers licence, insurance and registration."

Panic-stricken, Kenny couldn't speak as he dug out his wallet to get his licence and then leaned across to open the glove compartment to get his insurance papers.

His hands were shaking so badly, he had a hell of a time working his licence out of the wallet. He then handed the documents over to the cop and his shoulders slumped as he turned his eyes away and listlessly studied the dashboard in front of him.

The cop took a quick look at the papers in his hand before he spoke again.

"Sit tight, I'll be back in a moment."

Kenny managed to nod and watched the uniformed cop climb back into the passenger seat of the patrol car. The interior light came on and Kenny got a short view of the young cop's older partner, who was sitting behind the wheel, before the passenger door of the black and white closed.

He watched as the cop he'd been talking to pulled out a notebook and began to write in it while he gave the papers Kenny had provided another look.

Kenny closed his window partway, so the rain wouldn't come in, then slammed both fists into the steering wheel and silently repeated the words to himself.

'Stupid... fucking stupid...I'm so fucking stupid!

A few moments later the door of the cruiser opened again, and Kenny pressed the switch to lower the window all the way as the cop approached. He sincerely hoped that he was composed enough as he turned his head to face the cop.

The constable handed him back his papers through the window and began to speak.

"Nice truck. Seems brand new. Looks like you're the registered owner. You're kinda young to be driving around in something this nice. Mind telling me what your doing parked here?"

Kenny's brain raced to come up with a plausible answer.

What the hell could he say that would sound reasonable?

He realized he needed to respond quickly.

He said the first thing that came into his mind.

"It was raining so hard... I was having trouble seeing the road. I haven't been driving that long and I figured I'd just pull over and wait the worst of it out."

Kenny's brow furrowed.

Christ...that sounded so lame...

One sideways glance at the cop was enough to convince Kenny that he agreed with him.

Shit!

The cop didn't say anything for a couple of seconds.

"If you figure you really need to sit out the rain, you'll have to move out of here and find yourself a legal parking spot, my young friend."

Kenny fumbled with the keys in his eagerness to get the hell away for the cop and after a couple of aborted tries to get them into the ignition, he got the truck going. He put on his turn signal, carefully pulled away from the curb, and drove away.

In his mirror, he could see the cop standing in the rain beside the marked patrol unit with it's rotating light flashing, pensively watching him drive off.

When the cop got back into the car his partner reached for the defroster and flipped it on as he spoke.

"Christ, close the fucking door before we drown. What took you so long?"

The young cop closed the door and shook his head.

"I don't know exactly. The guy was just weird, really nervous."

"Around here - you find that unusual?

His partner put the cruiser into gear and switched off the rotating light as they pulled away.

"Well, what the hell. If he bothered you that much, you could always put in a check card on him. Can't hurt."

"I think I will, polite enough and all, but really up-tight. Just something weird about him I didn't like.

Kenny didn't look for a parking spot. He was so unnerved at having to deal with the cop that he headed straight for home.

Once safely there he poured himself a stiff drink and took the bottle with him into the office and sat down in front of his computer.

He didn't turn it on; instead he continued to verbally chastise himself for what had occurred earlier.

He worked his way through the rest of the bottle before he staggered off to bed.

The next morning, he was hungover, but he had regained his self-confidence to the point the he could stop beating himself up over the episode with the cop and had begun to think positively again.

Yes, it had been a stupid thing to do. But what was done was done. He couldn't change that now.

The cop hadn't given him a ticket or anything, so maybe he was making a big thing out of nothing.

The incident had taught him a lesson though.

The first thing he was going to do was set himself up with a cut-out. That couldn't wait. He could not risk leaving himself open to inquiry by police. That would fuck-up everything that came after.

He had to remain anonymous to the police. Yes, finding a cut-out had to be his first step.

He ate breakfast and felt a lot better for it, then when back into the office and sat down at his desk.

There, he closed his eyes and let his mind run back through what he had seen on the stroll.

The images of the various meat that had been on display rolled by and he briefly concentrated on each one, looking for some indication that a possible prospective cut-out was among them.

He knew what he wanted. A loner, young subservient and malleable. Someone he could easily dominate.

There had been one possibility.

A kid who had been standing off by himself, away from the others. The one he had been mainly concentrating on while he was jacking off.

Small, but cute.

Alone, not part of any group.

Kinda anxious, and vulnerable-looking for sure.

That night after he had made his hospital visit he drove back down to the stroll. He didn't risk parking, but instead circled the couple of blocks, driving slowly by the lineup of boys on offer.

He was looking specifically for the kid he had seen the night before.

The weather had changed for the better and although the sky was overcast, at least it wasn't raining.

On his third pass he spotted him, standing alone just like the night before, a fair distance away from the others.

Yes, it was him all right. Kenny slowed even more to give himself time to check the kid out more closely.

Yes, he looked like a good prospect. Beaten down for sure. A little worse for wear, could certainly use a bath and some new clothes. Looks like he hasn't had a decent meal in a week. Probably living on the street.

There was promise there though, small but well-defined, cute in a boy-next-door kinda way.

More importantly he looked delightfully defenceless, susceptible, probably malleable.

The kid had taken note of Kenny's crawling truck.

Unlike the others Kenny had watched being picked up by a cruising vehicle, those who had taken note of a probable john and immediately responded by crossing to the curb and approaching it; this kid seemed scared shitless and unable to move.

Kenny met his gaze and held it as he swung into the curb and stopped. He put the passenger window of his truck down and used his index finger to beckon to him.

The panicked expression on the kid's face as he hesitantly approached the truck gave Kenny an immediate woody.

Oh yes! This could be exactly what he was looking for.

The dinner with Ed in November had gone very well from Dave's perspective.

After several pre-meal drinks and a homecooked meal, he and Ed had left Cathy and Linda to clean up and retired to Dave's small home office for a cigar and a brandy.

Dave waited until they were well into enjoying both before he raised the subject of the upcoming promotions and the fact that there would be an opening in Major Crime for a Sergeant to replace him should he be promoted to fill the new vacancy of Staff /Sergeant.

He told Ed he figured he should apply for it and told him he had already spoken to Henderson about the possibility and that he had the Inspector's support for the transfer.

If Ed was interested.

Ed had taken a few seconds to think about it and then asked Dave several questions about what the job would entail exactly. Questions answered, Dave brought him up to speed on what was going on with the profiling and the trial run involving the opening of old cold-case files.

Even though he was reasonably happy where he was, in drugs, Ed knew that the Chief was a supporter of what Dave had been able to accomplish in the Major Crime unit to date and that his work there had propelled his old partner forward into a rapid promotion cycle.

Common sense suggested that it would likely be a good path for him to follow as well.

Before they had finished their cigars, Ed had agreed to the idea, if not with unbounded enthusiasm, certainly with a fair amount of fervour.

Once that topic was out of the way, Ed had immediately shifted the conversation to Cathy.

He had been aware that Linda's sister had moved in with Dave and Linda to help with Shaun's care, but he had never met her before that evening. As the banter between he two of them had progressed, it had quickly become apparent to Dave that his old partner was obviously keenly interested in the stunning and outgoing young lady with whom he'd shared dinner.

Initially Dave had been a little taken aback by Ed's clear interest in his sister-in-law. Cathy was a good deal younger than Ed after all, but on the other hand, there was no doubting that she was a very attractive woman.

When he mentally went back over the exchanges between the two of them during the earlier meal, Dave realized that Cathy had also demonstrated a great deal of interest in Ed, engaging him in conversation whenever the opportunity arose, more than he would have expected.

At the time, preoccupied with his own addenda for Ed, Dave hadn't paid a great deal of attention to the back and forth between Ed and his sister-in-law across the table. Now he took the time to relive it with a new set of eyes, he could easily see Ed's interest in Cathy. To anyone paying attention to their exchanges, the mutual attraction between the two would have been obvious.

Dave was somewhat intrigued by this development. He'd found himself both surprised and slightly amused by it.

He wasn't sure if it was a good turn of events, however. Something that should be encouraged or not.

Ed was a good-looking guy in a rugged kind of way and basically had a good heart, but he was also on the rebound and seemed to be drinking more than he had before his breakup. Conversely, Cathy was riding the wild side lately, so maybe a serious relationship was not what she wanted.

Dave decided to keep his eyes and ears open over the remainder of the evening before he formed any firm opinion on the possibilities of encouraging a budding relationship between the two of them and then he'd later discuss the situation with Linda when the two of them were alone.

Since November, the Ed and Cathy thing, which he had discussed with Linda on that first night when the two had met, had taken on a life of its own and whatever concerns he and Linda may have shared on that night, were no longer an issue.

Ed seemed to be completely smitten by Cathy and in turn she had begun dating him exclusively.

Within days of that shared meal, his sister-in-law and Ed had become an item and by December Ed, who loved kids, was soon joining Cathy whenever she looked after Shaun. He was also spending two or three evenings a week for dinner at Dave and Linda's.

The two couples thoroughly enjoyed each other's company.

Now almost a month old, her new relationship seemed to be having a positive effect on Cathy. She was eating better, had gained back some weight, was getting more sleep and seemed content once again.

At least outwardly, she radiated health and appeared very happy with her transition to a more stable lifestyle. To Dave and Linda, the transformation was impressive.

By December there had been several major changes in Dave's life, both at work and at home.

As promised, the promotions for both him and Ed had taken place toward the end of the month.

The test period for the work on cold-case files had come to a successful conclusion, with four murder charges having been laid. Additionally, two rapes and a serious assault were nearing the charging stage. As a result, the Chief had given the order to make the small unit permanent and there was currently an active discussion about the possibility of doubling the manpower presently allotted to it.

Ed had made the transfer from drugs to Major Crime and Dave was given a period of grace before taking up his new responsibilities as the unit's, newly created Staff/Sergeant position, to facilitate the training that would be necessary to prepare Ed for assuming the responsibilities of Dave's old job.

It would be quite a change for Ed, and Inspector Henderson had tasked Dave with ensuring that Ed would be fully prepped to take over the position before Dave relinquished it.

To this end, Dave had suggested that Ed be sent off to the FBI profiling course before coming to the unit. Henderson agreed and on the day his transfer took place, Ed left to travel down to the States.

Dave had driven Ed to the airport for the trip.

During the drive there, both admitted that they were inwardly somewhat concerned that they might not be able to reignite the outstanding working relationship they had enjoyed several years before, primarily since there was now a separation in their respective ranks. They discussed their feelings about the matter in great detail on the trip.

By the time Dave had dropped Ed off, any doubts there might be a problem in that regard had been dispelled and the two of them were both confident at their ability to make the change work. The were sure they could jointly organize their respective responsibilities while working closely together on all investigations.

When Ed returned from the course, Henderson instructed Dave to take the time necessary to bring him up to speed on both profiling and the current investigations underway by the cold case section, which had now been doubled in manpower.

CHAPTER NINETEEN

- MAY 1999 -

Each day seemed to be a repeat performance of the day before. Cloudy with sunny periods.

It had been an eventful five months for Kenny.

The old lady had finally kicked the bucket in February.

He had faithfully visited each day until she'd succumbed. Having to do it had nearly driven him crazy, but it had served its purpose.

He had inherited the works. Money would very definitely never be a concern for him from now on.

His full plan was still on hold of course, but sufficient progress had been made to satisfy him.

Setting up Robbie Brody, the kid he picked up in December, had occupied a good deal of his time and had also provided sufficient stimulation to ease his sexual demands, to the point that he found them controllable.

That, and the fact that he was getting close to being ready to make the final step toward the realization of his fantasy kept him in check.

He was pleased with the self-control he had exerted over that period. He had taken no more risks, instead steadfastly following his predetermined plan to the letter.

The minute Robbie had agreed to go with him that December night, Kenny had immediately pulled away from the curb and driven briskly away from the stroll.

At first, he had kept the conversation to a minimum. The kid was obviously nervous and Kenny's first task was to gain his confidence.

At the time, he'd wrinkled his nostrils at the smell of the kid. Needed a bath all right, but he'd dismissed that small irritant and spoke softly as he drove.

"You don't look like you've been at this very long..."

The kid glanced over at him and acknowledged the comment with a nod.

"Ya, well only a couple of weeks. Where are we going?"

Kenny liked that response.

The kid was already giving him control.

Now to slowly build confidence.

"Well you looked like you could use a bite to eat. You hungry? I thought maybe we could get a couple burgers, then maybe find a quiet place to talk while we eat. It looks like you're living kinda rough, and I figured I might lend you a helping hand.

I'm considering making you an offer."

The kid didn't respond for a few seconds then he sucked in a deep breath and retorted more loudly that he had intended.

It was bluster, and Kenny immediately recognized it as such.

"Twenty bucks for a blowjob..."

Kenny laughed.

"Right, well we can discuss that later, after we have a bite to eat. In the meantime, I'd like to get to know you a little better. How about we start with your name."

The question threw the kid.

Obviously, his previous contacts had been interested in other things and hadn't enquired as to his name.

"Ah...Robbie, Robbie Brody...and it's one hundred bucks for the night."

"OK Robbie, I'm Walter...and how bout I give you two hundred dollars right now, so you can stop worrying about the time and money for the rest of our time together?"

"Okay, sure, that works."

"Deal then."

Kenny handed over the cash he had previously put into his jacket pocket and then stretched out his right hand in an offered shake.

The kid tucked away the bills in his jeans and then accepted the proffered hand hesitantly. His grasp was weak, and the hand was damp.

Kenny shook it firmly and then released it.

Good, he's unnerved and already off balance.

"How old are you Robbie?"

Don't overload him...one question at a time, let him relax...gain his confidence.

"Nineteen."

Kenny laughed.

"Ya right! And I'm Santa Clause.

Look Robbie, if you and I are going to become pals, we are going to have be honest and upfront with each other. I dig that you say your nineteen.

Otherwise, you'd be jailbait and you figure that I might get upset by that. Well, I'm not, so why don't you just tell me your real age. Alright?"

The kid swivelled his head and looked directly at Kenny for the first time since he'd picked him up. It took a couple of seconds for him to respond.

"Sixteen... just turned a couple of months back"

Good, he's loosening it up.

"How come you're selling yourself. Are you on your own? Don't you have any folks?"

No response.

Shit! I'm coming across too eager. Just one question at a time.

"Just curious, if you don't want to tell me, that's okay. Like I said, if you don't want to talk, that's cool, I can drive you back and drop you off. You can keep the money."

The response came in a rush.

"No! It's OK. It's just that no one has really asked me this kind of stuff before.

I ran away from home. My old man is a drunk and when he got locked up, my mom took off with some guy. Moved back to Ontario with him.

I would've gone with them, but they didn't want me. I didn't know what to do.

They don't want me, then I don't give a shit about them either.

I got no one else to stay with.

Eventually, I had to find a way to make some cash, so I could eat. I only been doing this for the last couple of months."

He flushed deeply, paused and then continued.

"I'm gay and I like sex, so it's not so bad."

Kenny nodded.

Awesome, he's taken the hook!

"Tuff to have to do it to survive though.

Better if you got to pick who you had sex with too, instead of the other way around.

Well let's hit a MacDonald's and get those burgers. Tell me what you want, you can have whatever and as much of it as you can eat. Don't be shy, my treat."

They picked up the food at the drive-through and then Kenny drove to a nearby park. One that he had mapped out earlier.

Not surprisingly when you considered the weather over the past few weeks, the parking lot at the park was empty. Kenny shut the truck off and kept the conversation light while they ate.

Nothing personal.

Bitching about all the rain of late and drawing Robbie out very gently. Letting Robbie relax as he wolfed down his food like there was no tomorrow.

When the kid had finished Kenny started the truck and turned up the heater. As the truck warmed up, the kid, stomach bulging, began to unwind, his eyelids drooping.

"You look kinda tired Robbie. What say we get ourselves a hotel room and then you can have a relaxing bath while I nip out and pick you up a change of clothes. What you're wearing is looking shabby.

OK by you?"

"Sure."

Kenny already had the room reserved and he left the kid in the truck while he picked up the key from the desk, then he came back and got him out of the truck and took him up to the room.

Robbie looked a little nervous once the door was closed behind them and Kenny moved to set him at ease again.

"Ok, I'll head out and get you some new stuff to wear. Why don't you just go ahead and hop into the bath and have a good soak until I get back."

An hour and a half later, Kenny returned to the hotel room. Once he'd locked the door behind him, he took the packages he'd purchased over to the bathroom door.

He knocked lightly.

"Are you doing alright in there Robbie?"

It was obvious by the mumbled response that the kid had nodded off and he'd wakened him.

"I'll just put the bags down here on the floor and you can get them when you get out of the tub and change in there."

Kenny went back into the main room, kicked off his shoes, then settled himself down on the bed and used the remote to switch on the TV.

So far so good.

About twenty minutes later Robbie came out of the bathroom carrying the bags.

"I put my old stuff in this bag. What should I do with it?

"Just dump them into the garbage can over there. You won't be needing them, providing you and I can come to an agreement.

There will be a lot more clothes, and better ones for sure in your future, if things work out like I'm hoping they will."

Robbie did as he was told.

That's my boy. You just keep on letting me do the thinking for both of us.

He patted the bed beside him.

"Hop up here and join me. There's a good movie coming on shortly.

The kid hesitated for a second before replying.

"Do you want me to take off my clothes first?

Kenny laughed.

"No Robbie. I don't.

For the time being, you can stop worrying about that kind of thing.

I think you and I are going to become good friends. When that happens, and if you want to do something more, we can see what else develops.

In the meantime, let's just chill out and get to know each other a little better. If that's OK with you.

Oh, and I got us something to drink. I hope you're OK with rum and coke."

For the first time since Kenny had picked him up, the kid actually smiled.

"Great, sounds good to me."

Kenny rolled off the bed and crossed to the small desk where he'd left the bag containing the bottle and mixer.

"I'll mix us up a couple then before the show comes on."

H turned his back to the bed and poured out two healthy slugs of rum into the glasses and then slipped the small vial out of his shirt pocket and dumped about 1 milligram of Rohypnol into one of the glasses.

He had learned about the drug when it had been prescribed by Granny's doctor a couple of years ago, to help her sleep. Kenny had observed its affects on the old lady, liked what he saw and had then done some research on it via the net.

He'd found out that it was called *'The Date Rape Drug'* and figured a supply would come in handy in his preparations toward reaching his goal. He'd then begun to swipe every second pill provided by the nurse to Granny daily and had built up a good supply by the time the old lady had been shipped off to the hospital. He'd crushed and diluted these and put the resulting mixture aside for later use.

Kenny added Coke and then used a finger to stir the stuff into the kid's drink until it had been thoroughly mixed and absorbed. He then picked up both glasses, turned and crossed back to the bed and handed Robbie his.

He grinned broadly and raised his own glass.

"Down the hatch. This will put hair on your chest, as my old daddy used to say."

A half hour later, once Kenny was sure the drug had taken effect, he put his empty glass on the end table, shut the TV off and walked around to the other side of the bed were the comatose Robbie was passed out.

So malleable, and completely helpless now. I have complete control of him. What a delicious sight he is!

He prodded the kid a couple of times to be sure he was out completely, then grinned and began to strip him. Once his clothes had been draped over the chair next to him, Kenny paused and happily ran his eyes over the kid's tight body.

Awesome definition. Robbie had obviously been working out regularly before his unhappy little home had broken up.

Kenny then quickly stripped off his own clothes and let them drop to the floor.

His prick was rock hard, and he'd begun to masturbate at a leisurely rate as he used his free hand to run his fingers over the kid's body, eventually settling on his pert little cock.

In short order, it began to stiffen and although Kenny knew that the drug decreased blood pressure as a side effect, the kid was obviously young and virile enough to get a delightful hard-on.

Kenny chuckled with glee.

You are a horny little devil aren't you kid?"

Kenny had been so excited he came quickly, letting his spurting semen pool on the surface of the kid's flat belly.

He'd taken time to finish the kid with a hand-job and then cleaned him up before tucking him into the bed and climbing under the covers beside him on the other side.

When the kid woke up in the morning, as expected, he was disoriented for a bit.

Kenny was just coming out the bathroom. He was naked, using a towel to dry his hair.

"Morning sleepy head. How you feeling, you did a good amount of drinking last night? You hung over?"

Robbie didn't reply, shook his head to clear the cobwebs as Kenny continued.

"Hope you don't mind me stripping you and putting you to bed. You passed out, so I figured that was the best place for you and since I sleep nude, I figured you probably would too."

Robbie was trying to remember what had happened after they had started to watch the movie on TV.

It was all a blank to him.

His throat was dry, and he had trouble forming his words.

"No, that's cool. Jeez, I'm sorry I passed out. We were going to talk."

Kenny laughed and began to put on his clothes.

"No harm done. I'm starved. Why don't you grab a shower and freshen up?

We can talk after we've had breakfast."

They had breakfast in the hotel restaurant and were back in the room in just under an hour and a half.

Once the door had closed, Kenny flopped on to the bed.

"We can talk now if you like.

What did you want to talk about anyway?'

Robbie look a little confused for a second before he replied.

"You said something about making me an offer…"

Kenny raised his eyebrows.

"Oh that…right. Well let's see now.

I want you and I to be friends, very close friends. I like you kid, and I want to help you, and I'm financially stable and able to do that.

If you're up for it, and want to be my friend that is, then I'm prepared to fix you up with your own place, give you a nice allowance and buy you clothes and stuff and a car."

Robbie couldn't believe what he was hearing.

Was this guy pulling his leg or what?

He pursed his lips.

"That sounds great, and I don't want to sound ungrateful for the help your offering me or anything, but I can't help but wonder what is it that you want from me in return?'

Kenny put on his most sincere face.

"Just friendship is all, at least to start. After that, we'll see what happens.

I'm guessing you've figured I must be gay too by now, and you're right, I am. And I admit that I do like you already and find you attractive in that way.

That said, it's just friendship that I want from you unless you want it to be something more. No pressure *'dude'*.

For now, let's just take some time to find out if were compatible and see if we enjoy each other's company."

For the next week Kenny spent his days at the hotel and his nights at home.

During the days, he'd taken Robbie out extensively. They had gone to movies, arcades, skiing, indoor paintballing. They'd had a ball.

Kenny never laid a finger on him.

As Kenny anticipated, it was Robbie who had made the first move sexually.

On the seventh night at the hotel, Robbie asked if Kenny could spend the night with him.

In response Kenny shook his head.

"I don't know man. Are you sure that's what you want to happen?"

The kid flushed slightly and nodded.

"Ya, I'd like to try it for sure."

They didn't get a lot of sleep, but Kenny kept it simple and saw to it that Robbie was well looked after.

He did confirm that as he had suspected, Robbie liked to be dominated.

The kid was not only submissive, he enjoyed being subjugated and he thoroughly enjoyed taking it a little rough.

Kenny had a definite plan in mind for the kid's sex education and he'd sensed he couldn't move ahead with it too rapidly.

One step at a time, experiment a little, but always let Robbie be the one to ask for more.

For now, Kenny would simply maintain a reasonable level of heavy activity in their sex-play, but over time, he fully intended to lead Robbie further down the path leading to the enjoyment of a serious S&M relationship.

They checked out of the hotel the next morning and three hours later Kenny surprised the kid by showing him through the house he had recently decided to purchase in one of the better areas of East Vancouver. It was nothing fancy, just a simple bungalow. It did have an attached garage and fenced yard.

When they were in the last room he told Robbie that he was thinking of buying it for him.

The kid couldn't believe his luck. It seemed like a castle to Robbie.

"Would it really be mine, could I live here now?"

Kenny laughed.

"Not now, but in a week or so after the deal goes though, I would be able to give you the deed.

Like I told you, now that we're friends, things will begin to look up for you."

Robbie grinned from ear to ear.

Six days later they were back at the house. Robbie was clutching the deed to the place, in his name mind, in his hand.

Kenny had been busy. The fridge and cupboards were stocked with food and there were ten one-hundred-dollar bills neatly stacked up on the kitchen counter.

Kenny tapped the pile as they passed.

"Pocket money for you."

They spent that night together in the king-sized bed in the main bedroom at the house and Kenny kept himself in check.

He firmly dominated but was reasonably gentle with the kid. As much as he would have liked to, he introduced no seriously rough stuff into the repeated sex they'd enjoyed.

The session served to confirm to Kenny that he'd made the right choice in his selection of Robbie. The kid was at that horny age where he was always thinking about it, and while not usually the instigator, seemed eager for each new round, whenever Kenny suggested it.

The next day Kenny started Robbie taking lessons at a driving school. Two months later the kid got his license and Kenny bought him a second-hand mustang. The kid was ecstatic.

After that had been accomplished, Kenny changed his daily routine.

He began staying at his own home during the day and spending his nights in the east-end Vancouver house with Robbie.

To explain the change to Walter, he'd told his manager that he was enrolling in night-school courses which were being held In Vancouver, so he'd taken an apartment in town, so he wouldn't have to be driving back and forth every night.

Walter seemed to find that reasonable.

Kenny held to his intention of eventually striving to reach a complete sadomasochistic relationship between him and Robbie by making slow progress in that direction. Always carefully gauging Robbie's readiness to expand his horizons and concentrating on keeping the sex enjoyable for the kid.

It took restraint on his part, but it had to be enough for Kenny, he understood that it had to be a learning experience for Robbie. At least for the time being.

Sex aside, he had to turn Robbie into his reliable right arm.

While that meant sticking to his plan for training and absolutely dominating the kid before taking the next step in his plan to make later use of him; he also had to nurture the kid and build a very strong rapport with him both mentally and psychologically.

Whenever he was sorely tempted to take the sex to a rougher level than Robbie had already experienced, he had to be sure to simultaneously create an atmosphere of growing trust.

He would require Robbie to be completely dependent upon him. And trust would facilitate that. It would give him complete control over the kid, avoiding the likelihood of later problems.

Walter's house and office complex, which had been under construction across from the yard at the front of the property, was finally completed toward the end May. Walter and his new wife would soon move in, meaning Kenny's last problem regarding personal privacy at the house, would disappear.

Once that was a reality and he had the house to himself, he would be free to do what he liked in it.

He had some definite plans about that already.

A week prior to the anticipated completion of the project, Kenny approached the contractor and asked him if he would be interested in taking on some renovations that he was contemplating in the main house.

The guy had agreed to take on the job, before leaving the property.

The next day Kenny provided him with a rough drawing of what he wanted to achieve as far as the renovation in his house went.

It was not a major job.

Kenny explained that he wanted to expand the master bedroom by removing the shared wall between his room and the bedroom next door and a further addition to the house by adding another room through an extension off that to incorporate a completely new room.

He then mentioned that he wanted this additional area to have soundproofing in the ceiling and all walls.

The floor was to be covered in a thick, commercial grade of linoleum.

It was also to be windowless and accessible only by way of a single, secret doorway which would be concealed in a built-in bookshelf. This was to be incorporated in a section of the separating wall between the master suite renovations and the newly expanded space.

That the construction superintendent was obviously surprised by the idea of a soundproofed room with no windows and a hidden doorway, was clear by way of the expression on guy's face and his arched eyebrows, but he made no comment in relation to his surprise at the suggestion of such a construct.

He confirmed his willingness to take the project on as soon as the current work on Walter's house was completed, and predicted that once under way it should take no more than a couple of weeks.

As the project neared completion, Kenny decided on what lighting he wanted for the special room addition. He selected a very large crystal chandelier to be installed in the center of the high ceiling.

Kenny explained he whole thing away by saying that the extension was to provide a private sanctuary for what he referred to, as his space for meditation.

By this point, the construction superintendent was eager to get the job finished and took the suggestion of the unusual fitting in stride.

A job was a job and if the money was good, whatever the customer wanted, he was prepared to build.

This new hidden room was designed to play a central part in Kenny's overall plan and although he was impatient to get started on the actual acts he intended to consummate upon his intended victims, he was still determined not act impulsively.

Years of planning were about to come to fruition. It was just a matter of a little more time now. He could and would wait until all was in place, before he took that final delicious step and started on the road toward enjoying his life to the full.

While he waited for the renovations to be completed, he concentrated completely on working on the kid. By the time the room was ready, he wanted the Robbie properly schooled and ready to play his part in the upcoming process.

Then it would be time for the kid to really begin earning his keep.

Dave had been a little concerned about accepting his new Staff/

Sergeant position. Not because he didn't think he could handle it, but because he knew it would mean more supervising and less time for hands-on work in his specific fields of expertise, within the Major Crimes unit.

As Staff/Sergeant, he would be working directly with the head of the unit, sharing the overall responsibility for the direction of all ongoing operations and their supervision. He didn't foresee any problem getting along with Inspector Henderson. They seemed to have a good working relationship, but it would mean he would have to fight for time spent directly involved in the actual daily operations of Major Crime.

Dave had been given leeway to take the time to bring Ed up to speed once he'd returned from the States. While Ed had been away, Dave had been able to learn, prior to taking up the Staff/Sergeant position within the unit, exactly what Henderson was expecting from him.

His duties were to be primarily supervisory, but as he was already familiar with most sections of Major Crime there wasn't a great deal more he needed to learn to prepare himself in that area. As a result, Dave had been largely able to maintain his hands-on work in his special areas during the time Ed was on course.

It wasn't until mid-May that Dave had officially taken up his new job, and settled into the small office across the hall from Henderson's.

It seemed to Dave that for the remainder of the month, he and the Inspector seemed attached at the hip.

To his surprise, Dave quickly learned that there were a lot of politics involved in handling his new position. Apparently, toes in the department hierarchy could be easily bruised by decisions made at the Staff/Sergeant level and for one's own good, one had to always be aware of exactly what senior officers supported or conversely, did not support.

It was quite a learning curve for Dave and while he realized that the stuff he was picking up from his crusty, soon to be retired boss, was both informative and necessary for him to handle his new position it did occasionally give him pause to wonder if taking his promotion had been the right thing to do.

By the time the end of the month rolled around however, Henderson told him that he had absorbed sufficient knowledge about the unit to allow himself to back off a little. He suggested Dave should now spend some time working with the individual detectives in the unit, to bring himself up to speed on all the various current investigations.

He told Dave that from that point on, the two of them would meet each morning at nine in Henderson's office to jointly discuss the overnight incidents, and any progress made on individual cases. For the most part, the rest of the day would be Dave's to spend as he saw fit, baring any unusual situations that might arise.

Henderson also made it abundantly clear from the onset that he and Dave were going to be working as a team, and would become interchangeable as the immediate supervisor of Major Crime. This meant that they would need to be constantly keeping each other abreast of everything the unit was working on.

Dave raised one issue with the Inspector.

He explained that after a good deal of discussion, he and Ed had come up with the idea of making a change in how interviews and interrogations were conducted, once a suspect had been arrested by the unit. That arrest would have to be due to a solid evidence-based determination of guilt. Currently, the procedure was to have the detectives involved in the case make that first interview.

Based on the successes they'd had in getting written statements of guilt during their initial interviews when they had been partnered together earlier, something that normally led to an automatic conviction, they felt better results could be achieved within Major Crime, if they were also in attendance with the arresting detectives when all initial interviews for predetermined suspects by the squad were conducted.

This would provide the detectives involved with the benefit of their experience and over time, serve to introduce a set of standardized, time-tested interrogation techniques in all Major Crime arrest incidents.

If conducted when the suspect was off-balance and before he'd lawyered-up, this could improve the likelihood of getting a confession of guilt during those first interviews.

Henderson agreed to the idea, but warned Dave to tread carefully. He pointed out that senior detectives would see it as someone looking over their shoulders and doubting their abilities. When first introduced any change in procedure tended to create doubters.

To succeed, any new procedure would have to be first sold to them as some sort of team project.

"I would suggest that you take some time to prepare them, and make them an important part of the planning as to how it will work. Throw the idea out there when you're spending time with the individual teams.

Toss out a trial balloon and talk it around. Involve them in the planning. Wait until you have most of them onboard with a few test-runs of what you have come up with. Once that happens, you and I should make an evaluation, before we make any permanent change in the current procedure."

Dave nodded.

"Yes, Ed and I discussed a similar type of approach. We thought at first, we would just sit in and let the detectives begin the interrogations as usual, while we observed the interviews through the two-way glass and until we had assessed how things were going. When we were ready, we would then call the detectives out to join us and leave the suspect to stew while the four of us talked it out and jointly decided how we would handle the remainder of the interview."

Henderson smiled.

"You and Ed do realize that this means you are going to be working some very strange hours. While most of our arrests can be made during the day, of necessity some will have to take place at night."

Dave chuckled.

"Yes, we did consider that likelihood. Both of us are prepared to work some weird hours until we can figure out a permanent structure for a new procedure.

It shouldn't take us too long to reach the point where we have a system in place and all concerned have a grip on how these things need be done to produce optimum results. Once that happens, it should be smooth sailing and Ed and I will be able to supervise the process from a distance."

For Dave, a few new developments had occurred on the home front.

He and Linda had earlier decided to try for another child and mid-month they were pleased to have her pregnancy confirmed.

Shaun had entered the terrible-two's stage of growth and as a result now required a good deal more attention from the adults in the house.

Ed and Cathy had raised the idea of living together and had decided that they were ready to give it a try.

The four of them had then entertained the idea of Ed joining Cathy in her section of the house, rather than them finding a place together somewhere else.

They were more than willing to pay their way and there was certainly enough room. They all got on well, and as Linda succinctly pointed out, Ed was already spending most of his off time there anyway.

CHAPTER TWENTY

- June 1999 -

Warm, sunny days.

Kenny's adrenalin level was running high.

The realization that everything was finally falling into place, that the years of planning and researching towards the successful accomplishment of his end goal were about to pay off, was almost overwhelming.

He felt emboldened, tantalized and overflowing with anticipation to the point he had to continually remind himself to keep up an outward appearance of normal behavior when around others.

By the third week of the month, the construction crew had completed the renovations to his house. The new master bedroom had turned out exactly how he wanted it.

More importantly by far, the added room he'd envisioned behind the wall of bookshelves was going to be perfect for his purposes. His concept of a concealed doorway situated in a single panel of the bookshelves covering most of the one wall of the bedroom, had proven better than he'd hoped for. The builders had done an awesome job. No one would ever suspect that the extra space behind it even existed.

During the construction phase, he'd instructed the builders to add an en-suite bathroom for himself at one end of the same wall that contained the bookshelves and a second full bathroom on the other side of the wall in the adjacent safe room. This second bathroom was to share the wall between the two rooms, but could only be accessed from within the concealed space.

Kenny had bought and installed new furniture for his own room and had also purchased a second-hand queen-sized wrought-iron bed, which he had already installed in the very centre of the hidden room.

He had bought a new mattress for the old bed and a thick rubber sheet to cover it. He'd also installed restraints to both the headboard and footboard so that his future quarry could be fully restrained in a spread-eagled fashion on the bed.

There was to be no other furniture in the room except for a single metal chair against one wall, from which he could comfortably rest, when overtaxed by his indulgences. There, he could take time at his leisure to enjoy the view offered by the splayed, spread-eagled body, twisting and moaning in agony before him as the crystal chandelier delivered a sparkling array of shimmering light over the scene.

This bed was to be his alter. The place where he would be free to do as he wished, unhampered. Where he would prepare his victims for their demise. Where he would be able to enjoy, mutilate and torture each in turn in exquisite detail, before they were reluctantly, but necessarily dispatched and removed for disposal to make ready for their replacement on his alter.

His own little torture chamber!

The room was now done to his satisfaction. Kenny shifted his attention to the piggery and the attached butchering facilities in the outbuilding behind the house.

He had definite plans in mind for this area. An expansion of the pork production and sales started by his grandfather.

Kenny had done some more research online. He'd decided that he was going to try his hand in setting up a commercial sausage factory. Nothing too elaborate. Just a small operation.

He installed a low-profile, lockable cover for the bed of his pickup truck. With it in place to conceal his purchases from inquisitive eyes, he went shopping. First, he replenished and upgraded the basic selection of knives and saws he had on hand. Then, he ordered up a couple of large commercial walk-in freezers for delivery, a high-end meat grinder and a sausage-making apparatus.

With a view to pre-empting any curiosity on Walter's part about the time he would soon be spending in the outbuilding, he dropped in to see him, ostensibly to see the new house, but in fact, to find the opportunity to mention to him that he was planning on expanding the pork operation by providing more high-grade pork for some of his current customers.

Walter was a little surprised by the suggestion.

Since Kenny was rolling in cash, he couldn't help but wonder why the kid would want to spend his time looking after and butchering more pigs, but if that's what he wanted to do, it was OK with him and he said as much.

Kenny went on to say that he would be buying a small tractor to help with the expansion of the pig pen and as a result wanted Walter to take on the complete responsibility for the Landscaping operation in the future.

He suggested that, barring emergencies, he and Walter should meet once a month, so Kenny could keep up to speed on everything. He stressed that he would also continue to help with the machinery cleanup by spreading the shredded material coming in daily on the trucks and keeping the equipment washed and ready for next-day service.

He also informed his manager that, as the change would mean more responsibility for him, it would also come with a healthy increase in his salary.

Walter was more than pleased with the idea of this new working relationship.

During this period, Kenny had continued to spend his days at home and his nights at the house he'd bought for Robbie.

Real progress had been made with the kid. Robbie was coming along very nicely.

It had been mutually agreed that when Kenny arrived each evening now, he would be greeted by a completely subservient and nude Robbie, wearing only a dog's light-weight coke-chain and a dangling six-foot leather leash.

Robbie was no longer allowed to leave the house unless Kenny had first given specific permission and guidelines as to exactly what he could and could not do.

Their sexual activities had evolved considerably.

Kenny would take Robbie whenever he wished and during the act the kid often wore padded cuffs and was usually laid out on his stomach on the bed with his legs spread-eagled and secured to the footboard.

Robbie no longer had any say in what transpired during these sessions. There was no doubt as to who was in charge. He not only didn't mind, but was an eager partner in all of it.

The new regime was all-empowering for Kenny.

He had recently begun to introduce at least a touch of pain each time he coupled with the kid, beginning by squeezing his balls painfully while fondling and entering him and pulling the choke-chain tightly around his neck while he was experiencing his own climax.

The kid was really getting into it, moaning softly and blowing his load regularly each time they coupled. Kenny was delighted to find that

Robbie was getting off on it, just as much as he was. The kid was taking to it like a kid at the fair to cotton candy.

Of late, this new level of sex was intense for Kenny.

So much so that he had been very strongly tempted to finish the kid off on several occasions over the past week or so. So far, he'd successfully managed to resist that growing compulsion to act on that fervent yearning with Robbie. He'd been able to re-focus each time by reflecting upon his need to keep the kid alive. He had bigger plans for Robbie. Keeping the kid around was paramount if he wanted to reach his final goal.

His belief that another month or so would see the Robbie fully trained and submissive enough to play his major role in the overall selection methods Kenny had painstakingly planned for picking up the likely prospects he would require, was the only thing that now stabilized the pressure to take things that far.

By the end of the month Kenny had completed the expansion of the piggery, adding a commercial shower facility, doubling the size of the inner area, as well as that of the outside pen. He had used his new tractor and the old dump truck to remove all the old soil in the outer area and then replaced it with a foot of shredded material from the landscaping business prior to buying two dozen new animals and adding them to has current stock.

He'd also enlarged the butchering area, arranging it so it was more like a production line, at the end of which he had installed the sausage making equipment.

Having never given a second thought as to how sausages were made, he'd found his internet research on that part of the things very interesting.

He found that traditionally, the sausage casings were made from the cleaned intestines. These days, however, these natural casings are often replaced by other products. A sausage consists of meat, cut into pieces or ground, and filled into the casing along with other ingredients. In today's marketplace, the ingredients used in addition to the meat often included a cheap starch filler such as breadcrumbs along with seasonings and flavorings such as spices, and sometimes other materials.

The meat used in sausage making may be from any animal, but is most often pork, beef, or veal. The lean meat-to-fat ratio varies, dependent upon the style and producer.

Specialty sausages, were those which used other ingredients such as apple. That often the weight of the meat used in the mix exceeds the total weight of the sausage produced as a result. This being due to the drying process involved, which reduces water content.

Many traditional styles of sausage from Asia and mainland Europe use no bread-based filler and include only meat (lean meat and fat) and flavorings. The finest quality sausages contain only choice cuts of meat and seasoning. *'Fresh Sausages'* require freezing and /or refrigeration. They also require further cooking before they can be eaten. *'Fresh Smoked Sausages'*, those that are either smoked or cured, do not. Nor do they require any further cooking prior to being eaten.

Kenny liked the sounds of these.

After a good deal of added research on the subject, he'd selected and ordered all the equipment needed to carry out the process of preparing this specific type of sausage, from start to finish.

Completing the update was a new set of knives, three saws and a dozen meat-hanging hooks. He had also replaced all the doors of the area with new steel ones, installing substantial locks and added blinds to all the windows, so that he could have absolute privacy when he needed it in the future.

Several years before, his grandfather had created a separate incorporated company for the specific purpose of operating his initial pork meat sales. It was still in effect. At the time the old man had fulfilled the necessary requirements under the health act and arranged for the government inspections of his facilities necessary to have it licenced for that purpose.

So, Kenny had a credible setup already in place for sales. Now that he had expanded the operation to allow for a much larger product output, he decided to arrange for a new inspection of the upgraded facilities to make sure that everything about the sausage making setup was on the up and up.

All had gone well and after the resulting assessment he received the licencing to go ahead with an increase in his pork production as well as the production of sausage for the marketplace.

The changes in place, Kenny butchered over a couple of days to get himself up to speed with the new equipment and then had a refrigerated truck deliver the resulting meat to his customers.

He was now looking very much forward to running his first batch of sausage. He would have to have all the right ingredients for that before it could happen of course.

But hopefully that wouldn't be too long in coming.

Dave and Ed had been spending their free time working on the new procedure for conducting initial interrogations.

Over the first two weeks of the month, Dave had been rotating his time between the detective teams, with a view to becoming cognisant of the viability of each current investigation. He listed these in order as to their abundance of garnered evidence and how near they were to an arrest and by the end of the third week, was knowledgeable enough to be able to shift manpower away from the faint hopes and over to better prospects.

While sitting down with each team for an overview of their active files, he managed to bring up the topic of interrogating techniques and the importance of garnering confessions during the initial interviews with charged suspects.

As this was discussed as casual conversation, as expected, a general agreement by all concerned resulted from most of these exchanges.

By the last week, he and Ed had put together a report explaining the reasons for the adjustments that had been made on individual case loads. They coupled that with an overview of positive suggestions for improving overall success rates that had come out of Dave's interaction with all the squad's teams.

Special attention was given to the fact that everyone concerned had indicated that initial interrogations conducted with newly charged perpetrators were of primary importance and that certain techniques should come into play whenever these were held.

Dave circulated this report with all detectives along with a request for input as to exactly how these first interviews should be conducted, with the intention of having a standard procedure used on every occasion.

He hoped the request for their opinions would appeal to the individual teams and stimulate responses, which would then allow him to create a new standard policy that would be generally accepted without too much hassle.

Toward the end of the month he had received a fair stack of replies and could finally give a sigh of relief. His consultations seemed to have worked and most of the detectives appeared to be onboard with the idea of a standard approach to the initial interrogations of newly charged suspects.

He and Ed had already decided how they would approach the idea in individual cases when an arrest was made. They sold this to the detectives as a necessary process for the preparation of the most effective standard procedure for these interviews. It was to be a learning process to ensure that all the best techniques available from the array of seasoned investigators could be contained in any new procedure.

To accomplish this, either Dave or Ed would have to sign-off on the question of sufficient evidence to charge prior to and then sit in on all such future interviews.

The detectives would then conduct the initial stage of the interview as either Ed or Dave observed through the two-way glass. Upon entering the room, the team would lay out in point form the extent of the evidence they had against the suspect.

The detectives would then leave the interview room and join the observer on the other side of the two-way glass.

As the suspect stewed in the cramped overheated room, off balance, his mind filled with the overwhelming extent of the evidence, the three of them would observe him carefully and exchange individual observations quietly. During this period and with the goal of securing a confession when the interview continued, they would individually and collectively read the suspect for signs of stress to gauge the level of panic being reflected on the other side of the glass as they discussed the best way to proceed.

The main point of this exercise was to enable either Dave or Ed to evaluate the abilities of the various teams and to improve their overall success rate by sharing, in an non-intimidating manner, their own long-practiced techniques, not as instruction, but as part of a shared discussion.

If he and Ed could demonstrate to everyone on the squad, that due to these sessions, a credible increase clearance rate had been accomplished, the adoption of a new standard procedure would be readily acceptable to all.

On the home front, Ed had moved in with Cathy in her apartment at the house and the arrangement seemed to be working out well.

Always having someone around to take care of Shaun was now less of a hassle.

This was no small matter. The little guy was becoming quite a handful to manage for whomever happened to be providing his adult guidance at any given time.

Not that he was a bad child, but, as Dave was oft lovingly heard to say, because it seemed that *'The little bugger is full of piss and vinegar', 24 hours a day'*.

Murphy tolerated this change in the household, but the cat now spent a good deal of his time curled up on his elevated perch whenever Shaun was anywhere near striking distance. Up to now, this had been a safe spot, but recently there had been intrusion even at this altitude, in that Shaun had begun grasping and shaking the base of the perch.

Murphy was not amused by this incursion into his chosen refuge, and the adults in the house were quick to come to his aid whenever he complained of an attack from the little whirlwind.

And when that happened, complain he did, long and loud.

Luckily, the future living needs had been well considered prior to the earlier renovation of the house. As a result, the new quarters had been made large enough to allow for abundant space to ensure private time for any of the adults who wanted or needed it.

The positive change in Cathy had firmed up now. She seemed far healthier and more relaxed than she had been before Ed came into the picture. The dark rings under her eyes had disappeared and she had regained her lost weight. That the change had been positive was also reflected in the fact that her studies were going much better and her prospects for the future in her chosen field much improved.

Except for the odd time spent on the interview-standards project after hours, Dave worked steady dayshifts now with weekends off, as did Linda. Cathy and Ed were both working nights but were usually able to schedule the same days off each week, although these rarely fell on weekends.

CHAPTER TWENTY-ONE

- August 1999 -

A wonderful warm and sunny month.

By mid-August, Kenny was satisfied that his training program for Robbie had reached a successful conclusion. The kid was ready to fulfil his crucial role in the final realization of Kenny's plan for a safe and successful commencement of his fantasy world.

Kenny was sorely tempted to immediately launch into taking the first big step. Instead he leaned toward caution, deciding instead to take the remainder of the month to allow for a breather and to allow himself a safe interval to review his carefully prepared strategies, one last time.

Just to make certain that everything required was in place to allow for a smooth and unfettered rollout.

He had to be absolutely sure he had all bases covered.

He did not want any surprises.

He was about to begin the most important part of his life, after all.

So, he decided to do it on an auspicious day.

He would take the most fulfilling step in his life on a big day, his birthday, September the first. And what *an awesome birthday gift it would be! Beginning the path. Making his first kill driven by pleasure alone.*

During the final week of August, Kenny initiated a temporary change in their nightly routine.

He instructed Robbie to dress prior to his arrival at the house in the east-end. Instead of staying at home as usual, he and Robbie would get into the Mustang. Kenny would then drive them down to *'Boys town'* at the foot of Homer street.

The first time they did this, Kenny gave Robbie a rundown of what they were going to do once they arrived at the stroll.

"Were going to do this run every night for the rest of this week. Like tonight, I'll do the driving each time. I'll drive around the stroll a few times and I want you to take a good look at what's on offer. Your job will be to choose us a plaything once we get there."

He paused to let that sink in before continuing.

"We're going to spice things up a bit in the sex area, kinda expand our boundaries a little. We're looking for a guy to come and join us in a little three-way sex party. Not just any guy mind, we want someone pretty special.

You up for that?"

Robbie nodded.

"Sure, a threesome would be fun for sure."

Kenny grinned.

"I thought the idea would appeal to you.

Now, we're not going to choose anyone tonight, this is just kind of a recon. We're going to take our time picking someone out. We'll do this all week if we need to. We want a hot body.

We won't make the actual pickup until my birthday, not until the first of September.

So, we've got a whole week to decide who the lucky kid is going to be, you understand?'

Robbie nodded, and Kenny chuckled.

"Alright then, this is the type of guy I want you to be looking for.

Age-wise we want someone in their early to mid teens. No heavy druggies. Physically appealing for sure, a sweet boy-next-door type. A good build and healthy looking, but not too big and muscular. He should be a loner, not part of any group.

Kinda like you were, when I first picked you up.

Maybe a little nervous looking and new to the scene. No old hands, if you get my meaning."

"Ok, I know most of the regulars. We're looking for a new guy, young, a turn on, but not bigger than us then?"

"Right, now when we get there, I'll be concentrating on driving, while you're giving them the once-over. Feel free to let me know if you see something promising or have any questions.

I'm going to be moving at a reasonable speed. I don't want any of them to approach us tonight. So, to give you a chance to have a good look, I'll make several passes, probably two or three.

You just keep your eyes peeled for what we're looking for and remember, we have several days to make our selection. There's no rush for us to pick someone tonight.

Our end goal is to have some kid pinpointed and selected before the night of September first. That's when we'll pick him up."

It took four nights of crawling the stroll before Robbie made his choice and had it confirmed by Kenny on the last pass. Kenny was very pleased with the selection and they left for the east-end house early.

The first important hurdle had been completed.

They were both hyped over the prospect of an impending threesome and the sex they enjoyed that night at the house was both strenuous and exhausting.

As Kenny drove home early the next morning he found himself humming a favoured tune for seemingly no reason.

Things were going so well.

He was quite giddy by the time he pulled into the garage at home.

He was ravenous.

He made himself a humongous breakfast and then had a couple of stiff drinks, before he felt relaxed enough to climb into his bed and get some much-needed sleep.

Only one month had passed, but their involvement in the eight initial interviews conducted over that short period of time, those during which he, Ed, or both had taken to part, was already showing signs of success in the number of confessions that were being achieved.

Of the eight, four had managed to bring about a written confession from the guilty party. Three of those had been murders, two of which were cold cases and the other a recent rape.

It was early going yet for sure, but the statistics didn't lie and the uptick in the number of charges resulting from those confessions was encouraging.

At the end of the month, Dave, Ed, and Henderson sat down to review the progress.

Dave began the discussion.

"The stats look good. The idea of taking a standard approach to doing initial interviews with a view to eliciting confession appears to be working well. However, I don't think we should get too excited, just yet.

A couple more months should give us a better idea of how well it's working.

We know that, if investigated thoroughly, most murders and rapes should be relatively easy to solve. The guilty party is almost always someone the victim knows. Domestics, a member of the family, a friend or some close associate. Very rarely is it a random act. When we have a small number of probable suspects, it usually boils down to checking alibis to figure out the who. It then becomes a matter of finding enough evidence to build a solid case against that individual.

Getting a confession up front on that first interview, makes the securing of follow-up evidence necessary for a conviction much easier.

When we look at the eight cases we concluded by way of charges this month, four were a direct result of DNA or trace evidence. These will likely lead to conviction, without the aid of a confession. In the other four, it was a confession that led to supporting evidence and assisted in building a case that can be expected to result in a plea being entered by the guilty party. In those four cases, we can probably say that there would have been no charges laid, had it not been for the confessions achieved at the time of the initial interview."

Ed nodded his agreement.

"Yes, in most cases, I think a standardized interview procedure is going to bring about a more rapid clearance rate. A confession goes a long way toward the laying of charges. However, while it may be effective in the incidents that we have been dealing with involving these eight cases, it would be highly unlikely that we would be able to get a confession from the more professionally executed of the serious crimes.

We should be using a standardize procedure for all initial interviews involving the spontaneous everyday run-of-the-mill type of serious crimes.

But it makes sense to be sure to separate those out from the ones involving professional-type crimes. There we should be taking a different path, treating them each as unique.

I'm talking about the gang murders, serial killers and the like. The perpetrators in those crimes are not going to respond to the standard interview procedure we are looking at here. They are not likely going to be driven to providing us with a confession under any circumstances."

Dave interjected.

"Ed's right on that. The procedure we're putting together for use in the regular investigations is not likely to be effective in those unusual types of cases.

Gang members do not talk to police in interviews. They keep their mouths shut. Serial killers are even more likely to stay mute. Especially if they are of the *'organized'* type of serial killer.

These guys think they can always outwit the police. They plan and execute their crimes carefully. They leave little if any trace evidence. They know the game and how to play it. They have no intention of giving themselves up by way of a confession.

Just identifying one of them is like looking for a needle in a haystack.

And even if you do find him, good luck with building a case against him that will stick. There is virtually no likelihood of an *'organized'* serial killer providing a confession even if there is a massive amount of evidence against him.

Even after conviction, these types rarely confess to their crimes and if they do it is only to gain some type of advantage for themselves.

No, while I firmly believe that a standard interview procedure will certainly improve the relatively routine cases the squad normally finds itself investigating, the unique and specifically-tailored approach we already have in place for handling a serial killer would have to come into play when dealing with one of them.

When standardizing this new procedure, we will have to be careful to make it perfectly clear to all teams that there is a difference between the two approaches."

Henderson leaned back in his chair and smiled.

"You know, listening to you guys, one could almost think that you are looking forward to having a serial killer come into your crosshairs. Anyway, it sounds like this new interview concept is working out. Keep up the good work."

Dave glanced at Ed and then toward the Inspector.

"I wouldn't say we were anxious to go up against a serial killer, boss, but we're sure as hell going to be prepared to take him on, if one comes along."

Dave's home life turned a little hectic in August.

His father, who had beat cancer twice over the past ten years and had been in remission, was diagnosed with it again.

Both his mother and father were getting on in years and had given up their driver's licences. As a result, during the last two weeks of the month it had fallen to Dave and his brother to share the responsibility of getting them to and from several doctor and specialist appointments for examinations and tests.

While his father feigned the appearance of being fully confident that he would beat the big C yet again, it was obvious to Dave that both his dad and his mother were worried, and he began checking in on them more regularly than he had previously.

They were all currently awaiting the results of the latest tests and it was tense for everyone concerned.

He tried not to dwell on it, but the situation was worrying and always floating around in the back of Dave's mind.

CHAPTER TWENTY-TWO

- September 1999 -

It was a warm and cloudless month.

Kenny arrived earlier than usual at the east-end house on the night of September the first.

Eager, but also cautious, he did not want to have any personal, direct tie-in with the stroll from this point on. That meant sending Robbie out on his own to do the deed.

Before he despatched the kid, he planned to thoroughly coach him on exactly how to go about making the actual pickup.

Robbie was almost as excited about the impending threesome as Kenny. That was all well and good from Kenny's perspective. However, he didn't want the kid to get himself worked into a state before he sent him off to do the pickup.

He sat Robbie down.

"Ok, this is the big moment. Now, you don't want to screw this up, so I'm going to tell you precisely how to handle the entire thing. First, settle yourself down. You got to be thinking straight, before you leave here. You understand what I'm saying?"

Robbie didn't respond but nodded.

"Alright then, listen up."

Kenny took what appeared to be a full micky of rye out of his jacket pocket and put it down on the coffee table between them.

A quizzical expression formed on Robbie's face and he reached out a tentative hand to pick it up, but Kenny shook his head.

"Nope, that's not for you. You will be driving, remember?

So, no booze for you until you get back here to the house with the quarry. The rye is for him.

Now listen carefully to me Robbie, once the deal is done and the kid is in the car with you, you're going to offer him this bottle. However, a lot comes into play, before that happens.

The first thing you do is pull into the curb, drop the window and then beckon him over to the car. Remember, you don't want to be screwing around chatting. You want to get him in and pull back into traffic as quickly as you can and head directly back here.

When you get him to the window, ask him how much he wants for the whole night.

Be pleasant, smile, put him at ease. Tell him it's going to be a small party, just you, him and your boyfriend, for a night of fun. As you know, the going rate is a hundred for all night. If he agrees to that, get him into the car and come straight back here. If not, offer him two hundred.

If he still isn't ready to get in with you at that price, then just pull away and head home. We're both eager for this, but we're not going to screw it up by doing anything foolish.

If he turns you down, we'll simply repeat the selection process again and try with someone else, later.

Now, once he's in the car, you'll want to chat him up a bit and try to get him relaxed. When he settles in a bit, pass him the bottle and tell him to help himself.

Say it will help him get into the mood, that's there's lots more where that came from and a choice of drugs will also be available, once he gets to the party.

Look at me Robbie, and listen carefully.

It's extremely important that the kid takes a few good swigs from the bottle on the trip back to the house, I can't emphasise that enough. If he isn't into at least a couple of swallows, dump him and come straight home.

If all goes to plan up to that time, then you bring him here by way of the lane and directly into the garage. I'll move the truck out of there, so it will be empty for you.

Kenny picked up the bottle.

I've dosed up the booze in this bottle. A few sips will be enough to put him out, probably well before you get here, so don't be surprised if he dozes off.

That's what we want him to do.

Any questions?"

Robbie shook his head. He had learned long ago not to be overly inquisitive, and not to ever ask 'why' of Kenny. Just to do as he was told.

Kenny smiled.

"Right then, off you go, and remember to take it cool and get in an out of the stroll as quickly as possible."

Kenny was on pins-and-needles the instant Robbie left the house.

To say he was excited for what was to come, would a blatant understatement. This was a big day. After all the research and planning, he was finally taking the first concrete step toward turning his fantasy into a reality.

While he was sure of himself, he couldn't help but be worried about the part Robbie must, of necessity, play in the scheme of things. He hated that he had to rely on anyone other than himself, when it came to something this important.

The kid was not the brightest bulb in the box for sure. There was always a chance that he might screw up somehow.

The way he'd set this up, that was not a huge concern. Kenny could walk away from this without a problem if the kid blew it some how. All well and good.

But if that did happen, he would have to begin selecting a replacement for Robbie all over again. And, at this point, the thought of being forced to do that was hard to accept. He was just too close to the realization of all his dreams for that to happen now.

He poured himself a stiff drink and began to pace aimlessly.

Forty-five minuets later he heard the garage door activate and begin to open in response to the remote in Robbie's Mustang.

Kenny gulped the remainder of his drink and set the empty glass down on the coffee table before hurrying out to the interconnecting door between the house and the garage.

When he opened it, the overhead door was descending, and Robbie was just getting out of the driver's side of the Mustang.

One look at the kid told Kenny all had gone well.

Robbie was all smiles.

Kenny shifted his gaze from Robbie to the Mustang's passenger window. He could just make out the outline of a figure slumped down in the passenger seat.

He felt a surge of adrenalin flow through his body and he gave a little jig as he clapped his hands and hurried over to the door.

He pulled it open and then stood back a pace to allow himself a moment to savour the prospect of what was in front of him.

Jesus! I've already got a boner.

This is going to be so good!

Robbie joined him at the open door and Kenny, grinning broadly, reached in to take the slouched kid under his arms. His burden was heavier than he had anticipated.

The quarry had obviously lost control over his motor skills and was dead weight. It was like trying to lift a drunk. When Kenny awkwardly shifted him in his arms, he mumbled something unintelligible and then gave forth with a pathetic mewling sound.

Kenny loved it.

He turned to Robbie.

"I'll drag him out, you take his feet before they slide off the seat and together we'll carry him inside."

The car door began to close slowly, and Robbie grabbed it and held it wide as Kenny worked the confused kid out of the seat and hauled him free of the car.

Robbie then moved in to grasp his legs with one arm. After they'd shifted him out, he used his free hand to close the car door. Then using both hands he took a firmer hold on the kid's legs.

Walking backward, Kenny led the way to the interconnecting door to the house.

He reached it just as the overhead garage door dropped down and locked into place. He paused for a second to catch his breath and then, stooping slightly, he took the kid's full weight on one arm and used his free hand to open the door to the house and push it wide.

That accomplished, he shifted the deadweight yet again, until he could bring both hands into play and stand upright.

He and Robbie then carried the kid inside, Robbie kicking the door closed behind him.

They carted the semi-conscious bulk though the kitchen, down the hall and into the master bedroom.

In preparation for the arrival, Kenny had already stripped the bed and covered it with a rubber sheet. The two of them then unceremoniously swung the kid in an arc and released him conjointly, dumping him down onto the centre of the bed.

Kenny took a deep breath and shifted his gaze from the comatose kid to Robbie.

"I'm going to go back out and switch the car for the truck in the garage. You strip him while I'm gone. Play with him a bit, see if you can get him hard. I'm curious to find out if he can do that after taking the stuff.

How much did he drink by the way?

"About a quarter of the bottle, no more."

"It looks like it did a perfect job.

Good to know for next time."

Kenny looked back at the kid sprawled on the bed and ran his tongue over his lips slowly, before speaking.

"If he can get it up, go ahead and get him ready for us. Fix the restraints. Face down mind, I want that tight little ass of his ripe for the picking when I get back."

An impatient Kenny made the vehicle switch quickly. By the time he got back into the bedroom, the victim was nude, on his belly, and firmly shackled hand and foot.

Robbie was kneeling on the bed, one hand moving between the quarry's thighs.

As he heard Kenny entering the room, he turned his head and grinned.

"No problem getting it up and he seems to be digging it."

"Good.

Ok let's get out of our clothes and have some fun with him. Put your chain on, Robbie.

That stuff we gave him in the booze can last for as long as 24 hours, but to play it safe, we're gonna finish with him and get rid of him in four hours maximum.

I'll give him an antidote and take him back to the stroll."

Kenny wanted the passing mention of an antidote to register for Robbie, but to go unquestioned. To help that along, he quickly engaged Robbie with a question.

"How much did you have to pay him by the way?"

Robbie was eagerly undoing the belt on his jeans as he vaulted off the bed.

"Hundred bucks…no problem. He was up for it."

Kenny chuckled as he began to remove his clothes.

"Great, ok, you go ahead and have fun with him, I'm just going to wank and watch the action for awhile and then when I'm primed and ready. I'll join in."

Robbie was already hard as he slipped out of his underwear and eagerly climbed up on the bed to kneel between the quarry's splayed legs. Eager to get started he entered the kid roughly, and in seconds, his buttocks cheeks were tightly clenching on each stroke and he was blissfully and enthusiastically, thrusting away.

For some time, Kenny was content to gently stroke himself as he keenly watched the activity taking place on the bed. He was happy enough to let Robbie enjoy himself to the full, after all, this, would be Robbie's only kick at the can.

Robbie had no way of knowing it was just the preliminary for Kenny, and that Kenny's real fun, was to come later.

This is just the warmup for the main event!

An hour later Kenny joined the other two on the bed. He slipped up behind Robbie, who, for the fourth time, was happily taking the quarry from the rear. Kenny thrust forward, entering Robbie, sandwiching him between himself and the quarry. Robbie let out a soft whine of delight, followed by an appreciative moan and eagerly began to thrust forcefully back and forth between them.

Excited as he was with the prospect of how the evening was going to end, it didn't take long for Kenny to reach his climax. As he went over the top, he firmly hauled back on the chain around Robbie's neck, bringing a shuddering Robbie climaxed for one last time.

After they'd caught their breath, he and Robbie showered and returned to the bedroom. They dressed and then Kenny went over to the bed and checked out the quarry, who seemed to be sleeping uneasily.

Satisfied that he was still breathing well, Kenny nodded at Robbie.

"Get him cleaned up and dressed, then we'll take him out to the garage and put him into the truck and I'll drop him back at the stroll on my way home."

An hour later, as Kenny reached the gate leading into the compound he activated the remote above his visor and fixed his gaze to the driveway on the other side of the opening gate.

The roadway, which led to his house, divided the work yard from the new driveway which branched off to the right, and led to Walter's new quarters.

Kenny's concern was for any activity that might mean that someone was up and about in the house, despite the late hour. He did not want to be observed.

The initial portion of the branch road leading off was only dimly lit by the outer fringes of the strong glow provided by the halogen lights that illuminated the vehicle storage yard off to his left.

The house itself was shielded from the main driveway by a cedar hedge. If anyone had been up at the house, he was confident he would be able to pick up at least some indication of light.

The risk of him being seen was very slight.

Walter's place was some distance off the main drive and somewhat sheltered by a relatively juvenile cedar hedge.

He saw no sign of any lights or activity and he gave a sigh of relief as he drove through the gate and made his way quietly up the long driveway to his own house.

Kenny was very excited by the time he got the truck into the garage and the overhead door had dropped down into place, effectively leaving him free from any chance of outside scrutiny.

He'd done it. All the planning, all the careful preparations. It had gone like clockwork and now he was truly about to launch his project.

He was about to take the real first step toward experiencing his long-term goal. He was about to reap the benefits of all that prep work.

He was humming softly to himself as he climbed out of the truck and crossed to the wall. He lifted the dolly down off its hooks and wheeled it over to the passenger side of the truck before laying it flat on the cement.

He then bent and undid the two adjustable restraining straps and unfurled them to each side of the dolly. Then he crossed to the truck and pulled open the passenger door. Holding it wide open with his back, he reached in and took the limp form under the armpits and hauled the kid off the seat and laid him down on his back on the dolly.

He took one of the duel unfurled straps and then the other and fastened each tightly over the semi-comatose body.

A few minutes later he was in his master bedroom, where he released the hidden latch that opened the camouflaged bookcase panel leading into the soundproofed room. After it had sprung open, he wheeled the dolly through the opening and leaned it against the wall while he pushed the panel back into place and effectively locked out the real world.

This was to his safe place.

A place where he had complete and absolute control of everything that happened and could not ever be interrupted.

Here, he could do whatever he pleased, to whomever he pleased, for however long he pleased.

Happy Birthday Kenny!

Over the month, Dave had spent a fair amount of time shepherding his father though various doctor's appointments. The resulting diagnosis, delivered toward the end of September, indicated a new tumour had been caught early and was operable.

Surgery was now scheduled for mid-October. The cloud of immense pressure all involved had been suffering from the onset, had lifted immediately.

Things were going well for Dave at work.

The latest statistics more than confirmed the earlier indication that the new approach to the standardizing of initial interviews was resulting in the goal of achieving more confessions.

Of the active cases that had reached the courts, all had resulted in convictions, the clear majority by way of guilty pleas.

Additionally, in relation to cold cases, the number of charges laid, versus the prior month, had doubled. Confessions had been achieved for most of these and although none had yet come to trial, an overview indicated that all but two of them would probably lead to convictions also primarily due to the likelihood of guilty pleas.

Henderson had approached the Chief with the stats and had received the go-ahead for Dave and Ed to write up a proposal for a new standard procedure, which would henceforth be followed in the conduct of all Major Crime initial interviews.

As the month ended, the two of them were working on the proposal draft, which they expected to have finished by mid-October.

CHAPTER TWENTY-THREE

- December 1999 -

In October the first signs of the coming winter had settled in over the lower mainland of Vancouver, aided by the introduction of the occasional seasonable sweep of a stiff, cool and freshening, North-Easterly breeze.

By December, the cold of winter seemed to have set firmly into place.

A light skiff of snow now covered the tops of the surrounding mountains and anybody outside was well bundled up.

To many of the lower mainland dwellers, this time of year was depressing.

Not so this year for Kenny.

He felt like a new person.

A new man in every sense of the word.

It had all gone so superbly. More importantly it had given him an adrenalin rush that had reached levels he'd previously only ever dreamed of achieving.

A full three months after that wonderful birthday night, he was still riding high.

There were some minor changes he would make for the next one, now that he'd been through it once. Not big changes. More in relation to the timing of things.

Even now, he was a little taken-aback by the fact that he had not anticipated just how much he would enjoy the final part of the process. Quite surprised that he had found that portion even more satisfying than that of the initial sexual domination and the actual act of killing the target.

Surprised for sure, but not unpleasantly so.

Every day since that first ritual kill, he had excitedly relived the entire experience.

These delightful renditions had remarkably also replaced the repetitive reliving of the childhood accident that had, up to that point, continued to plague him with the horrible flashbacks he had suffered on a regular basis.

No more nightmares. Just happy dreams. What a pleasantly amazing and refreshing change that was!

He could now sit with a drink in his hand and close his eyes as the images would instantly form and play out.

Stripping himself and the quarry. Putting a blindfold on the quarry and then spread-eagling him in the centre of the rubber sheet on the bed. Repeatedly enjoying his complete sexual domination over the semi-conscious victim and lastly; the torture and mutilation that followed, something he so relished.

Of course, the best part of that first extended activity, was the final strangulation of the victim using a choke-chain.

This first time, he had kept the kid doped up and available for three days, before finally reaching a level of excitement while having sex, that he could no longer deny. So sublimely powerful that he'd had no choice but to commit that final act.

What he hadn't realized it at the time, the best was yet to come.

Funny really, when he thought about it after. He wouldn't have believed that would be the case.

I mean, what do most serial killers find the most difficult, the most demanding part of the game? Disposing of the body, once they're finished with it, of course. That's the hardest thing to do safely, the thing that they usually don't know how to handle and they screw up. It's what causes most of them to come to the attention of the police.

Not Kenny. He'd planned for that, planned right down to the very last detail and everything had gone like clockwork, just as he'd figured it.

During his mental reruns of that night, he often eagerly relived that final stage, step by step.

Use the dolly to take the body out to the building attached to the piggery.

Treat it just like you would any old pig.

Not much different at all. Just butcher it.

Save the good meat and freeze it.

Cut up the big bones and the skull, and dump that and the offal into the pigpen.

As good old Grandpa had told him way back when, those pigs will eat anything.

A couple of days later, after the pigs had cleaned up any remaining tidbits, scoop out any fragments mixed into the chipped material left in the pen with the tractor.

Put that through the big chipper to thoroughly shred it all and then truck what was left to a low spot on the property and dump it. Cover that with the day's fresh chipped tailings from the landscaping jobs and add a few more layers from loads the trucks bring in over the next week or so, and there won't be a visible trace left.

Then replenish the pen with new buckets of landscaping tailings.

Out of sight out of mind.

Good fucking luck finding a body after that process!

Dealing with any other traces of the quarry that remained, had been next on the list. Burn all the clothing and personal items in the burning barrel behind the piggery.

Empty the ashes into the tractor bucket once they had cooled and then dump that into one of the low areas on the property and cover it with a good load of the shredded material from the work yard.

That left only the quarry meat that had been tucked safely away into the freezer to deal with.

No challenge there.

On the next specialty sausage run, mix the minced pork going into the machine, in a three-to-one ratio, with the meat donated by the quarry once it had been thawed and well-minced.

Job done.

The sense of general contentment Kenny felt after his birthday present to himself was a revelation. He had never experienced anything like it before in his life.

He felt all-powerful.

All his needs were being met.

His goals achieved.

He was sleeping better.

He was eating better.

Since the experience, he had returned to his previous routine.

Nights at the house in the east end with Robbie and days at home where he continued with the spreading of shredded material over the low spots on the property and power-washed the equipment each day.

Most of any free time he had after that was now spent supplying the needs of the expanding pig population and looking after pork sales.

It was early days, but the volume of meat that he was supplying by the end of the month was already double what it had been at the start of the month.

He was now finding it difficult to meet the demand for the new sausage mixture he was producing for his regular clients. And by month end, he was receiving numerous enquiries about the possibility of a regular supply of the delicacy, from new clients.

He had little free time left out of each day.

Luckily, he found that he no longer needed the kick from the dark side of the internet that had previously taken up a good part of his normal routine. The real thing had been so much better. The porn just didn't do it for him any more.

The realization that he could do it again any time he felt like it, coupled with the nightly availability of Robbie, who was more than eager to act out whatever scenario Kenny desired, currently seemed to be sufficient to keep him sexually satisfied.

Not that he wouldn't want to repeat the quarry situation from time to time. That went without saying.

Counterbalancing that was the fact that, having successfully done it once, he no longer felt pressed to do it again immediately.

That pressure was gone.

His earlier internet research had implied that serial killers would go through periods of hiatus from the need to kill and that seemed to be ringing true for him.

He was fully confident that whenever that itch needed to be scratched in the future, he would have no trouble satisfying the compulsion in short order and with absolutely no risk of discovery.

They say you can't buy happiness.

Bullshit!

Money is exactly what makes this world go around.

Money had given him the freedom and means to do exactly as he wished.

Money had given him Robbie. The kid was his cut-out, and all it took to keep him happy was the money it took to provide him with his shelter and daily entertainment needs; video games and a computer to play with.

True enough perhaps, that attaining his goal had been costly, both in the time it took to plan and prepare properly and the luck to have a sufficient amount of cash in hand necessary to do it all safely.

But, it had been so worth it!

Life was good.

For the past month, Dave and Ed had been working shifts covering the hours between nine and midnight, Monday to Friday. Dave worked from nine to five and Ed, four to twelve. This allowed one of them to be available during that period and provided for a one-hour overlap, which they used to keep each other apprised of any new developments within their specific areas of interest.

This schedule changed temporarily in December.

During the first couple of weeks Dave attended a 'ViCLAS Specialist' course at the Canadian Police College in Ottawa.

The Violent Crime Linkage Analysis System (ViCLAS) was developed in Canada in the early 1990's, as an effective tool to be used to apprehend offenders of multiple violent crimes.

The ten-day course is offered by the college as a tool to train experts in the effective analysis of the information contained on the computerized ViCLAS system teaching users to ask the system the right questions, and to interpret the correct results.

It accomplishes this by improving the participant's knowledge of the behaviors of serious, serial offenders, and by providing insight into the application of the ViCLAS computer system to all active cases of homicide, sexual assault, missing persons, unidentified human remains, non-parental abductions and child luring.

Additionally, as he did every year, Henderson took the final two weeks of December as holidays. As a result, Dave replaced him in the capacity of Acting/Inspector of Major Crime.

While he was still able to interact with Ed, who had been moved up to A/Staff Sergeant as his replacement; being responsible for the oversight of the entire section meant that Dave found he had little time to work in-depth with the two specific areas of Major Crime which held his greatest interest.

While that frustrated him somewhat, this frustration was offset by the challenges offered by the day-to-day management demands necessary to oversee the varied responsibilities of the department's entire elite unit.

Sitting in the large corner office offered him a new perspective on the administration of the much larger group of investigators.

Only two departmental Inspectors were assigned a specific car on a full-time basis those heading the OAS (Operational Auxiliary Section) which oversaw the specialist Marine, Mounted, and Dog squads as well as VIP security details, and Major Crime.

These two positions were deemed important enough to require the use of one, as the officers in charge had to be on call for emergencies. Both unmarked units were fully decked out with the full emergency response equipment and had permanently assigned parking spots in the underground police garage. They were considered, within the department, as a definite perk.

As a result, while in the acting capacity, Dave's truck sat in the driveway at home and he drove the assigned unit to and from the office.

During Henderson's holiday, Dave had only been called out on one occasion, that of a family invasion that had gone wrong in the early hours of one morning, resulting in the gruesome deaths of the homeowners.

On the domestic front, now that his father had had the operation and was comfortably recuperating at home, things were going smoothly.

Linda, very pregnant, was going to take some time off starting in the new year to rest up at home before the baby was due to arrive. She and Cathy spent many hours preparing the house with festive trappings in anticipation of the first Christmas Shaun would likely remember later in life.

All four of the adults had the specific holidays surrounding Christmas off, although Dave was still on call. Everyone seemed to have picked up the holiday spirit, if not for themselves, certainly for the sake of Shaun who was bedazzled by the whole thing, and insanely spoiled by the many presents he found piled under the tree on Christmas morning.

On the twenty-sixth of the month, Ed presented Cathy with a ring and she readily accepted it.

No date was announced for the impending nuptials, but Linda and Cathy immediately put their heads together and by Christmas. had already done some preliminary planning.

CHAPTER TWENTY-FOUR

- January 2000 -
- Y2K -

Vancouver was in a deep freeze.

Under a cold spell that seemed likely to last for some time.

The Year 2000 problem, also known as the Y2K problem, the Millennium bug, the Y2K bug, or Y2K, was a class of computer bugs related to the formatting and storage of calendar data for dates beginning in the year 2000.

Problems were anticipated, and arose, because twentieth-century software had often represented the four-digit year with only the final two digits—making the year 2000 indistinguishable from 1900. The assumption of a twentieth-century date in such programs caused various errors, such as the incorrect display of dates and the inaccurate ordering of automated dated records or real-time events.

When January first of 2000 arrived, there were some problems, but because the glitches had been anticipated since 1997, numerous fixes had already been researched and put into place with the result that any problems that actually occurred, were generally regarded as minor.

While Kenny was aware of the dire predictions of expected problems, his new lifestyle meant that he was far less interested in going online, and he therefore gave it little concern.

He had much more important things to think about.

By mid-December, he had begun to feel the urge to select the next target for processing.

He had been sorely tempted to celebrate Christmas by way of picking up his next victim, but had eventually decided to put it off for a few days and use it to start the new year with a bang instead.

Accordingly, on New Year's Eve he arrived at the house in the east end just after five and instructed Robbie to head for the stroll to select a suitable subject for the evening's entertainment.

Kenny took pains to instruct the kid to carefully repeat the successful process that had worked so delightfully in September.

He was to follow the same procedure with no variations, and when the two of them had had their fun with the new boy, Kenny told him that he would take the target back to the stroll, just as he had done the last time.

To ensure that Robbie understood the importance of making no variation in the process of selecting and getting the new target back to the house safely, Kenny painstakingly went over the entire procedure from start to finish and made sure Robbie understood how important that was.

As far as Robbie was concerned, it was to be just a one-night deal again. Kenny however, had already promised himself that he was going to expand the length of the special time that followed.

That time he would spend a little longer enjoying the new target, once he got him back to his own house. He anticipated keeping this one alive longer and taking more time to enjoy the fun once he had him secured within his safe room.

This time it was not going to be just a three-day ride for Kenny.

No, this one was going to suffer longer than that, a good deal longer, before he was put out of his misery.

Kenny was tempted to fix himself a drink once he had dispatched Robbie, but decided against it. He wanted to be fully alert this time, so that he could soberly register and savor the entire session.

In short order, he was reliving the last time and his blissful anticipation of what was to come made him stiff as a board.

He was tempted to masturbate, but sensed that might lessen his enjoyment of what was to come, and he held himself in check.

When Kenny heard the garage door begin to open, in response to the remote on the visor in Robbie's Mustang, he hurried out to the interconnecting door between the house and the garage.

He flicked the light switch for the garage on and opened the interconnecting door for a quick look.

Robbie smiled through the windshield at him and gave thumbs up.

Kenny was ecstatic, and felt a rush of adrenalin surge through his body as he hurried down the steps and made his way to the passenger door of the mustang. He pulled it open and as he had done on the previous occasion and stepped back to allow himself a moment to savour the prospect in front of him.

Robbie had done well!

Young...couldn't be older than sixteen, more like fourteen!

Shoulder-length blonde hair. Could use a wash, but long enough to get a good grip on it while you were riding him. Maybe a little too muscular for his age, but too much was always better than too little.

And just look at that innocent angelic face!

Oh, this one is going to be just delightful.

Robbie had moved around the car and was standing beside him. Kenny heard him laugh and then felt his hand press up against his stiff cock through his pants.

"Man, you're sure as hell ready for this one."

Kenny grinned as he turned to face him.

"Yes, you did very well this time. This one will be delicious for sure."

Kenny turned back toward the figure in the car, reached out and raised a limp arm and then let it drop.

"Perfect...just like the last one. He's out like a light."

Robbie nodded.

"Ya, but I think he going to be a little more difficult to carry. He looks heaver than the last one."

Kenny grinned.

"I have a feeling that the effort is going to be worth it my friend. I can hardly wait to get him out of his clothes."

He was heftier, but between the two of them they easily managed to haul him out and get him inside down the hall and into the master bedroom. As he had done previously, Kenny had already prepared the room by stripping the bed and covering it with a rubber sheet.

They dumped the kid down onto the centre of the bed.

Impatient, Kenny started back to the doorway.

"Strip him. I'm going out to switch the car for the truck in the garage. Once you get him tied down, you can get started if you like. I'll be back in a jiffy."

By the time Kenny go back to the room, Robbie had then newbie stripped and manacled hand and foot, had stripped off his own clothes and was already blissfully pounding away against the firm orbs of the kid's elevated ass.

Kenny began to strip and then crossed to the bed and give Robbie his choke chain.

"Put it on."

Kenny hauled the last of clothing off and sat down to watch."

"How much it cost us this time?"

Robbie managed to respond huskily as he continued to hump the kid. "Same, just a hundred."

Kenny had already determined that he was going to take his time with this one. He forced himself to keep his hands at his sides, well away from his pulsing cock, letting the pressure build up without added stimulation.

Robbie reached culmination twice over the next half hour and when the exhausted kid rolled off the newbie, Kenny got up and joined them on the bed. He flipped Robbie over on his back and mounted him roughly.

Moaning softly, Robbie eagerly lifted his hips, welcoming each thrust.

When Kenny had finished in him, he got up and off the bed and caught his breath.

"I'm going for a shower. You go ahead and have some more fun with him. I'll take him back to the stroll when you've had enough."

Twenty minuets later Kenny and Robbie loaded the still comatose newbie into the back seat of the pickup. Once he was inside, Kenny climbed behind the wheel and pulled out of the garage, leaving Robbie to put the Mustang back inside.

On the off chance that Robbie was watching him leave, Kenny headed back in the direction of the stroll, but two blocks away from the house he turned and headed for home.

As eager as he was to get there, he kept to the speed limit and obeyed all the rules of the road.

While he figured he could probably explain away the kid in the back seat if he had to, he had no desire to attract the attention of any cops.

The drive was uneventful and when he got to the gate to the compound at the front of the property, he activated the remote above his visor and carefully turned his attention to the driveway on the other side of the opening gate.

As he pulled through, he shifted his gaze off to the right, toward the roadway leading to Walter's residence. He could see no sign of activity. Satisfied that he was not being observed, he drove directly through the gate and made his way swiftly up the long driveway to his own quarters.

A couple of minutes later he was pulling the truck into the garage.

He sat there for a second, waiting for the door to finish closing.

When it had, he gave a little sigh of relief and smiled.

It had gone well. Not a hitch. And now the real fun was about to start.

He was rock-hard by the time he climbed out of the truck and crossed to the wall to pull the dolly down off its hooks. He wheeled it over to the passenger side of the truck before laying it flat on the cement.

He was thinking of what was ahead as he undid the two adjustable restraining straps and spread them out to each side of the dolly. He took first one of the duel unfurled straps and then the other and fastened each tightly over the semi-comatose body.

Moments later, he was locked safely within the soundproofed room, where he had prepared for an expansion of his entertainment by earlier placing a few of his smaller knives beside the bed so he could do a little experimenting with some minor cutting while he had the kid alive.

He knew it would be messy and require more cleanup after, but felt it was worth the effort and was looking forward to how the unconscious quarry would react.

Happy new year Kenny!

The newbie was even better than he had been expecting.

So good.

Kenny managed to make it last almost two days before he finally weakened and poured his seed one last time into the newbie as he blissfully choked the little blonde to death.

Then the real fun began.

Over the holiday season, demand for his new sausages had been very heavy. He sorely needed more of the special meat for the recipe to make up another batch.

Making the preparations for same would not be onerous for him, luckily. In fact, he was very much looking forward to it.

It wasn't just the pigs who were going to be happy tonight!

He was riding high as he anticipated this next task.

He used the dolly to transport the body from the house out to the mini-slaughterhouse attached to the piggery.

One inside he turned on the overhead lights and began to hum softly as he carefully checked that all the windows were well curtained.

That done, he paused for a second to rub his hands together with keenness before unstrapping the body from the dolly and lifting it up onto the drain encircled cutting table.

He stripped off his clothes and put on a heavy leather apron and enjoyed a few minutes devouring the beauty of the body with his eyes as he ran his hands lovingly over every inch, savouring it one last time.

He then began to talk to himself as he selected his first knife and tested it for sharpness.

Just like any old pig.

He chuckled.

I was born to butcher.

An hour and a half later the job was done.

Kenny had taken his time and enjoyed every second of it.

He began to feed the grinder with the fresh meat and then packaged it all and moved it with the dolly over to one of the big freezers, before stacking it happily inside one the shelves in the corner.

That done, he turned to working with the saws to cut up the big bones and the skull. He loaded those with the offal into the large barrel and fastened it to the dolly before beginning the cleanup of all the equipment he'd used in the slaughter.

When he had finished with that to his satisfaction, he removed the apron and used the commercial shower facilities to scrub both it and himself clean and then hung the apron up on a peg, dried himself, and got back into his clothes.

Tired after his endeavours, but riding the rush, he stopped long enough to smoke a cigar and have a drink before he used the dolly to move the large barrel out the door and over to the outside run of the pigpen.

He opened the gate and rolled the dolly inside, unstrapped the barrel and tipped it over then using his foot to quickly roll it across the pen, allowing the contents to sluice out across the enclosure.

The barrel then went back onto the dolly and out through the gate, which he fastened securely.

The pigs, locked inside their inner enclosure could smell what was coming and had begun to squeal with anticipation.

Leaving the dolly, he hurried around and opened the door allowing the animals out and grinned as he watched them begin to feast.

He would have liked to watch them longer, but knew he needed to get back to work and finish the job as soon as he could.

He reluctantly went back out of the building.

Barrel cleaning came next. Once that was done, he would collect up all the kids clothing and use the burning barrel.

That would finish the night's work.

A job well done.

He would then crawl into bed for a well-earned sleep.

When he got up later in the afternoon, he would do the next specialty sausage run.

In a couple of days, he would use the tractor to scoop out any fragments mixed into the chipped material left in the pen.

Run that through the big chipper to thoroughly shred it all and then truck what was left to a low spot on the property, dump it and cover that with the day's fresh chipped tailings from the landscaping jobs.

All that remained to do then, was to freshen up the pen with a few buckets of landscaping tailings.

Upon Dave's return from the ViCLAS course he had approached Inspector Hamilton and discussed with him what he had learned.

One of the problems with the system was that it required a great deal of paperwork to enter the specific amount of information required to properly complete a single entry. Cops, famous for not being particularly stimulated by paperwork tended to avoid it when they could.

As a result, in many instances the system was simply not being used.

To circumvent this problem, Dave asked for a new data entry clerk to be assigned to Major Crime to ensure that this roadblock was removed and allowing all serious incidents falling within the guidelines of ViCLAS to be fed into the system.

Henderson agreed with the request, told Dave to put it in writing and said that he would endorse it and push it upstairs.

Y2K had been more of a concern for Dave than it had been for Kenny.

Therefore, he and Ed had both decided to work on New Years day.

It was with a sense of relief that they found the systems they were using hadn't seemed to have suffered any problems because of the year change.

As the two of them sat down in Dave's office afterward and drank coffee on the shift overlap, they happily discussed the current situation.

The number of charges being laid by the squad was way up over the same period last year.

Because of the number of clearances being achieved in the small unit, two additional retired detectives had been brought in on contract to add to the manpower strength of the cold-case staff.

Dave had been given the responsibility for personally picking them and he had been well pleased at the quality of the two finally selected. He was also delighted to find that one of the three female applicants who had applied, had made it though all the hoops leading to the final selection.

He had been wanting to add more women to the make up of Major Crime for some time and it was a good start in that direction.

When Dave arrived home that night he found that it would only be him, Linda and Shaun home for dinner. While he normally enjoyed being surrounded by the expanded household, it felt good for him and Linda to be on their own for a change, once they had settled Shaun down for the night.

Once they had him in bed they returned to the kitchen and Dave made Linda sit down and relax while he busied himself cleaning up the kitchen and depositing the dirty dishes and cutlery into the dishwasher.

That out of the way, the two of them flopped down in front of the television and watched the news. Dave nursing a brandy and Linda settling for a mug of hot water laced with a slice of lemon.

When the program finished they began to discuss his day something they routinely did now that Linda was off work.

Dave quickly brought her up to date and when he'd finished, she frowned.

"I called in to touch base with one of my supervisors today…"

Before he could respond, she raised her hand to dismiss what she knew was coming.

"I know, I know, I'm not working…I just wanted to see how things were going.

It was just a very short call. Anyway, I'm concerned about how effective our current polies are when it come to getting kids in need off the street quickly.

Especially the ones who have found it necessary to turn tricks to stay alive."

Dave scowled, but kept his silence. Linda continued.

"We seem to be doing fairly well with the girls. It's the boys that I'm concerned about. They tend to be harder to reach than the girls anyway, but of late its apparently getting worse."

Dave interjected.

"Ok, well then, when you get back to work you can have a looksee at what's happening. But in the meantime, Mrs. Richards, its someone else's problem, not yours."

He reached over and gave her a soft pat on her expanded tummy.

"You've got enough to worry about right there."

Linda looked down at his hand and smiled.

"For now, let's just get you on your feet long enough to get you to bed."

CHAPTER TWENTY-FIVE

- April 2000 -

The daily temperature had begun to rise perceptively. Spring was in the air.

Last time around, Kenny had made it through four months before his need to kill again had overwhelmed him. This time, the urge had become engulfing in less than three.

Over the last two weeks of March he had felt it building steadily.

On a couple of his regular nightly sessions with Robbie during that time, he'd come very close to a complete loss of control and had felt exceptionally strongly tempted to snuff the kid.

That would have been a bloody disaster.

Moreover, the demand for his special sausages had expanded yet again and he'd used up the last of his special-meat freezer supply. He needed more of that one unique ingredient that made his sausages so exclusive.

It was time again, and he'd already picked the date for his next party.

April Fool's day.

On the last day of March, he'd gotten home from Robbie's just before midnight. It had been a heavy session and he been exhausted by the time he'd driven home and had a bite to eat.

As soon as he'd finished with his meal he made his way to his bedroom and got into bed. However, he found that he was so excited for what was to come that next night that he couldn't find sleep, no matter how hard he tried.

He'd tossed and turned restlessly until three in the morning. Frustrated, he'd got a bottle and a glass and drank himself almost into a stupor, and finally closed his eyes just before five in the morning.

He woke at one-thirty on the afternoon of April first.

It was a grey, overcast and drizzly day, but Kenny, suffering from a massive hangover, was nevertheless wound up so tight with anticipation for what was coming, that he took no notice of the weather.

Feeling woozy after his bout with the bottle, he was angry with himself for getting plastered.

Once he'd showered, he took some pain-killers for his headache and then, determined to get himself back into top shape for the night to come, forced himself to eat a substantial meal.

Time dragged as he waited impatiently for the evenings entertainment to begin.

He had told Robbie to expect him at five and felt obliged to stick to that timeframe.

He kept switching his gaze between mindless TV shows and the clock, until four-thirty rolled around, and he could leave the house.

Even though he stuck to all the rules of the road, he still arrived at Robbie's ten minuets early. Kenny figured there was no need to run through the scenario of what the kid should do, yet again.

Robbie had it down pat.

He immediately sent him out to the stroll to select a prime subject for the evening's fun and games.

An hour later he and Robbie were hauling yet another comatose prime specimen out of the Mustang and into the house.

By one in the morning they'd both run themselves blissfully dry and Kenny had eagerly left for home to begin the best part of the night.

He kept the kid drugged and alive for a full five days. Enjoying him sexually and using the small knives on him repeatedly.

It was a good thing the room was soundproof, because even with low doses of drugs there was a lot of crying, begging and screaming.

After that, he eagerly began the best part.

It was the best yet, and it had gone without a hitch.

Kenny had now crossed the accepted threshold of three or more kills. He had truly reached his goal, and was now, a fully-fledged serial killer.

Linda and Dave welcomed their second child into the world on February sixteenth. It was a girl and they were delighted.

They named her Malinda Colleen.

Linda had gone off on maternity leave after the birth and everyone in the house had pitched in to keep Shaun occupied and looked after while she mainly concentrated on the new addition to the clan.

By April Malinda was two months old and very much a part of the family.

A preliminary conversation between Dave and Linda about his getting a snip job had begun.

It was early times yet, and even though he knew the vasectomy was both sensible and inevitable, Dave still got the willies when the topic was raised by his other half.

His only solace in the matter from within the household, seemed to be coming from Murphy the cat who, while seemingly sympathetic when Dave consulted with him, offered little real support.

At work, Inspector Henderson, who had been suffering from debilitating headaches for several weeks, booked off the second week of the month to facilitate a battery of tests designed to see if his doctor could get to the bottom of the problem.

Once again Dave and Ed had been bumped up in the command chain to fill the void.

Dave found himself more comfortable working out of the big corner office this time round. While he still missed the more hands-on supervision of the areas he enjoyed most, the challenge of overseeing the entire Major Crime section was challenging enough, and seemed almost routine to him now.

Although it was too early yet to seriously evaluate the effectiveness of having a data entry clerk doing the compiling and entry for the squads rough input to meet the ViCLAS systems needs, there had already been two serious cases that had been closed by way of the results of the extra effort.

It was encouraging, and had been noticed by the brass.

At the beginning of the final week of April, Henderson called Dave into his office.

When Dave entered the office, the Inspector asked him to shut the door and then waved him into a chair.

"Coffees coming."

Although Dave had seen his boss several times from a distance over the past week, he and Henderson had not had a one-on-one, due to the demands for their attention elsewhere.

Now that Dave was sitting down across from him he realized that the Inspector was looking unusually rough around the edges. He appeared to have lost some weight, and his skin had taken on a slight tinge of grey.

The coffee arrived and when the door was closed again Henderson, normally a man of few words, came right to her point.

"The results are in. Apparently, I've got myself a rapidly growing tumour up here."

He tapped his temple.

"Diagnosis is cancer. They give me no more than six months."

Dave was at a loss for words.

Before he could respond, Henderson waved his hand in the air.

"I'm not looking for sympathy. That's not what I called you in for. I've accepted it and so has the wife. It is what is.

Only my doctor, my wife, and now you, know about this so far, so I'd appreciate it if you kept it to yourself for now. The Chief is next on my list and once that's done, it will filter down from his office to the general population fairly quickly, I'm sure."

That doesn't apply to your wife of course. Linda will, of necessity, be a required sounding board for you, on that we can both agree. But please do that in a general way and play the whole thing low-key interdepartmentally, as and when the word does come down from upstairs.

If we expect this little project I'm about to suggest to you to succeed, you can't let on that you might know any more about it than anyone else does.

Dave's curiosity was piqued, but he stayed silent.

Henderson managed a small smile.

"So, let's get to why I did call you in."

Dave was still trying to deal with what he'd heard, and he reached for his mug and took a sip from it before he was able to look his boss back in the face.

Henderson gave him a second and then continued.

"I'm not going to be able to work much longer I'm afraid. At least that's what they tell me.

So, with that in mind, I got to thinking about my legacy and that led me to you frankly.

You will remember that we had a plan for you to take over from me, in a year or two.

Clearly, I'm going to be out of here long before we had figured."

Dave managed to shift his mind off his shock over the diagnosis and concentrate on what had just been said. He shook his head and thought for a second before speaking.

"I'm not sure that you should be worrying about me at a time like this..."

Henderson cut him off.

"It's exactly what I should be worrying about Dave.

I've been a member of this department for thirty-one years, eight of which I've spent in Major Crime. That's a helluva long time, and as quaint as it might sound, I care about its future.

Now, don't let this go to your head my friend, but I just happen to think you are the best thing to ever happen to this squad. I want that to continue. I want to see you stay here.

Let's face it, there is no way that the brass are going to be able to promote you again immediately, no matter how much the Chief may want to, and even though I'm going to push for exactly that.

The backlash from the middle ranks would be phenomenal if he did that. You and I might think you're ready, but common sense says that is not going to be happening."

Henderson paused and let that sink in before continuing.

"I have every intention of laying it on the line, telling it how I see it to the Chief when I meet with him. That will be no problem for me. I won't be worrying about burning any bridges, because they are already collapsed for me and I don't have any need of them now anyway.

And, lets face it, in consideration of what I'm facing, the Chief is going to be sympathetic to my cause.

The way I see it, he'll have two choices. He's either going to have to replace me by way of a transfer into Major Crime of an existing Inspector from outside the squad, or else promote someone with experience who is on the promotional list, up from Staff/Sergeant.

I've given it a good deal of thought, and it seems to me that your best bet for us is to have an Inspector transferred in, rather than the bump up of someone to Inspector from the Staff/Sergeant list.

Subsequently I intend to share my thoughts on that specific aspect with the Chief. Hopefully he will see it my way.

Additionally, I'm going to suggest that he select my replacement by way of a current Inspector who has had some minor experience with the detective division, but one who is of a seniority; that means he has no more than a couple of years left to put in before he pensions off.

That way you will still have a good chance to take the top spot once he goes.

I'm also going to push for someone who is already well into a 'pre-retirement' frame of mind and more importantly, who has already been promoted past his abilities within the department."

He paused to grin across his desk.

"Someone who the Chief considers likely to be happy with leaving you to do all the work and make all the important decisions, while he sits, happily on his duff, studying travel brochures in this office, in name only.

In other words, a guy who will keep out of your hair and let you run the squad your way."

Dave was gobsmacked.

He couldn't believe his ears.

Here was a man who had recently been told that he had only a short time to live and yet, Henderson was worrying about Dave's future, instead of fretting about his own.

Henderson leaned back in his chair and raised his hands and cupped them behind his head.

"I've got an appointment with the Chief this afternoon and I wanted to run this by you first, give you a heads up before the meeting.

Well, what do you think? Sound like its a scenario that might work out for you?"

Dave didn't respond for a few seconds. Moments later, he raised his arms, extended his hands out to his sides and shrugged.

"I really don't know what to say, to tell you the truth.

I'm so very sorry to hear of your prognosis. That goes without saying.

Other than that, I'm both surprised and appreciative of your confidence in me, and I thank you for your ongoing support. I also sincerely hope I can live up to that faith, if I should be successful in eventually stepping into your shoes."

Dave did discuss the situation with Linda that night over dinner. He kept his pledge to Henderson, telling her about the Inspector's situation but not going into detail about what his bosses leaving might mean for him.

Basically, they discussed the possibilities as to who might be stepping into the corner office once Henderson left, and how much he would miss working under Jim Henderson.

At ten the next morning, Dave received a call from the Chief's secretary and was sitting in a chair across from him by ten-fifteen.

He had half expected to find that the two deputies would already be in the room, but when the secretary closed the door, it was just him and the Chief.

Dave had no way of knowing how the meeting had gone between

Henderson and the Chief and decided to play it by ear and temper his responses.

The Chief offered him a coffee, but Dave declined.

That over with, the Chief pursed his lips and let out a soft sigh.

"I understand that Jim spoke with you yesterday about his situation."

Dave nodded.

"Yes, a hell of a thing. It always seems that we lose the good ones far too early."

The Chief leaned forward and rested his arms on the top of his desk.

"He seems to think a lot of you. Wanted me to promote you again and move you into his office when he goes."

Dave didn't respond, and the Chief continued.

"He didn't say so, but he knew that I couldn't do that, although, to be honest, I'd like to.

If I did do it, there would be dissention in the ranks and you'd be alienated. Not a good position to be in for either of us.

Anyway, he's came up with a backup proposal, one that he led me to believe he'd discussed in a general sense with you already.

I believe it's one that I can live with, providing you and I reach an understanding that, if any word of this conversation we're having here leaks out, we'll find ourselves in a helluva mess.

Something neither of us needs or wants.

We won't go into any details here. The less we talk about it the better. Suffice to say I will play my part in this and I've already got somebody in mind who might just fit the bill.

Now, there are going to be a few people with raised eyebrows when the transfer is made. Several inspectors are going to be unhappy for a start, as well as a few Staff/Sergeants who are currently on the promotional list, to say nothing about the Police Board.

Additionally, the two deputies are going to be nattering at me about the man I've chosen and trying to get me to reconsider. I can ride that out, and if you can do your part to make the squad run smoothly, despite who is sitting in the corner office down there, I think the whole thing will blow over in time.

If all goes well, when the new guy retires in two year's time, you'll be a shoe-in to replace him."

He frowned and leaned back in his chair.

"I've told Jim he can book off as of today.

You'll be acting until the new man arrives.

I'm sticking my neck out here Staff/Sergeant Richards. Don't make me regret it."

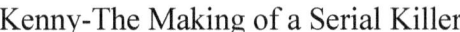

Book 3

CHAPTER TWENTY-SIX

- October 2000 -

Kenny found it necessary to have things properly structured.

Over the past six months he'd been experimenting with his periods of hiatus between kills. As a result, he had concluded that he needed to fulfill his needs monthly, if he wanted to reasonably satisfy his sexual needs.

He'd reached that decision on his birthday in September, shortly after he'd done his last one. That appeared to be a good balance, enough time to build up the sexual urge to a pinnacle, so that it could be properly savored and appreciated, but not so long as to cause him to become uneasy and moody.

He was both excited and pleased at having now picked a specific monthly date for each of his sessions. He was convinced such a plan would work well when it came to both his desires and the growing need to meet the special sausage production requirements.

From this point on, he would start each new month with a bang.

Rain seemed to be the order of the day for most of October. Frequently heavy. On other days, overcast and showery.

A couple of serious windstorms also hit the Vancouver lower-mainland during October.

By the first of the month, Kenny had a total of seven successful kills behind him.

Early on the morning of the eighth, he found himself happily humming as he went through the final processes of cleaning up after his last kill.

His only problem this time around, was getting the kid's effects burned in the barrel. The damned rain was pounding down. He had to keep pouring gas on the barrel's contents to sustain the fire.

It seemed to take forever to get it done.

During the third week of the month, the second of the windstorms hit with a vengeance and power had been knocked out, reportedly fromuprooted trees falling on wires in many locations of the lower mainland.

Kenny's was one of the households that found themselves in the dark as a result.

At first, he hadn't worried about it too much. He'd been through several short outages before. But when this one looked like it was going to last for days rather than hours, he immediately thought of the contents of his big commercial freezers and began to panic.

He certainly didn't want the meat to thaw before his next sausage run had been completed, and without power for his machines, he couldn't empty them and turn it into his special sausage mixture.

As a result, he'd scrambled to buy some large commercial generators.

Unfortunately, he soon found he wasn't the only one looking. In the end he had to get Walter to send one of the trucks across the provincial border into Alberta with instructions to pick three up there.

The whole operation had taken two days and Kenny was still without power when the truck came back.

By the time it was over, and he had temporary backup power, Kenny was a wreck.

For the whole time the power had been off, he had been unable to sleep. He'd kept checking the two big freezers to see how they were holding up. Each time he'd done it, the temperature dials had shown a steady, if slow, rise in temperature.

Once the portable generators were functioning, one for the house, one for the piggery and one for Walter's place, Kenny had finally been able to relax, and he slept for twelve hours straight.

The next day, normal power was restored, and the crisis was over.

Twenty-four hours later he had finished processing the contents of the freezers and shipped the outstanding orders to his customers.

That out of the way, he had once again meticulously cleaned the sausage-making equipment.

From his perspective, the whole system was organized to the point that it was all working like a well-oiled machine.

All the planning and effort had been worthwhile.

There was a physical change beginning to take place however, one that Kenny did not yet see coming.

'Boystown', was about to undergo a transformation, brought about by two factors.

The first was the subtle changes occurring in the commercial area where the stroll flourished. This had come about by way of the creeping gentrification taking place there, a move towards a reuse of the derelict industrial area, by way of a large upscale development to be known as 'Yaletown'.

This meant that increasing pressure to drive out the young male prostitutes was going to come increasingly into play over the next few years.

The second was the advent of cellular phones and their expanded usage, to the point that over the next decade they would probably become mainstream.

Once the cell phone was in common use and the price had come down to the point where everyone was carrying one, a kid wouldn't have to stand on a corner in the rain and snow to advertise his wares. He would be able to do it electronically.

Slowly but steadily, times were changing. By October of 2000 the writing was on the wall, but Kenny hadn't noticed it yet.

He was content.

Little Malinda was eight months old and along with her three-year-old brother, keeping the Richard's household busy.

In August, Ed and Cathy had decided it was time to get a place of their own. They had moved out in September.

After a good deal of discussion, Dave and Linda, both wanting to continue their careers, agreed to the idea of hiring a nanny for the kids and the day after Ed and Cathy vacated, Blessica Cruz, a petite, attractive twenty-two-year-old Filipino woman, took up residence in their secondary suite.

They'd hired Blessica under the Federal Temporary foreign workers program and although initially somewhat apprehensive about whether she would work out, in the end found themselves very pleased with the entire process.

Blessica turned out to be somewhat reserved, but eager and full of energy for her new task. She was delightfully polite, caring, and earnest in her care, concern and affection for the children.

Within a matter of weeks, she had completely settled in and it seemed that she had been with them for years. Any preconceived concerns quickly faded. By that time, Dave and Linda had complete faith in her abilities to handle the care of the children when they were at work.

Linda had come off her maternity leave and had been back at work since August.

Dave's vasectomy had become a reality in July.

He'd had an uncomfortable couple of days afterwards, accompanied by a goodly amount of friendly banter from within Major Crime, Linda's tongue-in-cheek sympathy and *'I told you so'* looks from Murphy the cat.

Dave had remained as Acting-Inspector for the squad up until September, but the replacement for Henderson was due to take place on October first.

It had been generally agreed in the lower ranks that a Staff/Sergeant was not likely to be raised to Inspector rank to fill the void. Rumors had been flying around for the last two weeks, but no one below the top floor really had any idea as to which current Inspector the Chief was likely going to put in the spot.

On the drive in to the office on the first, Dave had a few butterflies hovering around in his gut as he tossed around some of the names that had been popping up of late.

When he pulled the unmarked unit into the underground parking garage at headquarters and parked it in its reserved 'Insp. Major Crime' slot, he knew he was going to miss the car perk. He would be catching a ride home tonight with Ed and driving his own truck back and forth to work again after today.

As he rode up to his office in the elevator from the parking garage, he shifted his thoughts away from trying to guess who would end up in the big office he'd vacated the night before, and back to a more positive scenario.

ViCLAS results were more than justifying the upgrades he had put into place. Tips provided by the system were bearing fruit weekly and leading to some astonishing charges being laid in both current and cold cases. The entire department was now in full support of the new thrust to fully utilize the possibilities the program provided.

When he entered the reception area of Major Crime, Dave was immediately aware of an aura of general unease. The usual low-key banter that normally bubbled just below the surface was missing.

The small groups of detectives who habitually gathered in various parts of the section, were not in evidence and the silence was deafening.

The odd phone was still ringing, and the sound of the photocopier operating at the back of the office could be clearly heard.

Over-all apprehension was palatable.

Although he hadn't expected this change in the squad, he quickly realized that he should have.

A new man in charge.

Everyone was diligently working at his or her desk and with a few exceptions, on pins and needles, wondering what if any radical changes were about to come to descend upon them.

Brenda, the civilian secretary seated at her desk behind the counter, looked up as Dave reached over the top of the gate and popped it open, so he could enter the squad proper.

Brenda was a no-nonsense old-timer. She had been in her post for more than twenty years and Dave got along with her very well.

There was a blank expression on her face as she spoke. She kept her voice low, intentionally ensuring that he was the only one to hear her.

"Inspector Campbell would like to see you in his office first thing."

She had a twinkle in her eye as she raised her eyebrows and then slowly shook her head, before delivering a deep sigh.

"Better you than me!"

Dave paused before passing her desk and grinned as he let his eyes meet hers.

"Our new boss would be Doug Campbell then. Interesting times ahead."

He winked.

"Right, well I better go straight in then, hadn't I?"

What he knew of Doug Campbell began to roll through the back of Dave's mind as he crossed the open work area and moved down the hall toward the offices at the far end of the building. He was well aware of the multitude of eyes that were following his progress.

Fifty-three or fifty-four. Spent most of his career in the Patrol Division. Campbells only experience in the detective office had been with stolen autos and that had been over twenty years ago of short duration.

Never worked any of the serious Major crime desks.

Made the cut for Inspector ten years ago and had been moved to a position of acting as one of the Duty Officers for the patrol division, after hours. The Duty Officer position was a first placement for most new inspectors. Those who were actively on the march up the ladder normally spent less than a year in that position, before they were moved into a more specialized area of command.

Campbell had not been one of those.

In the end, he'd never been transferred to any other duty. He'd spent his last ten years working afternoon or night shifts, as a Duty Officer.

Within the department, Campbell was generally considered to be a cement-headed pompous ass, who was infamous for talking down to his subordinates.

A man who was clearly less than bright, but who thought very highly of himself and over the past ten years, had made it very clear that he believed he had been unfairly treated by various promotion boards and repeatedly passed over for promotions, that should have been his for the asking.

Physically unimposing as a policeman. Five nine, slightly overweight, completely bald, perpetual frown and introverted. Well-known for his bad temper and dislike for anyone who disagreed with him. Never wrong. The type of supervisor who always managed to find an underling scapegoat if anything he himself was responsible for went sideways.

An unforgiving man with a long memory.

Not someone you wanted to have on your bad side.

Dave didn't know what to think.

He'd never in his wildest dreams even remotely considered that the Chief would select this dolt to replace Henderson.

Dave entered his own office and closed his door softly behind him. He took his cap and overcoat off and hung them on the hook on the back of the door and then sucked in a deep breath.

What in heavens' name had the Chief been thinking?

Dave perched his butt on the corner of his desk and shifted his mind back to the last conversation he'd had with Henderson as to what he intended to recommend to the Chief - mentally rerunning parts of that discussion.

'... I'm going to suggest that he select my replacement by way of a current Inspector who has had some minor experience with the detective division, but one who is of a seniority that means he has no more than a couple of years left to put in before he pensions off.

That way you will still have a good chance to take the top spot once he goes.

I'm also going to push for someone who is already in a 'pre-retirement' frame of mind and more importantly, who has already been promoted past his abilities within the department.

Someone who the Chief considers likely to be happy with leaving you to do all the work and make all the important decisions, while he sits, happily on his duff, studying travel brochures in this office, in name only.

In other words, a guy who will keep out of your hair and let you run the squad your way.'

Then he reweighed what the Chief had said to him when he saw him last.

'... he's came up with a backup proposal, one that he led me to believe he'd discussed in a general sense with you already.

... the less we talk about it the better. Suffice to say I will play my part in this and I've already got somebody in mind who might just fit the bill.

... the two deputies are going to be nattering at me about the man I've chosen and trying to get me to reconsider. I can ride that out, and if you can do your part to make the squad run smoothly, despite who is sitting in the corner office down there, I think the whole thing will blow over in time.

...If all goes well, when the new guy retires in two year's time, you'll be a shoe-in to replace him.

I'm sticking me neck out here Staff/Sergeant Richards. Don't make me regret it.'

Dave rolled forward off his desk, left his office and walked down the hall.

He knocked and opened the door to the Inspector's office.

For better or worse, stepped directly into the lion's den.

CHAPTER TWENTY-SEVEN

- September 2005 -

Kenny turned twenty-eight on the first of the month.

As he had for the past five years, he celebrated his birthday by way of adding yet another victim to his tally.

Over that timeframe, he had been able to maintain his system without any serious hitches and his total kills now numbered sixty-eight.

As August was coming to an end, the hint of a problem had arisen - one that he recognized he would have to deal with before it got out of hand. It was a concern that he admitted he had initially recognized over several months but had been hesitant to deal with.

The problem was Robbie.

It was a two-fold concern.

Firstly, Robbie had matured, reaching an age that made him far less sexually desirable to Kenny.

Secondly, recently Robbie had begun to openly express disenchanted with the current state-of-affairs.

As Kenny got his real kicks from his monthly kills, his need for Robbie as a sex partner between kills was, while necessary for his daily comfort, certainly not paramount and in fact was waning.

Now, if that had been the only problem, he could have dismissed it as minor.

However, an uncooperative and moody Robbie was a risk that Kenny was not prepared to take. He sensed that he was losing the ability to fully dominate Robbie and that was completely unacceptable.

A Robbie deciding to vary the procedure for whatever reason by thinking on his own could only eventually lead to a screw-up which would leave Kenny vulnerable. Additionally, in mid-August, Robbie had casually mentioned to Kenny that he had noticed that none of the past targets he had selected for their nights of special fun, seemed to be currently working the stroll.

While he had made no further comment in that regard at the time, it seemed obvious to Kenny that Robbie was curious about this situation. It was a transient lifestyle for sure, which would go a long way to explaining their absence and Kenny had immediately pointed that out.

As he had done so, he'd carefully watched Robbie's facial expressions. By now, he could read the kid like a book, and he doubted that Robbie had found his answer a fully satisfactory explanation for the missing boys.

It was then that Kenny had decided that Robbie had become far to independent in thought for his own good. He had become more trouble than he was worth.

The problem would have to be nipped in the bud.

Things had been going along extremely well and this development was discouraging to say the least.

That said, Kenny had known from the start that this would probably happen at some point. He had also been fully aware that the concept of replacing Robbie would necessitate him again putting himself into direct contact with the stroll to select a replacement. With that contact would come all the risks the process would subsequently entail.

Kenny didn't like the idea one damn bit, but the alternative was far worse.

Which was why this month was going to be an extra special one.

Kenny got Robbie very drunk during their session with the September target at the house in the east-side.

When they were finished with the victim, Kenny presented Robbie with two pre-drawn documents to sign, explaining them away as necessary for tax purposes.

In fact, the two certificates actually served to sign away the ownership of both the house and Mustang on Robbie's part although the signature of the purchaser on each, remained blank.

That done, Kenny poured them each a nightcap before he got ready to leave for the night.

He saw to it that Robbie's drink contained a good dose of Rohypnol.

Kenny waited for it to take effect and then, with a good deal of effort loaded the semi-conscious forms of both Robbie and the night's target into his truck and put the Mustang into the garage before securing the house and heading for home.

Kenny took great care on the drive. He sure as hell didn't want to attract any attention with the two of them laid out in the back seat of the truck's cab.

As he stopped for an amber light two blocks away from the house, he took the opportunity to look up into his rear-view mirror to check on his cargo.

Out of the corner of his eye, he saw a cube-van headed toward him from across the intersection. The light turned red and Kenny realized that the van was not going to stop but had instead accelerated toward him through the intersection.

Kenny swore as he watched it shoot through the red light and as time stood still for a second, he prayed that the stupid bastard would make it safely through. He sure as hell didn't want to be involved in an accident now.

Luckily, traffic was light and there were no vehicles crossing on the green. The truck made it though without incident.

Well, yes and no.

As luck would have it, the intersection had red-light cameras and Kenny watched the camera across the intersection flash, indicating that the cube van had been recorded running the light.

Relieved, Kenny let out a nervous laugh.

Asshole got himself a ticket. Serves him right!

The remainder of the trip proved uneventful, but Kenny remained on pins-and-needles, until he had parked the truck safely in his own garage and closed the door.

The worst was over.

Now, once he had the two of them into the secure room, he could chill and get ready to thoroughly enjoy the rest of the night.

Kenny was highly aroused by the prospect and eager to get started.

Kenny did Robbie first.

The sex itself was old hat and not particularly exciting, although he did get an absolutely-stupendous, high when he was finally free to take Robbie all the way and actually haul the choke-chain tight while simultaneously finishing in Robbie's writhing body.

He then wrapped Robbie's corpse in a rubber sheet and dumped it on the floor, before re-placing him on the bed with the stripped quarry and shackling him securely in place.

Once that was done, he began to relax a little and spent a while just gazing appreciatively at his new victim as he rubbed his hands lovingly over the nude semi-conscious form.

He decided to wait for a couple of hours before doing this new one.

Letting the excitement re-build before he got started again. With that in mind he bent over the now passive form on the bed and kissed each of the firm buttock cheeks firmly, before turning his attention to dealing with Robbie's rubber-sheet wrapped form.

Because of the relatively high temperature of the day, he knew he would have to process the bodies quickly to save the meat. He'd determined to process them both at once, and as he would be keeping the new one for at least a couple of days before finishing with him, he needed to put Robbie into cold storage ASAP.

Whistling softly to himself, he used the dolly to cart Robbie out to the butchering building and left him, still wrapped in the rubber sheet, on the floor of one of the big commercial freezers.

On September the fourth, Kenny butchered the two bodies and immediately processed the meat, which resulted in his largest ever sausage run. It was a lot of work, but by the evening he had cleaned up and was in the process of burning the clothing and personal effects.

For the first time in years, Kenny's confidence had taken a hit. He was unhappy about, and lamenting the fact that Robbie was out of the picture and he now had to start all over in selecting a new cohort and all the trouble and risk that was likely to entail.

Subsequently, he put it off as long as he could, but by mid-month he was already beginning to feel the pressure to get the job done to ensure that he would be ready for the first of October.

The monthly routine he had set up was by this time, set in stone. He knew there was no way he would be mentally or physically able to skip the October first date for his next kill.

Finding the right kid turned out to be even harder than he'd envisioned.

He spent more than a week prowling the stroll before he was confident enough to make his move. By that time, he was a wreck. Over the period, he hadn't been able to eat or sleep properly and his self-confidence was at a low.

He was afraid of the risk, unsure of his ability to make a good choice and ended up rejecting his eventual choice at the very last minute on two separate nights, before, at his wits end, had let him in the truck.

It appeared that he had lucked in.

Joel Hurst, looked no more than fourteen but was sixteen and had a driver's licence; necessary, as he would have to be able to drive.

The kid was unquestionably cute, on the small size and baby-faced,' but the shorts and muscle shirt he was wearing when he'd climbed into the passenger seat of the truck, clearly outlined a good body.

Kenny figured he was new to the scene for sure. He hadn't been on the street until the last three days of Kenny's search. Kenny had spotted him standing off by himself. Obviously unsure of himself and scared shitless about being on the stroll.

He certainly appeared gay, all the mannerisms were clearly there. Effeminate to a degree, though not to the point of unattractiveness.

On that third night, when Kenny had finally pulled to the curb, he'd had to motion the kid to the truck several times, before he'd had the courage to approach.

By the time Kenny had Joel back at the house in east Vancouver he found out that the kid had been orphaned early in life and then been taken over by the province and bounced around from foster home to foster home for the last ten years.

He'd been both mentally and sexually abused in the last two and taken off from the final one just days before Kenny had spotted him on the stroll.

Kenny's self confidence had rebounded, and he was certain he had scooped up exactly what he'd been looking for.

It would be a busy week ahead, but if I really put my mind to it, Joel will be ready to go for the first of October.

Just after five in the evening on September the fifteenth, Inspector Dave Richards was waiting for Staff/Sergeant Ed Hamilton to join him for their regular, Monday to Friday afternoon change-of-shift meeting.

Dave was standing looking out the window of his corner office in Major Crime, scanning the bright blue and cloudless sky when Ed knocked and entered his office.

They exchanged greetings and moved across the room to sit at the small conference table.

It had been an eventful five years for both men.

The Chief had been true to his word and both had been promoted as planned. There had been some uneasy blips over that time, primary during the two years under the command of the, now retired, Inspector Campbell.

Nothing that Dave hadn't been able to handle by using *'kid gloves'* and a good deal of flattery, however.

Since Campbells retirement, things in the squad had been going very well.

Through attrition, Dave had taken great care to recruit bright and eager young detectives to replace the older, and in some cases, less productive pool he had inherited and statistically, the squad was currently performing well above expectation.

The day-to-day operation had become second nature to both Dave and Ed and both were becoming a little restless due to the lack of a new challenge.

That was about to change.

It was toward the end of the month, and it was Dave's wife Linda, who started the ball rolling.

She and Dave were at home cleaning up after dinner. Dave loading the dishwasher, while Linda wiped down the counters. They had been working silently for several minutes before she spoke

"An interesting report landed on my desk this morning..."

Dave looked up at her as he closed the door on the dishwasher.

"Oh, and what did it have to say?'

She tossed him the cloth she'd been using, and he rinsed it and draped it over the tap as she continued.

"...not that much really. It's what was implied that got my attention.

It was from one of the front-line social workers on the *'Boystown'* stroll."

She raised the wine bottle sitting on the table and waved it at him and Dave nodded as she refilled their glasses before settling down onto one of the chairs at the table. He left the sink and sat down across from her.

"And?"

Linda reached down and opened her briefcase, which she'd left by her chair when she got home. She pulled out a sheaf of stapled papers and passed them to him.

"I think maybe you should read it.

You remember way back when I said that we seemed to be losing a lot of the boys we had taken an interest in, far more than the number of girls? The statistics in this report seem to drive that point home rather strongly.

I'll let you form your own opinion before I tell you mine. Give it a read while I go check on Bless and the kids."

Dave took a sip of wine as he watched her walk out of the kitchen, then he picked up the report and began to read.

It was about ten pages long, the last four, a set of graphs.

He was aware of her coming back into the room some time later, but his interest had been piqued and he didn't look up as she sat down across from him and picked up her glass.

By this point, Dave had reached the graphs at the end and when he'd finished eyeballing them, he set the document down on the table and leaned back in his chair.

"Intriguing for sure...doesn't add up when you compare the males and the females...so what did you make of it. Something is out of whack, yes?"

Linda smiled and shook her head.

"Nope, you first."

Dave frowned and sat forward, resting his elbows on the table.

"You'd have a better idea than I would. Its your bailiwick, not mine."

Linda raised her eyebrows.

"Are you sure of that?"

He frowned.

Linda shrugged her shoulders.

"These boys are going somewhere. I know, I know, it's a transient lifestyle. They come, and they go. But just not as regularly or this often and none of them have come back. And did you notice...they are all recently arrived on the street, young, have similar physical descriptions and; in a general sense, are also very similar in appearance."

Dave nodded. He now knew where she was going with this.

"You think maybe, just maybe, we have a serial killer on our hands."

Linda nodded.

"These stats go back over at last seven years and if you base an assessment on the last five, you must accept that the numbers indicate one hell of an uptick over that time line."

Dave leaned back in his chair and crossed his arms. He thought for a few seconds before he responded.

"Ok, but we'd need to have more than this one report before we reach that conclusion. What are you suggesting?

"For now, a joint operation.

If this is what I think it might be, it's obviously something that you will end up running with.

For now, I would think maybe statistics and case load facts from me and from you, a discreet on-going street surveillance, on the stroll itself by one of your teams.

Let's see if we can nail anything down."

Dave took a deep breath.

"Ok, I'll get my team set up tomorrow.

You get some people working on the data relating to each of these *'missing-in-action'* boys. Bring home whatever you have each night and we'll discuss it. I don't think it will take more than a few weeks to reach a conclusion one way or another."

CHAPTER TWENTY-EIGHT

- October 2005 -

Kenny was ecstatic.

Joel was tuning out to be a gem, though yet, not an ideally polished one.

Perhaps a bit too early to be unquestionably convinced; but still delightfully effective at putting asunder a good deal of the worry and sweat he'd suffered over having to reset the stroll selection process.

Brighter than Robbie, quick to learn, all the while lacking in self confidence, subservient and crying out for affection.

Gay and horny.

What more could one ask for?

Kenny still had to be gentle with Joel during their initial sex acts. That went without saying, but was to be expected, at this early stage of their relationship.

As a result, their one-on-one couplings, did not provide the ideal satisfaction level Kenny had been used to with Robbie. But that would come in time.

Kenny had to build trust, after all.

He pointedly kept his sessions with the kid relatively mild in nature, unfortunately reducing the personal stimulation he got from them in the early stages. On the plus side, the kid was already freely open to being dominated, and Kenny was confident that it would surely work itself out over time.

Despite the short prep time, the October first of the month scheduled kill, had gone as smooth as silk. Joel had been eager for the idea of a threesome when Kenny suggested it and had turned out to be a natural.

Although he knew it soon had to be done, Kenny wasn't quite yet ready to transfer ownership of the Mustang and house to Joel by way of having him sign on the part of the purchaser, the two documents he had prepared and had Robbie sign for that purpose.

That was a big step.

It had to be accomplished for sure, to remove any easily traceable connections between the two of them. However, prior to committing to that, he would require a little more assurance of Joel's absolute loyalty.

He would have to make sure to get that out of the way before the next selection process was to take place to facilitate Joel's choosing of the November target.

A few little things to get tidied up, but all-in-all, reasonably doable.

By the fourth, Kenny had completed his sausage run and clean up.

He now had the rest of the month to get all the parameters set in place for Joel and satisfy himself that he could put any currently remaining concerns aside, for the foreseeable future.

By the end of the month, Kenny was still not completely convinced that he had the kid exactly where he wanted him. However, still uneasy about sending him out in the Mustang before it and the house had been legally put into his name; he went ahead with the ownership transfers anyway.

In mid-October, Dave, Linda, Ed, and the two younger detectives, Julia Arnold and Jack Stewart, who Dave had selected to set up the surveillance of the stroll met, in Dave's office.

Julia was thirty-two, stood five feet six. She had a trim athletic build exhibiting well-formed curves in all the right places. Her thick shoulder-length, dark-brown hair framed cute, if not outright striking facial features.

She wore dark-framed glasses, which seemed to be forever slipping down the bridge of her nose, requiring her to unconsciously push them back into place repeatedly, and spoke with a noticeable English accent.

For work, she normally dressed relatively casually in slacks and a sweater, neither of which were provocative in cut but certainly in their own way, accented her femininity.

Bubbly, full of energy, she didn't like to sit still. She could have a short fuse if she felt unnecessarily pandered to, patronized by a male colleague, or challenged about her ability.

When Julia walked into a room, men noticed.

She was once divorced and was currently in a long-standing relationship with Phil, her engineer boyfriend.

Her partner, Jack, was thirty-six.

Jack worked out daily. His broad-shouldered six-foot-four frame was well muscled. He kept his dark hair short and had chiselled, if somewhat boyish features, which made him look younger than his years,

Handsome, a quiet man of few words, cool, collected and very confident, he was a no-nonsense type, and was not known for his sense of humour. That aside, he was a skirt-chaser of some repute within the department and had a good number of successful conquests under his belt.

When they had initially been transferred in to the squad, primarily due to their very distinct personalities and reputations, Dave had wondered about what chemistry might raise its ugly head if he chose to pair the two of them up.

He'd been a little hesitant to make the move but, in the end, had taken the chance and to date, had never regretted it. Together they made a crack team, accepting of each others' strengths and each readily supportive of the other's shortcomings.

After making the introductions for the sake of the two detectives who had never met his wife, Dave took the lead.

"We are having this meeting so the rest of us can bring Jack and Julia up to speed on what we are trying to accomplish. In late September I tasked the two of them with setting up a continuous around-the-clock surveillance of the *'Boystown'* stroll. This was done to provide us with an idea of exactly what daily activity takes place down there.

I wanted that type of an overview because of a concern that The Ministry of Human Resources brought to our attention at the end of September. At that time, Linda showed me a report..."

Dave reached for a stack of paper sitting on the desk in front of him and scooped up the top two stapled items. He gave one each to his two detectives before continuing.

"...these copies are for you to read when you get the chance.

The long and short of this report suggests, only suggests mind, that a very large number of young male prostitutes have been simply disappearing from the stroll over a long period of time, roughly five years or more.

The numbers suggested in the original report are staggering. Included was a ratio comparing boys against girls involved in the sex trade, to attempt to illustrate just how glaring the rate of disparity is between the two sexes."

Dave paused and turned his full attention directly to the detective team, both of whom were by this point hanging on to his every word.

"After reading the report, both Linda and I felt that there might be a possibly, just a possibility that we might have a serial killer preying on the young males working the stroll."

Dave paused and let that settle in for a few seconds before he spoke again.

"At the time, I suggested that we accept that possibility and that we immediately look deeper into the situation to do our best to either confirm that possibility or dismiss it entirely.

With that in mind, on behalf of the ministry, Linda undertook to immediately review every single file they had opened for boys on the stroll over the past five years and then attempt to trace their current whereabouts if possible; if that was not possible, to garner as much information as they could on when, and under what circumstances they were in when last confirmed to be on the stroll."

He reached out with both hands and lifted the remaining stack of stapled reports that had been resting on the table in front of him.

"These are the copies of what they unearthed.

Linda, Ed and I have had only a brief chance to peruse them prior to this meeting, but we all agreed that they are disquieting in many ways.

To put it mildly, they do not inspire one to conclude that there isn't a reasonable concern as to the possibility that we may be very well looking at the work of a serial killer.

And if so, it is one on a massive and continuing scale.

With that in mind, I want to bring Jack and Julia into the full picture at this juncture.

Before I commit wholly to treating this as a serious investigation, I want all of us in this room to spend the next few days studying the information we now have before us, with a view to forming their own opinion of what it tells us.

As you do this, I want you to keep in mind some very salient facts; for example, we have not had a single reported incident confirming this situation, nor have we had even one body turn up that would indicate that such a thing is happening.

No crime scenes.

No complaints.

No bodies.

Conversely, consideration must be given to the fact that this is a marginal population, one that of necessity exists under the radar of not only the general population, but that of the police. That fact may well tend to explain why we might yet have no crime scenes, no complaints and no bodies, even though a serial killer is in fact at work.

Life on the stroll is populated by a highly transient group of people, many of whom are living day-to-day and as demonstrated by their choice of lifestyle, very likely have no practical fall-back position available to them.

In other words, it is unlikely that they have a better option accessible to them, one that would reasonably allow them to realistically drop out of the picture, without a trace of any kind.

Additional information for us to consider will be coming to us from the ministry as well over that time frame, and Jack and Julia will begin to review our footage of the stroll during this period.

If this turns out to be what we think it might be, it will be one of the biggest investigations this department has ever undertaken. That being the case, I must stress that it is imperative that what is said here between us now, must remain within these walls.

No leaks.

If this is a serial killer, we do not want to send him underground, because if we do, past case studies tell us that its highly unlikely we will ever catch him.

So, we keep what we know between us.

We'll give ourselves a week to reach a decision.

Linda won't be joining us again, as from this point on she will just be providing us with a continuous stream of updates on client files. She will not be directly involved with any investigative efforts that we may decide to undertake.

The rest of us will meet back here, same day and time, next week."

Each passing day had produced additional, more thorough examination of individual files by the ministry for Dave and Ed to study and analyse for any indication of obvious interest and investigative value. Jack and Julia worked overtime throughout, initially reading the reports in-depth and following that up by watching surveillance disks of life on the stroll, to see if they could determine any patterns that might indicate what was going on, one way or the other.

For all concerned the week passed quickly.

When the four gathered for their second meeting, Dave turned his attention to the two young detectives and opened the discussion.

"Ok, you've had a chance to thoroughly digest and access the reports and the tapes. What do you make of it?"

Julia responded.

"We both feel that its not only possible that we have a serial killer preying on the stroll, its probable."

Dave nodded and looked at Ed.

"Well then, that makes four of us.

And that means I've got to take this to the Chief and let him know what's going on. I'll need him to sign off on this before we take the next step.

I'll do that first thing in the morning and in anticipation of him giving me the green light, our next move will be to initiate the departmental investigative procedure on serial killers.

Ed, would you dig out the procedure tonight?

I wrote it up eons ago. I've made some updates since then, but the last time I did it was a couple of years ago and there will likely be new information available today, information that wasn't available the last time I looked at it.

With that in mind, spend your shift garnering any pertinent law-enforcement updates and revising our procedure accordingly.

I want us to be as up to speed as possible as we can be by morning.

Jack, you and Julia each take one of these follow-up reports home with you tonight..."

He selected two of the four stapled reports from the pile in front of him and passed them across the table to them.

"...these are updates to the ministry client reports we already have on hand; ones that they've delved deeper into over the past week. They provide a lot more detail in relation to several of the individuals overviewed in the last batch.

This is all we have to go on, at this stage. Somewhere in this information, is a key to opening the door to the case.

My suggestion would be for you to look for a specific thing when you go through them.

Using the additional information, see if you can nail down the shortest possible window of opportunity our serial killer was afforded, in relation to one or more of the boys. Look for those cases in which we can be sure of a specific timeframe between when they were first noted as having hit the stroll by ministry staff and then the date of their subsequent disappearances.

The ministry street workers check the stroll daily for new arrivals.

The dates these kids are first recorded by them can be expected to be very accurate in relation to when they first joined the stroll. So, pay particular attention to those individuals who we can definitely pinpoint as recent arrivals on the stroll and who then dropped out of sight before the ministry ever had a chance to interact with them for a second time.

What we want to do is to see if we can find a pattern of some kind.

For example, if we have the ministry registering a newbie client who arrived on a specific day, and who, at the initial contact, seemed responsive to their offer of assistance, and then he simply vanishes from the stroll two or three days later; that kind of information alone may give us a starting point for our investigation."

That should keep everyone busy until tomorrow. So, let's put it aside for now and look at what's coming at us.

Ed and I have both taken the FBI course on serial killers.

It was a while back, but I think we both have a fair understanding of what we are facing here.

You, on the other hand haven't and you should be forewarned as to just how difficult this type of investigation will likely be.

Simply put, it is like nothing else you've ever had to deal with. For the most part, normal procedures don't initially work when going after serial killers.

If they did, they wouldn't be able to continue murdering to the point of becoming serial killers.

In the morning we'll give you a general overview as to the investigational techniques that have historically brought the best results. That will at least give you a rough idea of how we will be handling it.

Okay, that will keep us all busy for now. We'll meet again after I've talked to the Chief, to go over the updated departmental procedure and ensure we are all up to speed on the best practices.

Once that's been done, we'll jointly review what pertinent information, if any, we've managed to garner from the additional reports provided to us by the ministry.

Get a good sleep tonight.

You're going to need it."

CHAPTER TWENTY-NINE

- Early November 2005 -

Over the past week, dull rainy days had returned to the Vancouver lower mainland.

Kenny did his best to write his recent moodiness off to the dismal weather, but the fact that he wasn't yet completely confident in Joel's ability to play his part in the first of the month kill, had been primarily responsible.

His concerns in that area proved to be unfounded, however.

The kid's choice of a victim turned out to be a reasonably good one.

And, everything went off smoothly.

By the afternoon of the fourth of the month, Kenny was finished with the sausage run and his cleanup. He had come out of his funk. His outlook for the future seemed considerably brighter than it had at any point since he'd had to put Robbie down and therein face the prospect of a fair amount of uncertainty and risk.

Everything seemed to be back on track again.

As he watched the personal effects turning to ash in the burning barrel, Kenny found himself looking forward to spending some quality time working on Joel sexually, with the aim of improving his gratification of the one-on-one nightly sessions during the time before they executed the December first quarry pickup.

On the morning of the fifth of November, Dave, Ed, Julia and Jack were once again gathered together around the small conference table in Dave's office. The aroma of fresh coffee filled the room.

In front of them, each had a revised copy of the departmental procedure manual on serial killers Ed had recently worked on. They had received their copies the day before and both Jack's and Julia's versions appeared well thumbed.

A large stack of file folders containing the ministry reports received to date sat in front of Jack with a smaller pile in front of Julia.

Dave had had his meeting with the Chief and he'd been given the green light to open an initial investigation of the situation. At the time, the Chief had asked if Dave wanted any additional manpower for the project, but Dave had declined the offer, explaining that at this stage he had sufficient for his needs. Instead, he said he'd keep the Chief posted as to necessary manpower allotments, if it appeared they were in fact dealing with a serial killer and as the investigation proceeded.

The Chief's interest had been definably piqued, and he'd instructed Dave to keep him in the loop.

Once the four of them had imbibed in a few sips of coffee, Dave lifted his own copy of Ed's rewrite.

"Ok, let's get started.

We've all had a chance to go over this and get up to speed on the latest methods and we have the Chief's agreement on proceeding to confirm what we are up against.

Ed has done an excellent job in updating our original manual to include the very latest methods of investigating serial killings.

First thing now, is for us to be sure we are all on the same page as we proceed with our investigation.

So, welcome to *'Serial Killer 101'*.

The topic of serial murder occupies a unique niche within the criminal justice population. In addition to the significant investigative challenges they bring to police agencies; serial murder cases tend to attract an over-abundance of attention from the media, mental health experts, academia, and the public.

Over the past several years, there has been significant, independent work conducted by a variety of experts to identify and analyze the many issues related to serial murder. Unfortunately, during that period there has not been any real concerted effort to reach a consensus between the police agencies and all those other experts, regarding these matters.

As luck would have it, the FBI very recently hosted a multi-disciplinary symposium in San Antonio, Texas. It took place from August the twenty-ninth 2005, through to September second, 2005.

The goal of the Symposium was to bring together a group of respected experts on serial murder from a variety of fields and specialties, with the intention of identifying any commonalities of knowledge.

One hundred and thirty-five experts attended the five-day event.

Those in attendance also included representatives of police agencies who had successfully investigated and apprehended serial killers as well as officers of the court, who had judged, prosecuted, and defended serial killers; and members of the media who's job it is to inform and educate the public when serial killers strike.

All were given an opportunity to share their expertise.

The attendees also reflected the international nature of the serial murder problem.

They came from ten different countries on five continents.

The agenda encompassed a variety of topics related to serial murder. These included common myths, definitions, typologies, pathology and causality, forensics as well as the role of the media, prosecution issues, investigative Task Force organization, and major case management issues.

Each day included panel discussions, case presentations, and discussion groups which addressed a variety of topics related to serial murder.

Courtesy of Ed, we can now take advantage of what came out of that symposium.

As at least some of this is new to all of us, I'm going to run over the pertinent points to ensure that as we begin, we share a basic understanding of what is ahead and how we are going to deal with it.

Any questions so far?"

Heads shook, and Dave continued.

"First a little background.

Serial murder is neither a new phenomenon, nor is it uniquely North American. Serial killers have been reported around the world for over a century. That said, serial murder is a relatively rare event, estimated to comprise less than one percent of all murders committed in any given year.

While rare, it repeatedly stimulates a macabre interest in the topic - one that far exceeds its scope.

A good portion of the general public's knowledge concerning serial murder comes from how it has been depicted in the movies we see. The problem with that is that in these, the story lines are created to heighten the interest of audiences, rather than to accurately portray serial murder.

By focusing on the atrocities inflicted on victims by *'deranged'* offenders, the public is captivated by the criminals and their crimes, which tends to lead to confusion as to the true dynamics of serial murder.

Historically we police had been subject to the same misinformation, albeit from a different source - the use of anecdotal information. Professionals involved in serial murder cases, such as investigators, prosecutors, and pathologists rarely have had more that a limited exposure to serial murder. Their experience is often based upon a single murder series, and the factors in that case are then often improperly extrapolated to other serial murders.

As a result, certain stereotypes and misconceptions take root when it comes to the actual nature of serial murder and the characteristics of serial killers.

A growing trend that compounds the fallacies surrounding serial murder is the *'talking heads'* phenomenon. Given creditability by the media, these self-proclaimed authorities profess to have an expertise in serial murder.

They appear frequently on television and in the print media and speculate on the motive for the murders and the characteristics of the possible offender, without being privy to the facts of the investigation. This often impairs law enforcement's investigative efforts.

The relative rarity of serial murder combined with inaccurate, anecdotal information and fictional portrayals of serial killers in the past has resulted in creating many common myths and misconceptions regarding serial murder.

For example, contrary to current belief, most serial killers are not reclusive, social misfits who live alone. They are not monsters and may appear quite normal. Many hide in plain sight within their communities. They often have families and homes, are gainfully employed, and appear to be normal members of the community.

Because many serial murderers can blend in so effortlessly, they are oftentimes overlooked by both the police and the public.

Serial killers are not all white males.

They come from all racial groups.

Serial killers are not always transient.

Most serial killers have a very defined geographic area of operation. They primarily conduct their killings within comfort zones that are defined by an anchor point, a residence or a place of employment. A small number of serial killers have much larger comfort zones, usually due to their employment, for example long-distance truckers. The difference between these types of offenders and other serial murderers is the nature of their traveling lifestyle, which provides them with many zones of comfort in which to operate. While it is commonly believed that serial killers cannot stop killing, some can and do.

However, these are relatively rare.

Any ability to do so is normally due to events or circumstances in their lives that inhibit them from pursuing more victims. These can include increased participation in family activities, sexual substitution, or other diversions.

It has been intimated that a serial killer must be either insane or an evil genius. In truth, serial killers tend to suffer from a variety of personality disorders, including psychopathy and anti-social personalities. When caught and facing trial however, most are not adjudicated as insane under the law. As in other populations, serial killers range in intelligence from borderline to above average levels.

Ask anyone if all serial killers want to be caught. They will inevitably say yes, but that is not the case.

When killing for the first time, its true that most are inexperienced. It seems to be the case that while most serial killers plan their offenses more thoroughly than other criminals, the learning curve is still very steep. They must select, target, approach, control, and dispose of their victims. The logistics involved in committing a murder and disposing of the body can become very complex, especially when there are multiple sites involved.

But they tend to gain experience and confidence with each additional kill, often moving on to succeed with few mistakes or problems.

As serial killers continue to offend while avoiding capture they can become empowered, feeling they will never be identified. As the series continues, investigations have determined they may begin to take shortcuts when committing their crimes. This may cause them to take more chances, which in turn may lead to them coming onto police radar.

It isn't that serial killers want to get caught; its simply that they feel that they cannot be caught.

As much as it would be great for us to take for granted that there is a single generic profile of a serial murderer, that's not the case. Serial killers differ in many ways, including their motivations for killing and their behavior at the crime scene.

That said, certain traits are common to some serial murderers.

These traits and behaviors are consistent with the psychopathic personality disorder. They include sensation-seeking, a lack of remorse or guilt, impulsivity, the need for control, and predatory behavior.

It's therefore vital for each of us to understand psychopathy and its relationship to serial murder.

Psychopathy is a personality disorder which is manifested in people who use a mixture of charm, manipulation, intimidation, and occasionally violence to control others, to satisfy their own selfish needs.

The degree of psychopathy an individual possesses can be measured through clinical assessment. This is done by measuring a distinct cluster of personality traits and socially-deviant behaviors of an individual.

These fall into four categories: interpersonal, affective, lifestyle, and anti-social.

The interpersonal traits include glibness, superficial charm, a grandiose sense of self-worth, pathological lying, and the manipulation of others.

The affective traits include a lack of remorse and/or guilt, shallow affect, a lack of empathy, and failure to accept responsibility.

The lifestyle behaviors include stimulation-seeking behavior, impulsivity, irresponsibility, parasitic orientation, and a lack of realistic life goals.

The anti-social behaviors include poor behavioral controls, early childhood behavior problems, juvenile delinquency, revocation of conditional release, and criminal versatility.

The combination of these individual personality traits, interpersonal styles, and socially deviant lifestyles are the framework of psychopathy.

They can manifest themselves differently in individual psychopaths.

Research has demonstrated that in those offenders who are psychopathic, scores vary, ranging from a high degree of psychopathy to some measure of psychopathy. However, not all violent offenders are psychopaths and not all psychopaths are violent offenders. If violent offenders are psychopathic, they can assault, rape, and murder without concern for legal, moral, or social consequences.

This allows them to be in absolute control, to do what they want, whenever they want.

The relationship between psychopathy and serial killers is particularly interesting.

Not all psychopaths become serial murderers. Rather, serial murderers may possess some or many of the traits consistent with psychopathy. Psychopaths who commit serial murder do not value human life and are extremely callous in their interactions with their victims. This is particularly evident in sexually motivated serial killers who repeatedly target, stalk, assault, and kill without any sense of remorse.

However, psychopathy alone does not explain the motivations of a serial killer.

Understanding psychopathy becomes particularly critical to law enforcement during a serial murder investigation and upon the arrest of a psychopathic serial killer. The crime scene behavior of psychopaths is likely to be distinct from other offenders. This distinct behavior can help us in linking serial cases.

Psychopaths are not sensitive to altruistic interview themes, such as sympathy for their victims or remorse/guilt over their crimes. They do however, possess certain personality traits that can be exploited. Specifically, their inherent narcissism, selfishness, and vanity. Exclusive themes in past successful interviews of psychopathic serial killers focused on praising their intelligence, cleverness, and skill in evading capture."

Dave noticed that despite holding their interest and the fact that the young team of detectives were making copious notes, Julia was beginning to fidget and more than a few eyes were beginning to glaze over.

He glanced up at the clock and smiled.

"Right, although the topic is interesting it tends to be dry when belaboured.

Let's break for lunch and meet back here at one."

They were all back in his office at a quarter to the hour.

Dave took this as a positive sign. He picked up where he'd left off.

"Motive.

It normally plays a large part in any investigation. Know the motive and you are on your way to knowing your perp. Most homicides are committed by someone known to the victim, so police immediately focus on the relationships closest to the victim. This is always a successful strategy to use in most murder investigations.

Unfortunately, motive in the case of a serial killer can be hard to nail down.

Most serial killers are not usually acquainted with or involved in a consensual relationship with their victims. Subsequently, we need to understand that motive can be extremely difficult to determine during a serial murder investigation.

A serial murderer may have multiple motives for committing his crimes.

Their motives could evolve both within a single murder as well as throughout the murder series. Any classification of motivations should be limited to observable behavior at the crime scene.

Even if a motive can be identified, it will not necessarily be helpful in identifying the serial murderer. Utilizing investigative resources to discern the motive instead of identifying the offender can derail the investigation. Investigators should not necessarily equate a serial murderer's motivation with the level of injury.

Regardless of the motive, most serial murderers commit their crimes primarily because they want to.

That said, serial killers can be motivated by many things.

These include anger demonstrated as rage or hostility towards certain subgroups of the population or simply with society. Or, criminal enterprise in which the offender benefits in status or monetary compensation by committing murder that is drug, gang, or organized-crime related.

It could also be for financial gain, where the offender benefits monetarily from each death. Examples of this would be *'black widow'* killings, robbery homicides, or multiple killings involving insurance or welfare fraud.

Ideology could be the motive; the intent to further the goals and ideals of a specific individual or group by way of the commission of multiple murders. Examples of these include terrorist groups. *The 'power/thrill'*, during which the killer feels empowered and/or excited when he kills his victims. Psychosis resulting from the offender suffering from a severe mental illness and who kills because of that illness during which they may experience auditory and/or visual hallucinations. Or, paranoid, grandiose, or bizarre delusions. And, often there is a sexually-based motivation, driven by the sexual needs and/or desires of the offender.

The serial killer selects a victim, regardless of the category, based upon availability, vulnerability, and desirability.

Availability is explained as the lifestyle of the victim or circumstances in which the victim is involved, which facilitates the offenders access to the victim.

Vulnerability is defined as the degree to which the victim is susceptible to attack by the offender.

Desirability is described as the appeal of the victim to the offender. It involves numerous factors based upon the motivation of the offender and may include issues dealing with the race, gender, ethnic background, age of the victim, or other specific preferences the offender predetermines."

Dave paused and took a sip of his now cold coffee, then leaned back in his chair and stretched.

In a few words, Julia quietly articulated what, albeit to varying degrees, all four of them were thinking.

"Needle in a haystack comes to mind."

Ed gave a thumbs-up and grinned.

"Nicely put."

Dave nodded and let out a deep sigh.

"OK, that's enough for now about who we are looking for.

Before we move on to how we are going to structure our investigation to find this bastard, let's shift to assessing what we have to go on so far.

Julia, you and Jack have been looking into that, so I'll turn the floor over to you."

Julia set her right hand on the files in front of her.

"Well, we haven't had a lot of time, but we've allotted what we had to two specific paths. The reports from the ministry and the round-the-clock surveillance we were able to get in place.

The reports based on the client files took priority.

We managed to go back chronologically over the last two years, with a view that those would probably be the most helpful. Having done that, we have been unable to trace any of the teens in the files we brought with us today.

They've simply vanished into thin air. On the stroll one day and gone, without a trace, shortly thereafter."

She paused to let them think that fact over and then continued.

"The sixteen files Jack and I have brought today have been selected out of the hundreds of client files that were opened by the ministry over the last two years only. That's as far back as we have had been able to go within the timeframe we had to make our search.

Of those, the seven I have in front of me are the ones that tell us the most. The ones in front of Jack are from the same period but appear to provide less firm information in them, than mine.

Keeping in mind what you said about trying to find any patterns and specifically trying to nail down a timeframe over which the victims are going missing, we have had some success, I think. It's early days yet of course but Jack and I believe that we have found at least a couple of starting points.

The ministry street-teams are very good at spotting new arrivals on the stroll and quickly registering them.

Without detailing the specific parameters that we had set for ourselves in our examination of each case, something we did with the knowledge that these may well change as the investigation develops, we did come up with a couple of indisputable facts.

Firstly, the boys we are concerned with are being picked up toward the end of each month and the selections took place over no more than a three-day period.

In each case, the victims selected were not seen on the stroll again after the first of the following month. It's important to note that each of my cases here, strongly confirms these facts and that, while the remainder, those in front of Jack, may not completely support that supposition; they do not don't dispel that probability."

She paused and turned toward Jack.

"As far as the second revelation goes, I'll pass that one on to Jack. He's done most of the reviewing of the surveillance coverage of the stroll itself."

Jack cleared his throat and nodded.

"The second interesting points we discovered, came about from the review of the surveillance material coupled with some follow-up interviews and discussions, held with the ministry street workers.

What we learned there seems to indicate that our killer is likely selecting only what are known on the street as *'recent clients'*. The ministry confirms that in the main, these boys tend to range between twelve and seventeen, have little, if any street smarts and are by far the most vulnerable.

We have also been able to at least nail down a few additional parameters about the victims.

For example, the most common service these kids supply to the *'Johns'* is oral sex. A vehicle pulls into the curb opposite them and beckons them over. After a short conversation, they hop into the passenger seat and the car pulls out.

Apparently, they find a quiet spot nearby, laneway or what-have-you and that's were the sex act takes place. This transaction is usually consummated quickly, and these kids are often back on the stroll in less than an hour, frequently in half that time.

In a minority of cases, anal sex is the soup-of-the-day and this usually takes a little longer.

On very rare occasions, a boy or boys, may be picked up for a *'Party'*, which can mean they will be gone for several hours or even over-night.

The deep furrows etched into the space between Dave's eyebrows seemed to disappear for the first time since the meeting began.

"Right. Well, its not a lot but at least it gives us something concrete to move forward on.

Okay, I'll have to give the Chief and update on what we have, first thing in the morning.

Ed, I'd like you to sit down with Jack and Julia at the same time and put your heads together. See if you can summarize and confirm exactly what we have so far and determine what kind of additional tools we need to bring into play now, if any. That may include additional manpower in various forms.

Tomorrow at eleven, we'll meet back here and share and discuss the remainder of the updated information we've found in the FBI symposium conclusions - specifically, those related to the procedures and structure we intend to use for the expanding investigation.

CHAPTER THIRTY

- Mid-November 2005 -

Grooming Joel meant Kenny needed to dedicate a fair amount of time with the kid during the day, assessing his needs with the goal of ensuring that the kid was generally happy with the new arrangement. Within a couple of weeks, he had a good idea of what would be required.

Initially they spent a few hours each day out and about enjoying various entertainment activities together before returning to the east-end home to relax, before getting into the sex sessions.

The video games he'd set up for Robbie seemed to appeal to Joel as much as they had to Robbie and kept him happily engrossed for hours. He found that whereas Robbie had leaned more toward alcohol, Joel preferred pot, and Kenny ensured that there was a good supply on hand.

Joel proved to be an eager learner and Kenny's early assessment of the kid's subservient sexual proclivity was correct.

The kid wanted attention so badly, he readily welcomed the contact, was very eager to please, and pretty much willing to try anything.

Recently Kenny had begun to use restraints during their couplings and had introduced the casual use of the choke chain.

Kenny was still taking it easy, letting the kid get used to complete subjugation in progressive steps. His initial restraint seemed to be proving worthwhile. The kid had a fabulous body and their sessions were becoming very hot.

Kenny felt that by the end of the month any remaining small kinks would be worked out.

On the morning of the sixth of November, Ed, Jack and Julia had joined Dave in his office and settled in around the small conference table.

As the two young detectives arranged several stacks of files in front of them, Dave opened the conversation.

"I've updated the Chief. I can't say that he's pleased that we've come up with the idea of having a probable serial killer working his turf, but he is ready to give us whatever we need to get the job done.

Before we get to deciding on what help we might ask him for, I want to go over the updated information from the recent FBI symposium as it relates to their conclusions regarding optimum procedures and structure needed to ensure a swift and successful conclusion to our problem.

The symposium participants listed the initial identification of a homicide series as the primary investigative challenge leading to the successful apprehension of a serial killer.

Generally, the first indication that a serial murderer is at work has resulted when two or more cases were linked by either forensic or behavioral evidence.

In most cases identifying a homicide series is a relatively simple task, when it takes place in rapidly-developing, high profile cases, which involves low-risk victims. That's because those cases are usually reported to the police upon discovery of the crimes and draw immediate media attention, which often results in the location of both crime scene and behavioral evidence.

Our case does not currently fall into that category.

It falls into a more challenging type.

Identifying serial killings involving high-risk victims which may be taking place in multiple jurisdictions can be very difficult.

There is no question that our victims maintain high-risk and transitory lifestyles. It is also quite likely that our crime scenes may be found in jurisdictions other than our own."

Dave briefly changed topics.

"Luckily for us, we have already been able to conclude that we have a probable serial killer at work. In our case, that means that we have already accomplished the symposium-listed primary investigative challenge.

But we still need to prove it, completing all the missing blanks in the five 'w's' and 'h' of any investigation that are required to facilitate the laying of criminal charges so that the perp can be taken off the streets and locked up.

So, lets keep those uppermost in mind as we move forward.

The who, the what, the where, the when, the why, and the how."

He paused and let his words sink in, before returning to the discussions of the symposium conclusions.

"OK, there is a recognition that these types of high-profile investigations present a multitude of leadership challenges for police forces, at all levels. They stress that it is imperative that strong management throughout the chain of command continually reinforce the supreme goal of the investigation - that being the arrest and prosecution of the offender.

During the investigation of serial killers, the roles of both investigators and supervisors needs to be clearly delineated.

At all times, the investigative function is the primary mission. All other activities have to be in support of that mission. To succeed, the actual investigation must be directed by competent homicide investigators, those that have previously demonstrated both the experience to direct and focus the investigative process.

While police administrators often think they should run these investigations themselves because of their importance, that approach simply doesn't work. Instead their sole responsibility should be to ensure that the investigators who know what they are doing have the resources to do their job.

Additionally, the job of any supervisors involved have to be primarily concerned with acting as buffers between investigators and the other levels of command."

He paused again.

"I've discussed this with the Chief and he has agreed with this premise. He's directed that I assume the position of lead investigator and that the three of you will head up whatever structure we feel we need manpower-wise. That means if you find it necessary to have the last say over any senior ranks who may partake in various areas over time, so be it. He'll see it happens."

Jack and Julia looked at each other.

Julia responded.

"Are you sure we should be an integral part of the team to run this? You have several senior detective teams you could have picked to do that. There is bound to be at least some backlash?

Dave smiled.

"I also discussed that with the Chief, as he raised the same concern.

I told him I wanted you two and I told him why.

You've worked homicide exclusively for the past two years and have been involved in this case since the inception. More important to me is the fact that you've both done well so far. I see no reason to make a change at this critical time in the investigation. If I were to select a more senior team, it would mean that they would have to be brought up to speed and we really don't have the time to play that kind of game now.

Based on what we now know, this guy is going to kill again before the end of this month.

The Chief's response was short and to the point.

You might say it was a test of his previous commitment to the process as laid out by the symposium, which I was surprised to learn, he has found time to read in its entirety.

He said, and I quote.

'Inspector Richards, I've designated you as the lead investigator on this case, and if these are the people you want in place, I support your decision."

Dave sat back in his chair and gazed across the table at them.

"Do either of you have a problem with my choice of personnel so far? If so, I'd like to hear it."

He let the silence fill the room for several seconds before continuing.

"Right, now that that's out of the way, lets get back to boning up on the symposium conclusions and get about catching this bastard.

We have to consider the various strategies outlined regarding what police executives may consider when preparing for these intense serial killer investigations. Although you, as investigators, will not be directly involved in the decisions around this, I will have to keep a keen eye on it, so I want you to be familiar with them.

So, here is an overview of what the brass has to do to get and keep things running smoothly:

When necessary, complete memorandums of understanding between different law enforcement agencies when they arise. This is necessary in order to obtain mutual support agreements and commitments of manpower, resources, and overtime.

Identify all resources that may be needed during the investigation and maintain up-to-date lists of available resources.

When it becomes necessary, create good working relationships with other departments, through networking, scheduled meetings, and joint training prior to calling on them.

Provide on-going training opportunities in the latest techniques and methods of homicide investigation.

The brass also has to see to it that all communication relating to any administrative issues are restricted to management personnel of the various agencies, so as not to distract investigators. Keep the intense pressure, often resulting during these high-profile investigations, away from the investigators as it tends to decrease logical decision-making.

The rest of the brass responsibilities are their concern and the Chief has indicated he will look after that end.

While these investigations are definitely a team effort, only the Task Force team leader and his inner circle will make decisions relating to the investigative process.

And what the hell is a Task Force you may ask?

Well…for now its the four of us, but that is probably going to change, and it will change rapidly. We'll discuss that next, but for now, let's break for lunch and meet back here at two."

Everyone was back on the dot of two. Julia was the first there and was still munching on a sandwich when others arrived

Dave got right to it.

"Task Force…

…once a serial murder series has been identified, it is important to create a Task Force. This unit that will be responsible for the many operational and investigative issues critical to the successful establishment of an organized investigation.

These types of investigations often end up involving more than one legal jurisdiction. We are not at the stage where we know that to be true in our situation; however, we should plan for that eventuality in the likelihood that it will occur.

The FBI symposium studied this concept in depth and they've concluded the following:

Right from the start, a lead police agency for the Task Force should be designated and assume the primary investigative role. The choice of that lead organization needs to be based upon several factors. Those include the number and viability of the cases, available resources, and investigative experience. Once established, subsequent law enforcement forces involved in the investigation must be represented by someone within the Task Force.

The chosen model for an effective and reliable investigation identifies a lead investigator and co-investigator, who, regardless of rank, are given complete control of the investigation. These investigators review all incoming information, collate the information, and assign leads.

I will assume the responsibility of lead investigator. Ed will act as co-investigator.

We will be bumping up one of our in-house sergeants to acting Staff/Sergeant to free us up from the majority of our normal duties in the interim.

As the lead investigators we will handle all crime scene activities and related leads, as each incident may be interwoven. It will also be our shared responsibility, all four of us, to ensure relevant information is distributed to the entire Task Force.

If the flow of incoming information becomes unmanageable due to an excessive influx of investigative tips, the lead investigators will delegate this responsibility to an experienced investigator or team of investigators, who will act as lead control officers.

Julia, you and Jack will fill that spot.

It will be up to you to choose which personal you want for each task as it arises. I want to emphasise that those choices will not be questioned or challenged in any way by anyone of the same or higher rank and that you should not necessarily use seniority as a guide in making your selections.

We do not want people who lack the skill or ability to do an effective job or who obviously have no desire to be involved in a major case in our Task Force.

Step one in the setup of the Task Force is for the lead investigators to implement a preplanned Task Force model. We will need to establish an information management system to track tips and leads in the case. We will have a dedicated computer system that should be able to account for the idiosyncrasies of the investigation while being flexible enough to handle any contingency.

All personnel we take on board must be familiar with its operation, and it needs to be be pre-tested to insure viability under investigative conditions.

While sufficient manpower is primary to the success of a Task Force, the overwhelming consensus from the attendees at the symposium was that the assignment of excessive numbers of personnel to the investigation may be counterproductive.

A small group of experienced homicide investigators, under the direction of the lead investigator(s), is far more effective than massive number of less experienced investigators or investigators who hold only previous experience in different areas of criminal activity. That is not to say the expert personnel will not be brought in for specific tasks as and when necessary."

When Dave glanced up from his notes, he saw that both Julia and Jack had heads down and were scribbling furiously on notepads. Julia was having her usual problem with her glasses and on several occasions, she had one hand pushing them back into place while the other was working her pen.

"Am I going too fast for you?"

The two heads across the table shook in the negative but didn't lift from the notepads in front of them.

Dave nodded to himself and continued.

There should be a distinct division of responsibility between the administration and investigation of the case.

The task of running the investigation is the sole responsibility of the lead investigator.

The Task Force administration is solely responsible for all the necessary support, including procurement of equipment, funding, and manpower. It will require and achieve authority for priority requests for services, from the forensic laboratory and all other service providers.

That said, the lead investigator and the administrators of the Task Force must have a close, cooperative working relationship despite the need to maintain their own areas of responsibility.

Jack, you and Julia will be responsible for selecting and assigning staff. One of your first picks should be that of choosing a person to act as liaison officer between us and the families of the victims. They may well have information that will prove crucial to our investigation.

You should be thinking about who that will be soon.

You will need someone in this spot who will raise the level of confidence in these families in the force's competency and determination to bring the killer to justice to the point that they will be supportive of the investigative efforts.

An investigator with exceptional interpersonal and communication skills is needed and his sole responsibility will be to maintain constant contact with the families, keeping them apprised of the progress of the investigation and any pending press releases that may be contemplated.

As the investigation grows you will also select someone who can be assigned to act as liaison with the numerous support entities both inside and outside the Task Force, including the prosecutor's office, the forensic laboratory, the medical examiner's office, and other law enforcement agencies. Prior to that you need to draw up a list of available experts in specific forensic and related fields and open liaison with them for use in the investigation.

Initially and while the flow of information is manageable, one individual can be assigned to multiple liaison duties.

I think that's enough for now.

I will be seeing the Chief before he leaves today regarding the provision of an adequate working space for the location of the Task Force. I've outlined what would be ideal, and he says he has some ideas. He told me he would confirm it one way or the other before the day was out.

I'll go over all the details of what we are going to need in equipment etc. once we have a better idea of what kind of space we've been allotted.

We'll need to get in there and get set up as quickly as possible. Hopefully we can get started on that first thing in the morning.

CHAPTER THIRTY-ONE

- Late November 2005 -

With six days still left before month's end, Joel was coming along nicely, very nicely indeed.

For the first time since he'd had to dump Robbie, Kenny felt fully confident that the problems that situation had created had been well and truly dealt with.

If anything, in some ways, Joel was proving to be the better of the two cut-outs.

He had become as subservient as Robbie and surprisingly even more eager when it came to the sadomasochistic aspect of their sex sessions, the parts Kenny enjoyed the most by far.

He was mentally quicker than Robbie, a fast and eager learner and, big bonus as far as Kenny was concerned, he kept both himself and the house cleaner than Robbie had.

The fact that he was a pothead played both ways. It was something that could go to excess if Kenny didn't keep an eye on it, but it also meant that Joel was usually high and laid back, making him even more easy to deal with.

As month-end approached, Kenny found himself relaxed and looking forward to the pick up of the next target.

When leaving the east-Vancouver house to return home just before midnight on the twenty-ninth, he told Joel to go easy with the weed the next day, pointing out to the kid that he would be driving that evening and could not risk the chance of being caught by a cop while driving stoned.

Joel was in love with the Mustang and Kenny knew that the possibility of losing his licence would be a strong deterrent.

The kid had taken the warning to heart. When Kenny arrived the next afternoon, Joel told him he hadn't indulged since he got up and it was clear to Kenny that the kid was straight.

After he sent Joel off in the Mustang on the evening of the thirtieth,

Kenny experienced anticipation and was understandably a little nervous, but that was to be expected.

The excitement of what was to come, coupled with the adrenalin pump he got each time before a new victim selection went down, inevitably made him a bit hyper each time it occurred.

Besides, he had added an additional safety factor into the method of the stroll pickup.

He'd given the kid a cell phone so that now, if anything untoward happened during the operation, they could immediately communicate, providing Kenny with better control but still allowing him to remain at arms-length from the act.

The phone had been provided with the proviso that it was only to be used when the pickup of a target was underway and only to call the home number of the east-side house to advise of any problems.

At all other times, Kenny kept the phone in his possession.

The three weeks between the sixth and the twenty-eighth of the month had flashed by in a blur for the members of the Task Force. The first week had been especially daunting.

There had been a good deal of overtime, all authorised without question by the Chief.

During that period, all their efforts had gone into moving upstairs into the area the Chief had ordered repurposed for use by the Task Force and getting it set up with desks computers, dedicated phones and office supplies.

It had turned out to be better than Dave had hoped for. The Chief had given them the exclusive use of the executive boardroom, which was located on the top floor and just two doors down the hall from his own office.

The room was large and unusual in the old building, had one long wall encompassing very large windows, providing natural light and a fairly good view over the building tops and out to the bay beyond.

It had fallen to Ed to oversee the equipment sourcing and supervision of the setup while Dave, Julia and Jack kept up with the investigation.

By the end of week two, they had added three civilian clerks to the team, two data-entry and one who would work general phones and secretarial. No additional police staff had been deemed necessary at that point, although there were several extra desks, phones and computers stacked against one wall, because they would probably be needed before the case was closed.

It was at the start of the third week before the four of them could get together and sit down as a team at the boardroom table, which had been moved out of the center of the room and placed against the windowed wall.

Everyone looked a little worse for wear, but eager to get back on track. The room had its own small kitchen and the smell of fresh coffee wafting up from their freshly poured mugs, added to the general ambiance.

Dave riffled the pages sitting in front of him and then set a selected sheet on top.

"I know you're all chafing at the bit to discuss recent developments, especially Ed, who has been out of the loop for the last couple of weeks, but before we do that, we have to deal with the remaining procedural overview regarding the proper operation of a Task Force.

I'll make this as painless as I can, but I urge you to turn your minds fully to it, so we can get it out of the way and get back to what this entire exercise is all in aid of."

Both Julia and Jack pushed the files in front of them aside and took out notepads. Dave waited until they had finished and then started in.

"As the investigation continues, the manpower requirements of the Task Force will increase for various reasons, including increasing the number of investigators and support staff.

As previously discussed, the use of fewer personnel may be more effective.

Therefore, restraint must be practiced by Task Force administrators to avoid the use of excess personnel. The lead investigator is in the best position to recognize when additional personnel are needed. The administrator's responsibility is to provide the authority for the permanent or temporary reassignment of the requested number of personnel to the Task Force.

When additional personnel are needed to expand the Task Force, the reassignment should not be temporary. To insure continuity of investigative information, it must be for the duration of the Task Force. That does not mean that specific, short term needs, such as a neighborhood door-to-door canvass or road block canvass, personnel cannot be reassigned temporarily to complete that specific task and then be returned to their normal duties.

In either event, the arrival of new personnel should be pre-planned, and a detailed case briefing provided. This briefing should include an explanation of the specific assignment, the work hours, and such details of the investigation that apply to their assignment, expected standards for report completion, and a complete list of contact numbers for report purposes.

It goes without saying that such personnel must be cautioned about discussing any case-sensitive information with anyone outside of Task Force members.

Arbitrary rotation of Task Force personnel must be avoided wherever possible, as it tends to negatively affect the continuity of the investigation, for obvious reasons. Rotation of personnel should only occur if requested by the investigator, or emergency coverage issues.

If for some reason the Task Force is disbanded and subsequently reinstated, the original investigators should be utilized."

Dave paused and looked up to check to make sure he wasn't going too fast for the notetakers.

As both Jack and Julia took advantage of the lull to grab a quick swallow of coffee, he continued.

"Information sharing among the Task Force members is paramount. We all need to be kept in the loop from this moment on. That means daily briefings, especially when there are different work shifts. Periodic summary briefings will also be necessary for managers and patrol officers. These can be accomplished via e-mails or at roll call and must be conducted by investigative personnel.

With that in mind, I'm now authorizing a liaison member to be brought onto our team, so the rest of us do not have to worry about it when liaison becomes necessary.

Julia, that falls within your bailiwick, you and Jack get that individual into place before the end of the day.

The facilities supplied by ViClas should not be overlooked during the investigation".

Dave paused and stretched briefly before moving on.

"A common problem in serial investigations occurs when data is not entered into the electronic database in a timely manner. Useful leads are lost when investigators are overloaded with information. Your computers are set up with a computerized case management system. It will effectively organize and collate lead information. It can analyse a tremendous amount of data.

Having sufficient personnel committed to ensure that data is being promptly recorded into the system in a timely manner is paramount. The system will also provide us with an up-to-the-minute overview of all the pertinent investigative information to date.

For that reason, we have two civilian data-entry clerks working with us and Ed has already given them their marching-orders.

For our part, we must see to it that all reports are written as soon as each investigative lead is completed. If reports are not finished by force members before the end of their shift, the lead investigator may not have time to review them. This will lead to a back-log of reports, containing pertinent and timely investigative information.

You don't go home until your reports are done.

All rough notes should be maintained and entered into evidence.

Next, let's look at resource use.

For some reason, the wide range of the analytical tools available to police are typically under-utilized at the onset of a serial murder investigation. Due to the voluminous amount of information characteristic of high profile investigations, critical lead information is often lost, therefore the implementation of a tested and reliable case management system, as previously discussed, coupled with competent analytical staff, is imperative.

Specialists in various areas will be required to offer critical support to the investigation by developing timelines on victims and suspects. That falls to you and Julia again Jack. Its up to you to see that information is sorted, compared, and charted to provide timely lead information. To handle that aspect, you will need a review team of experienced investigators to assist in filtering through the information as it is gathered. I have authorized bringing on one more detective team for that purpose. You need to see that they are also in place, before the end of the day. They will need to be brought up to speed and will be permanently assigned to the Task Force for the duration."

Dave set his notes down and smiled.

"That's it. Any questions you have about the topics I've covered over the past few days?"

There were none.

"Right, then let's get Ed up to date on what we've learned since he temporarily dropped out of the loop. Jack, I'm tired of talking and you're a man of few words, why don't you do that."

That brought a smile to three faces, although it seemed to go right over Jacks head.

He looked down at the single sheet in front of him briefly and then responded in typical fashion, nodding his head toward Julia before quietly but clearly annunciating each word.

"We have been able to further narrow the pickup time for the victims.

After going over a third year of ministry client files, Julia and I sat down again with two of the ministry street workers and between us concluded that these boys are not only being taken toward the end of the month, but in fact on the last day of each month.

This, regardless of the day of the week that falls on.

We have been able to nail down an ironclad pattern.

Its gets even better.

We now have twelve separate occurrences in which the streetworkers made face-to-face contact with the victims in the early evening hours of the last day of a month and subsequently recorded the fact that they had not been seen since on the stroll.

Additionally, a review of all the other missing kids in no way refutes that pattern.

Twelve is just too many to be just a coincidence."

Ed grinned and clapped his hands.

"Wow, we now have the exact date and time of the next killing! In the words of Arthur Conan Doyle's Sherlock, *'the game is afoot'.*"

Dave nodded.

"Very likely, unless of course he decides to change his MO."

Julia shook her head

"After at least three years of sticking to it…not very likely."

CHAPTER THIRTY-TWO

- Wednesday, November 30ᵗʰ, 2005 -

Kenny's well planned and choreographed world took a nose-dive on the last day of the month.

That evening began well enough.

He arrived at the east-end house shortly after five. He found Joel straight and up and eager for the night's activity.

They talked for a half hour or so, until Kenny felt the kid was settled down enough to carry out his mission. He then gave him the cell phone and sent him on his way to the stroll.

Twenty minutes later, while Joel, driving the Mustang, made his first pass along the string of tempting jailbait, he thought he spotted a familiar face, that of Jonathan Hunter.

Hunter, a fourteen-year-old aboriginal, had been billeted with him in his last foster home placement and although they had only been together for a couple of months before Joel had taken off, the two of them had become friends.

Hunter, who was gay and had recently come out, had been kicked out by his parents and upon his arrival at the foster house, had looked up to Joel as a sort of mentor. The two of them had quickly bonded and in short order were enjoying regular sex together.

Before Joel had done his bunk from the home, he'd told Hunter all about his plans to head for the stroll, so he could be out on his own. At the time, Hunter had begged to go with him, but Joel had counselled against it as he liked the kid, and until he was sure that he could make it himself on the stroll, he didn't want to have the responsibility for looking after the kid as well.

Joel made a quick swing around the block for a second pass and sure enough, it was a sodden Jonathan standing by himself in a door alcove.

Half obscured by the drizzling rain, shoulders hunched, the kid looked miserable.

Joel wheeled the Mustang into the curb and quickly sent the passenger window down.

"Johnny. You crazy bastard! What the hell are you doing out here. C'mon, get into the car out of the rain and warm up."

The kid raised his bowed head and squinted through the tangles of his drenched and matted hair. He paused for a second and then a grin formed on his face and he literally raced to the door and dropped into the passenger seat as Joel shut the window and turned up the heat.

"Christ man. I been looking for you for days. You said you were coming here. I been looking for you everywhere. I got a couple of guys picking me up, but I was scared shitless."

Joel turned his attention to the rear-view mirror, snapped his turn signal on and pulled back into the traffic.

"Easy my man, you're in good hands now. Let's just get out of this hellhole and find a place to park and I'll explain everything to you."

Hunter, who had been introduced to the wonder of booze at age nine, took note of the bottle of rum resting prominently in the console between the bucket seats and reached for it.

Joel caught the move out of the corner of his eye as he accelerated and quickly placed his right hand firmly over the bottle.

"No man. Don't touch that."

A hurt look filled Hunter's face as he reluctantly withdrew his hand.

"I could really use a shot or two…I'm freezing man."

Joel softened his voice as he replied.

"Not from that you don't. Its not what it looks like. The bottle has been doctored.

Just chill and give me a chance to find us a place to talk and I'll explain everything. Relax, everything is going to be all right."

Five minutes later Joel pulled the Mustang into a commercial alleyway and shoved it into park.

The heater was pumping out warmth, the kid had stopped shaking and his breathing, which had been laboured, seemed to be settling down.

Joel shifted in his seat and rested his right hand on Hunter's left shoulder and squeezed.

"Ok, so what's the story. Did you get booted out?"

Hunter shook his head.

"No, that bastard was making me blow him daily and I just got pissed off with it. I stood for it for as long as I could and then three days ago I took off and came looking for you.

Why weren't you here. You said you would be here.

I didn't know what the hell to do when I couldn't find you. I haven't eaten in two days…"

Joel raised his hand to the kids neck and squeezed gently.

"Easy, I was on the stroll until a short while ago.

Then I got lucky with a date. Got myself a sugar daddy. Young guy, good looking too.

Now I've got it made, a house of my own, anything I need, including this car and all the weed I can smoke."

Joel grinned.

"I'm sorry I wasn't here for you, but you can forget that now. You're coming with me and everything will be great, you'll see."

The windows inside the Mustang were all fogged up from the moisture. It wasn't until the cop car had pulled up behind them had turned on its overhead light bar that the two of them were even aware of its presence.

A second later a flashlight beam hit the driver's window.

Joel flinched and whispered to Hunter.

"Shit. Ok, just stay cool. Let me deal with this."

He hit the switch and the driver's window went down.

The cop let the beam of his light shift across from the driver to the passenger.

"Is the car yours?"

Joel nodded.

"Let's see your driver's licence and registration and some ID from your friend there."

Joel hauled out his wallet and passed over his DL and then reached across Hunter's legs and opened the glove compartment to pull out the vehicle registration. Hunter pulled his wallet out and took out his birth certificate. Joel took it from his hand and handed the documents through the open window to the cop, who glanced at them briefly and then turned on his heel and headed back to the marked patrol unit.

"Sit tight, I'll be back in a minute."

Joel put the window up and watched in his outside mirror as the cop walled back to his car. When he'd disappeared inside he turned to Hunter.

"Nothing to worry about. We haven't done anything wrong. I doubt that prick at the foster home has reported you missing. He's not very likely to want to have you picked up, considering what he's been making you do. But even if he has, they won't have told the cops about it yet.

He's just going to run the plates and check us out. It's all legit. He'll be gone before you know it."

In the patrol unit behind them the cop behind the wheel turned to his younger partner, who was riding shotgun, and handed him the documents.

"Run the plate and both names for wants. The driver is young, sixteen. Not the usual *'Chicken Hawk'*.

His partner frowned.

" *'Chicken Hawk'*?"

"Ya, that's what we call the Johns who go after these young guys. They're usually in their forties and like to go for the young fresh meat.

Even more interesting, the car is registered in his name.

Strange when you realize that I've seen the driver before not that long ago and he was working the stroll himself.

Seems to have come up in the world suddenly.

I think its worth doing a check card on them as well."

The younger cop nodded.

"Ok, but on rollcall they said that we were only to worry about vehicles who picked up young ones and then left the area with them.

These two are only a couple of blocks away. I know that we have three cars doing these checks tonight, but according to dispatch all three of us are now tied up with vehicles.

I'd hate to find out later that we missed the big one because all three of us were busy."

His older partner frowned.

"True, but this stop just seems weird.

For one thing they were just talking when I reached the car. I've been working car five for over five years. In that time, I've made hundreds of these checks. Experience tells me that if it had been a normal pickup, I would have expected to find the guy in the passenger seat with the driver's cock in his mouth or his ass by this point.

These kids were not stopped for sex and are both young. They don't fit the usual profile. It won't take that long for at least one of us to clear.

Do the check card."

Dispatch came back with no wants or warrants.

Ten minutes later, car five had cleared the alley and was back in service and watching the stroll.

Joel let out a sigh of relief and looked over at Hunter who was putting his ID back into his wallet with shaking fingers.

"See. No problem. Now let's get out of here and find somewhere quieter to talk."

Joel pulled out of the lot and turned in the opposite direction that the marked patrol unit had taken. Fifteen minutes later he pulled into the deserted parking lot of a park, well away from the stroll.

The inside of the Mustang was roasting by this point and he shut down the fan to minimum and shifted in his seat to look at Hunter.

"Ok, I'll make a call to my daddy to let him know what's going down. Just sit tight and relax."

He took out his phone and dialled the number of the east-end house. Kenny, who had begun to wonder about the delay in Joel's return, heard the phone ring and went into the kitchen to answer it. He waited until the recording clicked in and when he recognized Joel's voice in response he picked it up and interrupted him.

"What's wrong?"

Joel's voice came back down the line.

"Some exciting news. I found a buddy of mine from my old foster home working the stroll. He's done a bunk from his foster home.

Un... I think you're gonna like him. He's young, just fourteen, but he and I had a thing going and I know he's into having a good time.

I told him he could stay with me. It will be great, the three of us will have a ball."

Kenny froze for a few seconds.

Joel's voce came back on.

"You still there?

He'll be no problem and we can have a permanent set up for the three of us. It can be a regular thing. No more having to pick up off the stroll for our threesomes..."

Kenny closed his eyes as his mind raced.

In the background he heard another voice. He couldn't catch exactly what was said.

"That him talking?

Haven't you offered him a drink?"

Joel responded.

"Hell no, we don't need to put him out. He's up for it man, trust me. He's just a little nervous. A cop stopped us and checked us out and..."

Kenny cut him off abruptly.

"A cop stopped you?"

Sensing his displeasure, Joel responded quickly in hopes of easing the tension.

"Ya, no big deal. It happens pretty regular down here. He didn't hassle us or anything and he let us go, no problem."

Kenny knew he had to cap the conversation quickly to give himself time do some heavy thinking.

Not wanting Joel to pick up on his concerns, he did his best to sound upbeat.

"Oh, OK then. Look this may be for the best. I won't be able to stay tonight. I've got some business stuff to clear up. So, you go ahead and bring him home with you and have some fun. I'll talk to you tomorrow."

An obviously disappointed Joel replied.

"Shit, I wanted you to meet him.

How come you can't stay?

Can't you at least hang on for another ten minutes or so? We should be able to be there by then."

Kenny bit his lip and tasted blood.

He sucked in a deep breath and did his best to keep his voice level.

"No, I can't. It's a bit of an emergency. I was on the way out the door when you phoned.

I was going to leave you a note. Now I won't have to.

I gotta go.

I'll give you a call tomorrow."

Kenny hung up the phone.

In less than five minutes he was in his truck and headed for home.

Dave, Ed, Julia and Jack were ensconced in the room rented to hold the surveillance equipment that was in place to cover the activity on the stroll. All four were working four-to-midnight shifts and they expected to be pulling down at least some overtime.

Dave had arranged for the stroll area car, number five, to be temporarily seconded to the Task Force. In addition, he had borrowed two marked units from district two, to back them up. On parade the patrol constables manning the three two-man units had been taken aside to be briefed on their temporarily assignment.

Julia had taken them into the coffee room and given them their instructions.

Without going into any detail, she had told them what was expected of them.

They were to work on an allocated tac channel, not their normal radio channel. They were to observe the stroll from a distance and watch for all pickups of the younger kids made overnight. When they spotted one, they would in rotation, notify the other two units and then follow any vehicles involved in same, and *'IF'* these vehicles drove more the six blocks away from the stroll, pull them over and check the occupants.

They were seconded and not to concern themselves about any other duties, short of *'need assistance'* calls by other nearby units and instructed to leave unchecked, any vehicle that parked close to the stroll and stayed put in the area.

Only those vehicles which left the stroll and continued to drive after passing six blocks were to be given scrutiny.

If they ran into anything that seemed unusual, the borrowed units were to first discuss the situation with car number five, whose occupants were well versed in the normal activities of the stroll, and *'If* 'car five felt something wasn't right, they would then pass on the information by radio on the tac channel to the Task Force line, for any follow-up.

She did not advise them that Dave, Ed, she and Jack had also parked four unmarked units in the alley behind the building they were set up in and were prepared to use them to make stops as well, if all the marked units found themselves tied up at the same time.

It was deemed unlikely that they would need to step in and Dave preferred that marked units make all the stops, as such checks were not unusual in the area and they were far less likely to arouse any undue suspicion.

CHAPTER THIRTY-THREE

- Early Hours of December 1st, 2005 –

Kenny was fit-to-be-tied by the time he got home.

Over the next several hours, random thoughts continually circled around in his mind.

The bottom had fallen out.

In the wink of an eye everything had gone sideways.

What the hell was he going to do now to straighten it out?

He could go back to the house and dope the kid and bring him back home and do him. For that matter, he could dope them both up and kill the two of them. Stupid bloody Joel, too damn smart for his own good. It would serve him right.

No!

He couldn't do that. The cops had stopped the car. They knew the new kid was with Joel. If he didn't turn back up on the stroll, it would probably raise a red flag for the cops and they would have a direct line to Joel. If they got to Joel, he would spill the beans for sure and drag me into it.

Kenny was restless, couldn't sit down.

After several drinks, he gave up carrying the glass and bottle around with him and in frustration threw the glass against the wall where it shattered.

Ignoring the mess, he continued to stalk around the house, now drinking directly from the bottle.

Round and round his inner voiced ranted about the unfairness of it.

To have this happen now, after all the years of careful planning.

To have reached his goal, everything falling perfectly into place, only to have it snatched away from him.

Shortly after midnight, realizing that he was accomplishing nothing other than getting himself thoroughly drunk, he managed to get hold of himself. He put the bottle aside and forced himself to shift away from feeling sorry for himself and instead determined to concentrate on how to recoup the achievement of his goal.

He made two sandwiches and poured himself a glass of milk. Not because he was hungry but knowing that he needed nourishment and something in his stomach to soak up the excess booze he had consumed. By one in the morning he was finally able to think clearly and manage to examine the complexity of the quandary he found himself in.

The kid had to go back onto the stroll and he had to go back soon.

Now, how the hell was he going to swing that when Joel was so pleased with himself for getting the kid in the first place.

If it had been Robbie, it would have been easy, he'd just tell him to do it and he would, without question. But this Fucking Joel was something else.

He was too damn smart for his own good and I know damn well that he'll balk at taking the kid back unless I can find some pressing reason for that to become necessary.

And I need to do that fast.

He was still wide awake and pacing uncontrollably around the house at four in the morning.

Kenny picked up the phone and dialed the house in east-Van.

It rang five times before it was picked up and, in a sleep-filled voice, Joel said hello.

Kenny kept his voice level and with an upbeat lilt.

"Hey man, sorry to wake you. Sounds like you two had a great session."

Joel's words came out slurred and Kenny realized that it was more than sleep clouding his brain.

The realization pissed him off, but he left it alone.

Maybe having him high was a good thing. He wouldn't be thinking all that quickly.

"Look, I've been thinking about what you said last night.

You know about this new guy having taken off from his foster home and being only fourteen and all. That being the case, the ministry is probably going to be putting out a pick-up for him with the cops. If they do, the cops will come after you cause he's underage and you sure as hell don't want to have that happen. If they checked you earlier like you said, that means that they can tie you directly to him.

Look, what you need to do is to take him back to the stroll now so…"

Joel managed to respond.

"Shit, he's not gonna want to go back and I want to keep him with me, anyway. He's a good kid and great in bed and…"

Kenny had to take a deep breath before he could respond in a light tone.

"Hey man. I'm not saying he has to go back permanently. Hell, if after a few days no cops come looking for him on the stroll, then sure, you can bring him back.

I just don't want the cops hanging an underage endangerment type of charge on you.

You don't want that, do you?

It'll only be for a few days…"

It took a few seconds for Joel to mull that over and respond. As he waited, Kenny was tempted to push harder but thought better of it. Instead, he waited, silently if impatiently, and finally got a rejoinder.

"No shit…I don't want that. It would screw up everything. Okay, I'll do it, but he isn't going to like it."

Relieved, Kenny quickly brought the conversation to a close.

"OK man, get him in the car now and take him straight back to the stroll. Don't put it off for another moment or everything we've got going for us will be over.

It will only be for a few days and you can give him enough coin to keep himself safe until you pick him up again."

Kenny hung up.

Ok. For now, the immediate risk was tackled.

But that still left several problems that needed to be dealt with over then next few days.

Son-of-a-bitch!

No kill on the first of the month.

He'd needed that so badly emotionally.

Now all this other shit to deal with.

He should have never taken Joel on!

He had done his best to fix the immediate threat for now. Hopefully Joel would do as he was told and not fall back asleep. The kid was obviously high. He could see it getting even worse if the idiot somehow managed to get stopped by the cops for a second time, while he was taking the kid back to the stroll.

That could really fuck things up.

Kenny was exhausted and completely stressed out.

He told himself that he had done what he could. For the short term it was now out of his hands.

If Joel got the kid back to the stroll and himself back home without incident, then, maybe, just maybe, this whole debacle could be put behind him.

Yes, there were other problems to deal with, but he didn't need an intermediary to solve those. He would look after them himself.

He felt a little better. There was hope.

For the first time in several hours he could see at least the possibility of light at the end of the tunnel.

He climbed into bed for some much-needed sleep.

It was just before two in the morning when car five spotted the Mustang drop off the young native kid back onto the curb. As the car drove off, they reported the fact by way of the tac channel.

Dave looked over to Ed, who was had just put a check against the list in front of him and tossed his pen on the small table in front of him.

"That's the last one. Everyone is now accounted for."

Dave stifled a yawn and nodded. You could cut the cloud of disappointment filling the room with a knife as he responded.

"Ok, tell them to pack it in and head for headquarters. We'll debrief in the Task Force room."

The four Task Force members were the first to arrive at the station.

Everyone was tired, and the mood was glum. Dave had anticipated the sense of letdown and he moved immediately to do what he could to pull the rest of the group up out of the doldrums.

"Ok, we didn't get what we were hoping for. But, that aside, it appears that we did manage to see to it that another kid didn't get added to our killer's list of victims.

Who knows why?

Maybe it was simply due to our presence on the street. Perhaps we spooked him.

Maybe something just went wrong on his side of the equation.

Either way you see it, we came out on top.

What matters is that we don't appear to have another body out there somewhere.

If it was because we upset his applecart but putting a monkey-wrench into his little game, well that has got to be a real upset for him. Based on what comes out of the observations and what we already have, I'm going to be starting work on a profile for him.

Although we still don't have any crime scenes or bodies to work from, I think, after tonight, we will have enough to at least get a basic profile for him blocked in.

If it was because something went wrong for him outside of our project tonight, that means he's likely off base in his carefully laid out plans to do a kill on the first of the month. Based on what we know of him so far, I'd say that this is going to be very upsetting for him. He's been riding a high for the last several years and suddenly he's no longer in control.

A serial killer who is not in control makes mistakes and mistakes are what are going to help us bring him down.

In a few minutes the uniforms are going to arrive.

They don't know what we know, so they're not going to be disappointed in tonight's operation. It behooves us to be upbeat when they arrive and to see to it that whatever intel we and they have garnered by way of it, gives us enough information to allow us to advance our investigation.

I can't emphasize this enough.

These people are street cops. They will look at things with a different set of eyes and those eyes are experienced eyes. Something of what they have to say during the debrief could well break this case wide open.

Pay attention to them.

Don't lead them, let them express themselves in their own way.

So, everyone, grab a coffee, and brighten up.

When the patrol units arrive, they need to be carefully debriefed. I know that what went down tonight will tell us several things that we didn't know before, and every one of those details can make a difference.

Let them know that we appreciate the effort they've provided and listen carefully to what they have to say. Make sure that you take notes of what they saw and be sure that their reports are complete and ready for computer entry in the morning."

There was a knock at the office door and the first uniformed team entered the room.

Ed got up to pour them fresh coffees and when they had their preferred mix in their steaming mugs, he took them aside to a corner of the room to a smaller table and sat down with them.

Repeating the scenario, Julia took the next two and Jack similarly greeted the third team.

Dave retired to his own desk and set to work on sketching the first rough profile of their perp.

He was the last one out of the office and managed to climb into bed beside Linda's warm body just before five in the morning.

He knew he was in for a short sleep.

He had set a meeting for the Task Force members for eleven in the morning.

That would give the data entry clerks time to have entered all the information gathered overnight into the system, providing an up-to-date account of what they had learned to date.

CHAPTER THIRTY-FOUR

- Morning of December 1ˢᵗ, 2005 -

-

Kenny was badly hung over by the time he managed to drag himself out of bed at ten.

As his head began to clear, he chastised himself for losing his self control, for drinking too much and made a mental note to lay off the bottle until things were back on track.

After a couple of painkillers for his head and a hearty breakfast, consisting of a heaping plate of sausages, eggs and toast, he felt much better.

He sipped black coffee as he turned his mind to solving his current dilemma.

First up, was a call to Joel to find out if the kid had been returned safely to the stroll.

Kenny needed confirmation of that fact before he could confidently apply himself to working out how he was going to sort out the mess he'd inherited by way of Joel's idiotic move of picking up the kid in the first place.

Joel answered on the first ring.

"Hello."

Kenney took measure of the kid's voice and was relieved to find it seemingly unclouded by any recent trace of indulgence in weed.

"Is he back on the stroll?

The response, as if anticipated, was immediate.

"Ya, he was really pissed but I got it done. It went down fine."

Kenny felt a weight lifted off his shoulders and he gave an audible sigh of relief.

"OK. I want you to get the placed cleaned up. Change the bedding. We don't want any trace of him left in case the cops pick him up and then come calling on you. I'll be over at the usual time tonight."

"Right. OK. I'll do that.

Look, the kid is scared shitless down there. How long does he have to stay there, before he can come back here?"

Kenny had expected such an inquiry and had his answer ready.

"Like I said last night. A few days, to see if the cops come nosing around. You'd better hope that doesn't happen, because if it does, they will be visiting you shortly thereafter. "

He lightened the tone of his voice.

"Did you give him enough cash to help him make it through the wait?"

"Ya, but its not the cash so much that he's worried about.

It's just the stroll. He's likely to be bullied.

I talked to him about that and asked if the street workers had already spoken to him and registered him. He said yes, he'd talked to them, but he gave them phony information.

I told him if he was scared, he should talk to them again and register, because I know if he does that, they will at least give him a place to say overnight and see that he gets fed. They have to do that because of his age.

Was that OK?"

Kenny thought about it for a second, before answering the question.

"Sure, that's a good idea. He should give them his correct ID when he does that. Once he's in the ministry's care, the cops will lose interest in him and maybe this whole mess will just blow over.

Does he know how to keep in touch with you?"

"Ya, I gave him the number here."

"Alright when he calls, tell him to do that and tell him to keep his mouth shut about last night. Tell him if all goes well and no cops hassle him, you'll come get him and take him home with you in a week or so.

I'll see you tonight and we'll talk more about it."

After he hung up, Kenny sat staring blankly at the phone for several minutes.

It might be ok in the short term. The cops might not even see any reason to talk to the kid. And once he's under the protective wing of the ministry, if he keeps his trap shut, he's not going to attract any of their attention.

He's going to have to die of course. That goes without saying, and the sooner the better. He knows too much to be left sitting around.

So, two problems of immediate concern.

Get rid of the kid and deal with Joel.

He didn't have a lot of time to figure out how to deal with the kid.

So that had to be the immediate priority.

Joel he could handle in one of two ways.

He could simply kill the little bastard. But that would mean starting all over yet again to find a replacement cut-out. Experience had shown that hadn't proven all that simple. Nor had it worked out very well, the last time around.

Or, else he could see if he could salvage him.

If he was going to try to salvage Joel, he would first have to find a way to kill the kid without Joel knowing.

It was obvious that he was infatuated with the kid. If the kid went with the ministry and kept in touch with Joel, then a possibility could probably be arranged, which would allow for me to snatch the kid unbeknownst to Joel, then drug him and take him home and do him.

Of course, Joel would be unset by the kid's sudden disappearance, but Kenny was confident he could then step into the role of an empathetic-supporter and easily deal with that little problem.

Practice made perfect and by this point he would have no difficult in mimicking that kind of emotion.

It could go either way.

Whatever.

Offing the kid was the immediate problem.

The situation no longer seemed overwhelming to him. These were things he was quite capable of dealing with.

All things considered, Kenny was beginning to feel the return of control over his situation.

The data entry clerks had been working since just before nine and by eleven that morning, the four Task Force members had arrived at the office.

A little bleary-eyed, they were all were slurping coffee like there was no tomorrow.

That aside, everyone seemed to be eager to begin the assessment of the up-to-the-minute computer-generated overview of the case intel.

The printouts arrived just before eleven-thirty.

Dave handed them around the table.

"OK, let's just take the time to read through these individually before we put our heads together and jointly discuss them line by line.

Make notes and highlight anything that strikes you as interesting."

Jack was the last to put his pencil down.

The sound of rasping highlighters and pencil scratches had been the only sound within the room for a good half hour. Dave was encouraged to see that everyone had made several pages of notes.

"OK. Let's get started, Ed, you go first and then we'll go around the circle. Give us your highlights and we'll discuss each point. If we agree that we have any new fact nailed down securely or we have something we think is worth following up, I'll make a note of it.

Once we've all had our say, we'll go through what intel I've listed as a result. I'll use the facts discerned as part of working up a profile and we'll divvy up between you three for follow-up on what points need further investigation."

Ed and Julia had finished their input shortly before one o'clock. They broke for lunch and were back at it, starting with Jack's notes by one forty-five. Dave then finished his in about ten minutes, as many of the things he had noted either for follow-up or confirmed, had already been raised by one or more of the others.

He then pushed aside his copy of the printout and his rough notes and placed the lined notepad upon which he had made his final two lists directly in front of him.

"Right, lets go over what we know first and then we'll shift to the points that need further investigation.

We know we have a serial killer working the stroll. We know he has been active for several years. Even though he didn't succeed last night, most likely for one of the two reasons I mentioned earlier, we know that he has, at least over the past couple of years, picked up his targets on the first of each month. We know that our man lives driving distance from the stroll, very likely somewhere in the lower mainland area.

While we don't know for sure why he missed last night, courtesy of the check card and information provided by the uniforms in car five, we all agree that the Mustang they checked is very likely a vehicle of interest. We have also spotted it on our own October surveillance operations and it has been seen by car five on several occasions in the area before that. Because of the check done last night, we've now got solid info on both the car and its occupants.

I'm convinced that this car is being used to service our killer.

For several reasons I won't belabour now, I don't believe that the driver of the Mustang is our killer. He's too young for one and according to car five, he was himself working the street not that long ago.

That said, all four of us think this vehicle is in fact being used to pick up and deliver the victims to our killer and the only reason the kid who was in the passenger seat last night ever made it back to the stroll alive, was because car five pulled it over.

A total of six vehicles were followed further than six blocks from the stroll. The Mustang being one of them. Each of the other five ended up at private homes or at cheap hotels and/or motels.

Every kid that had been picked up was back on the stroll within a few hours. The last one back was the kid dropped off by the Mustang.

I think it's more than probable our killer panicked when he found out that the Mustang had been checked. That the young guy driving the car is just a go-for who was told to take him back to the stroll.

That the car check by car five saved that kid's life.

If I'm right, while we haven't identified our killer, we've finally found ourselves some substantive leads toward identifying him.

Jack, you get on to your contact at the ministry. Talk to the streetworkers. Find out all you can about the two kids who were in the mustang.

Julia, you take the Mustang. Trace the ownership and confirm the registered address. Have a covert look at the address and see if you spot the Mustang. Get what information you can on who currently owns the property and its sales history. Get the telephone number and printouts of incoming and outgoing calls covering the past year or so.

This may well be our crime scene, something we badly need if we are going to build a case once we identify this scumbag, so no direct contact with neighbours or anything at this point, stay under the radar.

Ed, you go over the files we hold on our suspected victims.

Focus on common characteristics. Let's see if we can't pinpoint exactly what our killer looks for in his targets. Also eyeball the Mustang by way of past check cards. We may be able to trace other drivers back over time. The kid behind the wheel last night was relatively new to the scene, the Mustang had been seen for some time, so we might expect to find a history identifying previous drivers.

As well, check the surveillance tapes and find out if we have any footage of the Mustang being used to specifically pick up any of our previous victims. That would remove all doubt and tie it directly to the crimes."

They'd been sitting for a long time. Dave's ass felt like it was part of his chair.

He leaned back and stretched.

"Any questions?"

Three heads shook.

Dave grinned, looked at Ed and quipped.

"All right...to quote Sherlock again, this time properly, *'Come Watson, come. The game is afoot'.*"

It lightened the atmosphere as Dave had hoped.

Everyone had a good laugh.

With a sigh of relief, Dave heaved himself out of his chair.

"Off you go.

I've got a dental appointment for this afternoon, so we'll meet back here in the morning, nine sharp."

CHAPTER THIRTY-FIVE

- Afternoon of December 1st, 2005 -

Kenny arrived at the house in east-Van in late afternoon at five on the dot.

He found Joel somewhat subdued. Apparently not sure what he had done wrong, but aware that Kenny wasn't pleased with him.

Good!

Kenny checked throughout, finding the house tidy and no trace of anything left in relation to the night before. Satisfied, he plunked down a bag containing a bottle of rum and a two-liter of coke on the coffee table in the living room and took out the contents.

He poured them each a drink, handed one to Joel and waved him into a chair.

Putting a concerned frown on his face, Kenny took a sip from his glass before he spoke.

"I've been thinking about this kid. I know you two are friends and all, so I want to help him.

Did you tell him to go to the ministry like I told you?"

Joel perked up a little.

"Ya, he was OK with that. He's scared shitless of the stroll. He was afraid that they would send him back to the same foster home, but I told him to tell them about the asshole who was diddling him there, and they put him into a different one.

He went there last night.

It's a place out in Richmond. He called me after he got there.

He doesn't like it. He wants to come back here."

Kenny nodded.

"Ya, I don't blame him. But that's not in the cards for a week or so."

Kenny took another sip and then put his glass down on the table.

"Do you think he would be happier somewhere else. Someplace on his own. I could get him a hotel room for a week.

Maybe close by here. That way you could go and visit him and keep him company now and then."

Joel, as Kenny had foreseen, welcomed the suggestion.

He grinned and nodded vigorously.

"Ya, that would be great. Like I told you he's a good kid. We could maybe both visit him, he wants to meet you."

Kenny smiled.

"Well, that's settled then.

I feel much better about things.

Get hold of him and tell him what we have in mind.

I'll make the arrangements to get a place for him set up on the way home tonight and you can pick him up and take him there.

If the kid's unhappy we should do it as soon as possible. Tomorrow morning would be good if he can manage it.

Just make sure that he doesn't tell anybody about the plan before you pick him up and don't go to the foster home itself. Arrange to meet him somewhere away from it."

Joel was half out of his chair.

"Can I call him and tell him now then?"

Kenny laughed.

"Sure, at the same time, you might as well arrange a time and place with him for the pickup in Richmond as early as possible in the morning for tomorrow.

Go ahead and do it now.

And when you get off the phone, get out of those clothes.

I'm as horny as a three-peckered rat."

Dave had been working long hours recently and although he would much rather have been back at the office working on his rough profile, the dentist's drill soon cleared his mind of thoughts about the case and brought him back to the real world.

Dave hated dentists.

By the time he was entering his driveway at home, the freezing was coming out and the damn thing was bloody sore.

He and Linda had not been seeing much of each other of late, due primarily to his need to work varying hours and the longer shifts needed to keep on top of the investigation.

He had arranged with her to take off a little early, so they would have the time to sit down to dinner with the kids as a family for a change.

Linda was understandably interested in the progress of the investigation and he had been keeping her current when their paths crossed. Dave was looking forward to bringing her up-to-date once the kids were finished eating and were off watching television with Blessica.

After a couple of glasses of wine with the meal, the damn tooth had quieted down to a dull ache and Dave could live with it.

He and Linda discussed the stroll investigation while the two of them cleared up the kitchen, Dave loading the dishwasher as Linda first carried the dirty dishes over to the sink and then wiped the table down.

By the time the cleanup was done they had shifted topics and Linda was sharing some of the current dilemmas she was having to deal with at work.

The household routine was well set by this time and domestically things were going very smoothly.

It felt good to have enough time to think about things other than the case and Dave felt fully relaxed by the time the two of them climbed into bed.

Their lovemaking over the past few weeks had been both sporadic and rushed and without voicing their feelings, both were eager to take advantage of this chance to change that.

They made love at a leisurely pace for what seemed like the first time in ages and afterwards, mutually satisfied with a job well done, they both slipped into deep sleep.

CHAPTER THIRTY-SIX

- December Second, 2005 -

On the way home the night before, Kenny had stopped long enough to get a place for the kid set up and then called Joel to let him know its location.

It was a dump, located on the east side, that Kenny had driven past many times in the past.

From what he'd seen previously, it was primarily used by hookers to turn tricks, and druggies living on welfare.

A dilapidated complex.

It was clearly on its last legs.

When he'd entered the office, the wizened old lump of shit behind the counter hadn't give him a second look.

He'd paid cash for a week and was able to get the unit he wanted.

Located at the end of the complex, in a dark alcove and far from the office and inquisitive eyes.

He figured, that, when the time came, he would be able to keep an unobtrusive eye on it from the parking lot of the corner store, which was located just across the road.

That was were he was parked at shortly after eleven in the morning of the 2nd.

Ten minutes later he watched the Mustang swing into the motel lot and pull into the parking space in front of the chosen unit.

Joel got out and walked back to the office on his own.

A few moments after, he came out carrying the key and made his way back to the passenger side of the car.

Kenny could make out the silhouette of a second person sitting there.

The door opened and the kid, wearing a hoody and with a backpack draped over his shoulder got out and he and Joel went inside.

A few minutes later, Joel came out alone and climbed into the car.

Kenny watched him pull away and head back in the direction of the east-Van house.

It was done.

Kenny lit a cigarette, smoked it leisurely and then tossed it out his window, before pulling out of the store lot and heading for home.

There, he planned on having a nap and some R&R before he headed back for his nightly visit with Joel.

He was a little early arriving at the east-Van house later that day.

The Mustang was parked in front and Kenny went down to end of the block and turned, then swung into the lane and pulled his truck into the garage at back.

Joel was surprised to see him, but eager to talk.

"Hey, I dropped Johnny off at the motel. He's happy to be on his own, but the place is a real hole. Its damn near as bad as being on the stroll.

The phone in the room doesn't even work."

Kenny nodded.

"Ya, sorry about that. I was trying to find something off the beaten track.

Not the best, but it will only be for a short while.

You don't think he'll do something stupid and fuck off out of there do you?"

Joel shrugged.

"Well like I said, he didn't think too much of it, but I figure he'll stick there. He's excited about seeing me regularly and is looking forward to meeting you."

Kenny smiled.

"Good, well, we'll let him settle in and then you can go visit him in a couple of days and make sure he's doing OK."

Kenny, who normally spent several hours when he visited, begged off early, blaming a headache and by midnight he was pulling into the motel parking lot.

The place looked half deserted. There was no one around.

He parked in the poorly lit space in front of the end unit and got out.

Using his key, he entered without knocking.

He was a little taken aback to find himself face to face with the kid, who was listlessly sitting on the sagging bed with has back propped up against the scarred headboard.

Kenny hadn't been expecting a Native.

Not really his type, but then beggars could not be choosers after all and on the positive side, siting there with his mouth hanging open in surprise at the sight of me, he was deliciously young and vulnerable looking.

Besides, he needed a supply of special meat for his grinder to do his next sausage run.

And, here it was on the hoof.

The kid had obviously not been expecting company and looked scared as hell.

Kenny kicked the door closed behind him, grinned broadly and held up a brown paper bag.

"Joel said you were unhappy with the room. I'm the friend he told you about.

He had some running around to do, so I've come to pick you up and take you back to his place.

He won't be home for an hour or so. He's going to give me a call when he gets back."

Kenny waved the bag.

"So, I've brought along something for us to drink to help pass the time."

Forty-five minutes later the kid was laid across the bed, out like a light.

Kenny stuffed all his personal things into his battered backpack and took it out to the truck, doing a quick look around as he walked and put it into the passenger seat.

It was all clear. No one was around.

He returned inside and dragged the kid up off the bed and onto his feet. He was more than a little wobbly and Kenny had to damn near carry him to the tuck, but as he took all his weight while shoving the semi-comatose form into the back of the cab, Kenny was surprised at how light he actually was.

Just over a half-hour later Kenny, humming happily to himself, was pulling into his own garage.

His confidence was fully restored.

Not a worry in his mind.

Things were back under his control.

As he went to work, unconcerned, he found himself idly wondering if brown meat was going to affect the taste of his next batch of sausage.

It was an intriguing thought.

He'd soon know the answer to that.

He wasn't going to take time much time with the Native kid. The sooner he was finished with him, the better. He'd only play with him overnight and then off him and deal with the disposal at first light.

Maybe catch a few winks here and there.

By ten after nine in the morning on the 2nd, Dave, Ed and the detective team were back sitting around the table, notebooks out and open in front of them.

Surprisingly they all looked well refreshed and were clearly pleased with themselves.

The vibes Dave was picking up from his team were good.

He had every reason to anticipate some good news and he wasn't to be disappointed.

Julia started the ball rolling. She was clearly eager, no preliminaries, right on topic.

"The Mustang is registered to Joel Hurst, lives in an older bungalow at an address in east-Van. He's the sixteen-year-old kid who was behind the wheel when it was stopped. I've scoped out the place and found the Mustang parked out front on the street.

I could see activity inside. Looked like just one person. I couldn't swear to it, but based on what we have so far, I would say that it was the Joel kid.

Interestingly, the house is also registered in this kid's name and both transfers of ownership are recent, done on the same day in October of this year."

She paused for a couple of seconds, shoving her glasses back up into place on the bridge of her nose, glancing from face-to-face around the table to allow those facts sink in, and then carried on.

"It gets better…I looked back at the history on the car and the house and found that both of them had been also previously been owned by the same individual, one Robbie Brody, who just happened to also be sixteen years old, when he purchased them in December of 1998.

Coincidences?

I don't think so.

I checked further back on the ownership of both, before Brody took possession, and the owners of the house and the Mustang, historically, are both different; I couldn't find any link between the two before then.

As he was detailed to follow up with the ministry on both Brody and Hurst, I passed this information on to Jack immediately, and I'll let him take it from here."

Jack cleared his voice.

"It turns out both Robbie Brody and Joel Hurst have other commonalities.

They were both sixteen and working the stroll before they became the proud owners of the Mustang and the house. Down and out, penniless, hooking, and living day to day with no real family contacts. They are also similar in physical appearance.

Most importantly, Robbie Brody seems to have disappeared off the stroll, in early December of 1998.

Its pretty hard to overlook the fact that these two homeless kids didn't just happen to each find a bundle of cash on the street, sufficient to buy the house and car.

It follows that these kids were obviously selected by our serial killer to run interference between him and the stroll. He chose them, set them up and used them to do the physical pickups of his target victims.

If our killer has indeed been using these two to do his stroll pickups, then the killings have been going on since at least 1988, meaning we are going to have to go back much farther than we have so far, in our search for victims.

First, our perp used Robbie Brody and then, I believe one can reasonably conclude, for some reason he needed a replacement for Brody. I figure he likely killed him and then promptly replaced him with Joel Hurst.

Julia has more for us."

He nodded to her and she stepped in.

"Just regarding the telephone records for the house. I used my contact with the company there and I expect a printout by tomorrow."

Dave shifted his eyes to Ed.

"How did you make out?"

"Julia also passed her info on the Mustang to me when she got it. No previous check cards on it, but we know from car five that its been around for a long time.

Ministry street works say they've seen it prowling around off and on for years. They also say that the Robbie kid was driving it then.

Courtesy of Julia's info, I did hit pay dirt going back over the surveillance coverage with the car as my target. Although we only have footage from about mid-October, it was enough.

We've got the Mustang making a pickup overnight on both the first of October and that of November.

The kids that got into the passenger seat of the car those two nights were never seen on the street again, and I can't find even the slightest trace of either of them after they stepped into the Mustang.

There is no doubt in my mind that this vehicle, by proxy, is being used to grab the kids off the stroll for our perp.

Oh, and the ministry staff have been working overtime checking on the next-of-kin of our confirmed missing kids and to date they can find no trace of any of them.

Our guy has been damn busy, that's all I can say.

As far as an overview of the physical attributes of all the missing kids goes, I've done up a list and, with the exception of only the last one, Jonathan Hunter, who was a Native, they all prove very similar and provide a good idea of what our guy likes to get his hands on.

The ministry tells me that Natives make up approximately forty percent of the kids working the stroll.

That means our guy could obviously have had one or more of them, if he wanted any, a long time ago.

He didn't.

So, it occurred to me that, perhaps our killer isn't really into them and maybe he wasn't particularly enthralled by Hurst's choice of Hunter the last time around.

That could be why the native kid ended up back on the stroll later that night.

His race may have saved his ass.

I'll give you each a copy of all the data."

Dave nodded.

"Could be. Either way, the Native kid did get back and maybe, just maybe during the time he was gone he got a look at our phantom killer.

We need to get hold of this Native kid, Jonathan Hunter. Where is he now?

Ed responded.

"I checked with the ministry.

He's not on the stroll.

Kid's only fourteen, if you can believe it.

He was a foster home runaway when he started turning tricks on the stroll.

He was taken into care by the ministry the day after he was dropped back off by the Mustang and they have placed him in a new foster home, out in Richmond.

I got onto the Mounties in Richmond this morning and asked them to pick him up and hold him for us. I haven't heard back yet."

Dave smiled and gave them a thumbs-up.

"Well done. We still don't know who our killer is, but it looks very much like we soon will. Let's take a break for lunch. Meet back here at hall-past one.

Ed, you better follow up with the Mounties.

This Native kid has taken off from foster homes before and he might do it again. We don't want to have him slip into the ether somewhere.

Julia, call your telephone person and put a rush on that phone printout. Hopefully it will give us a direct line on our killer.

In the meantime, I'm going to have to speak with the Chief. I'm sure he's going to be very happy with what we've got so far."

Julia spoke up.

"What about the house? It might be a crime scene. Should I arrange for a warrant to hit it?"

Dave let out a deep sigh.

"I've been thinking about that one.

We don't want our killer getting wind of the fact that we are getting close to him. If we do, he may go to ground or simply pull up stakes and move his operation elsewhere.

He'd sure as hell get a heads up if we hit the house.

And everything we now know about him tells us this the dude has access to the kind of money he would need to do that."

But you're right, it might well be a crime scene and we are in dire necd of one of those.

Let's leave it for now. My gut tells me no, but I will talk it over with the Chief when I see him and get his input as well.

We'll decide one way or the other, when we get back from lunch.

See you back here at one-thirty."

The Chief was delighted with recent progress in the investigation, and shared Dave's hesitancy to hit the east-Van house immediately.

It would have to be watched for sure however, as there was always a possibility that the killer might turn up there and they couldn't afford to miss such an opportunity.

He suggested that they just sit on it for a couple of days to play it safe.

The others were already in their chairs when Dave got back to the room allotted to the Task Force.

Dave looked across at Ed who was frowning.

"Any word on the kid from the Mounties?'

Ed shook his head.

"Nothing good, I'm afraid.

Apparently, he bolted right after breakfast, this morning. He took all his stuff with him, so it looks like he has no intention of coming back. They're going to check back later, but I think he's long gone by now.

He may be heading back to the stroll. I asked the ministry street teams to keep and eye out for him and scoop him if he turns up.

I'm not holding my breath."

Dave nodded.

"Shit, I was afraid of that. OK, we can't expect to win them all. Julia how'd you make out with your telephone guy?"

Up went the glasses to the bridge of her nose.

"Should have it by early tomorrow.

What did the Chief say about the warrant for the house? We going to hit it?"

Dave shook his head.

"No, not just yet. We don't want to spook our guy unnecessarily. Get the warrant anyway but leave the date of service open. That way we will be ready to do it on short notice if we need to.

In the meantime, we need to set up round-the-clock surveillance on it."

Julia nodded.

"It will take at least four teams."

"Yes, you and Jack get working on that.

The two of you can carry one shift per day. Pull another two out of the detective pool and to make up your fourth, I'd like you to second the two uniforms that were working car five the other night and have them assigned temporarily to the Task Force.

Go directly to the D1 Inspector for them. Tell him if he has any problems with losing them, he can discuss them with the Chief. Once you have them, brief them and get them into plain clothes and assign them their own unmarked pool car."

Julia smiled.

"They'll like that, and they deserve it. We wouldn't be where we are now if it hadn't been for that car check of the Mustang."

Dave beamed back at her.

"My thought exactly.

How soon can you manage it?"

Julia pursed her lips and pushed her glasses back into place yet again.

"Well, Jack and I could probably pull an early morning shift, say midnight to eight in the morning. And I might be able to get the other teams in place before tomorrow night at the earliest."

Dave shook his head. No, you and Jack can't take a shift tonight.

You're going to have your hands full just selecting your people and getting them briefed and scheduled to start coverage by tomorrow night.

Our killer likes to do his victims on the first of the month and he likes the 'soft' targets provided by the stroll. We've still got camera coverage going on down there.

Ed, perhaps you can make an early morning check on what we have on the stroll overnight, just to cover our asses. Julia, try to have your teams ready to go at the house for tomorrow night. I'll be satisfied if it's a go for then."

CHAPTER THIRTY-SEVEN

- December Third, 2005 -

It was getting on to one in the afternoon by the time Kenny had completed the sausage run and begun his cleanup. By four he was finished and on his way to his regular visit with Joel.

He'd been doing a lot of thinking about things while he'd been busy with his cleanup after the last kill.

He was refreshing those musings in his mind as he drove

Things had been a little tense of late to say the least, but it hadn't been his fault.

Even after the best of planning, things could and did go wrong. Besides he had already dealt effectively with the biggest problem, that of the Native kid.

For the moment, Joel remained a dilemma that would have to be handled, granted. But he'd faced that specific problem before and been able to handle it well.

So, the cops had checked the Mustang. It was likely just a routine patrol stop. He doubted that they would treat it as more than that.

Cops were stupid. He was smarter than all of them put together. He'd proven that for years and was confident that he could keep it up for as long as he wanted.

Which was another thing that he had been thinking about.

With the last kill, he had reached a total of seventy-two. Pretty damn impressive. Probably the most ever done by a serial killer.

The more he'd thought about that, the more he wanted to be certain that he was the best in the world at it. He deserved to be, and just to make sure he reached that pinnacle, he'd decided that he should have a firm target number to strive for.

Add to the challenge. Prove beyond a doubt that he had controlled his own destiny. Become a god in his own right.

In the end he'd settled on one hundred as a nice round number.

Surely that would top the list for successful kills by an individual worldwide.

Set a new standard.

Make him the master of all serial killers.

Reaching that conclusion had been very heartening and he was sure that it was the right choice to make.

That out of the way, he'd decided that he needed to take his overall planning to one more stage.

If he had not been quick to react over the screw-up Joel had made in picking up the Native kid, the cops may well have had themselves a lead to getting to him.

Something like that could happen again. If it did, he needed to have himself an escape plan in place.

To manage that he'd promised himself that he would give serious thought as to how to organize just that, first thing in the morning.

He'd also made his decision on Joel's fate.

He was not looking forward to having to yet again find a replacement to act as his cut-out, but an in-depth evaluation of their relationship had clearly indicated that Joel was likely to continue to be a loose cannon.

For years Robbie had been satisfied with an exclusive relationship with him. He had been, beyond all else, totally loyal. I'd had absolute control over him.

Joel did not have that level of commitment.

He was unpredictable in many ways. Ways that would almost ensure future screwups.

He had no other choice.

Joel was going to have to pay dearly for that lack of loyalty and his necessitating the search to find yet another cut-out. Joel was an affront to years of planning.

Kenny was going to enjoy every minute of the next few days.

If he could resist the temptation to finish the little prick off and he did not bleed out too soon, he would kill the little bastard very slowly and painfully indeed

The clean-up after was going to be one hell of a job, but it would be more than worth the effort.

And that would be number seventy-three.

The Task Force had grown exponentially overnight. When Dave entered the room, he found that eight more chairs had been arranged around the conference table. He knew all the new detectives by sight and in a glance was satisfied that Julia and Jack had made good choices.

The remaining two men, now sitting slightly to the side of the others, had to be the team from patrol car five. They were clearly finding the situation a little intimidating, but were nonetheless, in civvies, bright eyed, and bushy-tailed.

As Dave took his seat, Julia made the introductions all round.

Dave took interest in the name of the senior uniformed cop from car five, one fourth-class PC who went by the name of Steve Moody.

He addressed the two men directly.

"Welcome aboard. We owe you two a lot and when this investigation wraps up, I'm not going to forget it."

Clearly pleased, the pair both flushed slightly at the attention, but were clearly pleased with the individual recognition.

That over with, Dave welcomed the other new detective members of the Task Force and then looked to Julia.

"Is everyone up to date?"

Julia nodded and then because of the move, had to push her glasses up on her nose again.

Dave was seriously considering taking her aside later and advising her to get contacts.

As that thought rolled through his mind, she responded.

"We've been here since seven. Everyone is now up to speed."

Dave nodded.

Okay, lets get the ball rolling then.

"Ed, any news on the Native kid? Anything on the coverage of the stroll last night?"

"Negative to both."

"Julia, telephone printout?"

"Nope, not yet. But I will give my guy another call, when we wrap up here."

"Okay. I went by the house a couple of times overnight. The mustang is still sitting out front where you spotted it, Julia. My passes were only drive-bys. There were no lights on and I saw no sign of activity.

That made me a little nervous and I'm thinking that we should run our surveillance…"

He looked over at Julia.

"You set up to start that tonight?"

She responded.

'Ready to go."

"Right, well done.

Ok, as I was saying, I'm thinking we run the surveillance for just one night and if we don't see some kind of activity in the house during that timeframe, we date the warrant and hit it first thing in the morning.

I want this Joel kid in cuffs and in an interview room before he decides to disappear too. And I want a house- to-house around the target dwelling completed before the day is over.

Is everyone on board with that scenario?"

There were nods all round.

" With that in mind, I want everyone who is not working the watch on the house tonight to head on home and get a good sleep. The next few days are likely going to be hell on wheels for all of us and I want you to be well rested before the pressure hits.

I apologize to the teams that have to work overnight watching the house, but we all meet back here at eight in the morning and if there has not been any observable activity at the house overnight, we exercise the search warrant first thing in the morning.

Ed, I want a crime scene team on site with us when we hit it.

Give them a heads-up before you leave for home.

If there is nothing else, that's it for now.

I'll see you all in the morning."

CHAPTER THIRTY-EIGHT

- Morning of December 4th, 2005 -

Kenny had spent most of the night enjoying making Joel pay for his infidelity.

This was going to take days…

He'd finally left him at three in the morning, still in restraints on the bed in his special room, screaming in pain, bleeding from numerous cuts and slashes and begging for mercy.

He'd grabbed five hours of sleep and was, at eight o'clock, sitting in front of his computer screen surfing for specific data.

As a fall back, just in case things began to look too risky, it would be prudent to have a plan in place to divest himself of all his property and allow him to simply leave the country.

He was looking for information on what specific countries in the world did not have a reciprocal extradition agreement in place with Canada.

He was surprised and extremely pleased to find that there were well over one hundred of them.

After a little research, he liked the sound of Belize and entered the name into the search engine.

Up popped:

'Belize is a crown jewel carefully carved out by the British over three centuries, located on the Caribbean coast of northern Central America at 17°15' north of the equator and 88°45' west of the Prime Meridian on the Yucatán Peninsula. Central America is the isthmus that connects North America with South America. The country shares a land and sea border on the north with the Mexican state of Quintana Roo, a land border on the west with the Guatemalan department of El Petén, and a sea border on the south with the Guatemalan department of Izabal.

It is about two hours by air from Miami, or Dallas-Fort Worth. It is a two-day non-stop drive through Mexico from the Texas border. The land border with Mexico is at Chetumal City.

From Central America, Belize is a one-day drive from Guatemala City, or a half hour boat ride from the Izabal Department in Guatemala that features the beautiful tourist city of Puerto Barrios.

Belize is also located next door to Honduras. A two-hour boat ride from Punta Gorda in the Toledo district will land you at Puerto Cortez, Honduras. Commuter flights connect Belize to Chetumal City, Cancun and Merida in Mexico, Flores City (near Tikal) in Guatemala, and San Pedro Sula in Honduras.

To the east of Belize is the Caribbean Sea and Atlantic Ocean; the second-longest barrier reef in the world flanks much of the 386 kilometers (240 mi) of predominantly marshy coastline. Belize Map below is by Google Maps.

The area of the country totals 22,960 square kilometers (8,860 sq. mi), an area twice the size of Jamaica, and slightly larger than El Salvador or Massachusetts. The abundance of lagoons along the coasts and in the northern interior reduces the actual land area to 21,400 square kilometers (8,300 sq. mi). Being a small country, it is no wonder most people need to ask: Where Is Belize?

The land area of the country extends about 280 kilometers (170 mi) north-south and about 100 kilometers (62 mi) east-west, with a total land boundary length of 516 kilometers (321 mi). The undulating courses of two rivers, the Hondo and the Sarstoon, define much of the course of the country's northern and southern boundaries. The western border follows no natural features and runs a north-south imaginary line through lowland forest and highland mountainous plateau. This area is officially known as the adjacency line between Belize and Guatemala, the latter having a centuries old territorial claim on the former British colony. English is the official language of Belize, followed by Spanish. The Adjacency Zone is administered by the Organisation of American States (OAS).

The north of Belize consists mostly of flat wetlands and coastal plains, in places heavily forested. The flora is highly diverse considering the small geographical area. The south contains the mountain range of the Maya Mountains.

The highest point in Belize is Doyle's Delight at 1,124 m (3,688 ft.). The Caribbean coast is lined with a coral reef and some 450 islets and islands known locally as cayes (pronounced "keys"). They total about 690 square kilometers (270 sq. mi) and form the approximately 320-

kilometre (200 mi) long Belize Barrier Reef, the largest in the Western Hemisphere and second only in the world after the Australia's Great Barrier Reef.

Three of only four coral atolls in the Western Hemisphere are located off the coast of Belize. One of the natural wonders of the world, the Great Blue Hole is located here.

One writer on the site described the country in these words:

"Belize goes unnoticed by the rest of the world, and over the years the country has parlayed its obscurity into an attractive asset. For those shipwrecked on the shoals of life, Belize offers a new beginning.

The country teems with adventurous refugees who've set up shop in the middle of the Central American jungle. British innkeepers, Mennonite farmers, Chinese shopkeepers, Lebanese entrepreneurs, American missionaries, Canadian aid workers, and Dutch scientists live peacefully alongside the nation's longer-established residents, the Garifuna artists, Maya cacao growers, Mestizo plantation managers, and Creole politicians who make up the majority of the country's population. Belize draws the eccentric, the madcap, and the downright mad."

Kenny laughed uproariously, promptly highlighted the entire description and engaged his printer.

Now you're talking my language!

Who could ask for more.

Time to apply for a passport.

There had been no sign of activity at the house in east-Van overnight. The mustang was still parked out front and had not moved.

The Task Force units, using a tac channel to stay in contact, bolstered by a crime scene van with a full complement and accompanied by three two-man marked patrol units arrived in a convoy at eight-twenty-five.

Before they entered the block, one of the marked units entered the lane at the rear and took up a position with a clear view of the back door.

Once they were in position, they notified the others and the remaining units pulled up in front and quickly exited their vehicles and approached the front door. Of the pack, Jack and Julia were first up on the porch.

There was no response to repeated ringing of the doorbell by Julia and a final solid pounding on the front door itself, delivered by Jack. This information was transmitted to the unit at the back and then Dave nodded to one of the uniformed teams who were carrying a ram and they stepped up front and let go.

Ed, who was keeping the official log of the operation, noted that the door to the house went in at shortly before eight-thirty.

Julia led the way in, with Jack as backup.

Both had their guns out and down at their sides.

Jake give the warning.

"POLICE...EXERCISING A SEARCH WARRANT."

Ed, who had been holding two clear plastic bags containing sterile white coveralls, booties and caps passed one each to the two of them. They quickly got into the gear. Dave and Ed followed them in but stayed put in the entranceway as Julia and Jack checked the house room by room and in short order shouted that it was clear.

Dave looked at Ed and shook his head.

"Shit...no kid. Son-of-a-bitch."

Dave turned to two of the remaining uniformed teams and instructed them to double tape the house, stringing yellow *'POLICE- DO NOT CROSS'* around the house itself and then a second string around the entire property line. He directed the other patrol unit to begin a house to house down the street in both directions and the second team of new detectives to do the same along the far side of the back laneway.

He and Ed then also suited up in sterile dress and the four of them, Dave leading, began a room -to-room.

Dave's gut feeling was that if the kid was not in the house, he was probably dead.

It didn't take long for them to confirm that likelihood. The kid's stuff was everywhere. If he'd simply taken it on the lam, a goodly amount of it would have gone with him and the fact that the Mustang was still parked out front, also supported that concept.

Nevertheless, there was a good chance that the house was a crime scene and that's how they determined to play it.

Two of the uniform units were detailed to sit front and back to enforce the yellow tape and one of the newly added Task Force detective teams, who worked murder for Major Crime, were left to handle the site as the crime scene group unpacked their boxes and went to work.

Dave, Ed, Jack, Julia and the car five team headed back to the office.

They sat down, and Dave set the stage and began to assign follow-up responsibilities.

"Now that the tape is up at the house, we will have the media to deal with. The Chief and I will look after that. We'll set up an in-camera press conference here at the station and give them just the basics. Do our best to get them to agree to sit on it for twenty-four hours with a promise to provide everything we have at that time.

Hopefully we can black it out for at least that time frame.

I wouldn't count on that by the way. And even if we do manage it, our killer, just by the fact that we found no one at the house, is likely now aware that we have him in our sights and is already moving to tidy up loose ends and get out of town.

Ed, you stay here and co-ordinate all the information coming in from the teams at the house. We want a quick overview from the crime scene guys and feedback from the door-to-doors.

Someone must have seen something, vehicles coming and going etc.

"Julia, I want those phone records from the house asap. You've got your warrant. Go see your contact and get the printouts back here and go over them."

He nodded to the car five team.

You two stick with Ed. As info comes in, he will likely have follow-up tasks as a result and he will be assigning those to us as they come in.

All of you make sure that you keep Ed up to date with anything that looks like it might be interesting.

When I get back from the media scrum, I'll stay here with Ed to help him co-ordinate all additional investigative initiatives.

Before the end of the day, I want to know who our killer is and where he lives. I know the answer to those two questions is out there right now just waiting for us to grasp it.

CHAPTER THIRTY-NINE

- Afternoon of December 4th, 2005 -

Kenny's earlier euphoria over the possibility of clearing out and heading for Belize had gone through a reality check and he now realized that it had to be abandoned.

He was in his private sanctuary giving Joel a shot of Rohypnol shortly after noon to keep him under and the first indicators of an impending depression were settling in.

Only a fool could still think that the police weren't on his trail and he was no man's fool.

They weren't all that bright and he had been very careful. They probably didn't know exactly who he was yet, but it was only sensible for him to accept the likelihood that they did have at least some idea of what he had been doing.

Lacking any desire to engage further with Joel, he left the safe room and wandered around the house listlessly, thoughts going around and around in this mind, until just before five at night.

If they did know what he had been doing, then they were bound to keep digging and eventually they would manage to identify him. Once that happened, even if they didn't have enough evidence to charge him, they would persist in riding his ass and in so doing prevent him from continuing with his program of kills.

One thing for sure was that he was not going to give them the slightest opportunity to arrest him.

If Belize, now on the back burner as a long-range endgame, was not a viable option before that happened.

If it seemed that they were closing in on him in the interim, he needed a plan in place to ensure that any attempt at an arrest would fail.

If they came for him, they would have to come through the gate at the front of the property. As part of the fence line, he'd had the foresight to have a camera and intercom installed at the gate at the time it was built.

Other than himself, only Walter had remotes to operate the gate. The crew-chiefs of his work units also knew the code for the touch-pads required to activate the gate and they were under strict orders to be certain it was closed after each usage.

That meant that if the cops came for him, they were going to have to announce themselves at the gate to facilitate entry.

That would give him several minutes to prepare for their arrival.

His sanctuary, the safe room, would also provide him with a certain amount of time before they could reach him, more than enough time for him to do what he had to do to prevent them from physically taking him into custody.

So, that being the case, he would be the one to decide what happened to him, not them.

His destiny would remain totally within his own control.

That thought fortified him.

Pleased, he determined to make the necessary preparatory arrangements before the day was out, to facilitate that eventuality. In so doing, he was able to put aside his concerns about cops.

The dark cloud that had settled over him, dissipated somewhat.

Kenny realized that he hadn't eaten in some time and was suddenly ravenously hungry.

He prepared himself a plate of eggs and sausages. The sausages were from the most recent batch and after savouring the first couple of bites, Kenny decided he could sense just the faintest, slightly exotic, change in taste.

He considered it an improvement, was delighted and dug in with gusto.

Finished eating and feeling a little better, he was surprised to find that he felt sexual desire rekindle.

He placed the dirty dishes in the sink and then humming softly, ambled off down the hall to return to the safe room for another round of enjoying what was left of Joel.

When Dave returned from the Chief's office, he found Ed alone in the Task Force room and on the phone. He had a notepad in front of him and was scribbling on it as Dave dropped into a chair across from him.

Ed saw him and nodded, then cut the call off and grinned.

"Right, stuff is going well here. Before I enlighten you though, how did the media scrum go?"

Dave shrugged.

"Hard to say. We swore them to secrecy and told them it was off the record and just a heads up. Asked them to sit on it and after a fair bit of grumbling they agreed. Time will tell."

Ed nodded.

"About all you can expect.

Ok, here's what we've got so far.

The crime scene guys are still at it of course, say they will be there for a couple of days at least. But, they have already picked up a load of prints and traces of DNA. No matches of either yet of course but looking pretty good.

The door-to-doors picked up one good lead, to be specific, it was your boy from car five and his young partner.

Old guy, lives directly across the lane, says he's spotted a truck going in and out of the garage on several occasions.

He's a smoker and his wife won't let him smoke in the house, so he's out puffing on his second-floor back deck on a regular basis, night and day.

No plate, but he seems to know his vehicles well and he describes the truck as a red Ford Lariat, five or six years old.

The older constable from five, picked up on that and remembers that, back when he was new to the job and working the same car, he checked a vehicle of that description parked on the stroll.

This is several years back.

There was a young guy in it at the time and over the initial objections of his training officer, primarily because the guy struck him as more than a little strange, he decided to put in a check card on the truck and occupant.

I sent him off to dig it out and he and his partner found it. Completed on the night of December second of 1998. It provides us with a licence number and a name. They're currently running both.

Jack went with them and decided to run the plate through our traffic system to see if he could find anything that would put it in the area near the house in the east-end.

That was him on the phone. He's riding high.

Got a red-light camera hit that took place only a few blocks from the house on September the first of this year. Shows the truck plate clearly and even better, a full-frontal face shot of the driver.

He's taken it down to see if our tech boys can bring the quality of it up better than it is.

Julia has the phone printouts and is on her way in with them.

At that moment, Julia, pushing up her glasses with one hand while holding a clip of pages in her other, bustled into the office.

"I checked a few calls listed in and out to the house...three on December 1st between that address and two others stood out. I checked with Jack by phone and they tie things together, Joel, the foster home in Richmond, and our suspect.

We've got him. No doubt about it".

Dave had what he'd asked for.

Enough evidence to prove who the killer was and where he currently lived.

Dave called upstairs and updated the Chief.

CHAPTER FORTY

- Evening of December 4th, 2005 -

Finished his session with Joel by six-thirty at night, Kenny was in his office, researching how to apply for a passport.

He'd left the kid in the saferoom, still shackled, lying face-down and limp on the blood-soaked rubber sheet.

By that time, Joel was seemingly on his last legs due to blood loss.

His pitiful pleas for help now reduced to an unintelligible level of muffled whimpering.

His shivering form was hardly recognizable as that of a human.

It was more like a blubbering animal.

At seven in the evening, with light snow falling, the members of the Task Force, in eight unmarked cars and backed up by a secondary crime scene van, search and arrest warrants in hand; made a meet with a marked R.C.M.P. Suburban, two miles west of Kenny's property.

North Vancouver was Mountie jurisdiction. Inclusion of one of their members in the move on the house, was a matter of profession courtesy.

Due to the seriousness of the case, they had sent a patrol supervisor to observe and assist with uniformed backup, as necessary.

It was just short of seven-twenty, when the group of ten police units, lights off, slowly approached the front of the property. They stopped in line when Dave and Ed, in the lead car, spotted the closed, well lit, gated entrance to the compound.

Ed, behind the wheel, swiveled in his seat and turned to face Dave. "Shit!"

Dave squinting ahead through the now steady snow, nodded.

"Yes, looks like a pretty solid gate. Camera up on that main post on the left and what looks like a key-pad and intercom combination on the short post on the left side just before the gate.

Not going to be as easy as we thought I'm afraid. I can't see any house from here.

How big is this place anyway?

Ed shrugged.

"I heard something about acreage I think. But don't quote me."

Dave swore again, this time under his breath.

"Well, I guess it doesn't matter at this point. It is what it is.

You go back and update the others. I'll join you in a few minutes.

Once I figure out exactly how we're going to play this."

Five minutes later, the marked Mountie SUV, with Ed sitting in front, riding shotgun with the sergeant, moved up to the front of the line of cars and parked with its engine running.

Dave left the others, who were now back in their vehicles, and began to walk toward the gate on his own. He pulled up the collar of his coat and bowed his head as he moved into the glare of the floodlight at the gate, kicking his way through the several inches of accumulated snow and bent down to the intercom.

Up at the house, Kenny caught a flicker of movement in the image of the camera monitor sitting to his left on the desk, before the sound of the intercom buzzer filled his ears.

He froze momentarily, staring at the screen. It wasn't until the shadowy bundled up figure on the screen had buzzed for the third time that Kenny had made up his mind what to do.

He pushed the button to answer the intercom.

"Yes…"

Dave turned sideways to the camera as he answered.

"My car's broken down. I need to use a phone."

Kenny stared at the screen for a few seconds.

Ya, sure and I was born yesterday and I'm going to let you in.

Dave waited for response for a minute that seemed like and hour and then he stood erect, raised his arm and stepped a few paces to his left to be well clear of the driveway.

Kenny saw the move and got up out of his chair.

Panic grabbed him as he watched the big marked police suburban surge into the frame and launch itself directly at the gate.

Kenny was on the move before the big black push-bars framing the grill of the Suburban made contact, forcing the gate open, sending it reeling aside on it hinges.

Kenny realized he had stopped breathing. He managed to regain control of his faculties and then immediately raced down the hallway toward the saferoom.

The Suburban came to a stop and Dave hurried across to it and climbed into the back seat.

As he pulled the door closed behind him, the other units, lights back on, bulled in behind them.

Dave met the eyes of the R.C.M.P. sergeant in the rear-view mirror.

"Sorry I had to ask you to do that. No push-bars on our unmarked units. The city will pay for any damage you've suffered."

The big man grinned back at him.

"Not to worry, I've always wanted to do something like that."

Without further comment, he hit the gas and the parade of vehicles shot forward down the driveway.

Kenny downed the contents of the large glass in three huge gulps. He'd mixed the booze half and half with Rohypnol. He knew he would likely be dead in twenty minutes or so.

Tossing the glass aside, he quickly got to work.

The strong smell of gas fumes had filled the room by the time Kenny had drained the last few drops out of the ten-gallon plastic vessel.

He dropped the red container on the floor and turned back to survey the room briefly before crossing to the single chair and sitting down.

He was calm now.

The decision had been made and he was in total control.

He rested his gaze on the still squirming form on the bed in front of him.

It looked like Joel was still going to be among the living when the fire engulfed him.

Good, let the little prick suffer to his last breath.

Here we go, him getting his just desserts and me going out in a ball of fire, a blaze of glory, on my personal funeral pyre.

Kenny felt the first signs of the drug taking effect. He pulled out his lighter, savoured the sight in front of him for a couple of seconds, then flipped the top open, lit it and gently tossed it.

He watched it sail cross the room and land in a puddle of gas to one side of the door.

There was a moment when he thought it might not ignite, but then a terrific *'whoosh'* filled his ears and a stabbing flame flashed upward.

They had to kick in the locked front door. Minutes later they had determined that the house was unoccupied. Dave was standing in the mater bedroom detailing teams to check out the outbuildings and assigning inside responsibilities to the others, when Julia interrupted him.

"Inspector, do you smell smoke? I smell smoke."

Dave frowned and turned to face her. Before he could respond Julia had turned and moved toward the bookshelf.

"Look here…there is smoke coming out of the wall. Seeping out…"

She began to trace the wisps of smoke wither fingertips.

And I feel heat."

Dave turned to the R.C.M.P. sergeant, who had been leaning against the far wall, doing his best to stay out of the way.

"Son-of-a-bitch! Can you notify the local fire department?

The big man was already reaching for the mike on his shoulder.

Dave turned to the rest.

Ed, go and check outside. This is an outside wall were looking at. The fire must be outside, maybe in a lean-to or something. We might be able to put it out ourselves. We've got extinguishers in the cars.

"Right, the rest of you, out of the house, until we know what we are dealing with.

Check the out-buildings.

We need to find this guy. With fresh snow, if he's out there, he will have left tracks. Look for those first. If you find no tracks, then come back to the front of the house and we'll wait there until we get the fire department on scene."

Drifting back one at a time, all but Ed were gathered together in a tight circle about thirty feet from the house, staring at the roofline, expecting to see flames break thorough at any moment.

Ed, joined them seconds later.

"I looked at the back of the house and the outside. There is no sign of a fire back there. But the shape of the building doesn't fit with the inside wall where we saw the traces of smoke.

I think there is another room on the other side of the bookshelf in the master bedroom."

Dave nodded.

"Okay you guys stay here. I'll go inside and briefly check to see if the smoke is still coming out."

He returned a few minutes later.

"The odd little bit of smoke now and then, but less than before. I think you're right, the fire is not just inside the outside wall or something like that. There must be a room behind those bookshelves."

The sound of a wailing siren filled the silence that followed his words and he let out an impatient sigh.

"Thank Christ."

When the two trucks, lights and sirens operating, pulled up to the front of the house, the men inside began to pour out and Dave hurried across in the direction of the guy issuing the orders.

He quickly outlined the situation and the crew went into action.

A hose line with an auxiliary pump was run from the tank truck to the dug well at the side of the property. A second line was run from the truck to the house.

Dave led the Captain and two firemen into the house and showed them the spot where the smoke had first appeared.

The Captain turned to one of the firemen.

"Get a couple of axes."

Then he turned to Dave.

"We're going to have to cut our way in there.

I think we've probably got a room behind it, but one that's almost hermetically sealed.

Those wisps of smoke you first saw tell us there is a fire in there, but because it hasn't broken through the roof, my bet is that its smouldering."

Dave frowned, and the man continued.

"If you can seal a room and the fire doesn't cause a breach, it will eventually consume all the available oxygen and then either smoulder or go out. If the heat breaks a window or if there is another way for oxygen to still get in it can cause a flashover or backdraft."

Dave nodded.

"There are no windows."

"OK, but a fire can burn slowly until a door or window is opened and then the fuel in the room that is at a high temperature, can react quickly to the resulting inrush of oxygen.

We will need to hit it hard with water the instant we break our way in."

Dave nodded again.

"OK, do what you have to do, but try not to pour any more water in there than you need to.

We think this is a crime scene and we want to be able to work it as soon as you've finished."

Fire axes took the door down in six solid blows.

Two firemen, manning a swollen hose then hit the resulting burst of flames with a solid stream of water.

It was knocked down in a mater of minutes.

EPILOGUE

Two weeks after the fire, Dave, Ed and the Chief sat down to dinner with the senior Crown Prosecutor.

It was the Crown Prosecutor who had chosen the restaurant. One that offered a good deal of privacy and reflected the fact, by the prices it charged.

To say the least, it was a very unorthodox method of reaching a determination by the prosecution on the action to be taken, after a capital crime investigation had been completed.

That said, all the men gathered around the circular table in the private dining room had agreed it was probably for the best.

Dave had been doing most of the talking during the round of pre-meal cocktails.

The food would arrive shortly, and Dave had reached the point of capping the discussion.

"So, to capsulize; confirmed by dental records and a plethora of evidence, we have ourselves a confirmed dead serial killer. Over the past several years he's managed to kill somewhere between fifty and a hundred kids-all selected, from the *'Boystown'* stroll.

Our guy followed a ritualistic process of killing these kids at his home, where he had constructed a hidden saferoom. He processed the bodies rather uniquely, first butchering them and then using the meat to add to the pork sausage he sold commercially.

We know that from what we found in the fridge freezer in his house and the wrapped packages sitting in the large freezers in his butchering area.

The remaining tissue and bones were first fed to his pigs and then buried under wood chipping material, in several areas of his large forty-acre property.

What we are considering here is how we should handle the notifying of the public of what has taken place.

We've already given the media the basic facts of the case, without any mention of the sausage part.

Using DNA and trace evidence and prints recovered to date, we have positively identified twenty-three of the victims. Their next-of-kin, where it was possible to find them, have been notified. We have also done that in the case of approximately, its changing daily as the investigation goes on, another forty victims.

With no exceptions, the families we've contacted to date are satisfied with the fact that we have confirmed that the killer is dead and given them closure.

Remember, these kids were on the fringe of society, were often on their own or had been kicked out of there homes.

Unsurprisingly, they were not then and are not now, being particularly missed.

Our quandary at this point is, do we release the details of the sausage-making. If we do, the investigation will have to continue, and it could go on for months or even years, cost a bloody fortune, and serve little purpose in the end.

Or do we halt the investigation now and let sleeping dogs lie? "

The Chief added,

"Do we let the public know that a good number of them are unwitting cannibals, or do we wrap it up now and leave well enough alone?"

Other books by Patrick Laughy

Murder Mysteries

The Little Black Book
Alumni
Kenny-The Making of a Serial Killer
-A Trilogy-

Historical Fiction

The 4th Reich series
Books 1-7

Fantasy

Atlantis-Ship of the Gods-a trilogy

www.ingramcontent.com/pod-product-compliance
Lightning Source LLC
Chambersburg PA
CBHW060544180626
46817CB00002B/718